DAWN OF THE MUMMY

MARK L'ESTRANGE

Copyright (C) 2020 Mark L'Estrange

Layout design and Copyright (C) 2020 by Next Chapter

Published 2020 by Evenfall – A Next Chapter Imprint

Edited by Terry Hughes

Cover art by CoverMint

This book is a work of fiction. Names, characters, places, and incidents are the product of the author's imagination or are used fictitiously. Any resemblance to actual events, locales, or persons, living or dead, is purely coincidental.

All rights reserved. No part of this book may be reproduced or transmitted in any form or by any means, electronic or mechanical, including photocopying, recording, or by any information storage and retrieval system, without the author's permission.

*To my gorgeous babies: Jovi, Poppi, Bambi, Tigger and Gizmo.
Thank you for making every day so special.*

Chapter One

The renowned Egyptologist, Professor Erland Kautz, clutched his chest with his right hand as the latest in a series of attacks took hold. This one was by far the worst since his last operation and he knew deep down that the time he had left was short, regardless of what his cardiologist, Dr Freedman, assured him.

Each breath the professor took was more laboured than the last.

His chest felt as if a great weight were sitting on it, pressing down, and making it harder for him to take in his next lungful of air.

With a quivering hand, he reached across to the occasional table beside his chair and fumbled with the catch on the tiny round pill box he always kept by his side.

When he eventually managed to flick the lid open, several of the tiny white pills within spilled out on to the table. Erland pressed his index finger down hard on one of them and pinched it between his thumb and forefinger before carrying it over to his open mouth.

He dropped the pill beneath his raised tongue, and collapsed back in his chair, spent from the effort.

After a moment, he could feel his chest starting to relax and the awful pressure slowly eased away.

That was it!

As far as he was concerned, tonight was the night. It had to be – fate might not give him another chance.

Since his retirement from the lecturing circuit, Professor Kautz had spent his time devoted to the one passion he had left in life, studying and translating the scriptures of ancient Egypt.

In reality, it had always been his passion. Or, as some of his erstwhile colleagues used to refer to it behind his back, his obsession. He had fallen in love with the history of the land at a very early age, when he was fortunate enough to have been taken on a dig led by his great aunt, a formidable and austere Egyptologist, on behalf of the British museum.

From that day, the young Erland spent every free moment he had in Egypt, volunteering for digs, and working on excavations under the watchful eye of his great aunt, until her unfortunate death as a result of a landslide.

Erland focused his formal education on a single goal; to become as renowned in the field as his great aunt had been.

And he had succeeded. Most academics agreed he had surpassed her triumphs, becoming a world authority on the subject and highly sought after for guest lectures at the most important universities throughout the world.

Throughout his long and distinguished career, Erland had also come into contact with some less-than-scrupulous characters, who nonetheless were able to get their hands on some of the most authentic and best-preserved antiquities he had ever laid eyes on.

Their price was always high, but worth every penny, in his opinion.

Erland had spent a major proportion of his inheritance on such artefacts, but each purchase was, to him, a treasure.

He had donated so many finds to the major museum in the nearby town that they had even erected an extension, specifically for the display of his many endowments, in his honour.

But there were some rarities with which Erland could not bear to part.

These were the ones that he had taken special care not to reveal to anyone, not even those academic colleagues whom he considered his equal when it came to their hunger for knowledge about ancient Egypt.

Erland had gone to extreme lengths to acquire some of these items, and, although he was ashamed to admit it, even to himself, he had turned a blind eye to everything from bribery to murder itself to lay his hands on them.

As soon as he felt strong enough, the professor rose from his chair and walked slowly down the long corridor that led to his cellar.

Switching on the overhead light, Erland descended the wooden stairs to the cellar floor. Once there, he checked around and listened for the sound of approaching footsteps.

There were none.

He knew that all his servants had already left for the day but, whenever he decided to visit his secret chamber, a cloak of paranoia enveloped him, which always had the effect of making him believe that there were thieves hiding in the shadows.

As soon as he was satisfied that he was alone, he walked over to the far wall and slid back a mock-stone-covered panel in the wall, revealing a keypad concealed in the brickwork.

With bated breath, Erland tapped in his code and, within seconds, a large section of the wall pivoted silently to reveal a hidden chamber beneath the cellar.

Just like the Pharaohs of ancient Egypt, Erland had ensured

that the builders he had employed years earlier to carve out his underground hideout did not live long enough to reveal their endeavours to anyone.

It was a necessary, if somewhat regrettable, precaution, over which the professor had, to his credit, lost an immense amount of sleep.

As the stone door pivoted open, the underground chamber flooded with a dim light. The strip lights in the ceiling held tubes of a low wattage, to ensure that their glare did not damage any of the delicate artefacts on which the professor secretly worked.

Even after his generous donations to the museum, the professor's underground collection was immense. Most consisted of ancient scripts, pieces of jewellery, trinkets and relics, some of which were merely broken fragments although, to the professor, they were all priceless treasures.

But the pride of his collection stood at the far end of his chamber, still encased in its sarcophagus.

The mummy of Anlet-Un-Ri.

The sarcophagus had been unearthed in a dig in 1975 in the Valley of the Kings. At the time, the professor was an invited guest in Egypt, representing the British Museum, when the tomb of Mehet-Met-Too was discovered.

At the time of his death, Mehet-Met-Too had been only a boy. The third son of the pharaoh by his second wife was buried with all the grace and ceremony befitting a member of the royal household.

During the excavation of his tomb, some of the local workers discovered a separate tunnel that, on later inspection, led to the burial chamber of the servants of the young boy.

Among them stood the sarcophagus of Anlet-Un-Ri, a female warrior of distinction and a decorated soldier in the pharaoh's army.

Erland was immediately captivated by the find.

Chapter 1

There was something mysterious and almost mesmerising about the ornate carvings and intricate detail that had gone into the construction of her sarcophagus which, for a mere servant, even a decorated soldier, was extremely unusual.

A script discovered inside the chamber recounted how Anlet-Un-Ri had volunteered to be buried alive in the chamber to protect the young royal when he passed over, and that the warrior would without mercy tear asunder anyone who violated his tomb.

As Erland happened to be the only official on the site at the time, he bribed the workers to steal Anlet-Un-Ri's sarcophagus and hide it until he could find a way to have it exported to England without the knowledge of the authorities.

During the endeavour, several guards who would not accept bribes were killed, and in the morning, it was assumed that thieves had attempted to rob the tomb of the young royal and been chased off by the surviving guards on duty.

But there was another script of equal fascination that Erland discovered in the warrior's chamber on that night. One that he also kept hidden from the rest of the party.

It bore the ancient seal of the dead, and, although it was not the first of its kind to be discovered, it piqued Erland's interest enough that he knew he had to study it in secret.

Sure enough, his suspicions were confirmed when he finally managed to decipher the ancient parchment. It was indeed one of the missing parts of the ancient scripture of the dead, and the professor knew that its value as an artefact would mean more to him than diamonds or gold.

Since then, it had taken the professor more than forty years to piece together the ancient scripture, which was supposed to have been written by the high priests, from fragments he had managed to collect from the famed Book of the Dead.

Even when the priests wrote it, they knew that the whole contents could not be entrusted to any single individual, not even the monarch himself. So they devised a system whereby they created smaller individual scripts, each one on its own incapable of providing the reader with sufficient knowledge to appreciate the immense power the complete manuscript could impart.

These parts were then passed down from high priest to high priest, each endeavouring to secrete one piece of the overall scripture in the tomb of the next pharaoh who died during their time in office.

The secret of the forbidden scripts became legendary over the centuries.

But it was not until the first piece was unearthed in the mid-19th century, and eventually verified, that the leading authorities in Egyptology throughout the academic world finally acknowledged its existence.

The other extracts from the forbidden scripture were housed in various museums and universities throughout the world, depending on which country financed the excavation from which the script was unearthed.

Erland had used his not unsubstantial credibility as one of the world's most formidable experts in the field, to gain access to each parchment in turn. Those he was not able to decipher immediately, he copied and brought back with him to England so he could work on them in his own time, far away from prying eyes.

Unable to rely on the discretion of even his most trusted colleagues, Erland worked alone, unhindered by outside distractions.

Now, finally, he had mastered the cryptic message that the ancient priests had hidden within the various scripts.

Tonight would be his final unveiling, with a chosen audience of one – himself.

The professor moved to his desk where he had set out his copies of the ancient scripts.

Chapter 1

Without delay, he began to recite the long-dead language of the high priests of ancient Egypt.

Out of nowhere, a thunderstorm erupted above him. Even from down here in his hidden chamber, he could hear the roar of each ear-splitting clash growing louder with each word he spoke.

As he recited the ancient text, Erland could feel the dark power of the high priests flooding through his veins, demanding that he cease his blasphemy before it was too late.

But, for him, that time had already passed.

As he continued to read, he could hear the sound of movement behind him.

Erland turned in his chair and stared at the sarcophagus of Anlet-Un-Ri.

With an unsteady voice, he continued to recite the sacred text.

Suddenly, the sarcophagus began to shake.

At first, it was a minor movement, so slight it was barely perceptible.

But, as Erland continued with his forbidden task, the vibrations grew stronger, until, as he read out the last few lines, the lid of the casket shuddered open, and the mummy of Anlet-Un-Ri opened its eyes and turned its head to see who had awakened it from its eternal rest.

Even though this was a day that the professor had dreamt about since he first entered the chamber of the mummy, all those years ago, the sheer shock of seeing the mighty warrior come to life was more than his heart could stand.

Erland immediately felt a tingling in his chest, which he knew all too well was the first sign of another angina attack.

Keeping his eyes fixed on the mummy, he reached into his old-fashioned smoking jacket pocket for his pills but, to his horror, the box was not there.

Frantically, he searched his other pockets, all to no avail.

As the hammering in his chest grew more acute, it felt to Erland as if his heart was in competition with the mounting thunder outside.

It was only then that he remembered leaving his pill box on the table next to his armchair.

The distance would be only a short stroll to anyone else. But to him, in his present condition, it might as well be a marathon.

He looked up to see the mummy take its first tentative steps in more than 3,000 years. Although he knew he had nothing to fear from it, the sight of its eyes boring into him from behind its wrappings caused his heart to skip several beats.

As fear and panic took hold, the professor could feel a hand reach into his chest and squeeze his heart, cutting off the blood flow.

He tried to stand, but the effort was too much for him.

As he slumped back into his chair, his book of scriptures fell to the floor.

In his final seconds of life, Professor Erland Kautz knew that what he had done was both unearthly, as well as ungodly, and no human alive had the knowledge or power to stop it.

He had unleashed an undead spirit into the world, and although he had spent over half his life building towards this moment for all he was worth, he wished he could take it back.

As he closed his eyes for the final time, he prayed that God would forgive him.

Chapter Two

"Keep your fuckin' eyes on the road!" Scrapper demanded, reaching over and slapping Jeremy across the back of the head.

"Ow, that fuckin' 'urt," moaned Jeremy, gripping the wheel tighter to prevent the van swerving into a different lane.

"Ha, that was funny," Sara chimed in. "Smack him again."

Scrapper smiled at his girlfriend and raised his hand as if to comply with her wish.

"Leave it out, Scrapper – we want to arrive there in one piece." Phil turned around in the passenger seat and looked back at his mate. He knew that Scrapper would do anything to impress Sara, even though he always claimed that he was in full control and did only what he wanted when he wanted to do it.

Phil knew better than to antagonise his old school friend but, by the same token, he was not prepared to sit back while Scrapper used Phil's cousin Jeremy's head as a punch bag. Especially when he was the one driving.

On top of which, he had promised his aunt that he would look out for his cousin, even though Jeremy was a bit of a wimp and completely wet behind the ears. They had never exactly been close as children, and in fact, the more he saw of his cousin, the less he liked him.

But this was different.

This was a job, and they needed a driver with a clean license at short notice, and Jeremy was the only one who fit the bill.

Scrapper glared back at Phil, evidently deciding whether or not he was going to take exception at his instruction to leave Jeremy alone.

Phil could tell by the way his mate's eyes narrowed, that he was giving the matter due consideration. It would not be the first time Scrapper had lashed out at one of his own. But Phil had known him long enough to accept that it was usually the drugs talking, so he did not take it personally.

When the pair had been banged up in Feltham Young Offenders Institution, Scrapper had looked after Phil, and saved him from a beating-up on more than one occasion.

The fact that it was Scrapper who had led to them being locked up in the first place made no difference to him. Phil knew he was already a long way down the wrong road so, as far as he was concerned, he would have ended up behind bars sooner or later.

Since then, they had both been extremely lucky not to end up in prison. Phil was all too aware of that fact, although Scrapper believed it was down to his ingenuity that they had never been caught thus far.

Billy "Scrapper" Watson was a small-time crook, and purveyor of an assortment of narcotics. He had made several connections in the underworld over the years and believed himself to be a hard-man and gangster who commanded respect and loyalty from others in the same fraternity.

In reality, Scrapper was anything but.

The "contacts" he had made were strictly low-level crooks, not the type that he aspired to be, but the simple fact was that

Chapter 2

Billy would not have known a serious criminal if he tripped over one.

He had let it be known over the years that he had earned the name Scrapper because of all the fights he had been in, whereas, in reality, it was given to him in school because he was made to work weekends in his uncle's scrap-metal yard.

Usually, Scrapper relied on Phil as his bagman, and the two of them made their money carrying out odd jobs around London for whichever villain required their assistance.

Scrapper made it a habit not to ask too many questions, preferring to build up his reputation by never turning down an offer. Although this philosophy did not always sit well with Phil, he usually went along out of loyalty rather than commitment.

Their latest job was a little unusual in that it involved making an out-of-town collection, hence the need for a driver. Scrapper had never learnt how to drive, and Phil, who usually did the honours, was midway through a six-month ban for speeding.

Sara was not an option. Although she had finally passed her test after the seventh attempt, she could not handle anything bigger than the pink Mini her father had bought her and, even then, she had already crashed that three times in as many months.

So Phil had enlisted his cousin Jeremy for the night.

Up ahead, Phil saw the sign for Lewes. As they approached the turning, he could tell that Jeremy had not noticed it, by the fact he was not indicating, so rather than spark another outburst from Scrapper, Phil pointed it out to his cousin.

"Next left," he said.

"Oh, right," replied Jeremy, switching on the windscreen wipers. "Oh crap, why is everything in this van the wrong way round?"

Jeremy corrected his mistake before Scrapper noticed.

As they took the turning, the sign stated the town was only two miles away.

Phil turned in his seat. "Do we head straight into town?" he asked Scrapper, who was too busy making out with Sara to acknowledge the question. "Scrapper!" Phil shouted.

"What?" replied his mate, clearly annoyed at being interrupted.

"I asked you how far down the road do we go?"

Scrapper looked at the instructions on his phone.

"Er, about half a mile, then there's a turning for some place called Narrow Loft. We take that, then we drive past a petrol station, and it's the next turning on the right. Got that, dummy?" He was addressing Jeremy, who was too concerned with the lack of street lights since they had left the motorway even to notice.

Once more, Phil stepped in. "Jeremy, look out for a turning for Narrow Loft. I'll direct you from there."

Jeremy nodded, still concentrating on the darkened road ahead.

When they finally reached the petrol station, Jeremy began indicating for the next right.

The road took them along a gravel drive that led to a remote farmhouse a couple of hundred yards away. The farmhouse was in darkness, which Phil presumed meant that the owners were out or else they had already gone to bed, which, given the hour, was not unlikely.

"This is it," announced Scrapper, hitting the redial on his phone. "Pull over and turn off the engine."

Jeremy complied and they waited for Scrapper to receive his orders.

After a couple of minutes, another vehicle approached them from the opposite direction.

The car stopped directly in front of them, and a tall, dark figure emerged from the passenger seat. He looked around suspiciously, as if expecting police officers suddenly to burst out from the fields that surrounded them.

Once he was satisfied, the tall man walked around to the boot of the car and removed a black holdall, which he carried over towards the van.

"Move, dickhead!" yelled Scrapper, shoving Jeremy from behind towards his cousin.

Phil, realising what his mate was trying to do, opened his door and slid outside. Pulling his seat forward he called back to Scrapper.

"Get out my side, it'll be easier," he insisted.

Scrapper left Jeremy alone and crawled over Sara to exit on the passenger side of the van.

Once outside, Scrapper walked over to meet the tall man, swinging his shoulders from side to side as he went in an effort to look more imposing.

As the others watched, Scrapper held out his hand to shake the stranger's, but the tall man did not bother to reciprocate. The two men exchanged a couple of words, then the stranger held out the holdall, and Scrapper took it from him.

The tall man immediately turned his back on Scrapper and walked back to the car.

Scrapper stood and watched as the car reversed back up the road until the driver found a convenient spot to make a U-turn.

For a moment, Scrapper watched as the rear brake lights of the vehicle disappeared into the distance, then he turned back and climbed back into the van.

Phil jumped back inside and slammed his door.

"Right then," said Scrapper, holding on to his prize, "we're going to Vauxhall. Make it snappy!"

Chapter Three

THE SEDDON ACADEMY BOARDING SCHOOL FOR YOUNG ladies lay nestled in the Hampshire countryside, half a mile outside Clevedon. The school prided itself on teaching those in its charge all the refinements that accompanied good breeding, as well as providing the very best education money could buy.

At £10,000 per term, the fees alone ensured that only the wealthiest and most distinguished of parents applied to enrol their daughters into the Seddon Academy and, due to the strict limitations on class size and teacher-pupil ratios, the board was at liberty to refuse entry to offspring of those parents who, although wealthy enough, lacked the requisite elements of refinement and culture on which they insisted.

There had already been several high-profile reports in the media about the daughters of pop stars, sports personalities and television celebrities to whom the academy had declined enrolment.

When it came to the arts, only the most distinguished of stage actors, in the view of the board, need apply.

The majority of students came from a background of family money although, on occasion, the school would consider the offspring of those particularly outstanding in their field. These included doctors, lawyers, scientists, and the most eminent academics.

To the outside world, the Seddon Academy was a safe haven, where parents could entrust their daughters to be raised to the highest standards of academic and moral aptitude.

Within those hallowed halls, however, it was a somewhat different story.

As the grandfather clock in the main dining hall struck the hour of midnight, the eight members of the Seddon Swan Society prepared their charges for the penultimate stage of their initiation into the society.

The senior eight were all members of the upper sixth and due to leave the academy in the summer. Their A-level grades were guaranteed to secure them places at the top university of their choice. They were the cream of Seddon, and it was their duty to ensure that they left the swans in the very best of hands.

Cynthia Rollins was the head girl and had been throughout her time in the sixth form.

Like most of her fellow swans, she had been born with the cliché of the silver spoon in her mouth and had spent her life being overindulged by her parents.

Cynthia was a third-generation Swan and determined to live up to the traditions she had inherited in the best way she could.

As the clock sounded the last of the twelve chimes, Cynthia raised her arms behind her head, and pulled forward the white satin hood that was attached to her ceremonial gown.

Her seven-fellow swans, following her lead, did likewise.

The main dining room was illuminated by flickering candles placed along the individual dining tables, as well as on the sideboards that sat prominently against every spare inch of wall space and housed the dishes and cutlery necessary to serve the academy's celebration meals and guest nights.

Once she was satisfied that her fellow swans were

customarily resplendent in their ritual attire, Cynthia gave the signal for two of the order to leave the line and admit those waiting outside.

As the main doors were pulled open, 10 naked lower-sixth girls entered the room in silence. They walked over to where the remaining six swans waited and took up their place opposite them, as they had been instructed earlier, during rehearsal.

Being granted permission to join the swans was indeed a great honour, one bestowed only on those who had proved themselves worthy in the eyes of the previously chosen.

Until their official acceptance into the order, the 10 chosen were known as "ducklings" and if, for some reason, any of them did not make the cut, they would be referred to as "ugly ducklings" for the remainder of their time at the academy.

Everyone stood in silence until those who had opened the doors for the ducklings re-joined their sister swans.

"Little ducklings," began Cynthia, her voice booming throughout the long hall, "you have the privilege of being considered to gain access to the esteemed order of the swans. It is a society with a long and glorious tradition, the secrets of which you will be expected to carry to your graves. Do you understand?"

The 10 ducklings nodded in unison.

Cynthia smiled to herself. "Although you have all come this far, that does not mean that you are at the end of your journey. There is still a final initiation that shall be made known to you in due course. Only after that, if you survive, will you be granted acceptance into our great order. Do you understand?"

They nodded again.

Cynthia turned to her nearest Swan and indicated with a nod of her head for the girl to prepare for the next stage of the night's initiation.

The Swan turned and walked over to the nearest sideboard.

Chapter 3

On top of the sideboard, carefully laid out on a silver tray, were a new box of pencils and a large wooden ruler.

The girl grabbed the pencil box, a cruel smile crossing her face as she poured the contents into her hand. There were ten pencils in total.

Discarding the box, she turned and went back to the line, handing the wooden ruler to the Swan at the far end, who accepted it with a malicious smirk.

The first Swan then proceeded to stand in front of the first duckling in line.

After a moment's pause, she handed over the pencils and the duckling took them from her with trembling hands.

As if from a prearranged script, the duckling went down on her knees and placed the pencils on the floor in front of her horizontally, in two lines of five, with the leads pointed inwards.

The girl looked up at the Swan and waited for the older girl to nod her approval.

The young duckling leaned forward and placed her hands, palms down, on top of the pencils, so that she had five under each hand.

Slowly and purposefully, the Swan moved forward and placed her left foot on one of the girl's hands, pressing down with all her weight.

The girl screamed out in pain, but still tried to keep her voice as low as possible.

Once she was sure the duckling had her cries under control, the Swan lifted her other foot and slowly brought it over to hover over the duckling's other hand. She held it there for an agonising moment, before placing it on the girl's other hand and leaning forward, so that her full body weight was now pressing the pencils into the girl's palms.

The duckling sucked in a deep breath through clenched teeth.

The older girl, like her fellow swans, was wearing white

pumps to match her outfit. But the pressure of her weight pressing down on the girl's hands, trapped on top of the ridged pencils, made it feel to the duckling as if her aggressor was wearing heavy army boots.

The naked duckling waited patiently, trying to fight against the pain in her throbbing hands. She knew that this was only the first part of tonight's initiation, and she hoped it would prove to be the more painful of the two.

As she waited, the Swan with the ruler moved into position behind her.

"Raise your buttocks higher," came the order. It was Cynthia's voice once more.

The duckling complied.

Seconds later, the wooden ruler struck the girl's naked bottom, making her scream out once more.

Each Swan took it in turns to deliver two blows.

Once the ordeal was over, the duckling was allowed to go and stand to one side so that she could nurse her sore hands and bottom.

The scenario played out in the same manner for the remaining nine ducklings,.

Once the last one had received her strokes and been allowed to stand with the others, Cynthia moved to the front of the line, and stood with her hands on her hips, surveying the line of ducklings.

After a moment, she announced: "Well, it appears that you may all have what it takes after all, but time will tell."

The Swan who had been charged with standing on the girls' hands while they received their strokes now moved to stand next to Cynthia.

She whispered something in her ear that made Cynthia smile.

Carrie has just reminded me," she continued, "that due to

her having to attend to her own duty, she has missed out on delivering her share of whacks to you all."

Cynthia waited a moment for the realisation of what she was about to say to set in. Once she saw the understanding on the duckling's faces she continued.

"Therefore, in silence, I want all of you to bend forward and place your hands on your knees, and Carrie will pass among you and complete your punishment."

The ducklings all looked along their line and, one by one, they dropped forward as commanded to await their fate.

Chapter Four

"Please, take the greatest of care with that," Stanley Unwin, curator of the Clevedon Museum cried out nervously. He removed his glasses for the umpteenth time that morning with shaking hands and, using his sodden handkerchief, wiped away the beads of perspiration that had formed on his forehead.

Ted Casey raised his eyes to heaven, much to the amusement of his team, and turned to face the curator. "Please Mr Unwin, I can assure you that there is absolutely nothing to worry about. My lads have never dropped a consignment in their lives."

The curator rubbed his wire-framed glasses frantically before replacing them on his head.

He was a small-boned, wiry man of fifty, whose body appeared too small for the three-piece suit that hung shapelessly on his skinny frame.

Unwin was a nervous man at the best of times but the added stress of overseeing the museum's upcoming exhibition had turned him into a complete wreck.

It had not always been like this. Back in his mid-twenties, Stanley Unwin was one of the youngest lecturers at one of the country's oldest and most respected universities, with a master's degree in ancient history and a doctoral thesis that had just been approved and which he was about to commence.

Then, when he stood up on stage before a hall full of undergraduates to deliver his lectures, there was no sign of the bumbling, equivocating parody of an academic that his staff had come to know.

At the time, Unwin firmly believed that his life belonged in the world of academe.

Thoughts about the opposite sex were, to him, something he saved for bedtime, when he could be alone with his thoughts and those magazines he would buy from the newsagent in the next town. He preferred not to shop locally for such things. After all, he was an up-and-coming member of the community, and he knew that being caught with such pornography would lower his peers' opinion of him considerably.

He had never sought out the company of women for intimacy and, at the time, he firmly believed that he had no need for physical love, preferring his books and manuscripts as company.

But then, one fateful day, he allowed himself to be dragged out on a blind date by a colleague from the university.

Mildred Howes was the cousin of one of his fellow lecturers, and she had recently moved to the area after her previous fiancé called off their wedding at the last moment.

Mildred was a few years younger than Stanley, although she acted like someone much older. She was an excessive, overbearing kind of woman, who was evidently much put out by the fact that she had been dumped and was determined not to let that humiliation ever be repeated.

Once Mildred had established that Stanley was an honest, hard-working, decent sort of chap, she decided that they would make a lovely couple, and set about moulding him to her way of thinking.

The first time they made love was at Mildred's insistence.

Up until that time, Stanley was happy to coast along, making time for Mildred whenever she suggested that they go out, but he was never the one who instigated their dates, and Mildred grew concerned that he might be looking elsewhere for female company.

So, to cement their relationship, Mildred dragged Stanley to a party and force-fed him alcohol all night. He had never been a big drinker, and still was not in the habit of enjoying more than an occasional glass of wine with supper. But that night, Mildred managed to get several large cocktails down his throat and afterwards, she took him back to her place and virtually forced herself on him.

Stanley was too drunk to offer any resistance, and Mildred had learned enough about men to know what to do to make them excited, so during the night she managed to bring the hapless Stanley to ejaculation twice.

Once she confirmed she was pregnant, she gave Stanley an ultimatum. Either he made an honest woman of her or else she was going to make sure that everyone in his precious academic circle knew exactly what kind of a man he was.

Reluctantly, Stanley agreed, and watched as the rest of his life was mapped out for him.

During their 30-odd years of marriage, they had two daughters, Felicity and Tamara, both of whom soon realised how easy it was to get their own way with their father.

Stanley often found himself wedged between a rock and a hard place when he had his daughters on one side and his wife on the other, arguing for two different things.

His work had always been his means of escape, and so it was that Stanley threw himself into it, seeking ever-more cunning and astute excuses to spend more time at the university than at home. Evenings, weekends, even bank holidays presented a chance for him to create desperate and inventive reasons why he was needed at work.

As for Mildred and his daughters, they seemed happy enough so long as they were allowed all their selfish indulgences, with him footing the bill.

His diligence, however, did pay off, and when the opening for the job of curator at a major museum caught his eye, he was delighted to discover that several of his esteemed colleagues were on the board.

Now, he no longer needed an excuse to spend more time at work. It was his job to make sure that everything at the museum was running just so and, in order to do that, he had to sacrifice his precious family time to be there, just to keep an eye on things.

But there was another side to that coin that had reared its ugly head over the years.

Whether it was as a result of the constant haranguing by his wife and daughters for every little thing, or the sudden realisation of the significance of the responsibility which came with his post, Stanley Unwin had grown almost petrified of making a mistake at work.

His phobia, which seemed to grow worse with each passing year, not only ensured that he spent more time at the museum than was necessary, but also developed to the stage where it denied him sleep, making him wake several times during the night in a cold sweat, convinced that he had made some horrendous blunder that would cost the museum a fortune.

On occasion, he had actually jumped out of bed and driven to the museum in his dressing gown just to satisfy his paranoia.

Deep down, Unwin knew that his unhealthy obsession was having a detrimental effect on his wellbeing. But by the same token, as happens with most mental conditions, he was powerless to reason with himself.

All of which made the installation for the display of the

museum's latest acquisition a nightmare of epic proportions for him.

Ever since the estate of the late Professor Erland Kautz had cleared the probate process and the contents of his secret underground Egyptian chamber of treasures became the property of the museum, Unwin had slept barely a wink.

The late professor's collection included some priceless antiquities, which, although their provenance could not be ascertained, were now legally owned by the museum.

Because of the uncertainty over the origin of the artefacts, the museum had taken the unusual step of inviting a specialist from the museum in Cairo, who specialised in carbon-dating rare and ancient relics. It was hoped that, once these treasures had been authenticated, the museum's visitor numbers would go up and its revenue would thrive as a result.

The most important and magnificent find among the professor's treasures was, without doubt, the mummy of Anlet-Un-Ri, for which a special exhibition was being prepared in part of the wing built in the professor's honour years earlier.

Unwin watched with bated breath, as the sarcophagus that housed the mummy's remains, was slowly lowered onto a purpose-built gurney, guided by Casey's men.

As the hoist that held the immense casket came down, one of the straps gave way, causing the ancient structure to swing wildly from side to side.

Unwin could feel his heart exploding in his chest. He leapt forward, waving his hands in the air in a frantic effort to stop the sarcophagus from slipping out of its straps, missing the gurney and crashing to the concrete floor.

But his fear was unfounded.

Casey's team was quick to react and, within seconds, they had managed to guide the casket directly above the gurney. They waited until the natural motion of the hoist had eased, then signalled for their colleague to continue to lower it to safety.

Chapter 4

"Oh, my good God in heaven," Unwin called out, his breathing laboured as if he had just run a marathon. "Look what you're doing, please."

Ted Casey had to admit that the hoist strap snapping had been a foreseeable accident, and he intended to take it up with whoever on his team had been responsible for checking the equipment before leaving the depot. But he knew that even if two or even three of the straps had gone, the others were still capable of holding the structure, so there was no real danger.

Convincing the curator, however, would be another matter.

As he walked over to try to calm the man down and reassure him that everything was going to be all right, one of the museum security guards strode out of his office and made his way over to the him.

"Is everything all right Mr Unwin?" he asked, eyeing the approaching Casey suspiciously.

Bill Stead was a huge man, by any standards. At six foot six, he towered above most of his fellow human beings and, although he had a spare tyre around his middle, nature had given him shoulders that were as broad as he was tall.

The museum curator looked positively dainty next to the massive security guard.

By the time Casey reached them, Stanley Unwin was visibly shaking and obsessively cleaning his glasses yet again.

Casey nodded at the security guard but did not wait for an acknowledgement.

"Look, Mr Unwin, I've told you there's nothing for you to worry about. My team will handle this."

"But did you see what just happened?" Unwin screeched, his voice rising several octaves.

Casey held out his hands. "Rest assured, we calculate risks like that very carefully. Your display is in no danger whatsoever."

He could see that the curator was unconvinced, and to be fair, he could not blame him after what he had just witnessed.

Casey looked up at Stead, who had taken a protective stance behind his boss.

"Listen, how about taking Mr Unwin for a nice cup of tea, help to soothe his nerves?"

"My nerves are perfectly calm and well, thank you, Mr Casey," Unwin replied, his whole body shaking with rage.

Ted Casey scratched his head. There was obviously no placating the man and he was out of ideas.

Stead placed one of his enormous hands on Unwin's shoulder. "Perhaps a nice cup of tea ain't such a bad idea, after all," he offered sympathetically.

Unwin turned his head and glanced up at the huge man unsteadily.

The sight of the pair of them reminded Casey of the story of David and Goliath.

Eventually, Unwin nodded. "Yes, perhaps you're right, I have been feeling a little stressed today," he confessed.

Before he had a chance to change his mind, the big security guard turned him around and steered him back to his office.

Casey heaved a sigh of relief and went back to his crew.

"Come on," he called out. "That thing isn't going to move itself into place."

"You never know, boss," replied one of his men, "perhaps it will come back to life and walk in on its own, like they do in the horror films."

The rest of the crew laughed at their colleague's flight of fancy.

"All right, all right," said Casey. "Until you can convince it to do your job for you, get on with it."

Chapter Five

ANCIENT EGYPT

THE CROWD ROARED AS THE MIGHTY WARRIOR THREW another opponent to the ground. This was the third one to be vanquished in hand-to-hand combat since the competition started.

The victor, Anlet-Un-Ri, did not acknowledge the adulation of those in attendance, but simply turned to the three remaining men waiting in line and signalled for the next one to step forward.

Anlet-Un-Ri stood head and shoulders above most of the other guards who had gathered for the competition. She was a commander of the Pharaoh's second army and had earned her place among the male soldiers by proving her prowess and bravery on the battlefield.

The Pharaoh had promoted her on the insistence of his secondary wife, for whom Anlet-Un-Ri had once served as personal bodyguard.

However, there were still many among the Pharaoh's troops who refused to take their orders from a woman, regardless of her rank. Therefore, whenever it was felt necessary, the Pharaoh would arrange a tournament among those soldiers who objected the most, and the six winners would all face Anlet-Un-Ri in single combat.

This was now the third such tournament the Pharaoh had held for the amusement of his people and in the previous two, Anlet-Un-Ri had defeated all those who came against her.

There were those in the Pharaoh's household who felt that the competition was unnecessary, as the only reason Anlet-Un-Ri had to rise to the challenge was as a result of her sex. No male soldier had ever been challenged in such a manner.

But what no one else knew was that Anlet-Un-Ri had herself suggested to the Pharaoh that the competition take place. She had a thirst for battle which, between skirmishes, she found hard to quench.

The next challenger took two paces towards the female warrior. He was a large man by any standard, well over six feet tall, with broad shoulders and huge arms, but as he approached Anlet-Un-Ri, the expression on her face made his knees buckle beneath him.

There were those among the crowd who noticed his hesitation, and some began to call out to him, mocking his lack of steadfastness.

The warrior could feel the blood rising inside him and his face flushed with a mixture of anger and humiliation.

As the chanting from the crowd grew in volume, the challenger sprang forward. His speed and agility were commendable for such a large man, and before she had a chance to counter his move, the man had Anlet-Un-Ri in a vice-like grip, with his arms clasped around her waist; pinning her arms to her sides.

The soldier heaved and pushed to try to bring the big woman down, but she wrapped her leg around his, preventing the move. As he struggled in vain to topple the large woman, the crowd cheered even louder and laughed at his pitiful efforts.

Refusing to accept being outmanoeuvred, the man pushed

forward for all he was worth. But, even with only one leg on the ground, the giant female still managed to keep his efforts at bay.

Finally, he let go, and stood there before his opponent, breathing heavily. His bronzed chest rose and fell as he sucked in air, the perspiration dripping down him.

For her part, Anlet-Un-Ri merely stood her ground, smirking down at him.

It was then that the last two combatants came towards him, brandishing swords and spears.

The rules of the tournament allowed for the challengers to decide what weapons they were going to use, and until now, all the others had unsuccessfully tried brute force.

As the last two soldiers reached their colleague, one of them called to him and handed him a sword.

The three of them stood there, beneath the blazing sun, flaunting their weapons in front of the unarmed woman.

The crowd jeered loudly, protesting to the Pharaoh to stop the fight and punish the three men for not following the rules. But the Pharaoh merely studied the stance of the female warrior and smiled to himself when he saw she displayed no fear at the prospect of facing all three men alone.

Even so, the code of combat demanded that the three men wait until their foe chose her weapon before they attacked. But, before she had a chance to move, they advanced, circling around her.

The crowd was going crazy.

Weapons were thrown into the arena to allow Anlet-Un-Ri to even up the fight. But she chose to ignore them and stood her ground, her arms outstretched, her legs braced, as she moved her head from side to side, following the men's progress.

Without warning, as one, they attacked.

Anlet-Un-Ri stood still for a split second longer, and a loud gasp rose from those in attendance, convinced that she was not going to defend herself.

Sensing her chance, the female warrior grabbed hold of the closest spear coming at her from her right and used it to swing its holder off his feet and send him crashing into his colleague at his side.

As both men sprawled to the floor, Anlet-Un-Ri quickly turned her body sideways-on to the first combatant who was now lunging at her with his sword.

She grabbed him by his wrist and twisted hard. The man screamed out as the sword fell from his hand and landed on the ground. Still holding his wrist, Anlet-Un-Ri slapped the man around the face with her free hand, back and forth, as the crowd chanted for her.

When she was finished, the man fell to his knees, holding his broken wrist.

The other two soldiers had, by now, reformed and each grabbed a sword from those the crowd had hurled into the arena.

They took up positions on either side of the female warrior, now determined to make their strike count.

This time, Anlet-Un-Ri retrieved the sword she had taken from the first soldier and twirled it back and forth in her hand, making it swish ever louder as the speed of her movements increased.

The soldiers looked at one another, each willing the other to strike first.

The first soldier, who was still lying on the ground at his victor's feet, yelled at them to attack. The two men raised their weapons and shouted aggressively as they lunged toward their target.

Anlet-Un-Ri moved with such speed, it looked as if her sword was in two places at once. She met each strike as the two men rained blows down on her, forcing them to move back in fear of their lives.

As the three fought, the soldier on the ground slid along the

Chapter 5

sand, his broken wrist held firmly against his chest. As he reached out for a fallen sword, Anlet-Un-Ri's sandaled foot slammed down on his good wrist, pinning it, and the sword, to the ground.

Seizing their opportunity, the other two men moved in, swinging their swords through the air as if they were slicing through a veil.

Holding back, Anlet-Un-Ri stayed poised until she saw her chance of attack.

With one swing of her sword, she decapitated the nearer of the two soldiers.

His head bounced along the floor before coming to rest, with his lifeless eyes staring off to one side.

The movement was so swift that it took everyone by surprise.

For a moment, the crowd fell silent from the shock. Then they began to cheer once more.

The decapitated man stood in position for what seemed like an age before his headless body collapsed to the floor.

The second soldier, seeing the fate of his comrade, dropped his sword and ran towards the crowd, waving his arms for them to grant him a path to safety.

All eyes were on the fleeing soldier, so no one noticed Anlet-Un-Ri lift her arm back and fling her sword powerfully after him. The weapon turned end over end as it flew through the air before entering the back of the running man's head and exiting via his open mouth.

Again, the crowd went silent for a moment, before a chant began to erupt through those gathered, insisting that the female warrior deal with the soldier she had pinned down beneath her.

Anlet-Un-Ri waited for several minutes, allowing the waves of cheers from the crowd to wash over her, and cover her with glory.

Finally, she bent down and picked up the sword for which her assailant had been reaching.

The soldier begged and pleaded for his life, with tears streaming down his cheeks.

He began to pedal his legs frantically against the sand in a vain effort to escape, but with his good wrist held firmly in place under the large woman's foot, he soon realised he was going nowhere.

Anlet-Un-Ri raised her sword above her head, ready to strike the fatal blow.

The crowd cheered her on, eager for another kill to conclude the tournament.

But, after a moment, she tossed the sword to one side.

The spectators were obviously disappointed, but she was not fighting for their amusement.

The whimpering soldier thanked her for her compassion, and vowed to follow her on the battlefield, wherever she went.

But Anlet-Un-Ri was oblivious to his words.

She removed her foot from his hand and bent down. Grabbing him by his ears, she hoisted him up to his feet.

The man screamed as one pain replaced another.

Without pausing, the female warrior spun the man around, wrapped an arm across his neck and hoisted him off his feet as she squeezed his throat.

She held him there while he kicked and bucked in her grasp, his eyes growing wide in fear and panic.

Eventually, he stopped moving, and his lifeless body hung limp in her arms.

Anlet-Un-Ri held him there for a moment longer before releasing his corpse and letting it slump to the ground.

The roar from the crowd was deafening, but the warrior refused to acknowledge their adulation.

Instead, she walked over to the tented area where the

Chapter 5

Pharaoh sat with his entourage and stood before him to offer her lowest bow.

The Pharaoh stood and held out his arms for the crowd to be silent.

They obeyed immediately.

"Once more, my great warrior Anlet-Un-Ri has proved herself worthy to stand side by side with my army and defeat my enemies. We are proud and honoured to have her among our ranks, leading my second army."

The crowd cheered.

The Pharaoh allowed them to continue for a while, even though he knew that his champion would not bask in such glory.

Finally, he held his hand up for silence once more.

"But after today, having witnessed her immense proficiency in the field of combat against some of my finest soldiers, I hereby announce that when we next go into battle, Anlet-Un-Ri will march as the first female commander of my first army."

Another cheer rang out from the gathering, this one even louder still.

While the crowd cheered and clapped, the Pharaoh beckoned for his champion to approach him. As she did, he turned to one of his house guards who handed him a magnificent-looking sword, the handle of which was encrusted with precious stones.

For the first time, Anlet-Un-Ri appeared overwhelmed.

As she graciously received her weapon, she thanked her king and strapped it to her side. She removed the mighty sword from its scabbard to admire it, and as she did, the noise from the crowd rose even higher.

Anlet-Un-Ri held the magnificent weapon above her head, and, although it was too slight for anyone to notice, a smile spread across her lips.

Chapter Six

THE SUNLIGHT STREAMED THROUGH THE NARROW ceiling-high windows that circled three sides of the school gymnasium. Inside the air-conditioned room, the sound of rubber soles could be heard slapping and squeaking on the wooden floor, as the lower sixth jogged around the perimeter.

"That's the way, ladies – keep those knees high, backs straight." Physical training instructor Danielle Parker stood in the middle of the circle and watched the girls as they ran around her.

Physical exercise was considered just as important as good grades at the Seddon Academy. The Latin tag about a healthy mind in a healthy body was engraved above the entrance to the gymnasium.

Besides the well-equipped hall where the girls now were, the academy boasted four tennis courts, an Olympic indoor swimming pool, squash and badminton courts that also doubled for basketball and netball training, a running track and a weights room fitted with a dozen carefully chosen, state-of-the-art weight machines to help improve the girls' overall posture and deportment.

Chapter 6

Twice a week, on Mondays and Fridays, they even had yoga classes, which were run by a local specialist teacher.

Danielle Parker was, by far, the youngest teacher at Seddon. At twenty-three, she was only five years older than the upper-sixth students, which was why most of them came to her when they had difficult personal issues to discuss. Anything from boys to menstrual cycles, and everything in between.

It was an aspect of her duties that Danielle had never considered as part of her remit when she took up the post. But then, she had never gone to boarding school, so she had been lucky enough to have her mum and elder sister on hand to help her with such things.

She soon realised that the girls at Seddon had no such luxury, and it was an unwritten rule that, if they wished to discuss any such personal matters, they should either speak to the headmistress or the academy nurse. But both of them were in their late fifties and not the most sympathetic of people, from what Danielle had seen.

Nurse Baxby, for example, was a deeply religious woman, but her faith bordered on zealotry. Danielle had heard from some of the younger girls that she had told them that their monthly cycles were so heavy because they were a mark of sin and meant the girls must have been having impure thoughts throughout the month and that had led to their excessive bleeding.

As it was the medical room where the supply of sanitary towels was kept, the girls were forced to seek out Nurse Baxby's assistance when they needed them and, needless to say, she was always prepared with a stern look and another cautionary tale.

Some of the girls had even been known to bring back suitcases full of towels at the beginning of term, to avoid the confrontation. Which was ridiculous, because the school fees their parents shelled out each term included the supply of such items.

Even so, put in their position, Danielle could easily sympathise.

She clapped her hands together to gain the class's attention. "Okay, ladies, that should have warmed you up."

The girls stopped and turned in to face their teacher.

"Right then," she continued, "how about we all do some circuit training?"

There was a communal groan from the gathering.

Danielle let out a long moan, too, mimicking the girls. "Come on, you lot. It's not as if I'm asking you to run a marathon."

"But Miss," came a despondent reply from one of the group, "circuits are so boring."

Several nodded in agreement with their classmate.

Danielle held out her hands in an expression of mock sympathy. "Oh, I know, it's such a trial for you all. My heart bleeds, it really does."

"Now you're just making fun," ventured another girl.

Danielle pointed at her. "Full marks that girl, now come on, we'll do one quick circuit, and then we will split into teams and have an exciting game of netball. How's that?"

There were general nods and smiles of approval.

The girls gathered in groups of two next to each one of the dozen or so pieces of equipment spread around the court. Danielle blew her whistle and the first in line began her task.

As she walked around the room, checking that the girls were completing their exercise safely and thoroughly, Danielle would jump in every so often and complete the exercise herself. She knew whenever she joined in, most of the girls would stop and watch her, continuing with their own workout once she had completed hers.

Danielle felt that taking part brought her closer to the class, which in turn, made her seem more approachable to them. It seemed to have worked so far.

Chapter 6

At the far end of the gym class, she noticed Natalie Prewst struggling to get up one of the climbing ropes.

To be fair, it was one of the most strenuous exercises in the circuit, and Natalie was not a natural athlete by anyone's standards. But Danielle had noticed a distinct improvement in the girl's overall fitness since she had arrived at the school, so there was hope.

"Come on, slowcoach." Janice Cooper, Natalie's work-out buddy was standing at the bottom of the rope, holding it in place for her friend. "We're lagging behind because of you, fat-arse."

Danielle walked over to give Natalie a few well-chosen words of encouragement. They seemed to have worked in the past, and certainly could do no harm.

As she approached Janice, the young girl looked up sheepishly, obviously feeling bad about what she had just called her friend.

Her cheeks flushed. "Sorry Miss, but she knows I don't mean it really."

Danielle took hold of the rope. "I know that she knows, but it still isn't a very nice thing to say, is it?"

Janice looked at her feet. "No Miss, sorry Miss."

Danielle leaned in closer. "I think it's Natalie you need to apologise to," she whispered. "Perhaps later, not in front of the class. It will mean more then."

Janice looked up, smiling. "Yes Miss," she promised.

Danielle gazed up at the struggling Natalie.

She was more than halfway up, which was not bad going, considering.

"Come on Natalie," she called out, encouragingly. "You're almost there, just a few more feet. Big effort now."

Some of the girls waiting to use the rope, began to chant.

"Nat-a-lie... Nat-a-lie... Nat-a-lie..."

The echo of her name seemed to give the girl the boost she

needed. Taking in a deep breath, she reached up and grabbed the rope, hoisting herself up another six inches.

"Nat-a-lie… Nat-a-lie… Nat-a-lie…" they continued, with others starting to join in.

Soon, the entire gym was cheering the girl on.

Natalie glanced down for a moment, stunned at the sight of all her classmates encouraging her to make it.

With one last almighty effort, the girl boosted herself up another six inches, then another, and finally she reached out her hand and grabbed hold of the top of the apparatus.

The room exploded with cheers and clapping.

Natalie looked back down at the group, a big beaming smile on her red, sweaty face.

"Now try to come back down as slowly as you can," instructed Danielle, having to shout above the cacophony.

Natalie nodded, excitedly.

As she climbed down, Danielle noticed something that gave her pause to think.

The Seddon Academy gym kit was the same for all girls. It consisted of a white polo shirt with the academy crest on the right breast, short purple skirt, white socks and white plimsolls.

As Natalie slowly slid down the rope, Danielle could not help but notice the red welts showing beneath the girl's knickers.

Danielle instructed the rest of the girls to continue with their own exercises. Once they dispersed, she looked back up as Natalie grew closer to her eye level.

There was no mistaking it.

Someone had beaten the poor girl and, judging by the redness of the marks left behind, it had been relatively recently.

Danielle was horrified. She knew that the regulations at the academy were somewhat draconian by modern standards, but she had certainly not been aware of corporal punishment being administered.

Chapter 6

She managed to disguise her revulsion as Natalie landed on the floor beside her.

She looked up at her teacher with a beaming smile of pride. "I made it, Miss, did you see? I went all the way to the top for the first time."

Danielle placed a comforting hand on the girl's shoulder. "Yes, I did, and you were absolutely brilliant," she assured her.

Natalie was panting from her efforts, but Danielle could tell the excited teen still had more to say, so she allowed her time to catch her breath.

"Did you hear them all cheering for me? Wasn't it fantastic?"

"Yes, it was," agreed Danielle. "See what wonders you can achieve when you set your mind to it?"

The girl nodded, excitedly. "Next time, I'm going to do it twice. You just see if I don't."

Danielle could not understand who could possibly want to hurt such a sweet, innocent girl, but the evidence spoke for itself.

Well, whoever it was, Danielle was going to find out, one way or another.

Chapter Seven

THROUGHOUT THE REST OF THE DAY, DANIELLE COULD not get the thought of those red marks across Natalie's bottom out of her head. She even found her eyes filling with tears at one point during an afternoon class at the mere thought of someone hurting the poor girl.

The more she thought about it, the more she rationalised that someone at the academy had obviously been the perpetrator.

The question was, who?

She had often heard tales of bullying slipping under the wall of respectability on which the academy prided itself. But she hoped that the girls trusted her enough by now to come forward if they were a victim of such appalling treatment.

Later that afternoon, as she sat alone in her office drinking a cup of strong coffee, another thought entered her mind.

Natalie was sixteen and, being cooped up in a place like Seddon for months on end, with no one for company but other girls, it was not beyond the realms of possibility that she might be experimenting with one or more of them.

Many girls at her age were already sexually active, or, at the very least curious to learn about their options. At least in an all-girl school, there was no chance of anyone falling pregnant, and they had all watched the cringe-worthy documentaries on sexually transmitted diseases during their relationships and sexual health classes, so they should all know the importance of safe sex.

So if Natalie were in a relationship with one of the other girls, or several of them, as the case might be, then perhaps those marks on her bottom were as a result of a little overzealous foreplay.

The lower and upper sixth dormitories were located in a different part of the school from where the teachers had their rooms, so who knew what went on up there once the lights were out?

The more she thought about it, the less likely it seemed to Danielle that a girl like Natalie would be a willing participant in some sort of domination game.

Danielle did not consider herself to be a prude. She, too, had experimented with most things during university, including sub-dom and lesbianism, but they were all within a consensual relationship and no one had ever forced her into trying anything she did not agree with.

So, if that were the case with Natalie, fine. But Danielle had to make sure that the girl was not being coerced into anything she did not want to do.

The problem, of course, was how on earth Danielle could find out for sure, without asking the girl outright.

She could see no other feasible alternative.

In her position, many other young teachers would take their suspicions to the headmistress and leave her to deal with the situation as she felt appropriate.

But, regardless what the truth of the matter turned out to be, Danielle knew that Natalie would never forgive her if she told the head about her concerns.

No, this one was going to be down to Danielle alone and she was not relishing the prospect.

Danielle opened her computer and checked the timetable to see where Natalie's class would be now.

She glanced at the time on the bottom of her screen. It was a little after 5pm. Class would just have been released. Between five and seven each afternoon, the girls were given the freedom to go wherever they wanted within school grounds.

Although the girls were encouraged to think of that part of the afternoon as study time, the library was usually the quietest part of the school during those hours.

Danielle knew the group that Natalie tended to hang out with, so she scraped back her chair and made her way over to the tennis courts. Sure enough, she spotted Natalie with her usual group standing in line for their turn.

The last thing Danielle wanted to do was draw attention to the fact that she needed to see the girl, so she stayed where she was and waited until Natalie happened to glance in her direction. She waved her over, casually, smiling as she did so, to lessen any concern Natalie might have at being summoned, and asked her to come and have a chat with her in her office.

Once back in her office with the door shut, Danielle watched as Natalie shifted awkwardly on the hard wooden chair opposite her desk. The poor girl was obviously still in pain, which was no surprise considering how red those marks were.

Danielle took her seat.

She could see from Natalie's expression that she automatically thought that she was in trouble.

Danielle smiled at her. "Sorry I had to drag you away from tennis," she apologised.

Natalie shrugged. "That's okay, Miss, I only went along because the others wanted to play. I fancied staying in and reading this evening. Am I in trouble for something?"

Danielle assured her that she was not and saw Natalie

Chapter 7

physically relax as she said it. Danielle thought for a moment before continuing. She desperately wanted to ask the right questions without embarrassing the girl or making her feel too awkward.

Finally, she asked. "Natalie, do you often find yourself agreeing to do things you don't want to do?"

The girl thought for a moment, considering her response. "How do you mean, Miss? Like today when you asked us to do circuit training? I didn't want to do that, that's for sure, but I'm glad now that I did."

Danielle laughed. "So am I – you were brilliant this morning," she assured her. "But what I'm talking about more specifically is, does anyone ever ask you to take part in activities which are not part of the school curriculum that make you feel uneasy, or perhaps even scared?"

"Scared, Miss?" The girl appeared shocked.

"Yes, that's right. Scared that if you do not take part, they might make life hard for you in some way?"

Natalie shifted once more in her seat.

This time, Danielle felt that it was not all down to her sore bottom.

She leaned over her desk and looked directly in Natalie's eyes. "You can tell me. I promise, if you want, that it will not leave this office."

Natalie could not hold her teacher's gaze for long.

The girl bowed her head.

Danielle could just see her bottom lip starting to protrude.

She waited to give the girl a chance to speak up.

There was obviously something bothering her.

After a minute's silence, Danielle took a deep breath and continued.

"Natalie, I could not help but notice those cane marks on your bottom at gym class today. Do you want to tell me how you came by them?"

The young girl looked up, then immediately back down again. In that split second, Danielle had seen the embarrassment etched on her face that her secret had been discovered.

Danielle felt a slight sense of relief that her instincts had been correct. She would naturally have preferred for there to be no reason for this discussion, but now she was convinced that there was, she was determined to find out what was going on.

"Natalie," she offered, soothingly. "If you don't feel comfortable discussing it with me, I totally understand."

The girl looked back up, her face flushed with embarrassment.

"Would you rather I went and asked the headmistress to come in, or one of the other teachers?"

It was a cruel trick, but it had the desired effect.

"No, please, don't do that." Natalie almost exploded from her seat. Now she was physically shaking. "I'll tell you everything. Just please don't let anyone else know, please!"

"All right, all right," Danielle assured her. "I promised you that, if you want, we can keep this between us, and I meant it, so don't worry."

Natalie calmed down but she now looked to be on the verge of tears.

"I promise you," Danielle assured her, passing her a tissue across her desk, "that once you tell me, you'll feel a lot better."

Natalie nodded. "I'm a duckling," she announced, "last night, we had another initiation ceremony."

Danielle was horrified. She knew all about the proud history of the Swan Society at Seddon. A former student had even written a book about it, a copy of which now sat, prominently displayed, in the school library.

When she first arrived, Danielle had flicked through the book, but did not read it in any great detail. It mentioned initiation, and the importance of weeding out those unfit to carry on the tradition. But when it came to the ceremonies, the book did not mention anything like this.

"Wait a second," she said, "are you telling me that part of last night's initiation included you receiving those marks on your behind?"

Natalie nodded.

"And was it just you on the receiving end?"

"Oh no," replied the girl, matter-of-factly. "We all had to take it."

Danielle could feel her stomach churn. She had heard stories from some of her lecturers at university of some of the antics that had taken place at private schools. But they had been stories from the past, when beating children was virtually part of the curriculum.

Society had progressed since then. Or so she had thought.

How could an upstanding academic institution such as Seddon still allow these antiquated rituals to take place?

Danielle tried to calm down. She did not want to stress Natalie out any more by showing how disgusted she was by the girl's account.

"And would I be right in presuming that it was one of the swans who inflicted this punishment on you all?"

Natalie nodded again. "Yes, they all took it in turns, but it could have been worse."

"Worse!" Danielle could not believe her ears. "How could it possibly have been worse? Your bottom is red raw."

Natalie looked behind her as if to ensure that the door was still closed, and no one was within earshot. "They only used a wooden ruler, Miss. We have heard that they also have a riding crop, and a cat o' nine tails, so at least we didn't get those."

Danielle shook her head. She could not believe her ears. It was almost as if Natalie was making excuses for her abusers.

The members of the Swan Society were no secret at Seddon. Danielle knew that head girl Cynthia Rollings ran the show, and she could just imagine the cocky privileged little madam taking great pleasure in deciding what torture could be inflicted on her underlings.

The situation was delicate.

Under normal circumstances, notwithstanding the promise she had made to Natalie, Danielle would have had no qualms in reporting this outlandish behaviour to the head.

But she knew from past experience that Seddon marched to the beat of an altogether different drum from those considered appropriate by modern education standards.

Danielle had witnessed a pupil being berated in front of the rest of her class for receiving a poor mark in a test. The teacher had actually reduced the poor child to tears, but still did not let up.

Later, Danielle had spoken to the teacher in private to inform her that she did not approve of her methods.

To her astonishment, the next thing she knew, Danielle was summoned before the headmistress and she was berated in her turn for interfering in matters that did not concern her.

When she ventured that the welfare of the pupils at Seddon was her concern, she was reminded that she had been accepted into the academy on only a temporary contract. And if she wished to have it renewed at the end of the year, she needed to learn to adjust to the Seddon method of instilling discipline and character into their students.

Danielle leaned forward on her desk. "Natalie, if I ask you a question, will you be honest with me?"

Natalie looked up, shocked. "Of course, Miss."

"Do you even want to be part of this 'Swan' ritual, or whatever it is? Wouldn't you rather just be able to concentrate on your studies and leave all that to someone else?"

The girl looked horrified. "Oh, Miss, you can't be serious. Once you've been nominated as a duckling, you have no choice but to comply. It's considered a great honour to be chosen, and if you fail to make the grade, you're an *ugly* duckling for the whole of the upper sixth."

"Would that really be so terrible?"

Danielle knew the answer from the expression on the girl's face.

"All right, fine," she accepted finally. "I can tell you're adamant about becoming a Swan. But I hope you know that you can come and see me any time, in confidence, if you change your mind."

She placed special emphasis on the word confidence just to make sure the point made its way across.

Chapter Eight

STANLEY UNWIN SAT AT THE BREAKFAST TABLE blowing on his hot tea. He knew he should not have made a second cup, as he was running late. Not for work – he would still be in plenty of time for that. But he preferred to eat his breakfast alone and be out of the door before his wife and daughters deigned to make their presence known.

Even now it was too late. He could already hear them descending the stairs.

He considered leaving his tea, but he knew even that would instigate a sarcastic response from his wife.

Unwin steeled himself and took a large swallow. The hot liquid scalded his tongue and scorched its way down his gullet, burning a path down to his stomach.

He started coughing and spluttering just as the three women entered the room.

His younger child, Tamara, was the first to comment. "Daddy for goodness sake, if you're going to cough your guts up, must you do it at the table?"

"He's swallowed his tea too quickly," chimed in his wife.

Chapter 8

"How many times do I have to tell you not to rush your food? Anyone would think you were in a race."

"Is there any more tea in the pot?" asked Felicity, his elder daughter. "I'm simply gasping."

Before Unwin managed to catch his breath to answer, Mildred had lifted the lid to check inside.

"No," she replied, not trying to disguise the exasperation in her voice. "Your father was obviously too busy to put the kettle on for us."

Unwin finished coughing into his hanky. "I'm sorry, my dear," he spluttered, "I was just about to refill it…"

"Don't bother." She cut him off in mid-sentence. "Thinking about number one, as usual."

"Sorry." He put his head down and concentrated on his tea. There was no point in arguing.

While the three women prepared their breakfast, Unwin opened his newspaper and flicked through the pages until he found the article about the upcoming exhibition at the museum.

The reporter had telephoned him a couple of days before and arranged an interview.

Unwin felt that it had gone rather well and, as he read through it; he was happy to see that the interviewer had made precise notes of what he had been saying.

There was even a photograph of him standing in front of the hoarding announcing the forthcoming exhibition.

"Look girls," he announced proudly, holding up the article. "Your father made the local paper."

"What as, a peeping tom?" Felicity asked scornfully.

The three women laughed.

"You've not been caught soliciting again, have you, Father?" Tamara chimed in.

Unwin slammed his folded newspaper on the table. He could feel his cheeks burning. His daughters had absolutely no respect for him whatsoever, and he knew exactly where that attitude came from.

"Now girls," stammered Mildred, through her laughter, "that's no way to speak to your father… Even if it is true."

The two young women were both bent over with laughter.

Mildred stood there, holding her sides.

It was obvious that they all took great delight in poking fun at him, so Unwin stood up abruptly, almost sending his chair over. "I'm leaving now!" he announced loudly.

Not bothering to wait for an acknowledgement, he turned and marched out of the kitchen. While he straightened his tie in the hall mirror, he could still hear the three women laughing at his expense.

He slammed the front door behind him as he left.

On his drive in to the museum, he could still feel the rage boiling within him.

One day, one day they would push him too far, and then they would know. He did not need them, they needed him. He was the breadwinner. He was the one who kept the roof above their heads and put food on the table. Not to mention their enormous credit-card bills, which he was expected to pay without complaint.

He had insisted that the girls were too young to have their own accounts. After all, neither of them worked. Felicity was just about to go to university, and Tamara was still in the sixth form, so what on earth did they need credit cards for?

Naturally, it was Mildred who insisted that they he allowed them, in order to teach how to handle money responsibly, or so she had argued.

But what responsibility did they demonstrate when they used their cards willy-nilly without having to think about it?

Not that their mother was any better. Her clothes bill alone could feed a small army and, naturally, everything had to have matching accessories. It would not have been so bad if she at

Chapter 8

least managed to make good use of each outfit. But she would wear each one once, usually to one of her functions, then insist that she could not possibly be seen in it again.

At least the girls would wear their clothes until they were considered out of fashion.

He supposed he should be grateful for small mercies, but right now, he was not feeling in a particularly appreciative mood.

Unwin pulled his car into the staff car park and groaned inwardly when he saw that someone had taken his spot. The sign for the curator's bay had long since faded with age, but everyone knew that it was his, and they had no right to grab it.

He parked in the space next to it and slid out of his seat.

He looked the vehicle over.

He did not recognise it as belonging to any of his staff, but it appeared to be brand new.

As he walked around, he noticed the rental sticker in the back window. Perhaps one of his staff members was having car trouble and had to hire one while theirs was being repaired.

Even so, that did not excuse their deliberate lack of respect for his authority.

Unwin strode purposefully towards the staff entrance.

Someone was going to regret their careless actions this morning.

As he fumbled in his briefcase, trying to locate his staff pass, Unwin heard the door buzz as someone pressed the release from inside.

The door flew open.

It was Bill Stead. "Morning guv'nor," he said cheerily.

"Oh, yes, good morning Bill," Unwin replied. "Did you notice who parked in my space?"

The security guard leaned out, keeping the door ajar with his foot, and glanced along the side to where the space in question was.

"I see," he replied nonchalantly. "I wonder if it might be your visitor from the museum in Cairo. She arrived about half an hour ago."

Unwin's face dropped. "She's here already?"

Stead nodded.

"But I wasn't expecting her until tomorrow at the earliest."

The guard shrugged. "Perhaps she caught an earlier flight," he suggested.

Unwin did not answer. He merely rushed past the guard and made his way to his office.

"The visitor from Cairo," as Stead had put it, was actually a forensic specialist on loan from the museum, who had agreed to come to England to carbon-date and authenticate some of the treasures unearthed in Professor Kautz's secret underground chamber.

She was a visiting dignitary, as far as Unwin was concerned, and not to be here to welcome her when she arrived was an unforgivable oversight on his part.

The curator was breathing heavily by the time he reached his office door. He was about to reach for the handle but instead decided to knock first.

It seemed the right thing to do under the circumstances.

There was no reply to his knock, so he twisted the handle and gently eased the door open.

His office was empty.

It made no sense, Stead had told him the woman had arrived an hour ago, so where else could she be?

"Mr Unwin."

He almost jumped out of his skin. He turned to see the massive figure of the guard looming over him.

"She's already with the artefacts," Stead informed him, anticipating his question. "She said she didn't want to waste any time. I didn't think you would mind."

Unwin dumped his briefcase on a chair just inside his office and composed himself as he strode towards the Egyptian wing where the new exhibition was being constructed.

As he turned the last corner, Unwin saw the person whom he presumed was his special guest, bending down over an open chest, studying the contents through a magnifying glass.

He introduced himself, offering his hand.

The woman removed her plastic glove and face mask and shook his hand. "Good morning, Mr Unwin, I am Doctor Amina Anmali. I hope you have no objection but I took the liberty of starting work before your arrival – there is so much to do."

The woman looked a good deal younger than Unwin had been expecting.

She spoke perfect English, although with a heavy accent.

Under her white coat, she appeared small and petite in stature and, for the first time in ages, Unwin felt an immediate stirring in his groin when their hands met.

He tried not to blush and hoped that his dark-blue suit trousers covered his protrusion.

"May I offer you some refreshment, a cup of tea perhaps?"

The woman shook her head. "No thank you, I had a lovely breakfast at my hotel before coming here."

Unwin looked surprised. "I see, then you flew in yesterday, I take it. I wasn't expecting you until tomorrow."

"Yes, I had a chance of an early flight and could not wait to come and study this great find."

Unwin beamed with pride. "Yes indeed, we were very fortunate to be bequeathed these treasures. Of course, the professor was a great friend to the museum. This wing we're standing in now was actually built and named in his honour."

"So, I read in one of your pamphlets. He sounds like a very great man."

"Oh, he was," agreed Unwin. "Although, as with the collections of many eccentrics, the provenance of some of his treasures cannot always be relied on."

"Indeed."

Unwin was careful not to say too much. He was all too aware that there was a great deal of speculation among those in the know about some of the professor's most treasured <u>finds</u>.

The last thing he wanted was to initiate a legal battle between their two countries over the ownership of their latest acquisition.

In the background, the museum crew were busy setting up the awnings and backgrounds for the upcoming exhibition.

Unwin drew the woman's attention to it.

"What do you think of our scenery so far?" he asked, pointing out the workers behind her.

The woman smiled. She was not taken in by his clumsy subterfuge.

"It all looks very promising," she agreed. "But I trust I will be given adequate time to complete my work before it opens?"

"Yes, of course," Unwin nodded, "and if for any reason you require more time, I'm sure we can work something out. The main feature of our exhibition will be our mummy, naturally. But if you need to work on her once the exhibit is open to the public, you'll be welcome to come in when the museum is closed."

"Thank you, that would be most acceptable." The woman looked directly into Unwin's eyes as she spoke. Her gaze did not waver, even to blink.

Unwin felt mesmerised. It was as if he was suddenly drifting on an invisible cloud, moving closer towards her.

He did not dare to blink, either. Her eyes became large like swirling pools, cool and refreshing, urging him to dive straight in, and lose himself in them.

"Mr Unwin."

The booming voice of his head of security brought him out of his daydream.

Unwin shook the image from his mind.

When he looked up, the doctor had already replaced her mask and glove and was intensely studying something from the open chest before her.

"Er, yes," replied Unwin, still feeling woozy.

"There's a delivery out back needs your signature," the guard informed him.

Unwin raised his hand to his forehead.

He hoped this was not the start of a migraine coming on.

"Yes, coming," he responded, rubbing the bridge of his nose between his thumb and index finger as he followed the large man to the loading dock.

Chapter Nine

THE MAN WATCHED, HIDDEN FROM SIGHT BY THE bushes that covered this side of the museum car park.

His pale linen suit was crumpled and wrinkled from the flight over from Egypt.

He had not had anything to eat or drink since his dinner on the plane the previous night and now his belly gnawed with hunger, but he ignored it.

Kasim was on a mission of great importance, one of honour and dignity, and in such circumstances, mere hunger was very low on his list of priorities.

The doctor was clever. She had managed to give his people the slip two days ago in Cairo. It took them a while to discover she had booked an earlier flight than the one they believed she would be on.

But it was no matter.

He was here now, and he was determined to succeed in his task.

Kasim tensed as he heard the staff door open as it had countless times that evening.

It had to be her.

Chapter 9

From his vantage point he saw the figures of two young women emerge from the door.

Neither of them was the doctor.

Perhaps she intended to work through the night? It would not be the first time.

Her reputation for immersing herself in her passion to the detriment of her own physical health was well known among members of the board of antiquities.

Indeed, Doctor Anmali was considered almost inhuman amongst her peers, because of her capacity to work on a new discovery day and night, seemingly without need of sleep or sustenance.

But if this was going to be one of those occasions, then he knew he could not wait for her to show herself.

If necessary, he would have to find a way to break into the museum and confront her.

His was a sacred mission, and justice would not be denied indefinitely.

Kasim waited for another hour, during which time several other members of staff left for the night. He watched as the security staff changed over and noticed with interest that only one night guard appeared to have been left on duty.

After a while, he saw the night guard let the cleaners out.

It was now almost ten o'clock. The summer sky had given way to the dusk, and stars lit the sky above his head.

Still there was no sign of her.

Enough! He decided that fate had left the doctor alone inside the museum with only one solitary guard for company.

The security man had looked old and weak, too weak for such a duty.

Even so, Kasim wished he had a weapon with him. Under normal circumstances, he would have his revolver at hand, just in case of trouble. But, with the risk of being caught too great to consider it an option, he had reluctantly left his trusty gun back in Egypt.

He looked around him for something substantial he could use as a club.

There were some discarded building materials dumped in a corner of the car park. He went over to investigate and managed to find a piece of a broken wooden curtain rod.

He slapped it against his palm several times to test it.

It was not ideal, but it would do.

Carefully checking the area to ensure he was not being observed, Kasim crept forward, keeping the wall of the car park to his right.

There were now only two vehicles left in the park. One he had seen the security guard drive up in. The other, he suspected, must belong to the doctor.

He considered trying the car doors, to see if she had left one unlocked.

If so, he could get in and lie in wait for her, hiding on the floor at the back.

Just as he was about to reach for the nearest handle, he remembered that most cars now had motion alarms fitted, and the last thing he needed was to draw unwanted attention to himself.

He continued on his way, heading for the staff door.

As he reached it, he stopped and looked up at the building. There were still several windows open, which with luck meant the guard would be on patrol at some point to close them.

They did offer him a point of access, however. But he would need to find a ladder to reach them, so they were not going to be his first choice.

Then, he realised, there had to be a fire escape somewhere, which might mean there was a metal staircase on the outside of the building.

Kasim looked both ways along the side he was on.

Chapter 9

There was no sign of one, therefore, it had to be either at the front, or more likely, down one of the other sides.

While he was here, it made sense for him to try the staff door, just in case.

As he was about to test it, he heard a movement from the other side.

It was too late to run and hide, so he lifted his wooden pole, ready to attack.

He held his breath and waited.

The locking bolt shot back, and the door opened towards him, blocking his view of whoever was coming out.

The good thing, he realised, was that it also blocked their view of him, so he stayed still, poised to strike if the need arose.

He heard a young girl call out to the security guard, wishing him good night.

Seconds later, she appeared from behind the door, walking towards the entrance to the car park.

She had not seen him.

The staff door began to swing shut on its hinge.

There was no sign of the guard.

Perhaps the girl had let herself out?

After all, Kasim had heard her shout out to him. If he had been nearby, she would not have had to call out at all.

He took his chance.

Just as the door's lock was about to engage, he sprang forward and wrapped his fingers around the edge of the door. He pulled gently and the door hesitated for a second before giving way. Kasim managed to pull it open.

As he suspected, there was no sign of the old guard.

Kasim slipped inside and carefully pulled the door closed behind him.

Once inside, he looked about him.

There was a long corridor before him, with different types of props and scene-drops leaning against both sides. In the distance, he could see a small office, with a dim light coming from inside. Probably the security office.

Kasim wondered if he should take care of the guard before commencing his task.

But then he remembered his instructions. He would kill the guard only if it became necessary to conceal his presence.

Kasim walked along the side of the wall, keeping as close to the leaning props as possible. Several of them stuck out at right angles and would make excellent places for him to hide, should the occasion arise.

As he drew closer to the office, he could hear the sound of a television with the volume up high. The old man was probably hard of hearing, which in this case was a blessing Kasim had not expected.

He crept past the office and turned the corner that led him through a labyrinth of corridors, finally bringing him out in the storage area behind some of the exhibition galleries.

Kasim tried the first door he came to, but it was locked, as were the second and the third. Starting to grow frustrated, he decided that the next door would open for him, regardless.

He turned the handle and braced his shoulder against the wood, ready to ram it open.

But, to his relief, it opened without resistance.

Kasim found himself in the main entrance lobby of the museum.

At the front, next to the ticket booth, was a board with a map of the whole museum, illustrating where everything was.

Kasim studied the directions until he found what he was seeking. He could feel the excitement within him growing.

As he walked from room to room, ignoring the amassed treasures and the rich treasury of knowledge and learning that surrounded him, Kasim felt an eerie shiver run through his veins.

Being closed, the museum was illuminated only by the

Chapter 9

emergency lights, which were barely enough to let him see where he was going.

The faint buzz emanating from the fluorescent bulbs that lit many of the display cases and vitrines around the room was the only sound that filled his ears.

More than ever, he wished he had more with which to defend himself than his lump of wood.

Kasim walked on through several smaller rooms and turned a corner at the reptile section of the natural history wing. In the distance, he could see the awnings masking off the section that the museum had dedicated to their latest acquisition.

He could see the light reflected from behind the fabric shield.

Someone was still working there.

Kasim knew only too well who it was.

Stealthily, he crept towards the awning, and peered around the edge.

In the distance he could see Doctor Anmali bent over a desk, concentrating on whatever she had laid out on the table before her.

Even with her gown and mask on, Kasim recognised her instantly.

He gripped the club in his hand until his knuckles grew white.

Crouching, he edged his way forward, leaving the protection of the awning behind him. He kept to his left so as to remain out of the woman's peripheral vision.

There was an eerie silence in this part of the museum.

Kasim could hear his heartbeat in his ears.

Though he was treading as carefully as he could, he felt he could still hear his footfalls echoing in the silence.

Suddenly, the doctor looked up from her work and saw him. She did not appear at all surprised by his presence. It was almost as if she had been expecting his arrival.

Now the game was up, Kasim drew himself to his full height. The two of them stared at each other for a moment.

The woman pulled down her face mask. "I wondered how long it would be before one of you came here," she said. "I don't know what you hope to gain, but whatever it is, I cannot assist you."

Kasim moved closer until he was within reaching distance of the doctor.

"What you are doing here is sacrilege, and you know it." He spat the words through gritted teeth.

"Sacrilege? According to whom, exactly? A deluded bunch of fanatics like you and your group? What I am engaged in is scientific and historical research, nothing more."

Kasim moved closer, his wooden club held tightly in his hand.

The doctor did not flinch although she feared he was ready to strike.

Just then, they both heard a muffled creaking noise coming from behind the doctor.

They both turned, and stared off, into the dim light towards the far end of the exhibition.

Without looking back, the doctor began to walk towards the sound.

Kasim's club struck the back of her head before she had taken her third step.

She crumpled to the ground.

Kasim took a moment to check the doctor's pulse. He could feel something, but it was very faint.

No matter. If she died, she had only herself to blame.

He stood up and walked towards the area from where the sound had just come.

He wished more than ever now that he had remembered to bring a torch. But he had been in such a hurry to leave once he received the call that he barely remembered his passport.

Chapter 9

Kasim moved cautiously across the room, squinting in the dim light to try to see what lay ahead.

Finally, the sarcophagus came into sight. It stood tall and erect in one corner of the replica tomb that had doubtless been created by the museum's construction crew.

The front cover was ajar and stood at right angles to the main body. But, as its hinge was on his side, he could not see what was inside.

Kasim walked around the open casket until he stood directly in front of it.

Inside he saw the mummy of Anlet-Un-Ri.

The mummy towered over him. The wrappings, grey from thousands of years, together with the poor lighting, made it impossible for him to make out any definite details.

He stared at it, mesmerised. The life of Anlet-Un-Ri was a legend in his country – her death a mystery.

The location of her earthly remains had been disputed among scholars since as far back as the 18th dynasty, and yet here he was, a humble servant of his sect, standing before her.

Kasim fell to his knees and bowed down.

He uttered a silent prayer of thanks, during which he lifted his upper body and gazed up at the mummy, before lowering it again to continue his worship.

The third time he rose, something odd caught his attention.

Although it was too dark to tell for sure, the mummy appeared to have opened her eyes, and was staring down at him.

Kasim halted his mutterings and tried to focus through the shadowy darkness.

It was true – the mummy had come back to life!

Before he had a chance to jump up, the mummy took a tentative step outside her sarcophagus.

Kasim screamed, in spite of himself, no longer concerned with raising the alarm.

The mummy cleared her sarcophagus just as he found his feet.

One of her enormous arms shot forwards and her bound fingers wrapped themselves around Kasim's neck, lifting him clear off the floor until their faces were level.

There was nothing behind the ancient wrappings that resembled eyes, only black sunken pits. But to Kasim, hell itself poured forth from within them.

He struggled to scream, but the hold on his neck was too tight to let him emit a sound.

He fell into a world of darkness within seconds.

Chapter Ten

Scrapper sat in the dingy flat on the fifteenth floor of a tower block in one of the less salubrious parts of Brixton.

Outside, he could hear the noise coming from the evening rush hour, as every second driver apparently thought using their horns was just what was needed to get the congestion moving along.

Beside him on the torn leather sofa sat Phil, anxiously rubbing his hands together.

Scrapper gave his friend a gentle slap on the arm, and mouthed the words, "Calm down," to him.

He knew that Phil was uncomfortable about this meeting. But he was Scrapper's right hand, so he had to be there.

Scrapper himself was so excited, he was fit to burst.

This was finally his chance at the big time. His name had been bandied around town as a reliable delivery man, and finally, last night, he had received a call from one of the biggest families in south London. The Bixby family virtually ran the area, and nothing went down without their knowledge.

The police could not touch them, although it was not from

want of trying. But everyone knew that, if you grassed up a Bixby, the next funeral you went to was your own.

They had connections all over the country and their outfit was, by far, the largest suppliers of drugs in the entire south.

There were even rumours that they were thinking of a takeover bid that would give them the run of the home counties as well.

Now that was real ambition, and Scrapper could see himself slotting right in with the rest of the gang.

The problem had always been that he did not have any major connections in the game.

All his life he had strived to be part of something spectacular in the criminal underworld, but no one ever took him seriously enough. Being a nine-stone string-bean with acne did not exactly exude menace, but Scrapper had worked hard to earn himself a reputation as a hard man.

He had tried bodybuilding down at their local youth centre but, within a couple of weeks, he grew tired of some of the bigger blokes laughing at him behind his back because of the modest weights he was using.

He considered taking steroids, as some of the users told him he could create a killer body in a couple of months. But he had seen documentaries about some of the side effects of those, and they were not pretty.

Worst of all, they could give you erectile problems and that would do nothing to enhance his reputation.

So he looked for other ways to command respect.

He shaved his head. He would have liked a beard but, alas for him, his facial hair never reached an adequate consistency to look like anything other than peach-fuzz.

He had several tattoos, most of which depicted skulls and bleeding daggers, with a couple of naked women thrown in for good measure.

Scrapper had been in and out of young offender institutions,

Chapter 10

but he knew that, among the fraternity he wanted to be part of, only prison counted. At one point, he made up his mind that he would commit a criminal act serious enough to earn him a couple of years inside.

Not too long. But long enough to make his mark.

The crime had to be something dangerous. He read the papers and scanned the news channels to see what sort of crimes he could commit to garner the desired effect.

He decided on robbery.

But it had to be armed robbery.

Scrapper was hardly going to walk into prison with his head held high for mugging some old lady so he came up with a plan to rob a newsagent, using a knife.

A gun would be better, but he had no idea how to get hold of one.

He stole a large carving knife from his mother's kitchen and set out on his grown-up criminal career.

His plan was to hold the staff up at knife-point, empty the till, grab some fags, and make sure it was all caught on camera.

If one of the owners decided to be a hero, Scrapper even had a plan to stab them. Not anywhere fatal, perhaps in the arm, or the shoulder. Just enough to ensure he got a proper sentence when he was up before the beak.

But the first three shops he went into, he discovered that he did not have what it took to carry out such a crime.

On each occasion he marched in with his knife tucked inside his jeans, gripping the handle in anticipation for the moment he would pounce.

But every time the shop keeper asked him what he wanted, he froze, and ended up buying a pack of chewing gum, all of which he later discarded because he hated the stuff.

Scrapper had smoked pot since he was in secondary school, so he knew some of the local suppliers quite well. After his debacle with the abortive hold-ups, he decided to spread the word around that he wanted to become more than just a good customer.

He knew they were always looking for distributors and couriers, so it seemed to him another viable avenue for breaking into the business.

It took a while for any of them to trust him enough, but eventually he received his first call.

It was an easy job. He just had to pick up a small package from a flat in Battersea and take it across the river and deliver it to a bloke in Pimlico.

The operation went like clockwork, although Scrapper must have lost 10 pounds in sweat on the journey.

He was well paid and, most importantly, he did not ask any questions.

Scrapper had no idea what was in the package, and he did not care. For all he knew, it might have been a dummy run to see if he could be trusted.

A week went by before he received his next job. This was a slightly bigger consignment, which, he was told, would look too suspicious to carry on public transport, so he needed a vehicle.

Trouble was, Scrapper could not drive, which was why he enlisted the help of his old mate Phil. They made a good team, which meant Phil just doing whatever Scrapper said without question.

The pair of them carried on working together after that. The size and frequency of the jobs increased, which to Scrapper meant he was gaining a solid reputation that would eventually lead to his introduction to the big time.

Finally, his time had come.

Len Bixby was not a senior member of the gang. He was in fact a distant cousin of the family who was trusted with odds and ends here and there. But he was still a Bixby, and that was what mattered to Scrapper.

Across from them, seated in two unmatched armchairs, were

Chapter 10

Len's girlfriend, Amber, and another girl who had been introduced to them as Lucy.

Both girls were made up for a night on the town, complete with leather mini-skirts and fishnet stockings.

Scrapper had decided not to invite Sara to the meeting. He liked to have her around because she was stunning and sounded posh. But she had an annoying habit of saying stupid things in company, making him look like an idiot as a result.

And that was the last thing he wanted in such distinguished company.

Anyway, he was happy enough checking out Amber's friend, especially as every time she smiled at Phil, he looked away, embarrassed.

Len returned from the kitchen carrying five opened bottles of beer.

He handed them around before taking the arm of Amber's chair.

"Cheers," he said, holding up his bottle.

Everyone raised theirs in salute before they drank.

The beer was ice cold, and played havoc with Scrapper's sensitive teeth, but he supressed the urge to wince, and glugged back a couple of good swallows.

"Now to business," said Len. "I've got a bloke in the sticks who I've been supplying for about a year, and now 'e wants to branch out a bit, set up his own crew."

Scrapper shook his head. "Can't 'ave that," he announced confidently. "Is that the job? You want us to go an' take care of 'im?"

Phil turned to his mate, his brows knitted.

What the hell was Scrapper talking about?

They did not know how to "take care" of someone, as he put it. He was beginning to feel that this meeting was a bad idea. Phil was happy enough staying with Scrapper for the time being. But collecting and delivering weed was one thing. Sorting blokes out was another kettle of fish altogether.

Len shook his head. "What? No, nothin' like that," he replied, obviously surprised by Scrapper's question. "'e's lookin' to expand, that's all. I'll still be 'is supplier, that's the deal, only now he wants more gear to get things movin'"

"Right." Scrapper nodded knowingly.

"So, what I need," continued Len, "is a couple of reliable blokes 'oo can courier the stuff for me, no questions asked."

Scrapper finished another swallow of beer and released a loud belch.

Phil noticed Lucy wrinkle her nose, and Amber just shook her head in disbelief.

"Well, we're definitely your men," offered Scrapper, slapping Phil on the shoulder.

Len nodded. "Yea, I 'eard you did a job for a mate of mine in Vauxhall the other day. That was good work."

Scrapper held out his arms. "I'm a businessman," he exclaimed, much to the amusement of the two girls. "My word is my bond, an' I never let me business associates down."

Len nodded. "I'm glad to hear it," he replied.

Reaching under the cushion of the armchair, Len pulled out a handgun.

He held it towards Scrapper, by its barrel.

Scrapper handed his bottle to Phil, almost dropping it in his haste to jump out of his seat and grab the gun.

He had never seen, much less held, a real gun before.

Scrapper could not contain his excitement.

He hefted the weapon from one hand to the other, feeling the authority of the weight. Then he turned it over in his hand, pretending he was looking for something, before giving up. Next, he looked down the sights, pointing the gun towards the window behind Lucy's head.

"Careful," Len cautioned. "It's loaded."

Chapter 10

Scrapper carefully placed the gun on its side, on the arm of the sofa.

"You ever used one of 'em before?" asked Len.

Scrapper was loath to tell the truth, but he did not wish to create a bad impression by being caught out in a lie.

"Not as such," he answered, "A mate of mine's old man 'ad a couple 'e used to bring out now an' again, but 'e never let us fire them."

Len nodded.

Phil raised his eyes to heaven.

"Well, if all goes to plan, you shouldn't need one for this job, I just wanted to know 'ow you were fixed in case the need arose in the future."

Scrapper nodded.

He reached over to retrieve his beer from Phil.

As he moved, he nudged the gun by accident. Before he had a chance to react, the weapon fell off the arm and landed on the wooden floor with a loud thud.

Scrapper leaned towards Phil, covering his head with his hands, preparing for the report as the gun went off.

But it never did.

Once he realised all was safe, Scraper sat back up and straightened himself, desperately trying to appear as if he had not been ruffled by the weapon falling.

Len stood up and walked over to pick up the gun.

He held it in front of Scrapper. "Good job you left the safety on, ain't it?"

Len walked back to his chair.

The women burst out laughing at Scrapper's antics.

Scrapper joined in the laughter in an attempt to make the whole incident seem like a joke when, in reality, he knew he was the butt of it.

He grabbed back his beer and took another long swig to calm himself down.

Once they had all finished their drinks, Len stood up. "Right then, lads, I'll be in touch soon, now if you'll excuse us, me and the ladies are off out for the night."

Scrapper and Phil stood up.

Scrapper offered Len his hand, but Len ignored the gesture and placed his arm around his shoulders instead. "You won't let me down when I call, will yer?" he whispered in Scrapper's ear.

There was an edge of menace to his voice that made Scrapper tremble involuntarily.

Scrapper tried to turn to look back at Len, but their heads were to close together, and Len kept a tight hold of his shoulder, preventing him from moving back.

"No… not at all. You can rely on me," Scrapper stuttered."

"Good." Len led them to the front door.

Phil turned and smiled at the girls. "Nice to have met you," he said.

The two women stood up in unison and walked towards Phil.

"My friend here was wondering if you could talk," said Amber, glancing over at Lucy.

Lucy sidled up to Phil and linked her arm through his. "Fancy joining us up west?" she asked. "I get awfully lonely watching these two make out all the time."

Phil was taken aback. He could feel his cheeks redden.

Before he had a chance to answer, Scrapper called to him from the open front door.

Phil carefully slid his arm out of Lucy's and apologised.

As he walked towards the front door, he nodded at Len, then kept his head low.

Once outside, Scrapper slapped Phil on the back. "We're in, son – told yer so."

Phil shrugged him off. "What was all that bollocks with the gun?" he demanded.

Chapter 10

"What?" replied Scrapper, clearly shocked by his mate's question.

"What d'yer mean, what? That crap that bloke was talkin' about us needin' a gun in the future. Understand this – I ain't now, or ever, havin' anything to do with guns. Is that clear?"

Scrapper looked over his shoulder to make sure their argument could not be heard.

"Keep yer bleedin' voice down, will yer?" he urged. "I told yer this was the big time, right? So it stands to reason we may 'ave to be tooled up some day."

"Tooled up!" Phil mimicked. "Will you just listen to yerself? This ain't a fuckin' game of cowboys and Indians. That was a real gun that bloke 'ad, the type that kills people."

As they reached the lift lobby, two women with prams stepped out of the lift.

Phil kept the swing door open for them to pass through.

Once they were gone, the men stepped into the lift.

Scrapper hit the ground button. "Look, Phil, I ain't talkin' about killin' anyone, either, but if Len reckons we need to be armed for a job, we'd be daft not to listen."

Phil stared back at him. "Let me make this clear, the day that Len bloke, or anyone else, says we need a gun, I'm off the job, an' I'm serious."

Scrapper held his hands out. "Okay, okay, no sweat, bruv. Everythin's gonna be fine – just trust me."

Phil was far from convinced, but he decided to let it drop for now.

Somehow, he had a nasty feeling that they had just made a deal they would one day regret.

Chapter Eleven

Detective Inspector Dawn Cummings flashed her badge at the uniformed constable manning the entrance and parked her Astra in the nearest spot in the museum car park.

At 39, she was the only female senior officer at her station.

It was a position she was proud to hold, although her ambition had always been to reach the dizzy heights of commissioner one day. The fact that she had already failed the DCI exam twice was not lost on her or her superiors so, for now, she was happy to plod along and see what the future might hold.

Dawn was an eternal optimist, and lived by the saying, "Never say never," so she was open to whatever might be waiting for her around the corner.

She had lived in the home counties all her life and, other than a couple of brief secondments to London, Birmingham and Liverpool, she was happy to stay where she was. Her ambition aside, she was not willing to swap the idyllic peace and relative quiet of the countryside for the crowds, dirt and noise of the big cities.

As she slid out of her seat, Dawn placed the wallet holding

Chapter 11

her warrant card and badge into the band of her skirt, with the badge on the outside. This left her hands free to hold her pad and pen to take notes.

Over time, she had become aware of her failing memory, so it made sense to her to keep a record of details she felt pertinent while on the job.

As she walked towards the staff door, she could see the corpulent figure of DS Courtney waiting for her. In her opinion, he was not what might be termed "lightening in a bottle", but he was diligent and straightforward, and was one of the few DSs she had worked with who did not complain about having to do the donkey work.

"Morning, Scot."

"Morning, guv," he replied. "Sorry to drag you out of bed, but this looks like it might be a curly one."

"What have you got?"

Courtney flicked through his notes. "Body discovered early this morning inside the museum. The security guard who found him is still quite shaken, he's inside on his 15th cup of sweet tea, poor old bloke."

"Anything suspicious?" asked Dawn, moving aside to allow a couple of men in overalls and face masks inside.

"Well initially there was no obvious signs of assault and we thought perhaps the bloke had simply had a heart attack. But, on closer examination, the pathologist noticed bruising around his neck. Now he's saying it looks as if he was strangled."

"Witnesses?"

Courtney shook his head. "Only the artefacts and statues. Shame they can't talk."

"Have you managed to find out who the victim was?"

"Yep, he conveniently had his passport on him. Name's Kasim Kassimme and, according to the visa and stamp in his passport, he only arrived yesterday from Egypt."

"That's odd," replied Dawn. "Bloke arrives in a foreign

country, comes straight here and gets killed for his trouble. What's that about?"

The DS shook his head. "According to the guard, he did not recognise the victim, says he only came on duty last night, but according to him, the only member of staff left was a visiting academic, a Doctor Anmali," Courtney looked up at his boss. "Coincidentally, he thinks she's also from Egypt."

"Well, that can't be a coincidence, can it?"

"That's what I thought. According to the guard, she was working here until 11 last night. He said he doesn't know where she lives, but we've called the curator of the museum and he's on his way now. Hopefully he can fill in the details."

Dawn nodded.

Just then, the two forensic officers who had entered earlier appeared with a stretcher.

Dawn and the DS moved back to allow them to exit with the body.

They were followed by the pathologist, Doctor Fergusson.

When he saw Dawn, he smiled. "Good morning, Inspector, I'll have your man on the slab after breakfast. Shall we say two o'clock for the PM results?"

Dawn had always found the pathologist a little too brusque for her tastes, but he had a good reputation for not missing a single thing.

"Thanks, Doc, see you there."

They watched as the technicians loaded the dead man into their van and waited for them to slam the doors before they continued.

"So how does this security guard look to you?" Dawn asked her DS.

Courtney frowned. "How do you mean?"

"Well if he was the only one on site, do you think it's possible he's our assailant?"

The DS thought for a moment, then shook his head. "No

Chapter 11

way, he's badly shaken up – there's no way he's faking it. Once I'd finished questioning him, I told him he could go home, but he's too shaky to drive. We called his wife and she's on her way to pick him up."

They looked up as another car entered the car park.

The driver swung their vehicle towards where Dawn had parked, then slammed on the brakes when he noticed the space was taken.

There followed a crunching of gears, before the car reversed enough to take up another spot.

The two officers waited for the occupant to exit his vehicle and walk over to them.

Courtney showed his ID as the man approached.

"And who might you be?" asked Dawn, not bothering to show her badge.

The man was covered in perspiration, far more than was warranted by the early morning sunshine.

"My name is Stanley Unwin, I'm the curator of the museum." He removed a pocket handkerchief from the breast pocket of his jacket and used it to wipe his forehead. "What on earth is going on here?" he demanded. "The officer who called me said a body had been found inside."

"That's right, sir," replied Dawn. She turned to Courtney. "What was his name again?"

"A Mr Kasim Kassimme," the DS relayed, checking his notes.

"Apparently, he arrived in this country yesterday, from Egypt, and from what we can gather he made a beeline for this place," Dawn informed him. "Was he a guest of the museum?"

Unwin stood there for a moment and thought. "No, the name means nothing to me, he's certainly not one of my team."

"But you do have another visitor from Egypt working here?" Dawn asked.

Unwin nodded, surprised that the DI was so well informed. "That's correct, Dr Anmali is an archaeological forensic specialist. She's here to study and carbon-date some ancient relics that have recently come into our possession. We have her on loan from the museum in Cairo."

"And, to your knowledge, this Dr Anmali has nothing to do with our victim?"

"Not as far as I'm aware," Unwin replied. He fumbled in his pockets for another hanky. When the phone call from the police woke him up, he just grabbed the first suit he could find, which, typically was one of his heavy winter ones.

His hands shook as he mopped his brow once more.

His nervousness was not lost on either officer.

"Are you all right, sir?" asked Courtney.

Unwin stared at him. "All right!" he stammered. "Of course, I'm not all right. We have a major exhibition due to open to the public in a few days, and now you're telling me a complete stranger has been found dead in my museum. How can I be all right?"

"Not just dead, I'm afraid," Dawn informed him. "Murdered."

The news caused Unwin to take an unsteady step backwards.

The two officers looked at each other. The information had clearly been a shock to Unwin, judging by his response. Which was a good sign for them.

"Oh, my goodness, murdered," Unwin muttered to himself. He looked up. "How?"

"Well we're waiting on the post mortem to give us the full details," answered Dawn, "but from what we can ascertain so far, it looks as if it might have been strangulation."

Unwin's hand shot to his mouth. His eyes were wide behind his wire-rimmed glasses.

"We believe that Dr Anmali was the last person to leave last night," Courtney mentioned, scanning through his notes.

"Er, I don't know," Unwin said, still shaking. "I left at about six-thirty; she was definitely still here when I went home."

Chapter 11

"Your security guard confirmed the time for us," Dawn confirmed. "Do you happen to know where we can contact this lady?"

Unwin attempted to settle himself. He was aware that his demeanour did not conform to the dignity of his position.

A murder? On his premises!

He could only imagine what the bad publicity would be like, once the press got hold of it.

He could see the headline: *Murder at the Museum.*

It was like something out of a bad dream.

"Mr Unwin," urged Courtney.

"Yes, yes of course, please follow me into my office, I have all her contact details in there."

As they were about to enter the building, a white van with a security logo on the side turned the corner at speed and screeched to a halt at the command of the officer at the entrance.

Unwin looked back. "That's Bill Stead, our head of security, he can show you any details you need about the comings and goings of our staff."

Dawn placed her thumb and forefinger in her mouth and gave a deafening whistle.

The uniformed officer talking to the driver looked up and Dawn signalled for him to let the van through.

The three of them did not wait for the security guard to catch up but continued to Unwin's office.

Once inside, he found the details of where the doctor was staying, and Dawn copied them in her notebook.

While they were still there, there was a knock at the door.

"Come in," Unwin called.

Bill Stead entered the room. He glanced at the two officers and half-smiled before he began speaking. "Mr Unwin, I just heard. This is terrible."

"Yes, Bill," replied Unwin, "these officers will need your

assistance in seeing if we can identify this poor man and discover what he was doing here in the first place."

Stead nodded. "I've just had a quick word with old Stan, he's pretty shaken up, but he says his wife is on her way over to fetch him."

"Do you have any CCTV here in the museum?" asked Dawn.

Stead turned to face her.

The look he gave her made her feel uneasy, almost as if he was trying to imagine what she would look like naked.

She held his gaze until he looked away.

"Well, we do," he said, nervously, "but I'm afraid we only use it when the museum is open, so it wasn't on overnight."

"Terrific," said Dawn, not attempting to disguise the exasperation in her voice. "Do you keep a record of staff members and visitors, and when they enter or leave the building?"

Again, she saw an expression on the guard's face that made her feel uneasy.

Dawn had always considered herself to be a good judge of character, a skill that she had found invaluable as a copper, and there was definitely something off about this bloke.

"Yeah," replied Stead, "we keep a sign-in sheet. I'll check it for yesterday. What name am I looking for?"

"Kasim Kassimme," said Courtney.

Stead left the room.

"You don't think this man might have broken in, then?" asked Unwin. "I mean, if he was up to no good."

"We don't know anything for sure at the moment, other than the fact he's dead," Dawn answered, gazing around the office.

"Our people did have a look around this morning," Courtney chimed in. "There was no obvious sign of a break-in anywhere, so we have to presume for now that he entered some other way."

The security guard returned to the office. This time he did not bother to knock.

"I've checked out the sheet for yesterday. There was no one listed other than the museum staff, and that guest of yours, Mr Unwin."

"Thank you, Bill," said Unwin, "could you have a look round with the crew when they arrive and see if anything is missing?"

Stead nodded. "Will do, Mr Unwin," he assured the curator.

He left without looking at the two officers.

Chapter Twelve

THE ORB AND SCEPTRE WAS THE ONLY FIVE-STAR hotel in town, far beyond the pocket of a humble DI. Dawn had often driven past it, and made the mistake one night of thinking she deserved a large glass of the house red.

That was an error she did not intend to make twice.

How such places justified their pricing was beyond her, but she supposed it was one way to ensure their clientele list was at the higher end of the market.

Dawn showed her badge to the parking valet, who looked as if he had been up all night and desperately needed his bed.

He directed her to the overflow car park, which was practically empty, so she took a spot near the entrance.

The man on duty at the front desk was tall and slim, and was wearing a black and gold waistcoat with shiny gold buttons over his pressed white shirt and black tie.

Dawn showed him her ID card and asked what room Doctor Anmali was staying in.

"Certainly, Madam," he responded, his accent as crisp as his shirt. "Is she expecting you?"

Dawn shook her head. "Afraid not," she replied.

Chapter 12

The man checked the register, then lifted the handset in front of him, and punched three buttons.

After a few seconds, he said. "Oh, good morning, Doctor Anmali. Robert on the front desk here, we have a Detective Inspector Cummings who would like a word with you. Should I send her up?"

Dawn gazed around the large foyer while she waited.

Through the glass double doors that led to the dining room, she could see guests tucking into bacon and eggs, and her stomach rumbled spontaneously. She had not had time for so much as a cup of tea before she left her house that morning, and now she was beginning to feel it.

"Thank you," Robert said and put down the phone. "Inspector," he continued, turning to Dawn, "the doctor is in room three-two-five – it's on the third floor."

He waved his hand toward the lift lobby off to her left.

Dawn rode the lift with an elderly gentleman who rushed to catch it when he saw her entering the car. He was dressed in what appeared to be a very expensive suit and made a stab at polite conversation with her on the journey.

Although he was old enough to be her father, Dawn had an uncomfortable feeling that he was going to attempt to ask her out when the lift stopped at her floor, and she stepped out.

But fortunately, he merely wished her a good day.

Dawn walked down the corridor until she was outside the right door.

She knocked, and a moment later Doctor Anmali opened it, wearing a white towelling robe, with a matching hand-towel wrapped around her head, and white slippers, all with the hotel's insignia on them.

The officer was immediately struck by how beautiful the woman was.

Even without make-up, her skin radiated a healthy glow and her eyes were positively hypnotic.

Dawn showed her badge as she introduced herself. "Good morning, doctor. Sorry for the early-morning call."

Doctor Anmali stood back to allow Dawn to enter the room. "Not at all, Inspector, please come in."

Even in flats, Dawn towered over the minute figure of the academic.

The room was a large double, with an en-suite bathroom and a king-size bed.

There was a television mounted on the wall, a dresser with an arched mirror, two very comfortable-looking armchairs, and two good-sized wardrobes near the door.

"I was just about to have breakfast," the doctor explained. "Would you care to join me? They serve far too much for one person here."

She led Dawn out on to the balcony where there was a garden table and two chairs.

The furniture was solidly built of wrought iron and was painted dark green.

On top of the table was a tray with an assortment of rolls, buns and croissants, individual butter knobs wrapped in gold foil, assorted fruit preserves, each in their own individual jars, and a large plate piled high with various slices of different fruits arranged in an artistic pattern that reminded Dawn of a kaleidoscope.

On a separate tray sat a tall coffee pot, plus matching cups and saucers, sugar basin and cream jug.

Dawn could feel her belly start to rumble again, but this time she managed to talk over it.

"Thank you, this looks lovely," she observed.

They sat down and Doctor Anmali poured them each a cup of piping-hot coffee.

"I take it you are here to check my papers?" she asked, handing Dawn her coffee. "I can assure you they are all in order,

Chapter 12

I have a working visa for three months to cover my time at the museum."

Dawn blew on her coffee before taking a sip. "Sorry, Doctor Anmali, I should have said, the reason I am here is because there was a break-in at the museum last night."

"Oh, I see." The doctor held out the tray of assorted pastries.

Dawn chose a croissant and helped herself to a pot of strawberry preserve.

They talked and ate together.

"Could I ask what time you left the museum yesterday, please?"

The doctor thought for a moment. "I'm not sure, exactly, but I would hazard a guess that it could not have been much after eleven, as I arrived here by twenty past."

"Did you see anyone when you left?"

"Only the elderly security guard. He saw me to the door and buzzed me out."

"Were there any others members of staff still working?"

"Not that I was aware of. Mind you, I was only in one part of the museum, so if there were others elsewhere, there's every chance I did not see them."

Dawn thought for a moment.

The croissant went down a treat. As she shoved the last morsel into her mouth, the doctor gestured for her to help herself to some more.

This time she went for a sweet roll and some butter.

The doctor nibbled on a piece of watermelon, carefully removing the seeds from her mouth with a napkin.

All the while, Dawn could not help but notice the way she looked at her.

There was a hunger in the doctor's eyes which made Dawn shift in her seat more than once.

It was an ironic reversal, as she was usually the one who made suspects squirm when she interrogated them.

But then she reminded herself that the doctor was not a suspect.

Not at this moment in time, anyway.

"May I ask?" Doctor Anmali cut across her thoughts. "Was anything stolen?"

"Stolen?" repeated Dawn curiously.

"Yes, you said there had been a break-in at the museum," the doctor reminded her, "so I wondered if the thieves stole anything specific."

"Okay," said Dawn, catching up, "I see what you mean. When I said there'd been a break-in, I should have clarified that someone broke in and assaulted someone."

The doctor looked shocked. "Not that nice old security man?"

Dawn shook her head, biting off another chunk of roll.

She held her hand up while she chewed, not wishing to spray bread crumbs over the table.

"Sorry." She swallowed too soon and the bread caught in her throat.

Dawn emptied her coffee cup to dislodge it.

"Sorry." She tried again. "No, the victim was a gentleman from your country. Oddly enough, he arrived here in England only yesterday and, from what we can work out, he went straight to the museum."

Dawn watched to see if her revelation produced a reaction from the doctor.

There was nothing.

"I see, how strange," mulled the doctor. "I was not aware of being introduced to anyone else from my country yesterday at the museum. I did meet several of the staff, but I am pretty sure no one from Egypt."

"May I?" Dawn indicated the coffee pot.

"Please do."

"Well, that's the thing, we spoke to the curator and the head

She hoped that now the seed had been planted, Miss Hedges would see to it that such cases would not be repeated.

"I see," Miss Hedges replied, clearly relieved that Danielle had not pursued the matter further.

"I thought it best to bring the situation to your attention in an unofficial way, so to speak."

"Yes, Miss Parker, you did the right thing. Best not to embarrass the girls, as you say." The headmistress turned her head slightly, and gave Danielle a half-smile, before returning to her breakfast.

———

Later that morning, Miss Hedges summoned Cynthia Rollins to her office.

The head girl stopped in between classes.

Miss Hedges had always admired Cynthia. Everyone assumed that she was made head girl because her father was immensely rich and donated a huge amount each year to the academy, on top of the usual fees.

But it was more than that, as far as the head was concerned.

Cynthia lived and breathed the Seddon code of conduct. It was almost as if she had stepped out of the poster for the academy. She was always immaculately turned out, polite, courteous and, academically, she had constantly been in the top three of her year.

It was no surprise, therefore, that she had embraced the position of head Swan with the same enthusiasm and vigour that she displayed when taking on any new task for the academy.

That was why it was with some reluctance that Miss Hedges felt the need to address this issue. She had thought about the situation long and hard since her conversation with Danielle Parker at breakfast, and whereas, under normal circumstances, she would have thought no more about it, Miss Parker was one of those modern teachers who did not fully appreciate the importance of tradition.

Her style might be considered the most appropriate in some modern comprehensive but the problem with these young idealistic types was that they always found it difficult to blend in with a superior seat of education such as this.

But the headmistress knew that she could not afford to have any scandal attached to Seddon. Hence the need for this meeting.

The headmistress welcomed Cynthia into her office and, once she was sure that the door was securely fastened, she began.

"Cynthia, I am afraid we might have a slight problem."

"Really?" The head girl genuinely sounded concerned. "Anything I can help with?"

Miss Hedges smiled, warmly. "You are such a dear," she remarked. "I feel blessed to have you in charge of my upper sixth. Heaven knows how I am going to cope when you head off to university."

Cynthia blushed. "You are too kind, Headmistress."

"Not at all," the head assured her. "I am totally in earnest. Now, to the matter at hand." Miss Hedges chose her words carefully so as not to offend Cynthia. "An observation has been made, one which has subsequently been brought to my attention, that I believe concerns the ducklings."

Cynthia sat forward in her chair. "Oh, really, what sort of observation?"

"Miss Parker spoke to me this morning at breakfast. It appears she has noticed some marks on one of the girls. She did not specify which one, but I had the distinct impression she was referring to a lower-sixth girl."

"I see," responded Cynthia, thoughtfully. "And has one of them made a complaint to her?"

Chapter 13

Miss Hedges shook her head. "Nothing formal. At least, she did not mention it. She was simply concerned about how she might have received those marks."

Miss Hedges watched Cynthia's expression as the girl took it all in.

They understood each other, without having to discuss the specifics of what had taken place, and the headmistress felt she owed her head girl as much respect for her position as she received in return.

"And you believe that we are talking about ducklings?" Cynthia asked.

Miss Hedges nodded.

"Would you like me to investigate the matter?"

"No, nothing like that," replied the head hastily. "I just wished to make you aware of the situation, that's all."

Cynthia smiled. "I see. Well, thank you for letting me know, Headmistress."

The headmistress rose to her feet, and the head girl followed suit.

"I'm so glad you understand the delicacy of the situation, Cynthia. This really takes a great weight off my mind."

The two shook hands formally and Cynthia left.

Later that afternoon, Cynthia gathered the rest of the swans together for an informal chat.

They had a decision to make.

Chapter Fourteen

WHEN DOCTOR ANMALI ARRIVED AT THE MUSEUM, there were still several police vehicles in the car park. She showed her pass to the officer at the main entrance and he signalled for her to go through.

Inside she was met by a frantic curator. Unwin was obviously stressed out by the morning's events, which made him seem even more hyperactive than normal.

He rushed over to greet the doctor when he noticed her standing by his office.

"Doctor Anmali, I am so sorry about all this. We've had some terrible news – an intruder broke in here last night and somehow managed to end up dead on the floor, smack bang in the middle of the exhibition."

"That's truly awful," she agreed. "A police lady came to my hotel this morning to speak to me about it."

Unwin looked concerned. "I hope she didn't bother you too much," he said. "But you see, they wanted to know who was working late here last night, and as you were the last person to leave…"

"That is quite all right, there's no need to concern yourself,"

Chapter 14

she assured him. "Have they made any progress with their investigation?"

Unwin shook his head. "Well certainly none here," he pointed away to his left, in the direction of the Egyptian exhibition. "Their forensic people are still in there, scavenging around on the floor, looking for clues. They've cordoned off the entire area. They won't even let me send in the construction crew to measure up for the next background piece."

"I suppose under the circumstances we will have to be patient."

Unwin removed his wire-rimmed glasses and rubbed the bridge of his nose between his thumb and middle finger before replacing his spectacles.

They sat lopsided on his nose, but he did not appear to notice.

"Patience is the one thing we have in short supply," he moaned. "I've got the chairperson of the board breathing down my neck about the arrangements for the opening night. Apparently, it's too late to cancel or postpone, because the cut-off date for the caterers has already passed. Added to which, we've arranged extra security, as well as a clean-up crew to clear away any litter afterwards. And, to top it all, I've now got my head of display telling me that they've run out of material for one of the backdrops, and they can't find any more with the same dye lot."

Doctor Anmali placed her hand on his shoulder. "You really are in the wars at the moment, aren't you?" she offered, soothingly. "Have the police given you any indication as to when we might be able to enter the area?"

Unwin seemed to calm down the moment she touched him.

"The man in charge seems to think another couple of hours, but you can never tell with these people."

The woman smiled. "That will still leave us plenty of time," she assured him. "I made a good start yesterday, so by tomorrow

I should be able to liaise with your signage team to start creating the information boards."

Unwin smiled. "Oh, that is good news," he said, sounding relieved. "If everyone else pulled their weight as surely as you do, my troubles would be over."

"They're a good team," the doctor assured him. "I'm sure they will all pull together to make this a success."

Unwin nodded. "Yes, I'm sure you're right," he agreed.

"Mr Unwin," Bill Stead called to them from down the corridor. The big security guard strode up beside the doctor, dwarfing her with his enormous frame.

"Yes, Bill, what can I do for you?" asked Unwin.

"I've just finished writing up my plans for the revamp of our security arrangements and I left them on your desk. When you have a minute, could you let me know what you think?"

Stead was sanding directly behind the doctor, talking to the curator over her head.

Doctor Anmali felt a wave of discomfort flood over her.

There was something deeply sinister about the security guard that caused all of her senses to prickle simultaneously.

Not wishing to appear rude, she took a casual half-step forward, away from Stead.

"Thank you, Bill," replied the curator, "I'm sure they will be fine. I'll let you know what I think later."

There followed a moment of uncomfortable silence as the big security guard stayed put, as if awaiting fresh instructions.

Finally, Unwin asked him. "Is there anything else I can help you with at the moment?"

Stead appeared to be the only one of the three who did not feel awkward.

"I was wondering," Stead ventured, "as the exhibition area is still off limits, if the doctor might like a guided tour of the rest of the museum?"

The doctor turned to face the guard, which gave her an

Chapter 14

excuse to take another step back to increase the space between them.

"That is most kind of you, sir," she replied. "But I have some paperwork I need to deal with while I am waiting."

"Perhaps some other time, Bill," Unwin said.

Doctor Anmali could see by the expression on his face that the guard was not happy.

Before she and the curator had a chance to resume their conversation, Stead cut in again. "It's just I was thinking, with the police being here and all, we should make sure that we have everything in order."

"How do you mean?" asked Unwin curiously.

"It's just that the doctor here should really have had a fire and health and safety tour as soon as she arrived yesterday. We don't want the police to think we're being sloppy."

Unwin thought for a moment. "Actually," he said, "that's a good point. The last thing we need is for the police to report us to the Health and Safety Executive for breach of practice."

The doctor did not like the way this conversation was going.

She considered faking a headache but knew that it would not sound feasible after her just saying she needed to concentrate on paperwork.

But she could not fight the sensation that Stead just wanted an excuse to be alone with her. If so, whatever his ulterior motive was, the doctor felt sure that it would not be in her best interest to find out.

However, without an excuse, she felt trapped.

"Doctor." Unwin broke her train of thought. "Bill's right, it was careless of me not to arrange a tour for you yesterday. I'm probably already in breach of some health and safety law. Would you mind terribly if Bill took you now? It'll only be about an hour."

The doctor smiled. "Of course. I understand."

Reluctantly, she turned back to face Stead, straining to keep the smile on her face.

Along the way, Stead made a point of trying to impress the visitor with his extensive knowledge of fire regulations and possible escape scenarios.

Doctor Anmali listened politely and tried, whenever possible, not to make eye contact with the guard. With their pronounced height difference, such a task should have been relatively easy. But, to her annoyance, the guard made a point whenever he was explaining something specific, of bending down and peering straight at her, like a first-year teacher trying to connect with a distracted pupil.

The longer the tour went on, the more uncomfortable the doctor felt in his presence.

Eventually, they reached the end of the circuit, and Doctor Anmali could feel the tension sliding off her shoulders.

This was their final fire door, according to Stead. He led the way down the staircase to the bottom and walked along the short corridor to the exit.

"Now, if you'll just press against this bar here," he said, demonstrating, "we should be out in the open air and safe from whatever has caused the alarm to be activated."

The doctor placed her hand on the release bar.

Turning to face him, she asked: "If I open this, will that not in itself set off an alarm?"

Stead smiled. "Not to worry, Doctor, the perimeter alarms are turned off during the working day. Please go ahead."

Doctor Anmali shoved forward, still half-expecting the alarm to sound, which she surmised would doubtless be the guard's idea of a joke, to try to embarrass her.

Instead, the door refused to budge.

She pushed it harder, using both hands this time, but still nothing.

Before she knew it, Bill Stead placed an arm on either side of her tiny frame, grabbing the release bar just outside where she had hold of it.

As he tried to open the door, his huge frame leaned in against hers.

She knew this was no accident.

He continued to push the bar, each time pressing himself against her back.

"Mr Stead, would you please mind removing your arms from around me?" The doctor kept her voice steady, but inside she was starting to boil over.

"Just a few more good pushes and I think we'll be there," Stead replied casually, his groin area deliberately pushing into her back.

"Sir," announced the doctor, "I am not going to ask you again, now will you please comply with my request, before I do something we both end up regretting?"

There was scorn in the guard's laughter.

He was obviously confident that he was in control of the situation and that they were far enough from earshot for no one else to spoil his fun.

Stead bent down so that his mouth was merely inches from her ear.

"Look, why don't you just relax and enjoy it, mmm?"

The doctor could feel his hot breath on the side of her face. It smelled of stale cigarette smoke and bacon. She could feel her gag-reflex starting to cut in.

Before she had a chance to react, Stead licked the side of her face, his slippery wet tongue leaving a trail up her cheek.

Without warning, the doctor grabbed hold of the middle finger of Stead's left hand. She turned back in on herself and ducked under his arm, taking his hand with her. Like a player in some strange maypole dance, she twisted underneath his opposing arm and yanked his finger after her.

Stead dropped to his knees, fearing his finger would dislocate if he did not comply.

The movement had happened so quickly, the big security guard was still unsure how the petite doctor had managed to manoeuvre him into this position, without his being able to counter her attack.

The doctor spun around and moved behind him, his twisted finger sill clutched in her vice-like grip.

Stead screamed out in agony. He lifted his free hand behind him to try and reach his assailant, but as he did, the doctor pressed her index finger into his neck.

The big security guard felt the strength in his upper body draining away.

His arm sank to his side and his eyes grew heavy.

He could feel himself starting to pass out.

His tongue suddenly felt as if it had grown immeasurably, so that it was now too big for his mouth.

He could not scream any more.

He could not even make a sound.

From far away, he could hear a voice, soft and soothing, lulling him to sleep.

Stead tried to focus on the words being spoken, but he was losing his battle to stay awake, such was the power being imposed by the tiny finger on his neck.

He was strangely glad that he was already on his knees, for it would make his journey to the floor less of a trial.

The security guard sensed, more than felt, his body slump to one side.

That was the last thing he remembered before oblivion came.

Chapter Fifteen

DI CUMMINGS WALKED IN THROUGH THE MAIN entrance of the station. Her pass allowed her to use the officers' entrance around the back, but as she could not be bothered to search her pockets for it, she just flashed the desk sergeant a smile and he buzzed her through.

She made her way to the main office to speak to DS Courtney.

Dawn found him at his desk, speaking on the telephone.

A cup of black coffee and a half-eaten sandwich sat by his computer keyboard. She picked up the coffee and took a sniff of the dark liquid, pulling a face when she found its aroma was absolutely not a patch on the nectar to which she had been treated at the Orb and Sceptre.

She perched on the end of desk and listened in on his call.

The DS appeared to be speaking to someone about the man they had discovered dead at the museum that morning.

Courtney was speaking slower than he usually did, almost as if he were trying to explain something to a child. The DI surmised that he must be talking to someone who did not have English as their first language.

The conversation sounded painful, with the DS having to repeat himself several times before he received an understandable answer.

He leaned back in his chair and covered the mouthpiece with his hand. "All right, guv?" he asked.

"Who are you talking to?"

"Egyptian embassy," he replied. "Trying to see if they can link us up with Mr Kassimme's family and employers in Egypt."

"How're you getting on?"

Courtney looked up to heaven.

"Never mind," the DI replied to her own question. "Let me know what you find out."

The DS nodded. "Super's been on the blower, wants an update."

Dawn nodded and slid off the desk.

Superintendent Cecil Jacks had reached the dizzy heights of his grade as the result of being a fast-track entrant. It was obvious to anyone who had spent any reasonable amount of time on the beat that he knew very little about actual policing. However, he was quite the expert when it came to police procedure and could quote the Police and Criminal Evidence Act in his sleep.

For all that, Dawn actually liked him.

When she first came to the station, Jacks had taken the time to get to know her and made himself available whenever she needed any help or advice.

Being fast-track, he was very keen on motivating his officers to forge ahead and take advantage of all promotion avenues that might open up.

His dry sense of humour often rubbed people up the wrong way and had done so with several of the other officers. But Dawn's father had shared that same quirk, so she was already used to it when they first met.

She knocked on his door.

Chapter 15

"Come in."

"Good afternoon, sir. I believe you wanted to see me?"

"Ah yes, Cummings, come in, take a seat." He made a meal of sliding some paperwork into a folder and setting it to one side before he continued. "I just wanted an update on where we are with that dead body found this morning at the museum."

Dawn sat in the chair opposite him. "Still waiting for the PM report," she informed him. "But from what Doctor Fergusson told me this morning, he suspects foul play was involved."

"I see." Jacks scratched his chin and thought for a moment. "Have the forensic team finished up there yet, do you know?"

Dawn shook her head. "Not sure. Why do you ask?"

"I had a call earlier from the curator," Jacks said. "He wasn't making a complaint, you understand – it's just with this new exhibition of theirs on the horizon, and so much to do before the grand opening, he wanted my assurance that we would clear things up as soon as possible."

"Clear things up!" Dawn repeated, surprised by her senior officer's flippancy. "What exactly are you asking me to do? We only found the corpse this morning. So far, we know next to nothing about the victim, we've taken all the usual statements, there were no witnesses, there's no CCTV…"

Jacks held up his hand to cut her off.

"Yes, of course, I understand, I'm not trying to rush you," he assured her. "It's just that I know this exhibition is a big thing for the museum and indeed for the town. I just want to be able to tell people that we are working as fast as possible to clear this matter up, that's all."

Dawn pulled a face. "Sorry, which people might you be alluding to?"

Jacks looked embarrassed.

He let out a deep sigh. "No one specific," he explained. "But you do know that in my official capacity I sit on several boards, one of which is the regional arts council, so I know exactly how much time, money and effort has gone into this upcoming event."

Dawn bit her bottom lip.

It was a coping mechanism she had developed over the years to stop herself saying something without thinking it through first.

Finally, she said: "Well, you can assure the board from me that I'll do everything I can to make sure this incident causes as little disruption to the proceedings as possible."

She hoped she had managed to keep the sarcasm out of her voice.

Jacks smiled. "Thank you, Inspector, I appreciate your cooperation, and let me know if I can help – more manpower, overtime, that sort of thing."

As she walked back down the corridor away from Jacks' office, Dawn could feel her frustration level rising. She had to remind herself that, to all intents and purposes, Jacks was just a figurehead at the station, waiting patiently for his next promotion and not wanting to cause too many ripples on route.

He could have been a lot worse.

She knew from past experience that those in charge often preferred to make it seem as if they were leading from the front when, in reality, all they did was get in the way and disrupt the flow of investigations.

Dawn made her way to her desk.

She needed a coffee, but she was afraid that her morning brew had now spoiled all other coffee for her.

Courtney made his way over to her desk. "You look like you've lost a monkey and found a quid," he observed "What's up?"

Dawn waved his comment aside. "Nothing, just trying to understand how the wheels of power operate. What have you got for me?"

The DS referred to the paper he was carrying. "Well, I've

Chapter 15

managed to get through to someone at the embassy, they've promised to speak to their people back in Egypt and get back to me." He looked up from his paper. "I won't hold my breath."

"I take it they weren't very helpful."

Courtney shrugged. "It's not so much that they weren't helpful, it's just the bloke on the phone hardly spoke any English, and I didn't want to sound rude and suggest he find someone else to speak to me."

"Was he someone official, at least?"

The DS flushed. "I didn't ask, he was just the person who answered the phone."

"He was probably the cleaner," Dawn joked. Then she realised she had made her DS feel embarrassed and that was not her intention. "We'll give it a day and if you haven't heard back from them, we can always try again," she assured him.

"Right you are, guv," Courtney said. "Doc Fergusson called while you were in with the super."

"What did he have to say?"

"His initial report states it was strangulation, but get this – he reckons every single bone in the poor bloke's neck was broken. He said it was like someone had put his neck in a vice."

"So that suggests the assailant was incredibly strong?" Dawn remarked, thinking about it for a moment. "So, what are we looking for? A bodybuilder-type?"

"More like a power-lifter, according to the doc. He said he had never seen this kind of damage inflicted on another human being that didn't involve machinery of some type."

"And he's sure that no such outside agent is responsible for this?"

The DS shook his head. "That's the first thing I asked him, he said no. The attacker left deep imprints in the victim's neck which went all around, which means he must have huge hands. But according to the doc, if anything hard such as metal or stone were pressed against a victim's neck, they would have left a different pattern."

Dawn remembered her breakfast with Doctor Anmali.

"Well, at least she's off the suspect list," she thought.

Then she remembered something else. "Here, do you remember that big security guard at the museum this morning?"

Courtney nodded. "I was just about to say that. Are you thinking what I'm thinking?"

"Well, he's big enough," Dawn agreed. "Did you take his statement this morning?"

The DS nodded. "Yep, typed it up with the others when I got back. But there was nothing to speak of – he said he was at home all night with his missus. Left work at six, didn't come back to the museum until he was called this morning."

Dawn considered their options. "I think it might be a good idea if we paid his wife a visit, just to confirm his story."

Courtney nodded. "I've got his address on his statement."

"Fetch it – we'll go in my car."

The houses in the street where Bill Stead lived were fancier than Dawn had expected.

"This security lark must pay more than I thought," she commented as they pulled up outside his address.

They both stayed in the car for a moment and stared up at the impressive two-story detached property.

Finally, Dawn said. "Come on, let's see what his good lady has to say."

The young girl who opened the door looked no more than 16 or 17.

The two officers showed their badges and Dawn asked if she

Chapter 15

was Stead's wife, although she looked barely old enough to have left school.

Without answering, the girl held up her index finger, and turned to look behind her.

"Meees Steeead," she called out, in a foreign accent neither of them could place.

They waited as they heard someone descend the stairs. As she arrived at the door, the young girl gave the officers a timid smile and disappeared back inside the house.

"Yes, can I help you?" The woman was in her early thirties. Her dyed blond hair was piled up on top of her head, and she had a deep tan that looked manufactured. Her face was caked with make-up, which Dawn guessed must have taken her hours to apply and probably just as long to remove.

Her nails were extremely long, to the extent that both officers wondered how she managed to perform the simplest of tasks without their breaking or at the very least getting in the way.

She was wearing a leather mini-skirt over fishnet stockings, and shiny black stilettoes. Her top looked to be at least one size too small and could barely contain her ample bosom.

The officers lifted their badges, and the woman gave them a cursory glance.

"Is this about that murder at the museum last night?" she asked outright.

Dawn and Courtney exchanged glances.

"You know about that?" Dawn asked, casually.

"Yeah, me old man phoned me this morning. Sounds horrible."

In the background, a baby began to cry.

The woman groaned. "Just a minute," she said and turned to look behind her. "Marta, the baby's crying!" she yelled at the top of her voice. Without waiting for a reply, she faced front again. "Are you here to speak to him? He's still at work."

"No, that's fine," replied Dawn. "In fact, we were just wondering if you remembered what time he arrived home from work last night."

The woman's eyes widened in shock. "'Ere, you don't suspect 'im, do yer?"

The accent she had been trying hard to affect, presumably for their benefit, suddenly slipped.

Dawn shook her head. "It's nothing to be alarmed about," she assured her. "It's just a question of elimination. Now, do you remember what time he arrived back last night?"

The woman looked up and thought. "I think it was about half-seven."

Dawn noted it down. "Are you sure?"

"Yep," she confirmed confidently. "Coronation Street was just startin' when 'e came in."

"Is that his usual time to come home?"

The woman shrugged. "Depends. 'e usually stops off for a couple on 'is way 'ome, and sometimes 'is dad asks 'im to stop off at one of the 'ouses he rents out."

"His dad?" Dawn repeated questioningly.

The woman nodded. "Yeah, 'e owns the security firm an' they also run a cleanin' firm – that's where I met Bill. An' he also rents a couple of places that 'e's done up."

The baby was sill wailing in the background.

The woman turned. "Marta, fer fuck's sake can't you give 'im a bottle or something?"

She turned back. "Sorry about that. Kids, eh? Who'd 'ave 'em?"

"And once he came home, did your husband go out again?"

"Nah, we 'ad dinner, once Marta 'ad finally got round to makin' it, then we watched telly, then went to bed."

"What time was that?" asked Dawn.

The woman mused. "About 11.30, maybe a bit later."

"And you're sure there's no way your husband could have slipped out without you knowing?" Courtney enquired.

"Absolutely not, 'is lordship there 'ad us up at least three times during the night," she signalled over her shoulder with her thumb. "I 'ad to go an' wake Marta up twice to see to 'im, she could sleep through a brass band, that one."

"Your first?" enquired Courtney.

"And me last, if I 'ave anythin' to say about it. They just take over yer life."

Chapter Sixteen

ANCIENT EGYPT

THE TWO GUARDS ON DUTY AT THE ENTRANCE TO THE Pharaoh's palace stood sharply to attention when they saw the new head of the first army, Anlet-Un-Ri, approaching.

One of them gave the secret knock to inform the guards within to open the main door and allow the mighty soldier to enter.

Once she had done so, and the great door had been closed once more, one of the guards turned to his comrade and asked: "Did you see her the other day in the arena?"

"No," replied the other, clearly disappointed. "I was at my post all afternoon, just my luck. I heard she was magnificent."

"She was," agreed the first. "I've never seen anything like it. She was invincible."

"Did you hear that Pharaoh made her head of the first army as a reward?"

His comrade nodded.

"I know a group of soldiers who are not at all happy with the new arrangement."

"Doesn't surprise me," the other agreed. "But I'm willing to

Chapter 16

bet they won't challenge her in the arena for her new position. Not if they saw what I did."

"Some of them came here yesterday to appeal to Pharaoh, see if they can persuade him to change his mind."

"Did you hear what happened?"

The guard nodded. "According to one of the maidservants, Pharaoh invited them to prove their worth against her in a special tournament at the next God's feast day. He even said they could choose the style of combat."

"What happened?" asked his companion eagerly.

"They all refused. Bear in mind, there were six of them, and the priests from the holy temple, the chief advisers, and Pharaoh's wife and all her handmaidens were also present."

"That must have been awkward. Six seasoned commanders, all refusing to fight a woman, and in such company."

They both laughed.

"She's no ordinary woman, that one," the first guard observed. "I'll bet she's amazing in bed."

His colleague stared at him. "Are you mad?" he exclaimed. "Have you not heard the stories of her former lovers?"

"No, what?" his friend asked avidly.

The guard looked around to check there was no one else within earshot.

Once he was satisfied, he leaned closer to his friend.

"They reckon that, once she has had her fill of a man, she kills him."

"Kills him! How?"

"She fucks him to death."

The other guard laughed heartily. "I like being on duty with you – you're good company. Fucks him to death," he mimicked.

His friend looked at him sternly. "I'm not joking. I heard it from the mouth of the sister of one of her late lovers."

"That's ridiculous."

"Well, do you know anyone who has ever boasted about sleeping with her? I don't."

The other guard thought for a moment. "That doesn't mean they don't exist. Perhaps she just threatened them with death if they revealed the truth."

His companion shrugged. "Possible, I suppose. But still, I wouldn't want to take the risk, would you?"

"Oh, I don't know. I've climbed many mountains in my time, but I bet her summit would be hard to beat."

They laughed together, slapping each other on the back.

Inside the palace, Anlet-Un-Ri walked through the marbled corridors towards the great hall, where the Pharaoh received his most distinguished guests.

This was her first time inside the great palace as a soldier, rather than a guard for the royal household.

As long as she had served, she had never felt overawed by the magnificence of her surroundings.

She was a soldier and, as such, she had no need for such finery. Her world was one of warfare and battle, where the value of the individual was measured by how well they could wield a sword or how far they could throw a spear.

On the field of battle, riches gave you no advantage.

Anlet-Un-Ri was the illegitimate result of one of her father's illicit encounters. A merchant, he travelled throughout the kingdom, trading his wares and drinking himself into nightly unconsciousness.

Her mother was a passing ship who died giving birth to her. So her father took Anlet-Un-Ri back home to his wife and family, where she was shunned by his wife, scorned by the rest of his legitimate household and made to work for her bread.

The merchant already had four sons, fine, strong young men, who had all been tutored in the art of combat privately, by some of the finest masters money could buy.

They delighted in teasing and bullying their little half-sister, beating her without cause and releasing their sexual aggression on her once they considered her old enough.

But they could not break her spirit.

Over time, Anlet-Un-Ri watched her older siblings fight. She learned from their mistakes, and memorised their weaknesses. As she worked, she listened intently to the teachings of those employed to instruct them and practised what she had learnt once everyone else was asleep.

Her work was physically demanding, but she revelled in it, as it made her stronger.

By the time she was 10, she could carry more sacks of grain in one go than any male servant in her father's employ.

At 13, she was already taller by several inches than all of her older siblings, and she often caught glimpses of the fear in their eyes when they approached her. But still she allowed them to chastise and berate her, all the time pretending that she was afraid, cowering under their blows and pleading for mercy.

She was patient and bided her time.

When she was 15, a tournament was held, financed by some of the wealthiest merchants, in honour of the Pharaoh's birthday.

Her father was one of them and he proudly entered his four strapping sons in the name of his house.

As the tournament was about to get under way, Anlet-Un-Ri entered the arena.

Unlike the other combatants, who were all dressed in protective clothing, she had on only her working outfit, which was made of the flimsiest cloth and barely covered her modesty.

The crowd laughed and catcalled as she made her way towards the centre of the arena, to where her four half-brothers and the rest of the male participants waited patiently for the start of the tournament.

Her father, full of rage and embarrassment, ran into the

middle of the gathering, shouting at the top of lungs that he would beat her bloody if she did not cease her folly.

But, before he managed to reach Anlet-Un-Ri, the Pharaoh raised his hand and called for silence. He summoned the lone girl to his side and, in front of the crowd, asked her what she was doing entering such a fierce contest, where death was a potential outcome.

In response, Anlet-Un-Ri dropped to one knee in the sand and pledged her allegiance to the Pharaoh, stating that if he would but give her a chance, she would fight in his honour in the arena, as she hoped one day to do on his battlefields.

The Pharaoh was evidently bemused by her speech, but he could tell by the sincerity of her tone that she meant every word.

To everyone's surprise, he called to one of his guards and instructed him to lend the girl his sword for the tournament.

A gasp went through the crowd as Anlet-Un-Ri returned to the field and took up her position facing her opposition.

As the signal was given for battle to commence, one of her half-brothers, enraged by her audacity, ran at her, swinging his weapon overhead, clearly intent on finishing her off before anyone else had a chance.

Anlet-Un-Ri stayed still, her hands by her side, watching as her sibling approached.

At the last possible second, she launched a counterattack and plunged her sword into his chest, lifting him off the ground with one hand, before dropping his lifeless corpse to the ground.

The arena fell silent.

Her stepmother let out a wail of misery, but her father, wanting to avoid an embarrassing scene, ordered his servants to usher his wife back to their home.

Two slaves hurried into the arena to drag away the first of the fallen.

Chapter 16

Suddenly, a loud cry of anguish rang out, shattering the silence.

It was Anlet-Un-Ri's eldest half-brother.

He stared at her menacingly as he crept forward. Unlike his younger brother, he wanted to draw out his attack in an effort to strike fear into the young girl's heart before he dealt the fatal blow.

The rest of the fighters stood back to allow him to pass without hindrance.

Anlet-Un-Ri took up her stance, and waited patiently for him to reach her.

Their weapons clashed.

Her brother attacked, slashing down at her with all his might, grunting and heaving as he swung his specially made sword through the air, before bringing it down against hers.

Although he was the one on the attack, it was Anlet-Un-Ri who moved forward during their battle. She countered every move he made with perfect precision.

The crowd grew excited, the cheering started up once more and, as the battle raged, the huge crowd roared their approval of Anlet-Un-Ri's every skilful move.

Realising that their eldest brother was in peril, the remaining siblings launched their own attack at their half-sister. This time, from behind. But the crowd rose as one and screamed out a warning, just in time.

The young girl turned to her side and fought with all three brothers simultaneously, like a seasoned professional gladiator.

In the blazing heat, the brothers' protective armour became a hindrance and, after a while, each movement took more and more out of them.

The other fighters stood by and watched, mesmerised by the lightening reflexes of this young girl, as she danced and outmanoeuvred her older siblings, swinging her sword as if it were an extension of her arm.

One of the brothers managed to move close enough to slice his sword across the girl's belly.

The crowd groaned, convinced the fight would soon be over.

But, to everyone's astonishment, Anlet-Un-Ri continued to fight as if she were not even aware of the wound.

Her blood began to pour out, drenching the flimsy material of her clothing. But still she fought on, refusing to submit to the pain she must have been feeling.

As she twisted and turned to fend off each attack from all three sides, one of the straps on her cheap sandals snapped, and Anlet-Un-Ri's foot slipped out from underneath her. As she fell to the ground, she managed to just duck under a swinging blow from one of the brothers that would probably have removed her head had it made contact.

Again, the crowd gasped as one.

On her back now, the young girl grabbed her sword with both hands and, squinting against the sun, continued to fight back.

The three brothers advanced together, ready to take the final fatal blow.

They laughed scornfully, confident that at least one of them would now take revenge for their fallen brother.

Seizing her chance, Anlet-Un-Ri did a back-flip, and as she came up, she lunged forward, sending her sword through one of the men's stomachs, and forcing it out the other side.

Without stopping to draw breath, Anlet-Un-Ri used the weight of her now-dead half-brother to hoist herself back up on her feet. As he started to slump to the ground, she placed her foot on to his shoulder and wrenched her sword free.

As the other two looked on in disbelief, the girl spun around and slashed through the air, decapitating one of them where he stood before thrusting her sword into the stunned open mouth of the last one, sending it straight through and forcing it with her other hand out of the back of his head.

Chapter 16

The cheer from the crowd was deafening.

Inside the arena, Anlet-Un-Ri stood, covered in blood, some of it her own, the rest from her fallen opponents.

She knew her injuries were serious and that they required attention.

But the tournament was far from over.

More than 30 men, fresh, strong and ready to fight, stood between her and the winning purse.

Anlet-Un-Ri turned to face them.

Each man gripped his weapon firmly, ready to attack.

It appeared for a moment as if they had forgotten the rules of combat, and had all decided to turn on her, 30 against one.

Even without her gaping wound, Anlet-Un-Ri knew that she could never defeat so many all by herself.

She readied herself and struck a defensive pose.

Just then, the Pharaoh held up his hands once more.

The crowd fell silent, and the combatants all turned to face him.

"We have all witnessed a great battle this afternoon," he began. "It was not what we had been expecting, but I think you will all agree with me that this young girl has proved herself most worthy."

The crowd roared their approval.

The Pharaoh allowed the noise to continue for a while before asking for silence once more.

"Therefore, I have decided that Anlet-Un-Ri is to be given the honour of the title 'People's Champion', and she will join my secondary wife's household as her personal guard."

The arena erupted in cheers.

Anlet-Un-Ri could feel her head spinning through loss of blood, but she remained on her feet, and turned to salute the remaining fighters.

To a man, they all returned her acknowledgement.

The Pharaoh instructed his best physician to attend to the young girl's wounds.

The tournament was allowed to continue so as not to disappoint the crowd, who doubtless craved more blood.

Her father demanded compensation for the loss of his four sons. But the Pharaoh decreed that they had voluntarily joined the tournament, and therefore had accepted that death would be a possible result.

As promised, Anlet-Un-Ri became the personal guard of the Pharaoh's secondary wife, and she remained in that position until she joined the Pharaoh's army.

She had been proud to fight for the Pharaoh ever since.

It was not unusual for a leader from one of the armies to be summoned to the palace, but usually, it was after winning some great victory, so Anlet-Un-Ri was intrigued to find out why she had been called.

When she entered the great hall, her arrival was announced by a blast of trumpets.

It was all a little overwhelming for her as she was not used to such adulation and preferred the relatively distant recognition received by most troops in service.

At the far end of the hall, the Pharaoh sat on his throne, surrounded by his leading advisors, high priests, and various members of the royal household, several of whom Anlet-Un-Ri recognised from her time in the palace.

The Pharaoh bid her welcome, and offered her refreshment, which she politely refused.

"As you know," he began. "Preparations are under way for the interment of my precious boy, Mehet-Met-Too. His loss is felt greatly by his mother, my secondary wife, as well as the rest of the royal household."

"We all pray for his safe passage into the afterlife," Anlet-Un-Ri assured him.

"I commissioned several casks of a new wine to be placed

into his chamber when he is finally laid to rest," the Pharaoh continued. "It has a very fine, distinct flavour and, after your success in the latest tournament, I have decreed that you shall have some for your personal enjoyment."

The female warrior gave her deepest bow. "I am honoured, my prince."

The Pharaoh clapped his hands, and several wine maidens appeared, each carrying a large jug in her hands.

In all her time at the palace, Anlet-Un-Ri had never formed a taste for fine wines, preferring the harsh aftertaste of soldiers' beer.

But she thanked the Pharaoh once more for his great generosity, and after several more pleasantries were passed, she left with her wine maidens.

As she exited the main palace doors, the two guards from before snapped to attention.

One of them called out. "A beautiful wine for a beautiful lady."

Anlet-Un-Ri stopped in her tracks and the wine maidens did likewise.

She turned to the guard who had made the remark.

"What do you mean by that?" she demanded.

The second guard glanced nervously at his colleague, then edged slowly away from him, as if to show that he had no part in his friend's impudence.

But the first guard was evidently not worried. "I meant no disrespect," he assured her. "All I was saying was that I have heard tell of this wine, and it is extremely fine, a fitting tribute to a lovely lady such as yourself."

Anlet-Un-Ri walked slowly towards him.

The man's smirk slowly drained from his face as the enormous soldier towered over him. By the time she reached him, her breasts were in direct line with his eyes and, realising he had probably gone too far, the guard tried to veer his gaze off to one side, so as not to give any more offence.

"I am not a lady!" Anlet-Un-Ri stated, clearly agitated by his earlier comment. "I am a soldier in the Pharaoh's first army!"

By now, the guard was quivering where he stood.

Without warning, she reached down and grabbed him between the legs, her huge hand dwarfing his tiny sac.

The guard squealed and tried to lift himself on to his toes to ease the pressure.

But, in spite of his vulnerable position, he could feel his manhood swelling against her palm.

His ardour was not lost on Anlet-Un-Ri.

Feeling his growing member, she began to rub her hand up and down the shaft.

The guard moaned and closed his eyes.

"Would you like to come and share my trophy with me?" she asked.

The guard opened his eyes, still unsure if she was in earnest.

"Yes, please," he spluttered, still desperately aware of the delicate position she had him in.

All it would take was for her to clasp her huge hand around his manhood and squeeze tightly and he would be on his knees, begging for mercy.

"Very well," she replied. "Come and find me when you get off duty."

With that, she released her hold on him and turned away.

The two guards watched the Amazonian woman walk away, followed by her wine maidens.

"Are you insane?" asked the first guard. "Have the gods taken your senses and replaced them with the mind of a fish?"

The second guard was breathing heavily, more from relief than anything else. He bent forward, leaning on his spear and massaging his balls with his free hand. "You heard what she said?" he reminded his colleague. "She wants me."

"But for what?"

"What do you think? We're going to drink the nectar from those wine vessels, then we will feast on each other until she is begging me for mercy."

His friend laughed. "With her reputation, I wish you good fortune."

That evening, the guard made his way to Anlet-Un-Ri's quarters.

As commander of the first army, she was not forced to live in barracks with the other soldiers, although she personally had never had a problem with such arrangements.

Her private quarters were far more luxurious and, in her mind, more than equalled those owned by her father.

The Pharaoh had also given her two house-servants to cook, clean and take care of any wants and needs she might have.

The young lady who answered the guard's knock smiled when she saw him, and stood to one side to allow him to enter her mistress's home.

Once he was inside, the young woman led the guard to Anlet-Un-Ri's bedchamber, as she had earlier been instructed to do.

Outside, the sun was already setting and, inside, the room was lit by several candles dotted around. There were not enough to light the entire room, but the shadows they cast seemed to add to the mystery of the owner.

The guard entered the room.

The female soldier sat naked on a bed of furs, propped up on dozens of cushions.

Next to her were several of the wine jugs, and two goblets.

The guard gulped loudly at the naked form of the warrior. As she was so large, and a soldier who had seen many battles, he had somehow expected her skin to be bruised and battered and wrinkled from too much exposure to the sun.

But he could not have been more wrong.

Her olive skin was oiled and it shimmered in the soft glow of the candlelight. Her muscles rippled beneath her firm skin, not hard or bulbous like those of a man, but beautifully formed and feminine in a way he had not seen before.

She had removed her wig, and he saw that her head had recently been shaved.

As he drew closer, he noticed that she had applied make-up for his arrival. It made her eyes seem even bigger than normal, almost to the extent of appearing to dominate her whole face.

"Sit down," she said, her voice soft and gentle, almost purring. "Have some wine – it's delicious."

They drank wine and ate fruit and several tasty morsels served by the girl who had let the guard in.

The wine was good, and strong, better than anything the guard had ever tasted in his life. He could feel himself growing increasingly sleepy the more he drank, but he could not stop himself – it was so tempting.

After a while, Anlet-Un-Ri began to undress him. He did not resist but neither did he assist. Instead he allowed her to remove his garments in her own time, as she saw fit.

The feel of her big, strong, though incredibly soft, hands running over his nakedness as they lay on furs on the marble floor of the bedchamber caused every nerve ending in his body to catch fire.

She teased him mercilessly, rubbing warm oil into his skin, but stopping whenever she reached his private region and carrying on somewhere else instead.

The guard moaned and squirmed under her touch. He could feel his erection growing fit to burst, until he could take it no more.

He grabbed her hand and moved it along his belly down towards his groin.

This time, she did not torture him. Anlet-Un-Ri rubbed the oil between his legs, gently massaging it along the length of his shaft, stroking it back and forth until he was afraid he might explode.

Eventually, she sat astride him, and gently guided him inside her.

She clenched his hips between her thighs and began rocking back and forth.

The guard closed his eyes and followed the curve of her legs up to her buttocks. Once there, he gripped them hard and massaged them. He could feel the strength in her legs, and the muscles that lay beneath her soft skin.

He felt the woman fall forward and heard the slap of her hands landing on the floor on either side of his head.

The guard opened his eyes and was met by the sight of her voluptuous breasts swinging back and forth in front of his face. He reached up and grabbed them, kneading them between his fingers.

He attempted to lift his head far enough of the floor to take her nipples in his mouth, but Anlet-Un-Ri angled her body just enough to keep them out of reach.

As he was about to protest, she lifted one of her hands off the floor and placed it over his face. The size of her palm covered his mouth and nose, mashing it back against his face, so that now he could not breath.

She held him there, increasing the pressure whenever he attempted to move his head to one side, all the time riding him with greater ferocity.

The guard tried to cry out, but the noise was lost behind the woman's mighty hand.

He strained to take in a breath but could not. The feeling of asphyxiation seemed to cause his member to stiffen even more, and Anlet-Un-Ri took advantage of his new-found rigidity to help bring her to orgasm.

The guard tried several times to slap her hand away from his mouth, but with each attempt he could feel the strength ebbing from him.

Anlet-Un-Ri lifted her head and gasped as waves of ecstasy flooded over her.

Finally, she felt the man go limp beneath her. His arms fell to his sides, slapping against the floor, as the last of his life ebbed from his body.

His purpose fulfilled, Anlet-Un-Ri dismounted.

She slapped the guard across the face a couple of times, just to ensure that he was in fact dead. Once she was satisfied, she lay on her bed, poured herself another goblet of wine and drank heartily.

Chapter Seventeen

Doctor Anmali climbed out of the shower and wrapped a large cotton towel around herself.

She walked back into her bedroom, lifted the half-empty glass of red wine off the dressing table and took a large swallow.

She lifted her leg and placed her foot on the chair in front of her and began to dry herself off. Once she was finished, she placed the towel back on the rack and slipped into the complimentary dressing gown the hotel supplied.

She replenished her glass from the bottle she had opened earlier and took her drink out on to her balcony.

The evening air was chilly and there was a smell of rain in the air.

Even so, she decided to stay outside long enough to enjoy her drink.

She had managed to make good progress that day, in spite of the police presence hampering her start.

All in all, things could have been far more awkward than they turned out, especially if she had been found unconscious next to the dead body after Kasim had knocked her out.

Fortunately, she had woken a few minutes later with a sore head to find him lying dead several feet away.

She checked the casket, but there were no immediate signs of tampering.

The mummy of Anlet-Un-Ri stood in place as she had done for thousands of years.

Even so, the doctor was in no doubt as to what had caused Kasim's death. But he had brought it upon himself. She was equally sure that he had uttered the sacred words from the forbidden scriptures in Anlet-Un-Ri's presence, just to prove to himself that they had the power to bring the mummy back to life.

The doctor hoped it had been worth it because he had paid for it with his life.

When Doctor Anmali left the museum for the night, she made a point of not raising any concern with the elderly security guard on duty. She waved goodbye from her car as she turned out of the car park, leaving him to return to his office and his blaring television.

She checked her wound once she returned to her hotel. Her head felt tender to the touch, but at least there was no blood, so she avoided a trip to the hospital, and some very awkward questions.

So far, the police seemed satisfied with her account.

As for today's little incident with Bill Stead, she felt sure that he had learned his lesson. When she saw him later on in the afternoon, he avoided her gaze and went about his duty as if she were not there.

There had been no point in killing him. He was offensive, utterly without charm, an odious man. But harmless, as far as she was concerned.

Killing him would definitely have raised too many questions, even though she felt confident that she could have completed the task by making it look like a tragic accident.

Chapter 17

The incident would doubtless have prompted more questions from the delightful Detective Inspector Cummings. Now, there was a prospect she would not have objected to.

She wondered if the detective preferred the company of women to men. The doctor certainly hoped so.

She pondered the thought while she sipped her wine.

The hall clock chimed the midnight hour as the Seddon Swans, decked in their familiar white attire, stood in a line, watching the ducklings shuffle into place.

The lower-sixth had received a rude awakening 10 minutes earlier and had been instructed to make their way down the back stairs to congregate in hallway that led to the rear door of the academy.

They knew that something was up.

Being summoned two nights in a row for initiation was virtually unheard of. So, in their minds, this had to mean something more serious.

Their instructions had been clear: Come at once, do not make any noise, and come as you are.

One of the ducklings had automatically reached for her slippers and was hissed at by the Swan who had been chosen to bring them down.

"I said, come as you are, that means no stopping for slippers, or dressing gowns, or your favourite teddy-bear, or anything else. Now move!"

As they stood in line, awaiting their fate, the ducklings kept their eyes on the floor.

"Now it appears," began Cynthia, "that we have a tattletale in our midst."

Immediately, some of the ducklings began to look along the line at each other.

"Heads down," demanded Cynthia.

They obeyed immediately.

"There is one among you," she continued, "who does not seem to appreciate the importance of secrecy and loyalty within our sisterhood. One of you has seen fit to involve someone outside our set and give them vital information about our initiation procedures." She waited for the information to take hold.

There was a nervous shuffling of bare feet on the cold stone floor.

Cynthia turned to face the rest of her brood and smiled.

Turning back, she walked to her right to the beginning of the lower-sixth line-up and stood directly in front of the first girl.

The girl kept her head down.

Cynthia stood there for a moment before she slowly made her way along the line.

Some of the girls instinctively sucked in a deep breath as the head Swan approached. It did not signify guilt so much as fear and Cynthia was well aware of the power her position allowed her to wield.

"Now, just to be clear," Cynthia explained, "we're not interested in who it was among you who broke our sacred seal of trust. As you all should know by now, we are a sisterhood, and as such, we stand or fall together." She made her way to the end of the line, then swiftly turned on the spot and began the journey back. "Our only hope is that the guilty party feels truly sorry for their betrayal and, in time, finds some way of making sufficient recompense to the rest of the sisterhood for her disloyalty."

Natalie Prewst glanced sideways and caught the eye of her friend Janice Cooper.

She had told her earlier about Miss Parker asking to speak to her in her office, and how she suspected something was going on, and managed to wangle the truth out of her. But Miss Parker

Chapter 17

had assured her that she would not breathe a word about it to anyone, and they all trusted Miss Parker.

So what on earth was Cynthia talking about?

Janice caught her eye and instinctively knew without speaking what was on her friend's mind. Natalie was too honest for her own good, sometimes, and Janice was sure that she was about to spill the beans and admit everything.

When she was sure that none of the swans was watching, Janice shook her head, and then looked away so as not to draw unwanted attention.

She hoped that Natalie would keep her mouth shut.

It did not do to betray the sisterhood, and she did not want her friend to be an outcast for the last year of school.

Cynthia had now moved back to the middle of the line. "Heads up!" she commanded.

The ducklings obeyed.

From behind the head girl there came a rustling of plastic, as each of the swans tore off a refuse sack from a large roll.

When they were done, they all moved forward and presented the ducklings with one bag each. The ducklings looked at each other curiously.

Cynthia signalled to one of her fellow swans to take up position by the back door. When she nodded, the girl opened the door, revealing the pelting rain battering the surrounding shrubbery.

"Now then," Cynthia said, "you will each go outside and collect 100 dead leaves from the ground and bring them back in here. Then, we will count them in the dining room, and woe betide the girl who has so much as one fewer or one more than the required number. Do you all understand?"

The line of girls turned to look out at the rainy night.

If they did not know Cynthia better, they would have taken this to be a joke. But sending them outside in the rain with bare feet and no coat or umbrella for protection was right up her street.

Cynthia waited for the enormity of the task to sink in. Then she said: "Right, you have exactly half an hour. Off you go."

The ducklings marched out in their line, none of them daring to object or protest at how cruel their task was.

Once they were all outside, the door was slammed shut.

The girls cowered under the minimal cover afforded them by the arch above the back door. The stone slab beneath their bare feet was freezing from the night air and covered with mud and twigs that had blown in from the lawn.

They huddled together for comfort in the vain hope that the rain might ease off before they ventured out. But after a while, and with their time running out, they realised nature was not going to be so kind.

"Fuck this for a lark!" Joanne South was the first to move out on to the lawn. As she did so, she trod on a stone, and jumped back, squealing. "Ow, that fuckin' hurt."

One by one, the rest of the ducklings followed their friend.

Natalie and Janice managed to pair off away from the others. Once they were out of earshot, Natalie asked: "Do you think this is because I told Miss Parker?"

"What else?" snapped Janice, bending down to retrieve a fistful of leaves.

Natalie immediately felt guilty. "I should say something," she offered. "at least tell the other girls it's my fault."

Janice looked at her. "Only if you want to be strung up the flagpole. Are you nuts?"

Natalie went to kick a stone, then thought better of it. "They'll hate me," she said.

"Yes, they bloody well will, now stop whining and start collecting, we haven't got long left."

When the 30 minutes were up, Jacinda Singh, one of the

swans, opened the back door and summoned the ducklings back inside.

They all trooped in, soaked to the skin and dripping water everywhere.

They followed Jacinda into the dining room, refuse sacks in hand, where the rest of the swans were waiting.

Cynthia ordered them to spread out along one of the long tables and empty their sacks so that their leaves could be counted.

They complied obediently.

Each Swan stood behind a duckling and watched intently as their charge counted out their sodden leaves.

The process seemed to take for ever but eventually all leaves were accounted for.

All the ducklings with exactly 100 leaves breathed a huge sigh of relief.

Three of them did not.

Suzi Ansbach and Greta Clarke had only 98 and 99 leaves respectively to show for their efforts. And, somehow, Joanie Vintner had managed to collect 103.

Greta begged her nominated Swan to allow her a recount, but Cynthia overruled the request.

The three ducklings were segregated from the rest, and told to stand to one side, as their remaining friends looked on, cold, wet and shivering in their sodden nighties.

Suzi Ansbach, as the first one in line, lifted her nightie and bent over, awaiting her punishment.

The swans began to laugh. "Oh, no, little duckling," chortled Cynthia, "we cannot give any of you an excuse to go running to your favourite teacher and show her your bruised bottom, now can we?"

Confused, Suzi straightened up and smoothed down her gown.

Cynthia turned to her left and signalled for Colleen Sykes to proceed with the girls' punishment.

Colleen walked slowly towards the serving hatch, and lifted the shutter, revealing something covered by a tea towel in the middle of the counter.

Colleen turned and waited for Cynthia's nod, before whipping off the cloth and revealing a large glass jar, with what appeared to be some form of jelly inside.

The three ducklings were then blindfolded by their nominated Swan and ordered to tip their heads back and open their mouths.

The other ducklings looked on in horror as Colleen opened the jar, and using a pair of tongs, gripped hold of a dollop of the contents, and walked over to Suzi.

Again, she waited for Cynthia's approval before dropping the jellified lump into Suzi's mouth.

The girl immediately began to gag, and instinctively held her hand to her mouth, and went to bend forward to spit out the contents. But before she had a chance to, her Swan grabbed hold of her pony-tail and yanked her head back, so that she was forced to keep whatever it was inside her mouth.

"If you try to spit it out," Cynthia informed her, "you will be made to eat two instead of one, and so on, understand?"

Both Greta and Joanie, although unable to see what was happening, knew that the head Swan's warning was directed at them, too.

"Now, swallow!" demanded Cynthia.

Some of the other ducklings looked away as their friend coughed and spluttered as she tried to force whatever was in her mouth down her oesophagus. It took her several attempts, but eventually, she made it.

Suzi kept her hand over her mouth, for fear that the slimy lump would come back up.

By now, Greta had tears streaming down her cheeks,

knowing that she was next for whatever her friend had just endured.

Without warning, Colleen snuck up beside her and dropped a similar-sized dollop of jelly into her mouth. In anticipation of her gag-response, Greta's Swan had already taken hold of her charge's hair to keep her in place.

It worked.

Colleen waited for Greta to swallow before she repeated the treatment on Joanie.

Joanie's Swan did not bother trying to prevent her from expelling the jellified gloop form her mouth.

Joanie retched and bent forward, expelling the lump on to the floor.

"Oh, dear!" exclaimed Cynthia. "It seems we have a discipline problem to deal with, ladies."

At her command, the other swans circled Joanie and grabbed hold of her, pulling her on to the dining table, before pinning her down on her back.

Her blindfold was removed and the petrified girl stared up into the faces of her menacing captors.

Cynthia slid in between two of the swans and gazed down at the stricken girl.

"Now, if you so much as make a peep, you'll spend all of next year as an ugly duckling. Is that what you want?"

Joanie shook her head. She could feel tears building up behind her eyes but refused to let them flow.

The other ducklings looked on in disgust while Colleen bent down and used the tongs to scoop up the globule Joanie had just expelled. She carefully carried it over to the table and held it above the girl's face.

Joanie's eyes turned to see what was coming. The image she had conjured up in her head before her blindfold was removed did not do the lump justice.

She looked back at Colleen who by now had a cruel smile on her lips.

"Open!" demanded Cynthia.

Closing her eyes, Joanie reluctantly complied.

Collen dumped the blob into her open mouth, and one of the swans slapped her hand across Joanie's mouth while she swallowed.

The ducklings watched as Colleen retrieved a second dollop from the jar, and the process was repeated.

When they were sure that Joanie had complied, the swans released her and moved back.

Joanie sat up on the table and swung her legs on to the floor, before standing up.

Her head was spinning, and she could still feel the jellified goop sliding its way slowly down her towards her stomach. The thought of it made her retch, but she managed to fight of the nausea and swallowed.

She could feel her throat burn from the effort. But she managed to keep it down.

"D'you know," said Cynthia, turning to her fellow swans, "I really don't know what all the fuss is about. In some Arab cultures, those are treated as delicacies."

Chapter Eighteen

Scrapper stopped dead in his tracks and listened in the darkness.

He could not believe that he had managed to bump into that stupid side table, which then sent the ornament on top of it rolling across the floor.

The noise had obviously woken the old woman, because he could hear her shuffling around above him.

Perhaps, he considered, she might not realise what it was that had woken her up, and now that she was up, she had decided to go toilet. He had heard that old people need to pee countless times every night, so it sort of made sense.

He would just wait quietly in the darkness until she was safely back in bed, then give her another five minutes to fall asleep before he continued with his raid.

Scrapper hoped that he would locate her purse down here because he really did not want to be heading upstairs to rummage around where she had more chance of hearing him. At least from down here he could make a run for it if the old bird decided to venture down.

Mrs Riley had lived in the old house for as long as he could remember. All the local kids had always been afraid of her. When he was little, his older siblings had told him that she was a witch, and if she ever caught him out alone, she would have him in her cauldron before he had a chance to make a run for it.

Hers was the best house on the street for playing knock-down-ginger, because it was surrounded by thick bushes that they could hide behind while they watched the old woman answer the door.

When he was about eight, one of his mates from school went missing. All the kids knew it was Mrs Riley who had him, but none of the grown-ups would believe them.

They found his body weeks later, and they never caught the culprit. But he and his mates knew who was to blame, and they left off playing near her house for several years after that.

Scrapper had no idea how old she was, but he reckoned she had to be about 100 by now. Mind you, she had looked that old since the first time he saw her as a child.

What he did know for definite was that she withdrew her pension every week in cash from the local post office.

He had watched her queueing up often enough. Keeping everyone else waiting while she painstakingly counted out her money at the counter, and checking it twice before finally putting it in her purse.

He had watched her that very morning following the same routine.

That was when he had the idea.

Scrapper followed her from a safe distance while she went to a nearby corner shop and bought herself a loaf of bread and a pint of milk, plus a few assorted tins of food. Her total bill came to less than a fiver, so he knew that the rest of her pension must still be in her purse, somewhere in the house.

He had to admit to himself that, even now, it gave him the

creeps approaching her house. He could not honestly remember when he was last at her door, but it had to be more than 10 years ago, when he and some mates egged her house on Hallowe'en.

Fortunately for him, she had never bothered to have those bushes cut back, so once he entered her front garden, he was effectively screened off from the street. That gave him plenty of time to work on her front door.

It was only a Yale lock, so it took him less than five minutes to open it.

His time spent in Feltham had left him with more than a few tricks of the trade.

Once inside, he cursed himself for not having brought a torch with him. The old woman kept her curtains drawn virtually all the time, so inside was as black as pitch.

He waited for a while to allow his eyes to adjust before he set about his task.

Something at the back of his mind kept telling him to leave. He was not sure if it was just his childhood fears of the old woman, or the fact that he knew if he was done for breaking and entering, he would definitely go down this time.

It was all Sara's fault. She was always on at him to take her places he could not afford. It was not enough for her to spend an evening down the pub. No, it had to be a wine bar, and an expensive one at that.

He could get pissed for what they charged for one cocktail at those places.

When it was not going out for a drink, she was on at him to take her out to dinner, or to the theatre. He had told her he would not be seen dead in a theatre. What was he, five?

Kids went to the theatre to watch a pantomime at Christmas, and that was all they were good for. But she was always on at him about her friends and the places they went to, which was fine for them – most of them had rich parents who could afford to let them spend a fortune.

Her dad was loaded. He worked in banking or something like that. Scrapper had only met him once, and he knew straight off the bat that the bloke did not like him or the idea of him seeing his daughter.

Well, if Daddy only knew what he did to his precious daughter when they were alone back at his flat, he would have a heart attack on the spot.

Perhaps one day he would film them, secretly, and then send a copy of it to him.

That would doubtless mean the end for him and Sara, and that would be a shame because she gave an awesome blow-job when she was in the mood.

Even so, it might be worth it.

Then at least he would not have to resort to this sort of thing to make his money. He could wait for the big jobs to come along, where he could make a decent wodge, and seriously up his street-cred, at the same time.

"Hello."

He heard the old woman calling from upstairs.

She must have heard him drop that fucking ornament.

Now what?

"Is there anybody down there?"

Scrapper tried to hold his breath to lessen the chance of her hearing him.

He stood stock still and waited.

Then he heard the top stair creak. The stupid woman was coming down to see if anyone was down here. Had she never seen any true-crime documentaries? he wondered. Sensible people would threaten to call the police in the hope that it scared away any intruders. What would be the point of someone as old and frail as her venturing downstairs to see if someone was waiting to punch her lights out?

Chapter 18

He could probably knock her silly with a slap.

Scrapper heard the woman slowly start to descend the staircase.

He let out his breath. That plan had obviously failed.

What now?

He spun around in the darkness to check how close he was to the front door.

He groaned when he felt his thigh slam against the small table, this time sending it over. Scrapper reached out to grab it, but it was too dark and he heard it crash to the floor before he had a chance of grabbing it.

"Fuck!" he hissed under his breath.

Now the game was well and truly up.

"I know you're there – I can hear you. I'm coming down now."

There was nothing else for it, he would have to make a break for it. Luckily, the old woman had not seen him, so she could not give the police a description. Even if he had to rush past her on his way out, he doubted she could recognise him.

"I know who you are, young man."

Scrapper froze. How on earth could she know who he was?

Was she really a witch?

No, that was nonsense. Witches did not exist; they were just used in fairy tales to scare the children. Even so, he felt a cold tingle run down his spine as if someone had dropped an ice-cube down his collar.

He heard another creak.

She was getting closer. He had to make a break for it before she reached the bottom.

Scrapper strode purposefully towards the sitting room door. He had left it open when he entered the room so he knew that, once he stepped through the opening, the old woman would be able to see him. But in this light, and with her eyesight probably not being too great at her age, Scrapper knew he would be okay, so long as she did not see his face from close up.

Suddenly, he heard a cry in the darkness, followed by a crashing sound.

It was the old woman. She had fallen down the stairs.

This was all he needed.

Scrapper waited for a moment, listening out for any sound of movement.

There was nothing.

Carefully, he crept out into the hallway, and through the shadows he could just make out the figure of the old woman, crumpled at the foot of the stairs.

She was dead!

Brilliant. Now what was he supposed to do?

They would do him for murder! No, wait, he remembered his brief once telling him that they had to prove intent for it to be murder. He never intended to kill her. It was not his fault the stupid old biddy had decided to walk down her staircase at night, in the dark.

But if he had not made a noise, then she would not have come down.

They did not know that. No one knew he was there. He would just leave and pretend he was never there. He had worn gloves, so there would be no fingerprints.

What about DNA?

Scrapper rubbed the back of his glove against his forehead. He knew that he was sweating profusely. What if a drop of his sweat had dripped on to the floor? Or on a piece of furniture? They could find DNA in the tiniest droplet these days.

He chided himself for panicking.

Even so, he rubbed his glove on his jeans, just to make sure.

He thought for a moment. He had not touched anything, he had not left anything behind, no one had seen him enter, and he would make damn sure that no one saw him when he left.

It would be fine.

Scrapper took a deep breath and took a step towards the door.

As he passed the bottom of the stairs, he could not help himself, he had to take one last look at the old lady.

Her outstretched hand appeared to be clutching something.

He leaned in for a closer look.

Scrapper could not believe his luck – it was her purse. He could have searched for it down here until doomsday, and all the time she was probably sleeping with it next to her bed.

He leaned forward to take it, but then stopped himself.

If he took out the money, then there was a definite chance he might leave his DNA on the purse, and how would he explain that to the coppers when they dragged him in?

He decided if he wanted the money, he would have to take the purse with him. He could always dispose of it later.

No, he would have to destroy it to make sure there was no evidence.

He decided he was going to burn it, the first chance he had, once he was away from the house.

Scrapper reached down and grabbed hold of the purse.

He pulled, but the old woman would not let go. Was this rigor mortis? Had her hand frozen in place? Did such a thing occur this quickly after death?

He would have to break her fingers to make release her hold on his prize.

This was fast becoming too much like hard work. But he could not leave it now – he had touched it with his glove, the same glove he had wiped sweat on a second ago.

Now, he had to break her fingers.

Scrapper gave the purse a final tug, in the hope that it might come loose.

Suddenly, the old woman opened her eyes, and screamed at him.

The shock of her sudden resurrection made Scrapper let out a scream of his own.

He fell back against the wall behind him. The back of his head made contact with the solid plaster and for a moment he feared he would pass out from the force of the blow.

Scrapper lifted himself off the floor, his head throbbing. It was then he realised he had something in his hand.

It was the old woman's purse.

He stared at it in disbelief. Now he had it, he could make his escape.

But the old woman carried on screaming at the top of her lungs.

Scrapper panicked.

He desperately needed to shut her up before someone outside heard her. But how was he going to achieve that without smacking her?

Then it would be murder!

There was no way he could guarantee hitting her just hard enough to knock her out, but he had to do something, she would not shut up.

Scrapper fell to his knees and rammed the purse over the woman's mouth, to muffle her screams. The soft leather filled her gaping orifice, just enough to prevent her from making any sound.

He forced the hand that held the purse down hard, to ensure it stayed in place while he thought of what to do next.

"Shut up, you stupid old hag," he spat at her through clenched teeth. "Shut the fuck up or I'm gonna fuckin' kill yer."

The old woman stared at him with terrified eyes. Her frail hands grabbed hold of his wrist, and attempted to pull him off, but she was far too weak to make a difference.

Scrapper looked around for something to hit her with.

In the dim light, all he could make out were an umbrella stand and a coat rack by the front door.

As he searched, he felt the woman go limp beneath him.

Scrapper turned back to face her. Her eyes were still wide open, but unlike before, they had a glassy appearance that showed she was no longer alive.

Her hands fell away from his wrist and slumped to the floor on either side of her body.

He backed off. She was dead. This time he was sure of it.

But he had hardly touched her.

It must have been her heart. Well that was not his fault – there was no way he could have predicted her heart was about to give way.

Scrapper withdrew the purse from the old woman's mouth and stared at it in the gloom. It was probably all wet and sticky with the woman's saliva, but he could not see to be sure.

He wiped it on his jeans. Great, he thought, now I've got her DNA on me.

Plus, his gloves had been in her mouth, with his sweat on them, so now his DNA might very well be inside her mouth, waiting for the techies to swab it out and prove he was the one who caused her death.

Enough!

Scrapper was becoming too engrossed in DNA evidence. Now, he realised, he was the one watching too many of those crime shows on the telly.

Just be sensible, he told himself.

He shoved her purse into the inside pocket of his denim jacket and grabbed hold of her nightie and used it to wipe the inside of her mouth. As an afterthought, he ripped off the piece that he had used, and put it in the same pocket as the purse.

Scrapper cautiously opened the front door, just in case someone had heard the old woman's screams and they were waiting for him in the front garden. But there was no one there.

He closed the door behind him, slipping his finger inside the catch so that he could ease it back into its keep, without making a sound.

He waited, concealed behind the same bushes where he had hidden as a kid, until he was sure that the street was clear.

Slowly, Scrapper crept stealthily from behind the bushes, and lost himself in the night.

Chapter Nineteen

WHEN DOCTOR ANMALI ARRIVED FOR WORK AT THE museum, the roadway leading to the car park was blocked by a huge van bearing the symbol of the security company for which Bill Stead worked.

When she parked her car on the other side of the van, she could see the burly security guard talking in a group with some of his guards, as well as some men in work overalls.

The second he caught sight of her, he said something to one of the other guards and disappeared back towards the staff entrance.

Doctor Anmali waited for a car to pass, then opened her door and looked over to where the men were gathered.

The guard to whom Stead had just been speaking walked over to her.

"Good morning, Doctor," he said brightly. "I'm sorry about all this but we're installing a new barrier gate to keep unwanted strangers out after what happened the other night."

"I see," replied the doctor. She walked around her car and peered past the guard. The pavement was fenced off on either side of the entrance to stop anyone walking by while the barrier was being erected.

The barrier itself was not yet in place, but she could see that the workers had already fixed the holding panels to either side of the wall.

"Is it still okay for me to go in?" she asked, turning back to the guard.

"Yes, absolutely," he assured her. "I'll escort you in, health and safety and all that."

"What about my car, will it be all right out here?" She glanced around and could see parking notices along some of the lampposts down the road.

"That's no problem," the guard answered. "Mr Unwin has made arrangements with the council. You just need to put one of these in your window." He handed her a green-and-white temporary parking permit with the date stamped at the bottom.

She thanked him and placed it on her dashboard, making sure it was visible from the outside.

At the staff door she was met by Stanley Unwin who, as usual, looked harassed and, even though it was still early morning, Doctor Anmali could tell from the damp patches on his shirt, that he had been perspiring profusely.

"Good morning, Doctor," he greeted her. "I trust you had a restful night."

"Yes, thank you," the doctor replied, standing back to allow him to pass.

"Forgive me for rushing by," he said, apologetically. "Can you believe this? Our insurers insist we have one of these contraptions erected," he indicated with a nod of his head towards the entrance. "And now they're telling me there's a problem with our power supply for the remote opening. Does anything ever go right?"

"I am very sorry for all the stress this is causing you," she offered. "Perhaps when you come back inside, we can sit down with a soothing cup of herbal tea, and discuss the descriptions for the placards for the items I have inspected? In my handbag, I have some special tea bags I brought over from Egypt. I can highly recommend them."

Unwin took out a handkerchief to mop his brow. "That sounds like a lovely idea," he said, smiling. "I shall come and find you inside once I've dealt with this latest catastrophe."

Once inside, the doctor donned her white coat, gloves and mask, and set to work on the remaining artefacts she was attempting to carbon date in time for the grand opening.

She waved at the design team members who were busy setting up the new backgrounds for the exhibition. The images were just what she had expected. Painted scenes of vast desert landscapes, dotted with pyramids and the odd sphinx. Slaves carrying jugs on their shoulders, and others transporting their betters in ornate litters supported on their shoulders or carried down by their sides.

It was almost two hours before Unwin reappeared from outside.

By now, his entire suit looked as if it needed dry cleaning, and it was obvious to the doctor from the colour of the little man's bald head, that he had been standing for far too long in the sun.

They went to the staff room, and the doctor placed tea bags in two china mugs, both with the museum's crest on them, under the hot water machine.

She carried the two piping-hot mugs over to the table where Unwin was waiting patiently.

"Now," she began, "you'll want to wait a minute or two before you taste it. You need to allow the tea to infuse with the water for the perfect effect."

Unwin nodded, and stared into the dark-coloured liquid as if he were afraid he might miss the experience.

Once the tea was ready, the doctor took a sip first, and then encouraged Unwin to do the same. The tea was rather more bitter than he had been expecting, and he could not help but pull a face when he sipped it.

"It's an acquired taste," the doctor informed him, noticing his grimace. "But it does wonders for the nerves."

"It's very nice," Unwin lied, not wishing to offend his guest.

They discussed the layout for the placards as arranged, and Unwin seemed overjoyed with the doctor's suggestions. Although Unwin was a respected authority on history and antiquities in general, he was by no means an expert on Egyptology, so whenever the doctor mentioned something that he did not understand, he would simply nod and make encouraging noises through closed lips.

The doctor was not fooled in the slightest by Unwin's pretence, but she found it quite endearing that he did not want to demonstrate his lack of knowledge in front of her.

What's more, it amused her that he seemed incapable of meeting her gaze for more than a split second before having to look away.

Once the business at hand was completed, she asked. "Have the police made any headway concerning the poor man who died here the other night?"

Unwin knocked back the last of his tea, then shook his head. "Not that I'm aware of," he confessed. "At least, they haven't had any more questions to ask me. I suspect that two of them probably broke in and ended up fighting over the spoils. One killed the other, then ran off empty-handed when he realised what he had done."

The doctor nodded. "I suspect you might be right."

Dawn sat at her desk typing up the details of the interview with Stead's wife from the previous day. It was not much, but she needed something for her report, which was looking somewhat thin so far.

The superintendent loved his paperwork because he did not understand how officers could be out on the streets all day, chasing down leads, and not have anything to write about when they returned.

It was another example of his lack of on-the-job training, but at least he did not complain so long as you handed something in.

She looked up and saw DS Courtney enter the room. She waited for him to catch her eye, then signalled for him to come over.

Dawn sat back in her chair and linked her hands behind her head. She lifted her feet on to her desk and crossed them over. As she was wearing trousers, her movement succeeded only in revealing her ankles, but she still noticed Courtney glancing at them as he approached.

"I've got a lovely little job for you, sergeant," she informed him.

The DS groaned. "I know what that means," he muttered.

"Now don't be like that," Dawn teased him. "It's not that bad."

"Go on then," he said. "Put me out of my misery."

"Have you got a dinner jacket hiding in your wardrobe back home?" she asked.

Courtney frowned. "What?"

"A dinner jacket," Dawn repeated. "You know, black tie, penguin suit, starched white shirt, cufflinks, etcetera, etcetera,?"

"Are you winding me up?" Courtney enquired, furrowing his brow.

"Not at all, Sergeant, we're going to the ball tomorrow night, so it's best bib and tucker for both of us."

Courtney screwed up his face.

"The super wants a discreet police presence at the grand

exhibition opening tomorrow night at the museum. And you and I are it. He's even willing to spring for overtime – bet your missus will love that."

The DS sighed resignedly.

"Cheer up, Sergeant. Just think, you and me, dressed up to the nines, free champagne, posh nibbles served to us on silver trays. Not bad for a night's work."

The DS raised his eyebrows. "The super's gonna allow us to drink on duty?"

Dawn swung her legs back down on the floor. "Well he said he wants us to blend in, as long as you don't get carried away. I don't want to have to write you up the following morning."

Courtney thought for a moment. "Do I really 'ave to wear one of those stupid suits? I'll have to hire one."

Dawn laughed. "I suppose not," she replied. "So long as you're well turned out."

The DS heaved a sigh of relief.

"And speaking of the museum," Dawn continued, "where are we with the embassy? Have they got back to you yet with any details about our victim?"

Courtney looked embarrassed. "Oh yeah, sorry, I forgot to tell you, they called me this morning. Apparently, he worked in a museum in Cairo in their antiquities section. They had no idea what he was doing over here, though. They said he had booked a couple of weeks' holiday at short notice."

Dawn sat forward. "Hang on, that museum he worked at, was it the same one the doctor at our museum came from?"

Courtney shook his head. "Don't know," he admitted, "I've got his work address written down on my desk, we can always check. Which museum did the doctor work at?"

Dawn thought hard, but she could not remember if Doctor Anmali had mentioned it when they spoke. "Hang on a second," she said. "I'll have to check."

She clicked her mouse and scanned her recent documents

Chapter 19

until she found the entry for her meeting with the doctor. Reading through it, she discovered that the doctor had not informed her, after all. But then, to be fair, she had not asked, either.

"That's annoying," she exclaimed.

"No luck?" asked Courtney.

Dawn shook her head.

"Do you want me to go and ask her?" the DS offered.

Dawn thought for a moment. "No, I'll tell you what, call the curator at the museum and ask him. He must know. But make it clear that we are asking him discreetly and he is not to say anything to the doctor."

Courtney nodded. "Right, will do." He turned away and went back to his desk.

"DI Cummings, the very man."

Dawn swung her chair round and saw DI Trevor Ampstead standing behind her. He had already been at the station a couple of years before Dawn arrived, and considered himself, due to his seniority in years, if not in rank, to be something of a team leader to the other detectives.

He was supposed to be Dawn's mentor when she arrived. She was told by the superintendent that he would show her the ropes and answer any questions she might have about the local area.

In reality, all he wanted was to get her in bed, and he made that quite clear from the first day. He was by no means a charmer but Dawn had the distinct impression that his rank and position had brought him luck with the girls on more than one occasion. He certainly enjoyed throwing his weight about.

But she managed to relay her lack of interest without incident, for which she was grateful. The last thing she wanted when she arrived was to have to report a fellow officer and end up with a bad reputation.

Coppers of the same rank dealt with their own.

She smiled politely. "What can I do for you, Inspector?" she asked.

Ampstead perched himself on the end of her desk. "I've got an operation on tonight, nasty little bunch of narcotics dealers, got their own factory and everything. We're raiding the place and I could always use a little more senior muscle to help things go to plan."

While he spoke, his eyes flicked from her face to her breasts and back again. She had her jacket open, and she was aware that her unbuttoned blouse revealed the top of her bra. But she was not about to give him the satisfaction of making her feel uncomfortable and buttoning her blouse would definitely give him the smugness of thinking that he had done just that.

"So what do you need?" she asked.

The DI leaned in as if about to whisper a secret, but his voice remained at the same level. There was only one reason Ampstead wanted to draw closer, and he was useless at disguising it.

"Well, I've got the actual raid sorted, but I need someone to take charge of the back-up, just in case any of the toe rags tries to do a runner."

"Where's your sergeant?"

"He'll be with me, we've been on this for ages, just got a tip-off this morning, probably a rival supplier. Anyway, I can't deny him the pleasure of being with me when we cross the finish line."

"Okay." Dawn nodded. "Count me in. When and where?"

Ampstead smiled. "At-a-girl," he said condescendingly. "Briefing back here tonight at eight, I'll see you then." He allowed his eyes to slip once more towards Dawn's breasts. "Dress accordingly," he suggested, before slipping off her desk and walking back into the main office.

"I always do," Dawn replied to his back.

Chapter Twenty

Stanley Unwin arrived home after what had been a particularly hectic day. Everything that could possibly go wrong, it seemed, had decided to do so.

After that fiasco with the security company and the new entry gate, he needed to unwind, and fortunately Doctor Anmali had been there with her therapeutic tea. He had to admit, if only to himself, he thoroughly enjoyed spending time in her company.

It was such a shame she was over here for only a short visit. Even so, there might be a chance for them to get to know each other on a more personal level.

Perhaps dinner?

The mere thought made him blush. Such thoughts were beneath a happily married man.

His afternoon had been as fraught as his morning. He cursed himself for allowing his assistant to take the week off, but mother needed her, having just had a hip replacement, and she had always been a loyal and, above all, reliable member of staff, so he felt he owed her.

It was only by chance that afternoon that he checked over the arrangements for the opening night of the exhibition. The catering company were under the misapprehension that he wanted to order a bulk load of Champagne and wine for the occasion, when he had specified in his email that he wanted a sale-or-return contract.

It was too late to go hunting for a new supplier, which meant his having to plead with the event's organiser for hours.

On top of that, he had to confirm the number of extra security staff they would require, which he was sure he had already done with Bill Stead, although the security guard was claiming ignorance.

He then had to ensure that there would be adequate serving and catering staff, so that guests were not left gasping for a drink. This too, he had been under the impression that his assistant had already confirmed. But, when he checked, the company claimed they were still waiting for confirmation, so again he had to beg and plead as he had left it so late.

To top it all off, he ended up having an argument with his head lighting technician, who insisted that it was safe to allow cables to trail across the floor where people would be walking, so long as they were secured under a rubber strip.

Unwin was definitely at the end of his tether and, although he prided himself on never losing his temper with his staff, the technician probably realised at some point during the conversation that the curator was about to have a heart attack if he did not comply.

This in turn meant ordering more cables at short notice, which in turn took more out of the budget, on which Unwin had to sign off due to lack of time.

Ordinarily, he would have had to run this kind of added expense past the board, but there was just no time. He knew that he would be on the receiving end for this at the next meeting, but he hoped the other members would be sympathetic and appreciate that his back was up against it on this one.

He was ready for a hot meal, a stiff drink, and bed.

As he opened his front door, he was greeted by a cacophony of laughter and gushing compliments coming from his sitting room.

While he hung up his raincoat, he realised that one of the voices emanating from the room was not one he recognised.

The unknown man had a strong French accent, although he spoke perfect English.

When Unwin popped his head into the room, he nearly passed out from shock.

The furniture had all been moved back, and in its place were two rails of dresses, with matching accessories. There were in fact three strange men in attendance. The one that was doing all the talking, and what appeared to be two assistants, dressed identically in black trousers and black roll-neck sweaters.

Unwin stood there for a moment, unobserved, as his wife and two daughters gasped and gushed as the Frenchman revealed each new ensemble.

As Unwin gazed around the room, he saw a pile of boxes three feet high off to one side, and he watched as the assistants took it in turn to present the contents to his girls. The boxes were filled with an assortment of shoes, handbags, shawls, wraps and even jewellery.

Finally, his wife Mildred noticed him standing in the doorway.

"Stanley, you're home at last," she announced. "Come in and see how beautiful our daughters look in their new dresses for opening night."

On command, both Felicity and Tamara paraded themselves in front of him, turning and swishing as if they were marching down a catwalk.

Unwin had to admit they did look spectacular, but it was the thought of the cost of all this that was uppermost in his mind.

"This is Monsieur Claude, from Paris," Mildred explained. The man who had been fussing over them when Unwin came in took a deep bow. "He was over here on a buying trip, so we were very lucky to book him at the last minute."

Unwin gulped. Yes, this was going to cost him a fortune.

There was no point in creating a scene. The upshot would still be the same. The women would all have their outfits, he would receive a hefty bill, and he would still be in the wrong for complaining in the first place.

Unwin had been here before.

"Speaking of clothes, dear," he said, trying to catch his wife's attention. "Did you manage to fetch my dinner suit from the dry cleaners?"

His wife waved his question aside. "No Stanley, I've been far too busy with the girls. You can pick it up tomorrow on your way to work."

"But, my dear," he objected. "I need to be in early tomorrow to ensure the final arrangements are in order. Could you not collect it and bring it by the museum?"

Mildred turned to face him, her hands planted firmly on her generous hips.

"Do you really think I have nothing better to do with my time then run errands for you, Stanley Unwin? The girls and I have to have our hair done tomorrow, plus our nails, then I've got a couple of girls from the salon coming in the afternoon to sort out our make-up. Do you want your family to turn up at the museum looking like we've just been dragged through a hedge backwards?"

Unwin took in a deep breath. "Right you are, my dear," he replied dejectedly. "I'll just go up and draw my bath," he announced to no one in particular.

Before he went up, Unwin went to the kitchen and poured

himself a very large Scotch. He sipped it slowly while he ran his bath.

As he climbed into the scorching hot water, Unwin drained the rest of the glass. He

was not a man who overindulged in alcohol, regardless of the occasion. But he had the distinct impression that one glass was not going to clinch the deal tonight.

———

After the briefing, Dawn followed the uniformed officers who were acting as back-up out to their van. She took her seat in the front, next to the driver and, once everyone was on board, they set off for the rendezvous.

Ampstead and his crew were all fired up for the operation – she could tell by the way they reacted every time he mentioned nicking this particular gang, during his briefing. From what she understood, this had been a long time in coming and they had already had two failed attempts, when the villains had doubtless been tipped off.

But this time Ampstead was positive he was going to get a result.

One of his informers had managed to get himself arrested on a firearms charge, but Ampstead had managed to cut a deal with the CPS to have the charges reduced. So he now had someone banged up inside who owed him a favour and who could keep his ears open.

That's why Ampstead and his team regarded this tip-off as solid gold.

The traffic was fairly light, so they arrived at their destination within 15 minutes of leaving the station. The lock-up from where the gang was allegedly running their outfit was, not unexpectedly, on one of the less salubrious estates on the outskirts of the town.

Dawn knew the area well. When she first arrived at the station, she had assisted on several raids in the nearby blocks of flats with crimes including everything from prostitution to money-laundering, child abuse to gun-running. Fortunately, all those culprits were now behind bars, which at least kept them off the street for a while. But there always seemed to be an endless supply of scumbags to take their place.

It was a real shame, because the rest of the town, as well as the surrounding countryside, thrived in an atmosphere of picturesque tranquillity, where crime was something the residents witnessed only by watching the evening news.

The van with the uniformed back-up parked a couple of streets away from the laboratory. Dawn unclipped her radio. "Oscar-Delta 21, in position, awaiting instructions, over."

There was a brief crackle of static before Ampstead replied: "Alpha-Zulu 7, received, hold your place until I give the order, over."

"Roger, out." Dawn turned and looked back through the grille that separated her and the driver from the rest of the officers inside. "Sit tight, team, it should be any minute now. You know what to do when he gives the order?"

There was a mumbled response and several heads nodded.

Dawn could feel the adrenaline pumping through her veins and knew that, for some of the younger officers, their hearts would be throbbing ninety to the dozen. It was always the way on a job like this. Regardless of how mob-handed they were, no one knew how things were going to end until it was all over.

She knew that Ampstead had arranged for armed back-up, but they were all in the lead cars, so if things turned ugly, she knew that her team would have to rely on their training, guile, and above all, common sense to make it out in one piece.

They all had their vests on but, even so, they offered only partial protection.

For a country where it was illegal to carry a gun, she was

always amazed at how many villains seemed to be armed to the teeth.

The waiting seemed like an eternity.

The driver next to her drummed his fingers nervously against the steering wheel.

In the back, she could hear some of the officers whispering to each other

There was an occasional laugh, but they kept it down.

She knew it was just a coping mechanism.

Suddenly, the radio sparked into life. "We're on. Go! Go! Go!"

"Let's go!" Dawn did not have to give the order – everyone in the van had heard the voice on the radio.

The back doors crashed open, and the officers all jumped out one after the other. They did not wait for any further instructions. They already knew where they were supposed to be so they spread out and made their way there.

Dawn followed as some of the officers cut through the back alley that ran along a row of houses. They were masked from the properties by the fences at the end of each garden. But, as she ran, Dawn noticed several curtains twitching in the windows up above them.

She hoped that none of those belonged to look-outs for the gang and were just curious residents looking out for their own.

By the time her group was in place, surrounding the back of the lock-ups where the laboratory was housed, Dawn was breathing heavily and she could feel sweat trickling down the inside of her blouse.

She had not worn a vest for a while and she had forgotten how heavy and cumbersome they were to run in.

She wondered why she bothered to shower before coming out, as that would have to be the first thing she did when she reached home.

After a stiff drink or three.

From out of the dark, there came a terrific crash as a white van suddenly rammed through a closed garage door and sped across the street.

Instinctively, Dawn raced after it, followed by several of her uniformed team.

The street they were on had parked cars on either side, with barely room for another vehicle to pass from the other direction. The van spun out of control as it careered from one side of the road to the other, grinding metal against metal as it bounced off each car it hit.

She could hear Ampstead's voice on the radio, frantically calling for back-up to stop the escaping van. But Dawn was too involved in the pursuit to reply.

One of the other officers radioed the van's course, and this was followed by the police van driver stating that he was on his way.

They needed him to block the end of the road.

If the escaping van made it that far, it was only a couple of short streets from the main road, then they would have lost it altogether.

The white van driver finally seemed to regain control of his vehicle, and Dawn could hear the engine revving, followed by another loud metallic grinding noise, as the driver fought desperately with the gear-stick.

Just then, the police van appeared from the other end of the road and drove directly towards the white van.

The white van careered over the edge of the pavement and slammed into a pillar box.

There was a sickening crash of glass as the driver was propelled out through the windscreen and hit the post box head first.

Dawn and the others continued the chase. They were only a matter of yards away when the back doors of the van flew open and three men jumped out.

Chapter 20

Seeing the officers in close pursuit, the three men split up and ran off in different directions.

Dawn set her sights on the one to her left.

The man ran through someone's front garden, then along the side of the house and into the back garden. Dawn gave chase, losing him for a split second when he ducked behind the front of the house.

As Dawn reached the end of the wall, she saw a shovel flying towards her head.

She managed to duck low enough for the flying tool just to miss her, but the action made her lose her balance, and she crashed into a free-standing barbeque, twisting her ankle as she tried to prevent her fall.

Dawn landed on her back with a firm *whump* on the concrete patio.

The force of the landing knocked the wind out of her body, and she lay there for a moment, gasping for breath, tears streaming down her cheeks.

As Dawn raised her head, the man was approaching her, holding what appeared to be a baseball bat above his head.

As he grew closer, she could see through her bleary vision the maniacal expression on his face. It told her that he meant business. She assumed that he was probably too high on his own products to know or care that several other coppers were just around the corner.

Dawn turned to look back. She could hear all the commotion taking place in the street, but none of her colleagues seemed to have followed her in.

With the man almost on top of her, Dawn scrabbled around on the ground for something to defend herself with.

Just as her hand landed on a long barbeque fork, she heard a cry from one of her uniformed team, telling the man to drop his weapon and surrender.

The man turned to see who was giving the order but kept the bat high over his head.

Dawn took advantage of the momentary distraction, and lunged forward, thrusting the twin points of the fork into the man's groin.

The man let out an animal-like scream and immediately dropped to his knees in front of her, losing the bat as he fell.

Within seconds, two uniformed officers had grabbed and handcuffed the man, who was still wailing about the pain in his testicles. "She stabbed me in the fuckin' nuts," he whimpered.

When the ambulance arrived to deal with the driver of the white van, Ampstead insisted that the paramedics check over Dawn's injuries, as well.

They had already pronounced the driver dead at the scene, so technically there was no immediate urgency in taking him to the hospital.

They concluded that Dawn had in fact sprained her ankle and recommended that she soak it in ice-cold water when she arrived home. She could stand and walk, albeit with a slight limp, so they told her that unless she wanted a lift to the hospital for a full check-up, they could not tell from here if there was anything else wrong with her.

Dawn thanked them but declined the offer.

Ampstead was wandering around with a huge grin on his face. The raid had been a great success. Not only had they nicked the entire gang but, with the amount of gear and equipment they had recovered, he predicted this lot would be going down for a very long time, which would enhance his clear-up rate significantly.

As the vehicles with the men and women in white overalls began arriving, Ampstead was promising everybody free drinks at the pub that served as the local for the station, once all the charge sheets had been sorted and the evidence booked in.

There were general cheers among the team. Ampstead with his hand in his pocket must have been a rare event.

But Dawn settled for a lift back to the station so that she could pick up her car and drive home.

She needed that drink.

Chapter Twenty-One

Dawn eased herself back on her sofa and took a sip of her brandy. The fiery liquid slid its way down her throat, warming her from the inside.

The journey home from the station had been a painful one. Her back had started to stiffen up the moment she slipped behind the wheel of her car, and her ankle throbbed every time she depressed the accelerator.

She had considered taking a long soak to try to ease her back, but soon realised she was too tired, so she settled for a stiff drink and a couple of painkillers instead.

Taking the paramedic's advice, she managed to find an unopened bag of frozen peas underneath all the frozen dinners in her freezer, and wrapped it in a tea towel before applying it to her swollen ankle, securing it in place with the belt from her jeans.

She desperately needed a foot massage.

It was at times like this that Dawn regretted not having a man in her life. But she knew from past experience that they brought their own baggage with them and, most of the time, she could not be bothered.

Chapter 21

Dawn had often claimed her profession was the main reason she did not have a partner. At least, that was her most common excuse whenever her mum or sister asked why she had not settled down.

In fact, the job was part of the problem. The erratic hours, the overnight sessions, the constant threat of being on call at the drop of a hat – what man could put up with all that?

To some, it made sense for someone in her profession to date within her own field, working on the assumption that a fellow officer would at least be able to appreciate the importance of her commitment to the job.

The truth, however, was anything but.

Dawn had dated several coppers over the years and, regardless of their rank or position, they all had one overriding dynamic in common – they all expected her to play the part of the subservient female and adhere to their view of the world.

To most of them, women were a necessary evil in the police force, placed there to placate the women's lib brigade and keep them voting for the right party.

In reality, the majority of male colleagues still saw women in the force as the tea makers and receptionists. They used them, whenever possible, to sympathise with the mothers and wives when their loved ones ended up dead as the result of some brutal crime.

Dawn saw it happening all the time. She had lost count of how many male officers of both superior and inferior rank she had been forced to threaten with formal action because of their inappropriate behaviour.

The truth was that Dawn could take it all as good-hearted banter, but time had taught her that some men, especially those in uniform, sometimes saw that as weakness and would try to take advantage at every opportunity.

She had not ruled out falling in love some day and even

getting married. But, if it were to be at the cost of her career, he would have to be someone really special.

For now, she could do with a man she could call on when she wanted, and discard when not. She had often mused that someone should create an instant man, just add water. She could do with one right now to rub her aching feet and possibly fix her another drink. Then, once he was finished, she could retire him back to the cupboard until the next time.

She would call him Charles.

Charles, massage my aching feet... Yes, Madam.

Charles, fix me another drink... Yes, Madam.

Would Madam care for me to bring her to orgasm?

Mmmm, not tonight, thank you, Charles. You may return to your cupboard.

Job done.

She had obviously spent too much time fantasising about this and often wondered what a psychologist would make of her strange obsession.

Was it just her way of putting up walls to ensure that no man could ever come up to scratch?

Dawn could feel the second brandy taking effect. Her eyes were growing heavy and she could feel herself drifting off.

She told herself she needed to move off the sofa and make her way up to bed, but her body had different ideas. This would not be the first time she had fallen asleep on the couch and doubtless would not be the last. But she also knew from past experience that she would wake up feeling awkward and unsettled if she slept the night in her clothes.

Dawn considered undressing. It was a warm night so chances were that she would sleep naked, anyway. But then she remembered her makeshift ice pack. There was no way she could remove her jeans over that, which in turn meant having to take it off, and retying it, by which time her sleepiness would have passed, leaving her feeling restless for the rest of the night.

Chapter 21

She decided to wait a little while longer to allow the frozen peas to take their full effect. Then she would go to bed.

Dawn convinced herself she would not fall asleep where she was.

Sarah Janu busied herself mopping the floor of the museum, adjacent to the area where the new exhibition was to take place.

At 23, she was the eldest of her mother's four children. Her younger brother had already been conscripted into the army in Africa and, with their father long gone, Sarah did whatever she could to send home as much money as she could from her modest earnings as a cleaner.

She had allowed herself to be smuggled into Britain on a false passport, by a man her mother trusted would allow her to go to university to study medicine, which had always been her dream. But instead, once they had cleared customs, he had taken her to Birmingham, where she had been beaten and tortured until she agreed to give her body to any man who could afford the going rate.

Sarah had been forced to live in a tiny flat, along with several other girls from all over the world. Most could barely speak a word of English, so even basic communication between the girls was difficult. But, over time, Sarah realised that they had all been tricked into coming to Britain by members of the same gang of people-smugglers, whose only interest was in how much the girls could make for them.

The girls were allowed no privacy. Whether at work or in the flat, they had constant company from members of the gang, who took it in turns to watch them or drive them to visit clients. The gang often made threats to the girls of what would happen to them if they ever tried to escape and Sarah had witnessed at first hand the brutality of their actions when such instances occurred.

The other girls were made to watch whenever a beating was deemed in order. One girl in particular, of whom Sarah had grown rather fond while at the flat, was forever trying to escape any way she could.

On one particular occasion, she had tried to convince her client that she would do anything he wanted if he helped her escape her captors. Instead, the client informed the gang member who came to collect her once the job was over, and he dragged her into the flat by her hair, and stripped her in front of the girls, before tying her to the bed. Then, he and the other members of the gang present took turns to beat her with their belts, until her body was nothing more than a mass of bruises.

It was weeks before the poor girl was well enough to visit another client. But, even then, she refused to stop attempting to escape, no matter how many times she was cautioned by Sarah, and the other girls who spoke her language.

One night, she did not return from a visit to a client.

By the following day, Sarah was growing increasingly concerned for her safety and, after three days with no sight of her, she asked one of the gang members what had happened to her.

The man told her bluntly that the girl had tried to escape once too often, so they had decided to take care of her permanently.

Sarah had no way of knowing whether that was the truth. But she never saw her friend again.

One night, there was a raid at the flat. Police smashed the door down and arrested everybody. Sarah had been in the bathroom, about to take a wash, when she heard the commotion outside the door.

She carefully pushed the bathroom door shut.

The girls were not allowed the privacy of locking the door, as the lock had been removed, which they knew was to ensure that none of them attempted to escape through the tiny window.

Without pausing to think, Sarah prised open the loose bath panel from the side of the tub, and crawled into the tiny space it afforded her, before holding the panel back in place so that, from the outside, it would look normal.

She waited with bated breath and listened to the police searching through every room. The melee that took place outside was deafening. Some of the girls were screaming and crying. Their captors shouted insults and threats, telling the girls not to talk, or else.

The officer in charge barked orders at everyone, demanding compliance.

Sarah hesitated beneath the bath. If she came clean, there was a good chance she would be deported back to Africa, which would at least mean she could see her mother and siblings again. But, on the other hand, she also knew that this might be her one chance to break free and earn some money in her own right. Enough so that she could support her family back home, which she would never be able to do from there.

Maybe she could even earn enough so that she might one day be able to realise her dream and study to become a doctor.

Sarah decided to remain hidden and hope that she was not discovered.

When the police kicked open the bathroom door, she heard a gruff man's voice call out that it was clear.

She waited there for ages after the noise died down and everybody had left. She was petrified that there might still be someone lurking outside, just waiting for her to make her presence known.

Eventually, after she had not heard a sound for what seemed like hours, she forced open the panel and crept out from her hiding place.

The flat was empty and, for once, silent.

Sarah wasted no time. She grabbed her suitcase and crammed it with all her belongings. There was no time to fold it or sort it out. Everything went in together.

Once she was packed, she picked up her coat and left.

Halfway down the stairs, it struck her that she had nowhere to go, and no money. Then she remembered the salad drawer in the fridge. The girls had been warned not to look in there, but they knew that was where the gang members stashed their drugs.

Most of them snorted cocaine, but she knew, having seen them before, that they also kept a stash of tablets sorted into separate plastic bags, which they sometimes slipped to clients.

Sarah had no idea how or where to sell them, but she needed money, or at the very least, something to bargain with.

She ran back up the stairs and went straight to the kitchen.

When she drew open the salad drawer, Sarah could not believe her eyes. Besides the drugs, she found a wad of bank notes, rolled up and secured with an elastic band.

She grabbed the money and stuffed it into her pocket. Her hand hovered over the drugs, but then she had an epiphany. If, for some reason, she was caught, she could explain away the money, but the drugs could land her in serious trouble.

Leaving the drugs where they were, Sarah left the apartment.

As she began to descend the stairs once more, she heard the front door below open.

She froze where she was standing and, sure enough, one of the gang-members began to climb up towards her.

At first, he did not seem to notice her. His head was down as he climbed.

But before she had a chance to move, he lifted his head and their eyes locked.

Sarah could tell from the look on the man's face that, until that moment, he was unaware of what had taken place in the flat earlier. All he knew was that one of the girls was trying to escape, and that he could not allow.

There were only a few stairs between them, and Sarah knew she had no chance of escape – the staircase was far too narrow to allow for that.

The man's lips curled back in an evil grin, revealing two rows of yellowing teeth.

"Now, what 'ave we 'ere?" he said to no one in particular. "You know what 'appens when one of you tries anythin' foolish, don't yer?"

Sarah turned to run back up, but the man shot forward and grabbed hold of her ankle before had a chance to take her first step.

She yanked her leg, but his grip held.

Sarah let go of her suitcase and listened as it bounced down the stairs past the man, landing at the bottom, near the door.

The man pulled the hapless girl towards him. Sarah lost her balance, and hit the stairs hard with her rump, bouncing down as he yanked on her leg.

Without thinking, Sarah raised her other leg and shot it forward, catching the man in the chest. She kicked forward with all she had, knocking her assailant off his balance, sending him rolling back down the stairs.

By the time he had reached the bottom, the unnatural angle of his neck clearly showed it was broken.

Sarah wasted no time. She stepped around him, grabbed her suitcase, and casually walked out through the front door.

The money she had stolen paid for a night in an hotel and a hot dinner.

The following day, she bought a coach ticket to somewhere she had never heard of before. Somewhere out in the country, far away from gangs and prostitution and drugs.

This was where she was to make her fresh start.

Or so she thought.

It was there that she met Bill Stead, after applying for a cleaning job at his father's firm. He had come across as polite and very professional and explained how their company looked on their employees as more like family than just workers.

He offered her a job on the spot and, when she said she was looking for accommodation, he proudly announced that they had recently acquired some flats nearby, and he would be happy to show her.

The flat was more spacious and far more inviting than the squalid flea-trap where she had been imprisoned for so long, and Bill assured her that with employees' rates, it was well within her budget.

Everything seemed perfect.

Sarah was given two shifts – one cleaning the block where she was living and the other at night in the museum.

Over time she grew to know and trust Bill. So much so that when it came to calculating her earnings, she confided in him that she was an illegal immigrant, and therefore had no national insurance number.

Stead assured her that would not be a problem, and he would sort everything out for her.

That was when he showed his true colours.

The following night, Stead offered Sarah a lift home from the museum after her shift.

He insisted on walking her up to her flat, and then asked if he could come inside to use the bathroom.

Once inside, he struck.

Stead grabbed Sarah and dragged her into the bedroom. There he subjected her to hours of torture and degradation.

Once he was done, he told her that if she ever tried to report him, or leave, he would make sure she was deported.

Sarah was trapped, and she knew it. This was no better than her life as a prostitute, except for the fact that she was allowed to keep her earnings at the end of the month.

Chapter 21

Stead's deal was simple. She could keep the job, and the flat, in return for him having his way with her whenever, and wherever, he wanted.

That had been more than six months ago and, although Sarah was proud of the money that she managed to send home, she was too ashamed to tell anyone what she had to do to earn it.

Whenever Stead stayed late at the museum and offered her a ride home, she knew what it meant, and over time she had come to accept that this was her lot.

Sarah finished sweeping the floor, in preparation to beginning mopping it.

Given her circumstances, Sarah still took pride in her work, and she always ensured that her section of the museum was spotless before she left for the night.

She replaced her broom in the cupboard. Turning on the tap above the built-in sink, she poured a measure of floor cleaner into a bucket, and half-filled it with water. Once it was ready, Sarah took one of the mops from the stand supplied and carried it and the bucket over to where she had been sweeping.

She removed her rubber gloves from her apron pocket and pulled them on.

Just then, she heard a sound from behind.

Before she had a chance to turn, a large hand clamped around her mouth.

Sarah was hoisted off the floor and carried over to the nearest display case. Once she was draped over it, another hand lifted up her shirt, and grabbed hold of the waistband of her jogging bottoms, yanking them, and her panties, down her legs.

The hand covering her mouth fell away, but she did not take the opportunity to scream for help.

She knew all too well who it was behind her, and she knew what to expect next.

Stead released his throbbing organ from the confines of his

work-issue trousers and guided it in between Sarah's exposed thighs.

Once he felt himself inside her, he shoved forward, grabbing Sarah's slender hips with both hands.

During the assault, Sarah gazed up at the exhibition in front of her.

From this angle, she could just see inside the sarcophagus, which had been hinged open to assist the visiting doctor in accessing the mummy's covering.

As Sarah looked up, she was sure for a moment that the mummy opened its eyes. But she put it down to her imagination, and the fact that she needed to focus on something other than what was happening to her.

Stead continued to force himself back and forth inside Sarah until he was spent.

Breathing heavily, he withdrew and pulled up his shorts and trousers and fastened his belt around his waist.

Sarah stayed where she was until she was sure Stead had finished with her.

He slapped her across her bare buttocks. "Come on," he said, "work's not going to do itself."

With that, he walked away.

Sarah picked herself off the display unit and rearranged her clothing.

Before she began to mop the floor, she walked over to the front of the sarcophagus and looked up at the monstrous figure of the mummy within.

The harder she stared at the face, the more she expected the eyes suddenly to come to life, as she was almost sure she had seen them do earlier.

She did not know why. It just seemed plausible.

Chapter Twenty-Two

ANCIENT EGYPT

THE FOUR SOLDIERS SAT AROUND THE TABLE, hunched over in private conversation. Around them, men in uniform caroused with abandon, grabbing hold of the serving girls as they walked between their tables and raising their glasses to past victories, for which all of them took some credit.

The air was heavy with celebration.

The Pharaoh had commanded four full days of celebration in honour of his son's passing over to the afterlife.

Now that his tomb was complete, the final ceremony would take place the following day, where the boy's mortal remains would be placed in his sarcophagus for all eternity.

Even now, the tomb was being prepared with jewels and gold in abundance, enough to ensure his comfort on the other side.

Royal priests within the tomb recited ancient scripture from sunrise to sunset, to ensure the young prince's spiritual journey would be without incident.

Two stout guards were positioned at the entrance for, even though the sentence for disturbing the royal chamber was death, there were those within the city who were willing to risk all, just to get their hands on some of the precious treasures within.

The architects who designed the tomb had been well paid and all their written plans destroyed, so that no one could disturb the young prince once he had been laid to rest.

The slaves who toiled day and night to construct the labyrinthian passages that led down to the royal chamber had been paid off, if they could be trusted to keep their silence. Or put to death, if they could not.

To oversee the project was, in itself, an honour that all members of the royal guard coveted. That honour had gone to one who had been in the Pharaoh's service since childhood.

Now a fully-fledged soldier of the Pharaoh's guard, Asim sat in the tavern with his three most trusted comrades, dourly drinking their evening away.

They spoke together in hushed tones for, although everyone around them was too drunk to remember their conversation, they all appreciated the necessity for secrecy in a land where lust for the Pharaoh's reward could cause most men to betray their closest ally.

"That position should have been yours, Asim, everybody knows it."

"After all these years spent guarding the royal household, how many times has your blood covered the floor, in honour of protecting the royal household?"

"Khartar is right, my friend, this honour should be yours by right. The men were all looking forward to your promotion as head of the first army. Now they have to bow and scrape to the whims of a woman. It's a disgrace."

Asim nodded his head, keeping his eyes fixed on his goblet as he swirled the precious liquid around the rim.

"You should demand to see Pharaoh and put your case forward. We will all support you."

"Yes indeed, we'll get the first army to stand at the doors of the palace and scream your name until Pharaoh changes his mind."

Chapter 22

Asim drank heavily, draining his goblet. He signalled for the nearest serving girl to refill it. Taking their lead from him, the others did likewise.

Once the girl had completed her task and was out of earshot, Asim signalled his colleagues to lean towards him. "I know the Pharaoh much better than any of you, and I can tell you now that if the entire city demanded it, he would not change his mind once he has made a decree. His word is law."

"Yes, but, surely…"

Asim waved his friend's argument away. "You know as well as I do that the only dispensation Pharaoh would make, is if someone challenges that bitch to a duel."

The others looked at each other, aghast.

"Did you see what she did in the tournament? Against some of our bravest warriors?"

"That cat has sharp claws, my friend. She is not human."

"She cut through those soldiers as if she were slicing a cake. It would be madness to demand a duel against her."

Asim shook his head and tapped his temple with his index finger.

The other three stopped talking. They knew their friend had a plan of his own.

They waited for him to speak.

"What if she simply disappeared?" Asim ventured.

The others stared at each other with confused expressions on their faces.

Asim checked once more that no one else was within earshot before he continued to explain. "I have a plan, my friends. I have been working on it ever since the tournament. But I need the help of my three greatest comrades-in-arms to see it through to fruition."

"You can count on us, my friend."

"We are your greatest supporters."

"It would be our honour to assist you in any way."

Asim smiled. "I am one who is blessed by the gods with such good friends. More wine," he shouted to the room in general, catching the attention of another of the serving girls. "First, we drink, then I explain all. Tonight, my friends, we will make a blood bond that will make us brothers for eternity."

After sunset, Asim and his three willing comrades set their wheels in motion.

Khartar was given the unenviable task of gong to Anlet-Un-Ri's quarters and convincing her that her help was required down at the young prince's burial chamber.

She towered down over the soldier as she scrutinised his face for any sign of a trap or trick. These soldiers were not above playing idle pranks on their newly appointed commanders.

"Who demands my attendance?" the female warrior roared, taking Khartar by surprise.

Shaking where he stood, the soldier replied. "The royal priests say there is one more ritual they must complete before the night is over, and Asim truly believed the honour of partaking was his. But apparently, as the new head guard of the first army, it has to be you. The priests are insistent."

Anlet-Un-Ri considered the man's explanation for a moment.

His whole demeanour demonstrated that either he was lying or just plain afraid.

The female warrior was not unaccustomed to seeing men quake in her presence, so she put it down to the latter.

She grabbed the sword the Pharaoh had presented to her and followed Khartar to the entrance of the burial site for the deceased prince.

As she approached, the two guards on duty bowed their heads out of respect when they recognised the new leader of the first army.

Khartar guided Anlet-Un-Ri through the myriad passageways that led to the royal burial chamber, using the instructions his friend Asim had given him earlier. Due to her height, the female warrior found herself having to duck her head for most of the journey, but she still kept a watchful eye on her companion. Something did not feel right.

Anlet-Un-Ri had spent long enough in the royal household to appreciate the importance of the ceremonial rites that the priests insisted take place at such times. But she often wondered if they were in fact all necessary, or merely the priests' way of justifying their necessity in the eyes of the Pharaoh.

All the same, if this was part of her duty now as head of the first army, then she supposed it was something she would have to accept and grow accustomed to.

Finally, they reached the main chamber.

Anlet-Un-Ri recognised Asim and his two other cohorts, and they each acknowledged each other in turn.

The priest, dressed in ceremonial robes, had his face covered, and appeared lost in prayer. In front of him knelt a dozen slaves, their heads bowed, as they repeated each line of scripture the priest spoke.

Asim approached his new commander. "Welcome, Anlet-Un-Ri," he said, respectfully, bowing his head. "I apologise for the lateness of the hour, but the priest informed us only a little while ago that an officer of your rank needs to be here for the final part of the ceremony."

Anlet-Un-Ri eyed him suspiciously. He sounded sincere enough, but when she glanced over at the priest for acknowledgement that this indeed had been his instructions, the man still had his head bowed in prayer.

"I thought the prayers ended at sunset," she informed Asim, holding his gaze. "It is already dark outside."

Asim smiled. "You are correct, and it has been my honour to be chosen by Pharaoh to take part in the ceremony during the day's devotions but, as I explained, the final prayer ceremony cannot take place without Pharaoh's most senior protector in attendance. It is to symbolise the protection the little prince will need on his long journey into the afterlife."

Anlet-Un-Ri shrugged. "Let's start then, this poor priest must be in need of his bed."

The slaves were ordered to stand to one side. Meanwhile, Asim and his friends set out purple fabrics, woven through with gold thread, over the seats that had been carved into the rock.

Asim indicated for his female commander to sit in the middle, as befitted her position.

Khartar and the other two soldiers began to pour wine into goblets, which had already been placed on the altar at the far end of the chamber.

Once the goblets were full, they carried them over to the priest who said a blessing over them.

The contents of one of the goblets was then poured over the sacred stone slab in the middle of the chamber, where the royal child's remains would be placed the following day.

Then one goblet was given to Anlet-Un-Ri, another to Asim, and then one to the priest himself.

They waited while the priest recited more of the ancient scripture, then, when he raised his goblet, Asim and the soldiers did likewise, so the female warrior followed their lead.

The priest kissed his goblet before tipping his head back and draining it.

The others did the same.

The ceremony continued for what seemed an age to Anlet-Un-Ri.

As the priest continued to recite ancient scripture, the slaves stood silently against the wall and bowed their heads in unison, whenever a response was required.

After a while, Anlet-Un-Ri felt her eyes growing heavy. Not wishing to show disrespect, she fought to keep them open, but she soon realised it was not just her eyes, but her entire body that seemed to be losing the battle against sleep.

Chapter 22

She felt her head loll forward and her chin slammed into her chest.

Lifting her head back up took all the strength she had in her.

The chamber began to swim before her eyes.

The priest's incantations grew further and further away, melting into the distance like metal in a fire.

Eventually, unable to combat her fatigue, Anlet-Un-Ri slumped forward on to the floor.

Asim was the first to stand up. He moved over to where the prone female lay and nudged her with his foot. She did not move.

He signalled to the priest to stop his prayers and the holy man obeyed.

The three others rallied to Asim's side, and each took it in turns to kick and poke the fallen warrior.

"Is she dead?" asked Khartar.

"No," replied Asim, "she is merely in a deep trance."

"When will she awake?" asked one of the others.

Asim turned to look at him. "When it is too late."

The priest was handed a heavy purse of gold, and the man bowed his head and left the chamber. His work was done.

Asim ordered the slaves to lift the mighty warrior and carry her through to a secret chamber that he had commissioned, privately, under the seal of the Pharaoh.

No one else knew of its existence and the architect had been well paid to ensure that remained the case.

Within the chamber lay a large sarcophagus.

The slaves were ordered to bind the slumbering commander with linen strips until her entire body was obscured beneath the wrappings. Then they were instructed to place her inside the sarcophagus and secure the door.

Finally, the slaves were made to lift the entire structure to a standing position, as only those of noble birth were entitled to rest lying down in the royal chamber.

Once back outside, in the moonlight, Asim gave the signal, and the slaves were attacked and slaughtered by the soldiers and the two guards on duty.

Their bodies were disposed of as if they had never been.

The following day, in a ceremony that took up all the daylight hours, the boy prince Mehet-Met-Too was enshrined in his royal chamber with all the pomp and ceremony due to someone of his position.

Once the ceremony was over, the tomb was sealed and any sign of the entrance was obliterated to the extent that anyone passing the site would be completely unaware of its existence.

Chapter Twenty-Three

AMIN SALAH CLIMBED FROM HIS TAXI AND WAITED while the driver unpacked his bags from the boot. Although it had been an extremely mild day, the Egyptian felt a slight shiver as the evening wind cut through his light linen suit.

The doorman greeted him as Salah approached the main doors of the Orb and Sceptre hotel. It was late, so most of the guests had already retired for the night.

"I will arrange a porter for your bags, sir," the doorman assured him.

Salah thanked him and walked to the front desk where he was greeted by the receptionist. The girl on duty looked no older than a teenager and her pristine uniform looked brand new.

Salah smiled and handed her his passport. "I hope very much that you have a room booked in my name," he announced, smiling.

The young girl checked the computer. "Yes sir," she replied pleasantly, "We have you booked for three nights, with an option to extend."

"That's correct – my business in town may take longer than expected."

The girl handed him a key-card for his door and told the porter the room number.

"Would it be possible to have a large Scotch sent up to my room?" Salah enquired.

"Certainly, sir," the receptionist confirmed, "I'll have it sent straight up. Will there be anything else?"

"No thank you, it's been a long day, I just need a nightcap to send me off to sleep."

Once inside his room, Salah unpacked his bags and hung his clothes in the wardrobe.

It had indeed been a long day for him, but as soon as the embassy had informed his office of the death of Kasim Kassimme, Salah knew that he would be expected to spring into action.

Kasim was a fool. A loyal and industrious worker, but a fool nonetheless.

When news of the discovery of the mummy of Anlet-Un-Ri first reached Egypt, Salah had been given the mission of arranging a private viewing through the museum where her remains were due to be exhibited.

The arrangements were progressing steadily, though not at the speed that the sect would have liked. But these things often took time. The most important thing was not to raise suspicion, and acting overly keen might have that very affect.

The sect appreciated that patience was the key.

The life of the female warrior was not particularly well-documented, although records of her military career had been found. But even so, her death was shrouded in mystery. It was rumoured that one of the ancient priests had given her the onerous duty of carrying the Eye of Aken on behalf of the young prince, Mehet-Met-Too.

This ancient religious symbol was considered by many to be the key to ensuring the dead safe passage to the afterlife. According to the Book of the Dead, those who held the symbol

Chapter 23

could pass through the Hall of Truth on route to the Divine Ferryman without having to answer any questions.

However, it was also written that forces within the Hall of Truth would constantly be trying to take the ancient symbol away from its carrier, and that was why the greatest warrior in Egypt at the time was entrusted with the task.

History did not record the actual ritual at which the symbol was passed, but what was known was that the Pharaoh summoned Anlet-Un-Ri just days before the burial ceremony, and she was last seen in the vicinity of the royal chamber the night before by some passing guards and then never seen again.

If the legend was true, then there was every chance that the ancient symbol might be secreted somewhere beneath the mummy's wrappings and, if so, then the sect had to have it at all costs.

So, a plan was put into operation whereby a member of the sect would be the first to study the mummy under scientific conditions. But, somehow, Doctor Anmali had been asked to attend instead.

The easiest option at that point would have been to exterminate the doctor, but the leaders of the sect agreed that to do so would only raise unwanted suspicion. For that reason, it was decided that a sect member, who was also a senior member of the Egyptian Archaeological Society, would visit the museum where the mummy was housed and discreetly examine the wrappings for any sign of the Eye of Aken.

Being in his position, it was the easiest thing in the world for Salah to request an invitation to the opening of the exhibition, but then Kasim had somehow managed to get it into his head that the sect needed to be more robust in its actions. So, before anyone could stop him, he booked a flight over to England, and that was the last of him.

Kasim had been a relatively new member of the sect and his was an honorary title handed down to him as the eldest male in his family following the death of his much-respected uncle, a previous member.

But, unlike his noble and dignified uncle, Kasim was too hot-tempered and impatient. He always seemed to want to rush in, whereas the sect had maintained its order over centuries by being patient and waiting for the right moment before striking.

To Kasim, the removal of anything discovered in an Egyptian tomb was a desecration. Especially if it was taken out of Egypt, regardless of whether or not the government gave its approval.

The fact that there was no documentation giving permission to remove Anlet-Un-Ri, let alone the Eye of Aken, made his zeal for their retrieval all the more frenzied.

Even so, the members of the sect were still anxious to discover who had killed him.

Theirs was not the only organisation in Egypt that upheld a noble and ancient duty and, although there were some that were known for resorting to violence in order to accomplish their missions, a warning would have been forthcoming before action was taken.

Enquiries had already been made but, as yet, no one was admitting to the murder.

So Salah knew that he needed to be on his guard while he was over here, just in case the assassin was still lying in wait.

The noise in the club was deafening but Scrapper was lost in the vibe. This was his kind of place, and these were his kind of people.

It was almost two o'clock in the morning, but Scrapper was only just starting to feel alive. The pot he had smoked earlier was really starting to take effect, and the three double shots he had swallowed since arriving at midnight helped to enhance the overall buzz.

Chapter 23

Phil stood in a corner of the room, trying to have a conversation with a couple of girls, but losing out to the volume of the thumping bass line surrounding them. These were not exactly ideal circumstances for getting to know someone, let alone holding an intelligent conversation.

Phil loved a good rave just as much as Scrapper but, for some reason, he had not been in the mood tonight. But Scrapper had insisted that they go out. He had some fresh gear on him and money in his pocket, and whenever Scrapper had cash, he just loved to flash it around.

Through the haze from the smoke machine, Scrapper recognised a connection. Barry was always good for some top-notch gear, and at this time of night he would be willing to cut an old mate like Scrapper a pretty decent deal.

Scrapper made a beeline for his mate and patted his pocket as if to signify that he had money to spend. Old Mrs Riley's purse had been loaded, and all in cold, hard cash. It was all well and good grabbing someone's credit card, but Scrapper never felt that he made enough from them. The going rates seemed to change like the weather. One minute he would be offered a hundred quid, the next, only fifty, and there were only so many fences he could trust to keep their mouths shut about where they got them from if they got busted.

As he had expected, Barry was unloading a stash of gear which he had apparently just collected from one of his best sources.

They negotiated a deal and Scrapper shoved his prize into his pocket.

The two men bumped fists and parted before security could notice them loitering.

Scrapper made his way over towards where Phil was speaking to the two girls. Ignoring them, Scrapper signalled to his friend that he had some stuff and was going outside to roll a fresh spliff.

The two girls were obviously not impressed by the new arrival. Scrapper was dripping with sweat from all the jumping he had been doing on the dancefloor, and his shirt was stuck to his scrawny body, with huge damp patches showing through the fabric.

Phil was obviously not keen to leave the conversation he was attempting to have with the girls. But he knew only too well that once Scrapper had an idea, it was futile arguing with him.

He considered asking the two girls to join them outside. They both looked like the kind of girls who might enjoy a fun experience. No one who came to these places did so purely for the music. Plus which, Phil had the distinct impression from the way one of the girls was looking at him, that she might be interested in more than just his conversation.

Phil tried to convey his idea to Scrapper, but his friend was already walking back towards the exit, beckoning Phil to follow.

There was no point in trying to shout above the noise, and even if Scrapper could hear him, Phil was hardly going to suggest seeing if the girls wanted to join them out loud.

He considered just asking them on his own, but he knew from past experience that Scrapper could be very tight when it came to sharing his stash, unless there were something in it for him in return.

As he had basically ignored the two girls when he came over, Phil doubted that things would end well if he carried out his plan.

Phil excused himself and looked at the girl who liked him when he promised to return.

He found Scrapper in the alley at the side of the club.

There were a couple of groups of clubbers scattered along the passage, but they were all too busy focusing on their own nefarious activities to concern themselves with whatever Scrapper and Phil were up to.

Scrapper lit his spliff, and breathed in, deeply holding the

Chapter 23

smoke in his mouth for a few seconds before releasing it. "Premium quality, bruv," he announced, handing it over to Phil.

Phil took a drag. He had to admit it was good stuff.

"I was thinking of inviting those two girls out here. What do you think?"

Scrapper exhaled his second puff. "Fine with me, just so long as they don't expect any of this."

It was just as Phil had expected. "Never mind," he muttered under his breath.

Just then, Scrapper felt his phone vibrating in his back pocket.

He took it out and squinted at the screen, then exclaimed: "Shit!"

"What's up?"

"I missed a fuckin' call from Len. Bollocks!"

"Can't you call him back?" Phil ventured, offering Scrapper back his roll-up.

Scrapper refused the spliff and waved his friend away. "I need to think, fuck, what's my excuse for not pickin' up the fuckin' phone when he called?"

Phil shrugged. "Say you were out clubbin'. It's not even a lie, you can't hear fuck-all in there."

Scrapper considered Phil's suggestion for a moment.

It did make sense, and it was the truth. But with a man like Len Bixby you only received one chance, and Scrapper knew he might have just missed his.

"Fuck! Fuck! Fuck! Fuck!" he called out, kicking the brick wall in front of him.

Phil could feel his cheeks redden. Scrapper's paranoia could set in at any time, and it usually ended in him acting in an embarrassing manner. Phil glanced up and down the alleyway. No one else along the line seemed at all fazed by his friend's erratic behaviour.

"The sooner you call him back, the better," Phil offered.

"I know, I know, fuck it!" Scrapper hit the number and waited.

After a few seconds, Len answered. "Thought you were avoiding me," he said sourly.

"No way, man, no way," Scrapper assured him. "I was in a club and didn't hear me phone. I am so sorry, it won't 'appen again."

"Don't worry about it," Len assured him. "Are you ready for the details?"

"Yes, yes, absolutely, go ahead."

"The stuff will be delivered to you tomorrow at four, make sure you're in, the courier will not wait around. The details of where you are to take it, and who you need to hand it to, will all be inside the bag. You do have a car, I presume?"

"Oh, yes, no worries there," Scrapper lied.

"Good," Len continued. "It's out of London so the drive should take you two to three hours, dependin' on how fast you go. Do not get stopped for speedin'!"

"No chance, I'm safe."

"The bloke the delivery is for will be expecting you after midnight, so don't trot up any earlier. If you get there too soon, just find somewhere safe to wait until it's time. Got it?"

"Yep, no problem, you can rely on me Len, honest."

There was a pause on the other end.

For a moment, Scrapper thought the call had been disconnected. "Hello, are you still there, Len?"

"Do not let me down!" There was menace in Len's voice and Scrapper did not have to second-guess the emphasis.

Before he had a chance to answer, the line went dead.

Chapter Twenty-Four

Marigold Hedges stood in the middle of the stage, with her fellow teachers seated behind her.

Morning assembly at Seddon Academy was a vital part of the day, as far as she was concerned, even when there were no new announcements to make. It was her chance to connect with all her girls at one time.

Marigold had never seen herself as one of those headmistresses who merely acted as a figure-head and spent the majority of their time locked behind their office door.

As far as she was concerned, it was her duty, as well as her pleasure, always to be visible to her charges and accessible at all times when possible.

Having finished her daily announcement, Marigold moved her head to one side of the microphone and cleared her throat.

"Now then, ladies, I have some exciting news for some of you."

She paused while a murmur of anticipation ran through the crowd.

"Tonight, our local museum will be holding a grand opening for a new exhibition and I have been fortunate enough to secure some invitations so that a group of you may accompany some of your teachers and me to this wonderful spectacle."

She paused to enjoy the "oohs" and "ahs" from the girls.

"Has she asked you along?" whispered Pascale Bouvier, the French teacher.

"No," replied Danielle. "Why, are you going?"

"Please, to a dusty old museum to see a three-thousand-year old pile of bones. I'd rather stick pins in my eyes."

Danielle had to stifle a laugh.

She noticed Miss Ogilvy further down the line leaning forward to stare disapprovingly in her direction.

Danielle held her fist to her mouth and pretended to cough.

Marigold, it seemed, had not heard the noise. "Now I realise that you will all want to go, but I'm afraid that just isn't possible as there are limited numbers being allowed this evening. Therefore, further visits will be arranged once the museum is open to the public."

Halfway down the school hall, an arm shot up.

"Yes, Miss Higgins."

The girl stood up, as was expected of anyone who either asked or answered a question during assembly.

"When will we find out if we are one of the lucky ones for tonight, Headmistress?"

Marigold smiled. "I have placed a list of names on the main noticeboard. Please do not all rush there after assembly, it's not going anywhere."

"I wonder when we will be put out of our misery?" Pascale said behind her hand.

"Oh, come on," whispered Danielle, "it won't be that bad."

"I'll remind you of that if you're picked."

Again, Danielle noticed Miss Ogilvy leaning forward. Considering she was seven chairs away, she appeared to possess incredibly sharp hearing.

Chapter 24

This time, Danielle did not bother to cover up the fact she had been speaking.

After assembly, the teachers stayed back, as was the usual protocol, to have their daily informal chat with the headmistress.

"Now then ladies, as I said earlier, tonight's opening will be a splendid affair. We can expect attendance from the local press, as well as the mayor and her consort, so it is imperative that we make a good impression and ensure that the girls on display act with impeccable manners."

"She makes them sound like show ponies," Pascale whispered, turning her head to one side, towards Danielle, then straight back to the front, as if she were trying to relieve a stiff neck.

But it was not enough to fool the headmistress, who noticed the sly movement and turned her attention directly at the two women.

Thinking on her feet, Danielle immediately put her hand up.

"Yes, Miss Parker." The headmistress eyed her subordinate suspiciously.

"Which girls have you chosen for this evening's event?"

"Ah, well now, in view of the circumstances, as I have already described, I thought it best, for tonight, to choose those attending from the upper sixth. It'll give them a chance to break out their evening attire."

Danielle nodded. "I see, and who exactly have you chosen?"

"Well…" the headmistress shuffled through the papers in her hand. In her haste to find the correct piece, she dropped several sheets which fluttered through the air, towards the stage.

Before anyone else could move, Miss Ogilvy was out of her seat and on her hands and knees, gathering up the runaway sheets.

She shuffled them into a uniform order before handing them

back to the headmistress.

"Thank you, Miss Ogilvy," Marigold responded, placing the sheet in her hand on the top of the pile. "Here we are. Now then, let's see, there's Cynthia Rollins, Carrie Anne Grant, Colleen Sykes. Jacinda Singh…"

Before she had a chance to proceed further, Pascale broke in.

"Excuse me Headmistress," she asked, raising her hand as an afterthought. "Are there any girls on the list who are not swans?"

Marigold became flustered. The directness and sheer impertinence of the question took her by surprise.

It was not the place of one of her juniors to question her authority in this way.

Marigold scanned the list in front of her, as if she was not already fully aware of the answer.

Finally, she looked up. "The swans are the very cream of the academy. I think this is an excellent opportunity to show them off in public."

Marigold could hear her pulse thudding in her ears. She waited a moment to allow her heartbeat to slow down. "Do you have some objection to my choice, Miss Bouvier?"

Pascale shook her head. "Of course not, headmistress, I just think it might have been nice to allow some of the other girls, especially those who have worked hard and excelled, to go along, too."

"Did you not hear Miss Hedges say that there are only limited numbers allowed?" Miss Ogilvy called out from down the line. Her lips were pursed, and her complexion was turning puce.

"Yes, thank you, Miss Ogilvy. My hearing is perfectly fine." Pascale turned back to face front. "I just wonder if by choosing the swans alone, it might send out the wrong message to the other girls who have strived so hard this term to improve their grades."

Chapter 24

It was obvious to those in line that their colleague, Miss Ogilvy, could barely contain her contempt for their young counterpart, as she appeared on the point of exploding.

The maths teacher rose to her feet but did not turn to look at her colleague.

Instead, she faced forward as if making an announcement to the empty auditorium.

"Becoming a Swan is something to which all girls in this academy should aspire, and those who manage to attain such a position deserve to be rewarded."

There followed a moment's silence as the teachers all looked at each other, bewildered. Even the headmistress seemed a little taken aback by Miss Ogilvy's sudden outburst.

Marigold waited for her to take her seat again before she continued.

"Quite so," she responded half-heartedly.

Nurse Baxby, who was sitting next to Miss Ogilvy, placed a gentle palm on her colleague's hand. It seemed to relax the maths teacher, who turned to the nurse and smiled.

"Now," continued Marigold, "concerning the chaperones for this evening. As I said earlier, we have limited invitations, so I am afraid there is only room for a few of you." She looked up and smiled sheepishly. "I of course will be attending in my official capacity as a board member, and I thought perhaps..." Marigold looked down once more, at the papers in front of her, as if she had forgotten whose names she had on her list.

"Here it comes," whispered Pascale. "Wait for it, any second now."

Danielle managed to stifle her laugh. The last thing she wanted was another outburst from the maths teacher.

"Miss Ogilvy and Miss Parker," Marigold finally announced. "I wondered if the two of you might care to accompany the girls and keep a watchful eye on them? Not that they'll need watching, I'm sure."

Once more, Miss Ogilvy was on her feet before anyone else had a chance to draw breath. "Oh, yes, thank you, Headmistress, it will be an honour, thank you."

Feeling as if she had no choice, Danielle rose to her feet, too. "Yes," she responded. "Thank you Headmistress – it will be my pleasure."

In truth, the last thing she wanted was to have to spend the evening among the chosen company. But what could she say?

Danielle blamed herself for not preparing a credible excuse. But the fact was, she never imagined she would be chosen to begin with.

As they left the school hall, the teachers all branched out in different directions towards whichever class they were teaching.

As Danielle made her way towards the gym, she felt a slight tug at her elbow.

She turned to see Pascale standing behind her with a hangdog expression on her face.

Danielle made sure that no one was within earshot, before leaning over towards her friend. "And you can stop taking the piss, and all," she muttered.

Pascale laughed. "Why on earth didn't you make up an excuse?"

"I couldn't think of anything on the spur of the moment."

"Seriously?" Pascale gazed at her friend dejectedly. "Oh, Headmistress, I am so sorry, but I think my time of the month has just begun and, by tonight I'll be in too much pain to go out socialising."

The tone of her voice sounded so sincere that for a second Danielle forgot that she was merely providing a demonstration.

"Well, thanks for nothing, pal," she said.

"Mon pleasure, mademoiselle," Pascale replied, curtseying before she turned and headed back to her class.

———

Chapter 24

When Dawn woke that morning, her back felt as if it were about to go into spasm.

As predicted, she had fallen asleep on the couch, and she half-remembered waking in the middle of the night for a second before turning over and falling back to sleep.

She lifted her legs off the couch and realised that she still had the bag of peas tied to her ankle. Only now, they were no longer frozen, and felt as if they were nothing more than a bag of water sloshing around her foot.

Dawn carefully untied them and, holding them away from her, she carried them into the kitchen and plonked them in the waste bin.

She stood there for a moment, trying to judge just how much pain she was in.

At least she was able to walk, but her ankle still throbbed each time she put weight on that foot.

Her back was another story. The pain there was permanent, regardless of whether she moved or not. Dawn guessed that she must have taken a harder fall than she realised the previous night. She had often heard from other colleagues that when the adrenaline is pumping, injuries often remain hidden until everything calms down.

Dawn switched on the kettle to make herself a coffee.

She opened the cupboard and took out a box of painkillers. While the kettle boiled, Dawn read the label. As she suspected, it advised that they should not be taken on an empty stomach but, ever since she was a teenager, Dawn had not been able to stomach food first thing in the morning.

She decided she would have to risk it, because the pain in her back was not going away on its own.

After coffee, Dawn took a long, hot shower. The steaming spray felt good on her back but it hurt whenever she bent down to soap herself. She tried standing on one leg and lifting the other to lather it up, but she almost lost her balance on the first attempt, so she shelved that idea.

Falling over in the shower was not going to enhance her chances of a speedy recovery.

The drive into the station was torture. Dawn had opted for flats instead of heels, to make walking easier. But each time she depressed the accelerator or brake, the pain in her ankle intensified.

She made a mental note to tell Courtney that, if they needed to drive anywhere, he was chauffeur.

Once inside the office, Courtney followed Dawn as she limped her way to her desk.

"You okay, guv?" he asked, concerned.

"I'll live," she replied, lowering herself gingerly into her seat. "A little slip last night on that raid."

"I hear it was a resounding success."

"Yeah, I think Ampstead was happy."

"The blokes were talking about it this morning, apparently they netted gear in that makeshift lab with a street value of over three million quid. Super's even threatened to buy us all a round tonight."

Dawn laughed. "Well, there's a first for everything, I suppose. But don't forget, we've got that exhibition opening tonight."

Courtney's face dropped. "Oh, yes. How could I forget?"

It was obvious to Dawn from his expression that he had in fact forgotten.

"Have you got a posh suit all ready and waiting?" she asked, looking his usual crumpled attire up and down.

Courtney flushed. "I'm on it, don't worry. Anyway, I heard back from the museum in Cairo where Doctor Anmali works. Seems our victim had never worked there, although they very kindly gave me some contact numbers for a couple of other museums, so I am going to try them now."

Chapter 24

Dawn nodded. "Good stuff. Well, at least we know the good doctor wasn't lying when she said she didn't know him."

"From her place of business, anyway," Courtney reminded her. "They may have still known each other socially, or through their work. Do you think local museums hold joint conferences or Skype meetings?" Courtney mused.

Dawn shook her head. "No idea, but anything is possible, and speaking of anything being possible, any chance you could make me a strong black coffee, one heaped sugar?"

Courtney could not remember his superior ever asking for such a favour before.

There were some senior officers who loved to throw their weight around and would often make demands of their junior officers that were not strictly part of their duty, including making their tea or coffee, fetching lunch for them or even collecting their dry cleaning.

But for Dawn to make such a request, Courtney knew she must be in some real discomfort.

"Of course," he replied. "Anything you need, just ask – that foot must be really playing up."

"It's more the ankle," Dawn admitted. "But my foot's not far behind."

Courtney nodded. "Maybe," he ventured, "we should consider telling the Super that you're not fit for tonight. You should really rest up and keep your weight off it."

"Your sympathy is most touching," Dawn replied, with more than a hint of sarcasm in her voice. "But you're going, with or without me. Now, coffee, please."

Courtney pulled a face. "Okay, okay."

As he slid off the desk and began to walk away, Dawn called after him.

"And when you've done that, call your wife and make sure your best suit is in a fit state for the evening. I won't be seen out in public with a scruff."

Chapter Twenty-Five

Stanley Unwin arrived for work and drew his car up to the front of the new security gates.

The man on duty in the security box saluted upon recognising him, and from his position, Unwin could see the man hitting the "open" button to allow him access.

Nothing happened.

Unwin frowned and glared at the man, who held his hand up in response as if trying to figure out how to operate the controls.

Unwin waited, his fingers rapidly drumming the steering wheel.

A woman with a pram and a toddler on a harness approached Unwin's car from the left, obviously wishing to pass. But with his car blocking the way, she had no option other than to wait, or attempt to walk around him, which would mean her taking her charges into the street.

At first, Unwin pretended not to see her, too embarrassed by the fact he was causing her such inconvenience.

Finally, he turned, and pretended to notice her for the first

Chapter 25

time. He mouthed an apology and offered a small wave. The woman looked peeved, to say the least.

The security gate still had not moved.

Now Unwin noticed the guard inside the box on the telephone, speaking to someone and shrugging his shoulders.

Unwin turned back to the woman. The toddler was attempting to run away, pulling at his harness, the strain of the action etched into his cherubic face, while the woman made a grab for him, without letting go of her pram.

There was nothing else for it. Unwin looked back over his shoulder and slipped his gear stick into reverse. He eased his car back until there was ample room for the woman to pass, which she did without acknowledging his assistance.

Once she had passed, Unwin moved his car back into position.

He undid his seat belt and slid out of his seat, making his way around to the security gates.

From his new vantage position, he could hear the man inside the security box, shouting down the phone. "I've tried that twice already. They won't budge, I'm telling you."

He sounded exasperated by the situation, and Unwin could tell from the tone of his voice that he was fast losing patience with the person on the other end of the line.

When the guard saw Unwin standing on the other side of the gate, he told the person on the other end that he was going to use the manual override and slammed the handset back into its cradle.

"I'm sorry about all this, Mr Unwin," he offered apologetically, emerging from his box. "I've told them that the stupid thing doesn't seem to want to work."

Unwin released a pent-up breath. "Well, what are we going to do now? I need this operational in time for this evening, I've got the caterers arriving at four."

The guard held up a long, black metal wrench. "Not to worry

sir, I'll use this for now and, as soon as Bill arrives, I'll let him know."

"Tell him I want to see him the minute he arrives," Unwin instructed.

He made his way back to his car while the guard approached the recalcitrant gates.

It took what seemed like an eternity for the guard to open the gates manually.

Once he had inserted the wrench in the socket, he frantically began turning it, but it appeared to Unwin that it took three turns of the tool to make the gates budge just an inch.

When the gap was finally large enough for him to drive through, he parked his car in his designated spot and made his way into the museum.

Before heading to his office, he went straight to the area that housed the new exhibition.

The sight that greeted him as he turned the corner was one of chaos and despair.

By the time he had left work the previous evening, everything looked ready, minus a few touches here and there. But now, for whatever reason, several of the awnings had been taken down, the backdrop was nowhere to be seen and two of the statues he had commissioned, at great expense, were laying on their sides, instead of standing upright.

Unwin could feel his whole body shaking with a combination of rage and fear.

Seeing the arrival of the curator, and his quite natural response to the state of the exhibition, Doctor Anmali walked over to him and placed a tender hand on his arm.

The gesture seemed to have an immediate effect. Unwin could feel himself calming down from inside. Her touch was miraculous.

He turned momentarily to look at her, once again feeling himself being swept up in the beauty of her dark eyes.

Chapter 25

Softly, she said: "I know – it seems as if disaster has struck. But it looks much worse than it is. They found a leak first thing this morning, so they had to clear away the exhibits until it could be traced and repaired."

Unwin nodded dumbly.

He managed to drag his gaze away from the doctor and looked once more at the shambolic debris that had, only yesterday, been the jewel in the museum's crown.

"It's all been sorted out," continued the doctor, still holding his arm. "The display team is even now touching up the area where there was water damage, and everything will be back in place in plenty of time for this evening. So please don't worry yourself."

Unwin turned back to her. "I've got the caterers coming at four," he said distractedly.

Doctor Anmali frowned. "Okay," she offered, to reassure him, "I'm sure everything will be fine long before then."

They heard the sound of loud footsteps on the parquet flooring.

The doctor turned first and saw the looming figure of Bill Stead heading towards them.

She turned back to Unwin. "Now, if you'll excuse me, I need to finish clearing away my mini-lab. I don't want any of my samples to become contaminated."

Unwin smiled, though he was still reeling from the shock of seeing the display in such a state.

Stead came up behind him.

They both watched the petite figure of Doctor Anmali walk back to her equipment.

"Sorry, Mr Unwin," Stead began, "Derick told me about what happened this morning. I can't understand it – the electrician told me yesterday it was all in order."

Unwin turned to face him, having shaken the mesmerising image of the withdrawing doctor from his mind. "Well, evidently, he or she lied," Unwin retorted. "Now what are we going to do about it?"

Stead held his hands up. "I've already put in a call, the electrician is on 'is way, and this time I promise you I won't just take 'is word fer it, I'll make sure I test the mechanism personally before I sign the job off."

Unwin nodded. "Just make sure that everything is singing and dancing no later than four."

"Of course, Mr Unwin. You can leave it to me – I'll see to it."

"See that you do, Bill, see that you do." With that, Unwin walked away towards his office.

Stead stared after the little man, a look of sheer malice on his face.

Oh, how he would delight in smacking that little shit about. One good punch and he would send him into the middle of next week.

But Stead knew that he had to keep on the right side of the little man.

This was a huge contract for his father's firm and he had put Bill in charge of it. And he had made it clear, in no uncertain terms, that it was his responsibility to keep the client happy at all times. If he screwed up, son or no son, he would be out on his ear.

His father was not the type to allow something as paltry as family ties get in the way of business. His elder brother had already learned that the hard way.

If his dad sacked him, he knew he would lose everything. Not just his job, but his house, his car and the money he made, which was far more than someone with his lack of qualifications could make anywhere else.

Not to mention that, if he lost all that, Carol would not stick around. As for the baby, well, neither of them was what you might call natural parents, and they both knew it. Again, it was his mum and dad who insisted on him supplying a grandchild.

Chapter 25

But that alone would not be enough to keep him in his dad's good graces if he blew this contract, there was no doubt in his mind about that.

So Stead had decided he would go into business for himself.

Not in a big way – at least, not to start with.

He had done his research. His dad had several contracts on the outskirts of town, supplying bouncers for clubs and some especially rowdy pubs. Through them, Bill had got to know the who's who for the local drug scene. And, according to his sources, there was plenty of demand but the supply was a little dry.

His job working for his dad's firm was the perfect cover. He had access to any number of vacant properties where he could sell his wares, not to mention company vans that would not raise an eyelid driving to and from the prearranged drop-offs.

Best of all, his dad would be supplying the cash for his initial investment, and he didn't even know it. Stead had been skimming money off the top for ages, which was one of the benefits he derived from paying people cash in hand. Barely a week went by when they did not need to call in emergency back-up, whether it was guards for a new contract or cleaners to do a deep clean after a fire or flood.

On such occasions, in order to expedite matters, his father allowed him discretion to bring in outside crews temporarily, and they were usually working off the books, so Stead would take a slice of the pie for himself.

He had also discovered a very lucrative side line in renting out some of their vacant properties on an ad-hoc basis. Several of the local working girls were willing to pay top dollar for a short-term let where they could take their clients, especially over weekends.

Stead always insisted on being present whenever genuine potential renters wanted to view properties, so he knew exactly when such apartments were vacant.

Over time, the money he had amassed had grown, until now he was finally ready to launch his new investment, drugs.

He had already made contact with a big player in London, who was happy to act as his supplier and, by this time tomorrow, he would have his first shipment ready and waiting.

The anticipation of his latest venture was one of the main things keeping his temper in check and preventing him from chucking in the towel and finally telling people like Stanley Unwin what he really thought of them.

That day would come, he could taste it. But first, he had to give his business time to grow.

———

Scrapper paced his bedroom floor, constantly glancing at the Mickey Mouse clock on the wall, urging the hands to move faster.

After his night out clubbing with Phil, Scrapper had slept in until 11 that morning. Once he had showered and made himself something to eat, he glanced through the local paper that his mother had left opened on the kitchen counter.

The lead story was the murder of old Mrs Riley.

The police had found her body the previous morning, just as he had left it. But now they were convinced she had met her end as a result of foul play and they were appealing for witnesses to come forward.

Scrapper skipped through the details on her life and focused on anything to do with the forensics. But, as usual, the police were being very cagey with the details, so as not to tip off the culprit.

As he sat there, spooning in the last of his cornflakes, Scrapper felt an icy trickle of sweat slide down his back.

He shrugged it off and threw the paper to one side.

There was nothing to link him to the old woman's murder – he was no idiot.

He knew his fingerprints were on file from when he went into Feltham. They never destroyed them, no matter what his brief had said. Besides, it was not that long ago, so the chances were he was definitely still in the system.

But he had worn gloves and kept them on throughout. Although, now he came to think of it, they were old and worn, so what if he had left behind a partial thumb or even palm print? Could they trace him from that?

Who was he kidding? They could trace anything these days.

But fingerprints were not the real issue, everything these days was all about DNA. Tracking you down from your semen, or saliva, or even sweat.

Scrapper suddenly became aware of the perspiration leaking from every pore in his face. He looked down and noticed a few droplets diving off his nose and chin, splashing on the kitchen lino.

That was how you left DNA.

He quickly grabbed some kitchen towel and rubbed his face dry. In his mind, if he did not ensure now that his face was clean, there was a chance he might have left a few droplets on the old woman.

Scrapper continued to scrub his face until the paper towel fell apart.

He was being insane. If he had left any perspiration behind, then it was too late to do anything about it now.

In a fit of anger, he threw his cereal bowl in the sink. It smashed on contact with the metal surface. He knew his mum would go spare, but right now he had more important things on his mind.

Tonight was his chance to join the big time. Once he had delivered the package that Len's courier was dropping off to him this afternoon, his name would be spread around as a reliable contact, someone who could be trusted.

This was the start of his time in the limelight and, if he had left any DNA on that stupid old bitch, it would all be over before it began.

He should have torched the place and her with it. They could not pick DNA out of ashes.

Since then, Scrapper had spent the rest of the afternoon pacing his bedroom in agitated frustration, waiting for either Len's call or a knock at the door from the Old Bill.

He had his music turned up full blast. Scrapper had no comprehension of the words being bellowed through his speakers, but he did not care. The thudding bass helped to calm him down.

Usually, by now, he would have had his first spliff of the day, but he was conscious of keeping a cool head for tonight. Nothing could be allowed to go wrong. He had already made arrangements with Phil to ensure that his dopey cousin would be ready with the van as soon as they were needed.

Phil was not happy about using his cousin like this, but he understood that, without him, they could not make the delivery.

In the end, Scrapper stared out of the window to pass the time.

Finally, his phone buzzed.

Scrapper fumbled in his jean pocket, trying to retrieve it. His hands were so wet with sweat they made it almost impossible for him to grab hold of the handset.

Furious with himself, he rubbed his palms down his jeans, then tried again.

This time, the phone came free.

It was a text from Len: "Courier waiting, space No 9."

Scrapper ran out of the flat and along the corridor towards the bank of lifts at the far end. As he reached them, an elderly couple emerged from one. Scrapper waited impatiently while the

Chapter 25

old man went back inside the car to retrieve the rest of their shopping.

By the time he was ready to exit once more, the lift door began to close.

Scrapper barged past him so as not to lose the lift.

He heard the old man muttering something to his wife about young hooligans as the door closed.

Once he was downstairs, Scrapper stopped in his tracks and took out his phone.

He reread Len's message. "Space Number nine," he repeated, thoughtfully. "What does that mean?"

Then it struck him. Len must be referring to parking space number nine.

The painted numbers of the allocated parking bays outside the tower block had long since faded into obscurity, so Scrapper wondered how the courier had known which bay to use. But as he emerged from the concrete structure into the open, he noticed a motorcycle parked halfway down the road.

The rider was dressed in black leather, head to toe, with a darkened visor pulled down the front of his crash helmet, which obscured his face.

When he noticed the biker, Scrapper instinctively raised his hand and waved. But the biker turned his head away, as if he had not seen him.

Realising his rookie error, Scrapper shoved both hands in his pockets, and casually began walking towards the waiting courier.

When he was within a couple of feet, the biker turned back to face him, before dismounting and opening the large back box behind his seat.

As Scrapper waited, nervously looking over his shoulder, the biker came forward and handed him a large black holdall. Scrapper took it without question and the biker instantly remounted and started his engine, before riding off, away from the estate.

The whole episode took less than ten seconds, and Scrapper found himself standing in the middle of the bays, surrounded by parked cars, with a holdall containing what he surmised was a vast quantity of illegal drugs.

The strangeness of his situation spurred him into action.

Scrapper swung the holdall over his left shoulder and casually walked back to the bank of lifts.

Chapter Twenty-Six

MARIGOLD HEDGES GATHERED THE SWANS TOGETHER after school and arranged for a light tea to be prepared for them in the dining room.

The girls sat huddled around the table, chatting excitedly about the evening's events.

Miss Humphries supervised the service, and her staff busied themselves serving tea, sandwiches and cake. Once everyone had been served, Miss Hedges thanked the head chef for her assistance and the rest of the staff were dismissed.

"Now, ladies," began the headmistress, "I trust that you are all looking forward to this evening's festivities?"

The girls nodded enthusiastically. "Yes, thank you, Headmistress, we are." Cynthia spoke on behalf of the girls. "And we would all like to say thank you for choosing us to represent the academy this evening. We will not let you down."

Miss Hedges held up her hand. "I have no doubt whatsoever, ladies, that each and every one of you will make me very proud, as you always do."

The girls smiled and blushed, accepting the compliment as they had been taught.

"There are just a couple of things I wish to go over with you before tonight."

Miss Hedges settled her glasses on the end of her nose and leafed through a leather-bound folder she had with her.

The girls waited patiently.

Miss Hedges found the sheet she had been looking for. "Now, firstly," she began, "the local press will be there this evening, so there is every chance that at least some of you will have your picture taken for the local paper."

There was excited shrieks from the group.

The headmistress allowed the chatter to die down before she continued: "The mayor will also be present, accompanied by her consort and the usual entourage, no doubt, and members of the arts council board, which I sit on, as you may well know. Plus several invited dignitaries from local businesses, the list of which I don't seem to have."

Miss Hedges riffled through the papers in her file but was unable to locate the sheet she was missing.

"Never mind," she said, absentmindedly. "Now, the reason I arranged this tea is twofold. Firstly, as you will be at the exhibition, you will miss dinner. However, I have asked Miss Humphries to lay on a light supper for you upon our return. Which brings me to my other point. There will, of course, be refreshments provided at the opening, and this will include champagne and wine."

Again, there followed more excited whoops and hoorahs from the gathering.

"Naturally," Miss Hedges continued once there was calm, "you must all remain on your best behaviour. Therefore, you will each be allowed to enjoy one glass of your choice, and one only. There will of course be non-alcoholic options, should you be thirsty. And may I suggest for those of you who have not tried alcohol before, that you nibble on something while you drink, to help soak it up."

The girls nodded their understanding.

"And please, if you are photographed with a glass in your hand, please ensure that you do not strike a pose holding it up to the camera or anything else of that vulgar nature."

"Rest assured, Headmistress, we promise we will all remember our three Ds."

"Decorum. Deportment. Deference," the girls chanted in unison.

Miss Hedges smiled proudly. "Thank you, ladies, I know you would never do anything to bring embarrassment on me or on the good name of the academy."

She had to stop to wipe away a tear.

"Right then," she continued, once she had regained her composure. "The bus leaves promptly at five forty-five. Mr Franks will not wait for stragglers so, once you have finished your tea, go and make yourselves glamorous, and make sure you wear a shawl or something else to keep you warm – these museums can be very chilly."

———

Dawn fell back on her bed and stared up at the ceiling. The hot shower had been just what the doctor ordered. Standing under the hot spray had certainly helped to ease the dull pain in her back. That and the eight pain-killers she had swallowed since waking up.

Her ankle was not giving in, either. The drive home had been torturous.

Fortunately, she had convinced DS Courtney to collect her on his way to the exhibition, to save her from having to drive any more that day. It also meant that she would not have to worry about how much she drank at the opening as alcohol was nature's painkiller, as far as she was concerned.

She lifted her legs up off the ground and studied her ankles side by side.

From this angle they both appeared to be the same size and shape, so she decided it was probably just badly bruised rather than sprained. She decided that if she could find another frozen bag of vegetables in her freezer, she might try the same procedure as last night.

She sat at her dressing table with her towel wrapped around her and dried her hair with her hairdryer. After scolding Courtney over his sense of dress for the evening, Dawn suddenly remembered that she had not yet been through her wardrobe to see if she had something suitable to wear.

Dawn had never been a great one for dresses, preferring trousers and skirts with matching jackets to help project her image of professionalism. In reality, she found that for all the grandstanding by MPs on television, claiming that the modern police force was an equal-opportunities organisation, where women would be treated as if they were men, she knew better. She still felt every male eye in the room on her whenever she wore a skirt that rode above her knees at one of the never-ending succession of conferences she was made to attend.

Therefore, usually trousers were a better option.

But tonight was different, and part of her actually wanted to get dressed up, if only for her own benefit. Dawn could not remember the last time she went out, other than with the rest of the squad for a couple of pints across the road.

She limped over to her wardrobe to survey her options.

The one and only "little black dress" she owned had been a hasty purchase for a friend's birthday bash. But there was no way she could get away with wearing it tonight, certainly not with the super in attendance.

She plucked it out, nonetheless, and held it against herself.

It was tempting but, when all was said and done, she was supposed to be working.

Chapter 26

Dawn put it back and slid the hangers along the rail, searching for an alternative.

She had more dresses on the rail than she remembered and each one instantly brought back the memory of when she bought it, and for what occasion. They were all lovely, but none really suited a black-tie event.

Then she remembered.

Her passing-out parade after-party had been such an affair, and she distinctly remembered the black cocktail dress she had bought for the occasion.

She had worn it on only that one occasion, then, after dry cleaning, it went straight back in its box.

Dawn lowered herself to the floor and looked under her bed.

She had a jumble of various plastic containers underneath, most of which held spare towels, sheets, and blankets. But, right at the back she could see what she wanted.

Moving to the head of her bed, Dawn reached underneath and snagged hold of the classy-looking box in which the dress had come. She placed it on her bed and removed the lid.

The dress still looked pristine in its original zippered cover.

Dawn took it out and hung it up to have a proper look at it.

It would be perfect, so long as it still fitted her. She remembered that, back when she passed her exams, she was a keen gym bunny and used to attend several fitness classes each week, something she had not done for a while.

Dawn regularly monitored her weight, so she knew she was only a few pounds heavier than her first days on the beat. But, if she were honest, she had noticed the lack of tone along her hips and thighs.

Sighing deeply, Dawn slipped the dress off its hanger and pulled it on.

The material was a little unforgiving, but she managed to force up the zip without too much effort.

Dawn stood there for a moment and admired herself in the mirror.

She would do.

After carefully applying her make-up, she found the black kitten-heels she had also bought for her passing-out party. She had had them on her feet only a couple of times, so they looked almost like new as well.

Dawn slipped them on her feet and stood up to walk back and forth across the room, just to make sure the shoes were going to last the evening.

It was no good. The more she walked, the harder it became. Her ankle was not going to hold out all night in those shoes.

Her options now were limited. If she had to disregard all her heels, the flats she was left with did not really complement her dress.

Perhaps, she wondered, she could go in her heels, and take them off when she arrived, holding them for the rest of the evening.

That could be a thing.

Loads of women at parties removed their shoes when they grew too painful to wear.

On the other hand, what she did have were several pairs of ballet pumps. So she took out all the black ones and sized them up, picking the cleanest pair and giving them a quick polish, making sure not to get any on her dress.

She completed her outfit with a short leather biker-style jacket with gold zips. It gave her the perfect combination of demureness underneath and kick-ass over the top.

As she waited for Courtney to collect her, Dawn emptied her usual handbag and made sure that her warrant card, keys and purse were transferred over to the evening clutch bag she was taking.

Courtney's expression when she opened the door told her immediately that she had made the right choice.

Chapter 26

Unwin felt as if he had spent the entire day running around like the proverbial headless chicken. After overseeing the reconstruction of the recovered scenery for tonight's exhibition, he watched while the display team set out the signage to direct the guests towards the main exhibition.

He had rope-chains set up to accommodate those who decided to enter by the main entrance. The invitations clearly expressed that parking was available around the back of the main building, which was why the staff entrance was being set up to resemble a great pyramid, just for the evening. But he did not want guests who might arrive by taxi at the front door to have to shuffle round to the back in their elegant attire.

Later, he met the electrician who had been summoned to repair the automatic gates for the car park.

It was obvious to him that Bill Stead was unable to convey the importance of having them up and running by the afternoon, so he felt it his duty to step in and convey his disappointment, and elicit a sound promise from the electrician that he would not leave until the job was done to Unwin's satisfaction.

Stead was all right when dealing with his security team and taking in deliveries, but when it came to negotiating with skilled labour, a firmer hand was needed.

He was just about to sit down for a very late lunch when he remembered his evening suit.

Naturally, the electrician had disconnected the power to the gates while he worked on them, and typically, he had done so when they were closed. Therefore, Unwin ended up catching a bus into town to collect his suit from the dry cleaners.

He decided to catch a cab back to the museum to save time and it was only by chance while he was waiting in the cab office that he noticed his trousers were not on the hanger. A quick dash back to the dry cleaners, followed by an argument with the assistant on duty, finally resulted in him having the compete ensemble.

When he arrived back at the museum, he was overjoyed to find the pyramid surround for the staff entrance in situ, and the electronic gates working.

The electrician was more than happy to stay there and demonstrate to him that he had fixed the problem and, after the third display, Unwin was finally satisfied.

As the electrician's van left the complex, the caterer's truck came around the corner.

Unwin spent the next couple of hours supervising the construction of the bar and tables for the food. The majority of the waiting staff, all of whom, apparently, doubled as porters conveying the tables, chairs, and stalls for the evening, were eastern European, and appeared to Unwin to have very little English between them.

Even their supervisor barked orders to them in their mother tongue, and struggled to understand his instructions, even when Unwin relayed them at a fraction of his normal talking speed.

Eventually, they had everything set out the way he wanted, or near to it.

With time getting on, Unwin returned to his office to change.

As he entered, he saw his sandwich box lying on his desk and heaved a sigh. It was too late to eat his lunch now, and he knew that, if he attempted to do so while he was changing, he would drop mayonnaise onto his lapel, or worse.

Just as he was tying his shoelaces, his desk phone rang.

"Clevedon Museum, Mr Unwin speaking."

"Stanley!" The shrill voice of his wife echoed through the headset. "You're not going to believe this – the Rolls we ordered to take us to the opening has broken down, and now the company say that all they can offer us is a Mercedes. I told them it was not good enough and they needed to find us a

Chapter 26

replacement Rolls, but the insolent fool on the other end insisted that they couldn't do so in time."

Unwin rubbed his forehead.

On top of everything else, he did not need this.

"Perhaps you could call a mini-cab, dear," he suggested, regretting the suggestion as soon as the words left his mouth.

"A WHAT?" Mildred Unwin bellowed down the line.

Unwin could feel the onset of a headache. He had gone for too long without food or water and his wife's shouting was not helping.

"I only thought that under the circumstances…"

"The girls and I have spent all day preparing for this evening, and after all that, you expect us to travel in some dirty little mini-cab, so we can emerge at the other end, smelling of stale beer and kebabs? I don't think so!"

Unwin inhaled, deeply. "But you said so yourself my dear, they cannot arrange another Rolls in time, and it's probably too late now to book another car from anywhere else." Then he had another brainwave. "Could you not drive here in your car?"

Again, he wished he had kept his idea to himself.

"How can I possibly drive in this dress, and you expect the girls to squish themselves up in the back? We'll all look as if we've been dragged through a hedge backwards by the time we get there. You'll have to come and get us in the Daimler. At least it has a modicum of elegance about it. You have had it washed lately?"

Unwin almost dropped the handset. "Mildred, you cannot be serious, I've still got a hundred and one things to do, and the guests will be arriving at any minute, I have to be here to greet them."

He could hear his wife on the other end taking a deep breath.

"Well whose idea was it to give your PA the week off? You've only got yourself to blame. Surely you can ask someone there to step in on your behalf, it'll only take you 10 minutes to get here."

"In cross-town traffic?" he objected. "During rush hour?"

"Well, the sooner you leave, the sooner you'll get back. Now I don't want to hear another word on the subject, you're coming, and that's that!"

Before he could protest any further, he heard the receiver being slammed down at the other end.

Unwin looked at his watch.

There was no time to spare. He knew that his life would not be worth living if he refused his wife's demands, regardless of how unreasonable they were.

His options were not just limited, they were non-existent.

Just then, there was a knock on his door. "Come in," he answered absentmindedly.

Doctor Anmali appeared in the doorway and the sight of her quite took his breath away.

She was wearing a fine silk dress that looked rather like an Indian sari, with layers of the gossamer fabric wrapped around her body, covering her from her neck to her knees.

Her legs were bare, and she wore black court shoes. Her hair had been wound around her head and built up into a high chignon, around which she wore a jewelled band of gold that perfectly matched her necklace and earrings.

"Will I do?" she asked modestly, striking a pose in the doorway.

"My dear doctor, you are an event," Unwin mumbled, captivated by her loveliness.

She took a slight bow. "Well, thank you, sir," she replied. "I was wondering if you had time to go over my address before the evening gets under way. You said 10 minutes would do, and I think I have kept it under that."

Unwin shook himself back into consciousness. "Doctor, I...

It's not fair of me to ask this of you, I know, but I'm in a terrible bind."

Doctor Anmali looked intrigued. "Anything I can do to help?"

Unwin felt terribly embarrassed to ask her, but she seemed his only hope.

"I need to pop out just for a moment or two. It's quite unavoidable, I'm afraid, and I was wondering if you would possibly do me an enormous favour and act as greeter when the guests start arriving. I need someone to hold the fort in my absence, and... Well, you would be perfect."

The doctor smiled, wryly. "Well, I have no official training as a greeter, but I would be happy to look after things until you get back."

Unwin ran around the desk and grabbed her hand, pumping it gratefully.

He quickly filled her in on what she needed to do and thanked her profusely over and over as he spoke.

As they approached the staff entrance, Unwin could see the extra security staff he had organised for the evening unloading from one of their company vans.

He turned to the doctor. "Bill, the head security guard, has his instructions, so he will deploy the extra manpower, and I must warn you that the catering staff appear to have little English between them, so that lady over there is their supervisor," he pointed to the woman who was busy organising the various platters of appetisers which her staff had set out. "But just between us, her English is nothing to write home about, either."

Doctor Anmali ushered him out. "Please do not worry," she assured him. "You just do whatever it is you have to, and I'll see you back here."

He thanked her again and made for his car.

Before he had taken a couple of steps, he spun back around.

"The pamphlets, how stupid of me, the pamphlets for tonight's exhibition are still in my office."

The doctor held up her hand to stop him walking back. "Don't worry, I'll find them."

Unwin stayed in place. "Four large cardboard boxes, just behind the door," he called out.

She waved him on. "Just go, it'll all be fine," she promised.

Reluctantly, he finally left.

Chapter Twenty-Seven

REG FRANKS WAITED BESIDE SEDDON ACADEMY'S ONE-and-only minibus for the group for tonight's outing to arrive. For a man in his late sixties, he was very grateful for his job as the school's general handyman.

He had always been an early riser, so having to wake up each morning an hour before anyone else so that he could check the elderly boiler was no trouble at all. For the rest of the day, he was his own man. No one at the school noticed him shuffling around in his overalls, moving from one task to the next, and he made a point of not acknowledging any of the girls.

He had been given fair warning by the headmistress when he applied for the position that she would not tolerate any liaison between him and the girls. He was actually quite flattered that she would even think that someone of his age might be of interest to a young girl.

But he still believed it was better to be safe than sorry. So he kept to himself and carried on with his work. The position came with accommodation, which in itself was a godsend.

Franks had joined the Navy at the age of eighteen and stayed there until he was forty.

When he first ventured back into civilian life, he had no clue what he wanted to do with the rest of his life, so he just bummed around for the next 10 years, working on fishing boats around the coast.

There was nowhere in the world he wanted to see that he had not already visited so, for a while, he was happy enough living the simple life of a fisherman.

Being good with his hands, when he had had enough of smelling like raw fish all day, he joined an agency as a handyman, and it was from there that he ended up applying for the job he now had.

Tonight, was one of those rare occasions when he did not enjoy his role.

For such occasions as this, Miss Hedges insisted that Franks wore the chauffeur's uniform she had arranged to have specially made for him. It was a deep purple, with shiny gold buttons down the front, and a peaked cap to complete the ensemble.

He felt like a right idiot in it. But, fortunately for him, these occasions were few and far between. So, on balance, it was a small price to pay.

Finally, the main doors opened, and Franks saw the girls and their teachers readying themselves to leave for the evening.

He stood smartly to attention by the open door of the bus, ready to help them up the steps and on to the bus.

The girls marched out in single file, and when they were all alongside the bus, they all turned like soldiers on parade and waited for Miss Hedges to stand before them.

The two teachers accompanying the headmistress stood a little behind, as if afraid of spoiling her view of the girls.

"You all look magnificent," Miss Hedges began, beaming proudly as she looked back and forth along the line. "You will all do the academy proud, I know it. Now, on the bus, quick-sticks. It's all right to be fashionably late, but we must not be seen to be excessively tardy."

Chapter 27

Franks took his cue and began helping the girls on to the bus, advising them all to take care as they climbed aboard.

Once everyone had boarded and taken their seats, the headmistress took one last look down the aisle and made a final head count, before turning to Franks and giving him the all clear to leave.

When they arrived at the museum, Franks followed the signs for the rear car park and was waved in by the guards on duty.

Before allowing the girls to alight, the headmistress decided on one last address.

"Now please do not forget what I told you earlier," she said sternly. She held up an index finger. "One glass of wine or champagne each and, for those of you who have never tasted champagne, may I suggest you drink it slowly – it goes down very easily."

The girls all nodded their understanding.

Franks pulled back on the lever to open the doors, then took up his position once more to help everyone off.

The headmistress led the girls to the entrance, with Miss Ogilvy and Miss Parker bringing up the rear. Miss Parker was the only one to thank him on her way out. He smiled and touched the rim of his cap in response.

Franks watched them go in, then removed his hat, and ran his hand through his hair to bring it back to life. He plonked himself down on the bottom step off the bus, took out his pipe and lit it.

They were met at the door by Doctor Anmali, who welcomed them and directed them to the cloakroom and bar area.

"Where's Mr Unwin?" enquired Miss Hedges. "I thought he would be here to meet everyone."

Doctor Anmali smiled. "A slight delay, I'm afraid," she replied, handing out leaflets. "He should be along shortly."

Clearly not impressed by the doctor's excuse, Miss Hedges ushered the girls inside.

Doctor Anmali was herself starting to wonder when Unwin would make an appearance. He had already been gone far longer than she thought he would from the way he had been talking.

The museum was starting to fill up as most of the guests had arrived.

As temporary hostess, she felt that she should really be mingling, and making sure that everyone had a drink, but her main priority was as a "greeter", and she could not be in two places at once.

She saw another car pull into the car park, but soon realised it was not the Curator's.

Doctor Anmali watched as the driver parked and the passenger climbed out.

She immediately recognised the female DI who had interviewed her at her hotel.

As the DI walked towards the entrance, accompanied by DS Courtney, doctor Anmali noticed that she was limping slightly. As the DI drew nearer, the doctor smiled. "Hello again," she said brightly.

"Wow," responded Dawn, "I'm sorry, did I say that out loud?" she placed a hand over her mouth in embarrassment. "What I meant to say was, I love your outfit."

"Well, thank you, yours is very elegant, too, if I may say so."

"Oh, this old thing," laughed Dawn "It's the only thing in my wardrobe that looks half-decent, so I was not really spoiled for choice."

"It's very fetching," the doctor assured her, holding out a pamphlet.

Even in flats, and with the doctor wearing heels, Dawn towered over her diminutive figure. Their eyes locked and stayed that way until DS Courtney cleared his throat behind her.

"Ah, yes," Dawn said, slightly flustered, "this is my sergeant. As you've probably guessed by now, we're here on official business, so no partying for us."

Chapter 27

Courtney smiled at the doctor and took the proffered pamphlet.

Doctor Anmali looked surprised. "Are we expecting trouble?" she asked, concerned.

Dawn shook her head. "God, I hope not, the super just wants a discreet police presence because of that poor bloke who got killed here the other day."

"Oh yes, of course. How is your investigation coming along?"

Dawn looked awkwardly at Courtney. She knew only too well that they could not discuss active investigations with the public. But somehow she felt captivated by the petite Egyptian, almost to the point of being under her spell, and it made her want to answer all her questions without keeping anything from her.

"I'm sorry, Miss," Courtney broke in, "I'm afraid we can't discuss it."

The doctor flushed. "Of course, how stupid of me, please forgive me."

"That's fine," Dawn assured her. "There's nothing to forgive."

The doctor showed them in. "See you later, perhaps," she called after Dawn.

Dawn turned back. "Yes, I hope so. I'll probably be here until the last knockings, anyway."

As they walked towards the cloakroom, Courtney looked over at his superior. "Are you okay, guv?" he asked, with genuine concern in his voice.

Dawn shot him a glance. "Of course, I am, what makes you ask?"

Realising he must have hit a nerve, Courtney shrugged. "Nothing."

The DS waited while Dawn handed in her coat. "What now?" he asked forlornly.

"I guess we get a drink and try and blend in with the cream of Clevedon society, lucky us."

The next car Doctor Anmali saw entering the car park was the Curator's.

She heaved a sigh of relief. Not that playing the part of greeter had been particularly arduous, but she was much more at home just staying in the background at these events. Her introduction speech later would be more than enough to take her out of her comfort zone.

She watched as Unwin attempted to swing his car into his reserved spot, only to find another car already there.

Inside the car, tempers were already frayed, and this latest insult did not go unnoticed.

"Isn't that space marked out for you, Stanley!" demanded Mildred.

"Yes dear, but it appears someone can't read."

"Well make sure we are not too far away from the entrance. I don't want the girls' dresses getting windswept on the way in."

"I'll have to park wherever I can find a spot. As you can see, we're almost full tonight. what with the caterer's vans and everything."

"Well, you should have put one of those security johnnies on notice to make sure no one stole your spot. What's the point of being curator if you can't even be guaranteed a private parking place, I ask you?"

"Yes dear. Well, here we are. Have you all got enough room to get out?"

Frankly, Unwin was beyond caring by this point. When he had arrived home, as instructed, he sat on the drive and honked his horn to let his wife and daughters know that he had arrived. Then, after a couple of minutes, when no one had emerged from the house, he honked again.

After another couple of minutes, he climbed out and marched to the front door, hammering on it with his fist.

When there was still no response from within, he took out his key and let himself in, where he found his wife and two daughters, standing in the kitchen, dolled up to the nines, drinking champagne as if they had all the time in the world.

Unwin almost exploded on the spot. "Didn't any of you hear me sounding the horn? I've been out there for ages?"

"Well, how are we supposed to hear you from in here?" replied Mildred. "And besides, you honk to show your support for a march, not to announce your arrival in a quiet residential area. At least, that's what civilised people do."

They continued drinking and chatting as if Unwin were no longer present.

"Well come on," he shouted. "We need to get going, the reception has already started and I'm not there to greet my guests."

Tamara knocked back her head and drained her glass. "I need to pee," she announced, placing her glass back on the table, and heading towards the stairs.

Unwin looked on in disbelief. "Can't you hold it in, for goodness sake?"

"Don't shout at her," Mildred scolded. "You know she has a shy bladder and hurrying her will just make things worse."

"Felicity," Tamara called down from halfway up the stairs, "can you come and help me with my dress?"

Felicity finished her drink, and called back before the bubbles had evaporated, so her response sounded like a cross between a burp and a gulp."

"Oh, for the love of all that's holy!" Unwin shouted, looking at his wristwatch.

"Stop being so dramatic Stanley," his wife chided him. "Anyone would think you were hosting the Oscars or something."

It was another 20 minutes before they finally left the house.

Unwin could feel his blood pressure rise to the point of

exploding by the time he finally put the key in the ignition and started the engine.

He tried to drive in silence, and just concentrate on making it there in one piece. But the constant interruptions, mainly by his wife, but with his daughters also chipping in every now and then, caused him almost to run two red lights in his haste.

Finally, when they arrived at the museum, Unwin felt himself begin to calm down.

Once he had seen his wife and daughters in, he could concentrate on his guests.

Unwin allowed Mildred and the two girls to walk on ahead. As they reached the entrance, Mildred immediately turned her back to doctor Anmali, and asked for her assistance in removing her stole.

Bemused, the doctor did as she was asked before Unwin managed to intervene.

"This is Doctor Anmali, a special guest of the museum, from Egypt." He tried to keep the irritation from his tone but did not succeed entirely.

"Oh," said Mildred, feeling foolish. "I thought she was the coat-girl. Why didn't you say?" She turned back to face the doctor. "I'm so sorry, dear," she apologised. "My stupid husband should have told me."

"Please do not concern yourself," the doctor assured her. "You are not the first tonight to make that assumption," she lied, trying to save Unwin some face. "If you would care to take a pamphlet, the cloakroom where you can leave your coats is just ahead."

Unwin stayed back after the three of them had entered. "I am so very sorry about that," he apologised. "And about how long it took for me to come back, I really did not anticipate taking so long."

"No problem," the doctor assured him, graciously.

"Has everyone arrived?"

Chapter 27

"We're still waiting on the mayor and her entourage."

Unwin consulted his watch once more. "Really, I thought for sure she would have been here by now."

Just then, he noticed the mayor and a host of followers turning the corner of the building and marching towards him.

Unwin opened his mouth in shock, then closed it without speaking.

From behind the group emerged a security guard, trying to appear discreet as he overtook them all and headed towards the staff entrance.

He reached Unwin ahead of the rest.

"What's going on?" demanded Unwin. "Why is our mayor walking around the building as if she's surveying the architecture?"

The guard was not a young man, and clearly looked as if he could do with losing some weight. He tried to catch his breath so he could speak before the others reached him.

"Sorry... sir... we can't find... the keys for the main door... We've been... having to send... people around all evening."

Unwin was speechless.

Within seconds, his complexion grew even more puce than that of the out-of-breath guard.

Before he had a chance to react, the mayor was upon him.

Unwin barged the guard out of the way and made as if to genuflect, then obviously thought better of it and began to rise before stopping halfway.

Doctor Anmali managed to cover her mouth before any laughter could escape.

She felt sorry for the little man, but he was in such a panic that he was behaving with a total lack of dignity.

"My dear Mayor Winthrop," he began, "I cannot apologise enough for this complete lack of protocol for one of such eminence. I assure you, heads will roll for this."

The mayor smiled. "Please do not concern yourself," she assured him. "But if we could go inside now."

"Of course, naturally, at once." He stood to one side. "May I introduce Doctor Anmali from the Cairo Museum of Archaeology, here by special invitation as a leading authority on ancient Egypt."

The doctor curtseyed, and shook the offered hand, before guiding the party inside.

From across the road, Amin Salah watched the goings on through the lenses of his binoculars. When he first arrived at the museum, he was surprised to see Doctor Anmali standing at the entrance to welcome the arrivals. He recognised her immediately from the profile the sect had created for her and, although she did not know him, he was reluctant to make his presence at the event known to someone who would doubtless remember seeing him enter.

As far as he was concerned, it was necessary for the success of his enterprise that he remain inconspicuous and blend into the crowd so that no one noticed his comings and goings. He knew that there was still a chance he might bump into the doctor during the course of the evening. But if that happened then so be it, there was no way he could guarantee their paths would not cross in a crowded exhibition.

Once the mayor and her group had entered, Salah noticed that both the curator and the doctor followed them inside.

He waited for a few moments to see if she would emerge again but, when she did not, he decided to grab his chance.

Salah locked his binoculars in the glove box of his rented car and checked to ensure he had his invitation before climbing out. He had already decided not to take advantage of the car park provided, just in case he needed to make a quick exit and the main gates were closed. Plus which, if he did end up being the last one at the museum, he did not want his car to be the only one left in the car park as that, too, would raise an eyebrow.

Chapter 27

He showed his invitation to the guard on duty at the gates and was nodded through.

As he reached the entrance, he waited for a moment then, when he was sure the coast was clear, he slipped in unnoticed and lost himself in the crowd.

Chapter Twenty-Eight

Much to Unwin's relief, the rest of the evening went without any major hiccups.

The local press was there, as arranged, and Unwin made sure that the reporter and photographer were both well supplied with canapés and drinks. Several shots were taken of the board members with the mayor in the middle. Mildred insisted on having one taken with the girls and Unwin, making sure that the photographer was aware of exactly who her husband was.

The Seddon Swans lined up graciously, surrounding their headmistress and fellow teachers. The photographer surreptitiously made sure that he also took several individual shots of the girls, especially Cynthia and Colleen, who were both more than happy to pose for him.

When it was the turn of Jacinda Singh to have hers taken, the photographer had to ask Bill Stead to move out of the way. The burly security guard had been staring at the young girl since she first walked in.

When the other swans noticed him staring at their friend, they glanced at each other and laughed, not even attempting to hide what they found so amusing.

Chapter 28

Stead pulled himself up to his full height, trying desperately to appear as if he was totally unaware of being the butt of their schoolgirl humour.

He pretended he was answering a call on his walkie-talkie as he strode away through the crowd.

As expected, the speeches from the mayor, and those board members asked to address the guests, took far too long, and there were some, not too well concealed, yawns escaping from the onlookers.

Unwin took everyone on a brief guided tour of the museum. He purposely kept to the ground floor, as he did not want to risk any accidents among those ladies with long flowing dresses trying to negotiate the stairs.

His tour ended with the latest jewel in the museum's crown, the mummy of Anlet-Un-Ri. He handed the master-of-ceremonies duty over to Doctor Anmali, who tentatively climbed the podium that had been erected for the evening and adjusted the microphone for her height.

Three rows of chairs had been set out in semi-circular fashion, enough to seat 50 guests. Once everyone was seated comfortably, she began.

Unlike most of the other speeches, hers was informative, entertaining and above all else, relatively short. She explained how very little was officially known about the life of Anlet-Un-Ri, mainly because she was not of noble birth, so the historians of the day were not apt to include much about her. Nonetheless, as a member of the Pharaoh's first army, her rise through the ranks was well documented.

She explained how, having had a chance to read the notes of Professor Kautz, they knew roughly when she died, as the life and death of the young prince Mehet-Met-Too was well documented, and her burial site was situated adjacent to his.

The doctor expounded several theories as to why the unknown mummy was buried the way she had been, but once again she explained that her submissions were mere conjecture, based on the evidence that she had studied thus far.

When she was done, she received a ripple of applause from those gathered, to which she put her hands together, as if about to recite a prayer, and made a gracious bow.

The lights were dimmed, which seemed to startle several members of the audience, judging by the gasps emitted, and the music began.

From out of the darkness, a deep voice began to narrate the introduction to the unveiling of the mummy. The recording had been made by a well-known actor who happened to live in Clevedon and was full of emphasis and structure, and his words echoed around the gathering to create a spectral ambiance.

On cue, the display team took their places, and slowly began to open the sarcophagus, revealing the gigantic form of the mummy.

Loud gasps could be heard coming from the crowd, and there was even the faint sound of chairs being scraped back on the floor, as some instinctively tried to move away from the mummy.

The narration continued for a few minutes longer, leaving everyone to focus on the hideous creature looming above them, until eventually it faded away along with the end of the music.

The lights went back up to full power.

There was another smattering of applause from the audience as they began to rise to their feet once more.

Unwin came over to congratulate the doctor on her speech. He was clearly relieved that the main event had gone so well.

Doctor Anmali stayed near the sarcophagus and answered questions from the more curious among the gathering. She could not help but notice Dawn hanging back behind the crowd, studying the various glass cases that housed some of the smaller artefacts bequeathed to the museum from the professor's collection.

Chapter 28

As the last person moved away from the doctor, Dawn was standing only a few feet away. She looked up and smiled at the doctor. "That was a brilliant speech you gave, Doctor," she said sincerely.

"Why thank you, Inspector, I hoped it would not be too dry or boring for those not familiar with the subject."

"No, really, it was perfect – just the right length and interesting enough for the non-academics like me to follow."

Doctor Anmali moved a step closer.

Dawn automatically made to move back but stopped herself. She had always prized her own space and hated it when anyone encroached on that, but there was something so alluring about the doctor that she did not feel at all threatened by her behaviour.

"I could not help but notice," the doctor whispered, "but you appear to be limping slightly."

"Oh, that, yes, I had a little accident last night chasing a suspect. Managed to land straight on my back, after twisting my ankle."

"Are you in a great deal of pain?"

Dawn thought about it for a moment. It was true that her last dose of painkillers was wearing off and, even after three glasses of Champagne, her back was still throbbing.

"Is it that obvious?" she asked, pulling a face.

"If you will allow me," the doctor offered, "I have some balm back at my hotel that I brought over from Egypt. It is an ancient recipe that has been passed down through the generations of my family. I'm sure it will alleviate your suffering far better than your modern painkillers."

"That's very kind of you," Dawn said, "but my colleague gave me a lift here, and I would feel bad asking him to detour out to your hotel on the way back. Besides which, I'm not sure I can reach the parts of my back where it would do the most good."

The doctor raised her eyebrows. "Do you not have a partner who could assist you?"

Dawn shrugged. "Not right now, I'm afraid. I wish I could blame my job, but if I'm being honest, I've never really understood the male species."

The doctor laughed. "They are a mystery to all womankind, I think."

They both shared a laugh.

After a moment, the doctor nodded towards the glass in Dawn's hand.

"I see you're empty, may I refresh your drink?"

Dawn automatically looked around for the superintendent. The last time she had seen him this evening was when he was busy hanging on to every word the mayor was saying while she spouted off her knowledge of ancient hieroglyphics.

He had at least acknowledged her presence with a nod of his head, but that had been it thus far. Ordinarily, she would never drink on duty, but tonight did not feel like proper work, even though she was technically on overtime.

So long as she did not make a fool of herself, it should be fine.

Besides, the first three glasses had not taken effect yet.

"Thank you," she replied, holding out her flute. "That would be lovely."

Doctor Anmali took her glass and made her way through the crowd towards the bar area.

Dawn walked over to the open sarcophagus and stood before the mighty figure of Anlet-Un-Ri. She traced a path up the mummy's body with her eyes, until she came to the head.

She stared at the mummy's eyes, which were no more than tiny slits in the ancient fabric in which she was covered.

For a moment, she almost felt as if they were about to open.

"I see you've found our murderer, guv."

Chapter 28

The sound of DS Courtney's voice in her ear shocked her out of her reverie.

"What?" she said distractedly.

Courtney nodded toward the mummy. "Well, she's the right height and build for our suspect, and the body was found just a few feet away. Sounds like an open-and-shut case to me."

Dawn turned to face him. "I'll leave you to make the arrest then, Sergeant, I can't wait to read your report."

Just then, the doctor returned with two glasses of champagne. She handed one to Dawn and held the other one out to Courtney.

The DS refused politely, and lifted his own glass which appeared to contain Scotch.

The doctor clinked glasses with him and then Dawn and took a sip herself.

They spoke together for a few minutes until Courtney mentioned that he wanted to have a look around the rest of the museum, as he was there.

When he had gone, both women took another sip of their drinks.

Dawn could not help but notice the way the doctor's lips moved as she savoured the taste of the Champagne. She circled her lips with her tongue several times, leaving her lipstick with a vibrant sheen.

"Please do not think me forward, Inspector, but may I make a suggestion?"

"You may," replied Sawn, "so long as you stop calling me Inspector. My name is Dawn."

The doctor smiled. "Well, Dawn, would it be presumptuous of me if I offered to apply my special balm for you, back at my hotel? I could give you a lift in my car, then drive you home afterwards."

Dawn felt a knot forming in the pit of her stomach.

Was the academic coming on to her?

She cleared the thought from her mind. For all she knew, it might be perfectly natural for one woman to offer such a service to another, in her country, and she did not wish to seem rude.

"Well, I, that is, it's very kind of you to offer, but I'd feel too guilty making you drive me home after all that."

Dawn almost bit her tongue.

Now she realised that she was the one who was sounding suggestive.

She could feel her cheeks flush.

"Well, in that case," continued the doctor, her voice calm and with no hint of having noticed anything provocative in Dawn's last comment. "You can always call a taxi from my hotel, if you prefer."

Dawn nodded. "If you're sure you won't be too tired after this evening."

The doctor shook her head. "Not at all, the stressful part of the evening is over for me, and I hate to see you in pain when I am sure that my soothing balm can help you."

Dawn put her glass forward, and they clinked again.

"Well, if you're absolutely sure it won't be putting you out, I'd love to take you up on your kind offer, thank you."

"My absolute pleasure."

While they were talking, neither of them noticed Cynthia Rollins inspecting the glass cabinets on the other side of the sarcophagus.

Some of the items within them were most likely priceless, which explained why they were locked inside, but others just appeared to be lumps of old rock, none of which resembled anything much at all.

She felt her way around the edges of some of the cabinets with her fingers.

The vast majority had lids, which, although secured, appeared as if they might give way with a slight amount of persuasion.

She looked up to make sure that no one was watching her.

Once she was certain the coast was clear, she applied pressure with both thumbs underneath the lip of one of the cabinets.

She felt the catch starting to give, so she stopped and stood back, pretending to admire the contents from a different angle.

An idea was already starting to take form in her mind.

This was perfect.

Cynthia moved away from the cabinet and quickly sought out the rest of her fellow swans.

Once together, they huddled in a far corner, away from prying eyes and big ears.

"Ladies, I have the perfect plan for our ducklings' last initiation test."

"Marvellous," enthused Carrie-Anne.

"Yes," the others agreed.

"Well," Cynthia began, "I think we should get them to break into this museum and steal something from one of the glass cabinets."

The others looked at each other with open mouths.

"Isn't that a little risky for our lot?" asked Sarah Posen, frowning. "One of them is bound to get caught and then we'll all be for it."

Cynthia could tell by their faces that some of the others seemed to agree with their friend.

"When you say, break in," began Josephine Mathews, "I take it you mean at night?"

"Certainly at night," replied Cynthia sharply. "There's no challenge in breaking in during the day when the place is already open to the public."

"But how do you suggest they break in at night?" asked Jacinda Singh curiously.

"Ah, well now, that pretty much depends on you."

"Me?"

"Don't look so surprised," said Cynthia, raising her eyebrows. "You're our only chance of this even getting off the ground."

"How?" asked Jacinda, looking genuinely shocked.

Cynthia sidled up to her friend. "Well," she began, "for a start, we need to know the lay of the land about this place after hours. You know, what sort of alarms they have, how many guards are left on patrol, that sort of thing."

"Fine," Jacinda agreed. "But how am I supposed to find out such things?"

"Well," continued Cynthia, with a sly wink. "You know that big security guard who's been mooning around after you all night?"

The others began to giggle.

Jacinda already suspected what her friend was going to suggest.

She opened her mouth wide in shock.

Cynthia held up her hand. "All you have to do is ask him a few searching questions. I'm sure he won't be in the least bit suspicious."

"Yuck! You're not serious?"

"Come on," goaded Cynthia. "I'm not asking you to give up your virtue."

"Bit too late for that," chuckled Geraldine Simms.

"Shut-up, Gerrie," Jacinda hissed. "This isn't funny."

"Ask a couple of simple questions," Cynthia insisted. "That's all you need to do, and then we'll come and rescue you. But you'll have to hurry, I can't see us being here more than another half hour or so."

Jacinda looked at her fellow swans for support but help seemed to be in short supply.

"Remember," Cynthia reminded her, "the sacrifices we make for our fellow swans will repay us tenfold throughout the rest of our lives."

Jacinda sighed. She, like the rest of the girls, knew all the sayings about the Swan sisterhood back to front, though none of them had the slightest idea who originally dreamt them up. Cynthia, in particular seemed to have adopted Miss Hedges' habit of quoting them whenever she felt the girls were not keen to do something.

Even though Jacinda felt this present assignment was way above the call of duty, she knew that, if she refused, the rest of her time at Seddon would not be worth living.

"A Swan can glide through the stormiest of waters without causing a ripple," Cynthia threw in, for good measure.

The other girls nodded solemnly.

Jacinda shook her head in resignation. She had heard all the Swan sayings a thousand times from Miss Hedges. They were constantly repeated to you from the first time you were chosen as a potential duckling, which in her case was in year two.

But what it really boiled down to was that when you were needed to take one for the team, you did so without complaint.

Or, certainly in this case, any concern for personal safety or reputation.

Jacinda had noticed Stead mooning over her during the evening. She only pretended not to have done so to try to avoid her task.

She still could not believe that Cynthia wanted her to go through with it. The man was a gargoyle and, what's more, he looked as if he had been sweating lavishly for most of the day and had not had time to change his shirt.

Whenever he had appeared beside her during the exhibition, Jacinda had smelled his body odour long before she saw him approach.

The thought of having to stand within close proximity of him and try to hold a conversation turned her stomach.

This was one time she wished she had not been included in the party.

Chapter Twenty-Nine

"WHAT DO YOU MEAN, IT WON'T FUCKIN' START?" Scrapper screamed. "It has to fuckin' start, we can't stay here in the middle of nowhere – I've got a delivery to make."

"I told you it had been giving me trouble," Jeremy pointed out, trying the key in the ignition again, without success. "You insisted it'd be fine."

From out of nowhere, Scrapper leaned over the driver's seat and slapped Jeremy hard across the back of his head. "Just fuckin' get on with it," he yelled.

"Calm down," Phil called out, reaching over to protect his cousin should Scrapper try another swing. "It's not his fault the stupid thing won't start."

"So, what are we supposed to fuckin' do now?"

"I'll call the breakdown people," suggested Jeremy, rubbing the spot where he had been struck.

"And what if they don't get 'ere fer 'ours?" Scrapper's voice was slowly rising in pitch every time he shouted. He did not realise it himself, but it was blatantly obvious to anyone within hearing distance that he was on the edge of hysteria.

After he had collected the package from the biker earlier that day, he had grown paranoid waiting for Phil and his cousin to turn up. Every passing second, he thought he heard a knock at the door.

It had been several hours yet before they needed to leave, so Scrapper was left at home with the bag of goodies, trying to figure out how to best pass the time.

He found himself hiding the bag somewhere in his room then, 10 minutes later, he would move it somewhere else, convinced that his first choice would be too easy for the coppers to find. This scenario played out over and over again until he was finally convinced that nowhere in his room was safe.

Finally, unable to control himself any longer, he lit a spliff.

It was part of what he had left over from the club the previous night, and he mixed it with some stuff he found in his parents' room when he was looking for spare cash.

He had always known that his parents smoked weed, his dad especially, and sometimes the gear he managed to get hold of was of a supreme quality.

Scrapper felt himself drifting off within minutes.

He slept throughout the rest of the afternoon and into the evening, and woke up only when his mother shook him to say that Phil had arrived.

By then, he had received a text from Len telling him where the drop-off was to take place.

Everything was going according to plan until Jeremy's van decided to break down on the motorway.

Now they were stuck. There was no way that Scrapper was going to phone Len and tell him he was not even capable of making a simple drop-off. But, by the same token, if they were delayed by too much, the bloke expecting the bag would probably call Len himself.

Scrapper could not believe he had managed to land himself in such a position. Having to rely on Phil's cousin was a bad idea from the start. But who else did he know with a vehicle, who could be relied on to keep their mouth shut?

He desperately needed another spliff.

Scrapper could hear Jeremy on his phone talking to the breakdown people.

"Tell 'em it's an emergency. Tell 'em we need to get going, fast," Scrapper shouted over Jeremy's head.

Jeremy ignored him. Sticking a finger in his ear, he pressed his mobile against the other one, and strained to hear what the operator was saying. In the end, he opened the door and slid out of the van because he knew Scrapper was not going to shut up.

The hard shoulder where the van was parked had overhead lighting, so at least oncoming traffic should be able to see them. Even so, when he came off the phone, Jeremy said that the operator had suggested that they leave the van and sit on the nearby embankment to await the patrol from the breakdown service.

It seemed like good advice, but Scrapper could not sit still.

He continued walking back and forth beside the van, muttering incoherently to himself.

Jeremy turned to his cousin. "Just so you know, this is the last favour I do for this so-called friend of yours."

Phil patted Jeremy on his back. "Don't worry, mate, after this, I'm not sure I want any part of his shenanigans either. He's getting in a little too deep for my liking."

"I don't know why you've stuck with him for so long. He's a fucking nutter."

Phil shrugged. "He was good to me when we were banged up – that's supposed to be a bond you never break."

Jeremy turned to face his cousin. "You know, he's going to end up getting himself killed one day. Just make sure you're not caught in the cross-hairs."

Chapter 29

Amin Salah stood before the open sarcophagus of Anlet-Un-Ri and scrutinised the ancient wrappings that covered her corpse. If she was indeed in possession of the Eye of Aken, then it had to be secreted beneath them, otherwise it would surely have been discovered by now.

During the doctor's speech, Salah had listened intently for any mention of the ancient symbol, but there had been none. This might be his only chance of searching for the treasure before the mummy was sent for a forensic X-ray examination that would reveal everything hidden beneath her coverings.

The doctor had not mentioned when such an operation was planned, but Salah knew from experience that, with a find such as this, it would not be too long.

It irritated him, as it did the rest of his sect, that an object such as this, that had been illegally removed from Egypt, could not be returned by order of his government. But such was the problem during these difficult diplomatic times, that no one wanted to say or do anything that might offend the other side.

Were there any way of launching an operation to steal the mummy back before any further tests could be carried out on it, Salah and his sect would have been at the forefront of it.

The alternative was his sacred mission to search for the symbol himself and to carry it back to Egypt in secret.

During Doctor Anmali's speech, Salah ensured that he was at the back of the audience, so he was relatively safe in the knowledge that she had not seen him. In fact, he had managed to circumnavigate the entire exhibition without raising an eyebrow.

Previous visits to England had taught him that in polite English company, no one approached you so long as you looked the part and smiled at the right time.

Salah checked over his shoulder to ensure that no one else had noticed him. Once he was reassured, he moved closer to study the form of the mummy.

He knew that the most likely place the symbol would have been placed was over the warrior's chest, nearest the heart.

Salah peered closely at the mummy's chest area, searching for anything unusual that projected beyond its natural form.

From ancient depictions of it discovered within the various versions of the Book of the Dead that had been uncovered over the centuries, Salah knew that the Eye was relatively flat in shape, and thus would not stick out too prominently, especially underneath the multiple layers of cloth that covered the mummy.

But any sign of its presence from this distance would give him great hope.

"She's really quite magnificent, isn't she?"

He spun around on the spot and came face to face with Doctor Anmali.

A master of deception, Salah smiled shyly down at the diminutive woman before turning his attention back to Anlet-Un-Ri. "She is certainly that," he agreed, "I can't remember the last time I saw such a specimen up close, in this country. They usually hide them behind glass screens to keep the inquisitive at bay."

"I believe that may well be the museum's intention, once all the forensic tests have been completed," replied the doctor.

Salah nodded knowingly. "Do I take it that you will be carrying out those tests yourself, in the fullness of time?"

"Oh no, I was merely invited over from my museum in Cairo to complete the initial investigation. There were many other fine artefacts found along with the mummy that I have been fortunate enough to study. They just wanted reassurance that it was fit to stand for this exhibition without suffering any further deterioration."

Salah nodded. "I see."

"Have you also been invited over here from Egypt?" Doctor Anmali asked. "I was informed by the curator that we should expect some representatives from the antiquities department but, as yet, I haven't seen any."

Salah felt a lump in his throat.

He could not afford for his cover to be blown, especially as, in such a crowded area, there was nothing he could do to silence the inquisitive doctor.

"I am originally from Egypt," he confirmed, "but I have been lecturing at a number of major universities around the county for many years now. It's been very enjoyable and, I must admit, highly lucrative, but I must confess I look forward to returning home permanently one day."

The doctor held out her hand. "Doctor Amina Anmali," she said. "Very pleased to make your acquaintance."

Salah took her hand. "Professor Kiron Shah," he lied. "The pleasure is mine."

His false name was not an off-the-cuff decision. The sect had supplied him with two sets of fake identities in case he ran into trouble. This was just one of them. He had made a point of studying the details on the plane journey over.

Amina smiled. "I hope you enjoy the rest of the exhibition," she said.

"Thank you, I'm sure I will."

Salah watched her as she walked away, before being swallowed by the crowd gathered around one of the other exhibits.

He sincerely hoped that their meeting had been merely a coincidence.

If he suspected for a moment that the good doctor was on to him, he might have to take the regrettable step of silencing her.

———

The rest of the swans stood huddled in a group while they watched their companion in the distance, speaking to the big security guard. Even from this distance they could tell, from Jacinda's body language, that she was way out of her comfort zone.

But she was hanging in there for the team, and that was what counted.

On several occasions, they had noticed Stead casually attempting to slip his arm around her shoulders while he was pointing something out to her. But, on each occasion, Jacinda managed to sidestep the familiarity while continuing with the conversation.

Guests had already begun to drift away, so the crowd was thinning out enough for there to be less chance of Cynthia and the girls losing sight of their colleague.

"Do you think she's found out enough yet?" asked Josephine, sounding concerned.

"Yes, perhaps we should move in now, and rescue her," agreed Colleen.

Cynthia held up her hand. "Just a little while longer," she insisted. "If she doesn't have all the answers by the time that she and lover-boy are finished, tonight's entertainment can't take place."

Some of the others exchanged nervous glances behind their leader's back.

They had all been game initially but, whenever Jacinda glanced in their direction, they could see how uncomfortable she was becoming, the longer she spent in the guard's company.

"I trust you ladies are taking advantage of this wonderful experience, and gaining some useful knowledge about the culture of the ancient Egyptians?"

The girls all whirled around together to find Miss Ogilvy lurking behind them.

"Yes, thank you, Miss," they answered together.

The maths teacher was standing between them and the mummy.

Chapter 29

Cynthia noticed the doctor who had given the earlier address explaining something to three women who were all dressed up as if they were attending a Paris fashion event rather than the opening of an exhibition in a museum.

"We were just about to go and listen to some more interesting facts, over there." Cynthia pointed to the small gathering, hoping that Miss Ogilvy would follow her lead. The last thing she wanted was for the maths teacher to realise that one of their number was missing.

There were no hard-and-fast rules about them all staying together throughout the evening.

However, if only one of them appeared to be separated, it might raise eyebrows from the teaching staff, followed by awkward questions.

Before the maths teacher had a chance to turn back, Cynthia guided the rest of the girls towards where the doctor was giving her talk, and Miss Ogilvy followed them.

"But what was the point of all these elaborate shenanigans?" asked Felicity Unwin. "Surely, once you're dead, you're dead. Does it matter what your corpse looks like?"

Doctor Anmali smiled. "Consider when a body is laid out in a coffin ready for the funeral," she explained. "Even if the deceased is being cremated, the family still insist that the undertaker dress their loved one up for the occasion."

Felicity considered the explanation and nodded.

"Added to that," continued the doctor, "the afterlife was incredibly important to the ancient Egyptians, so the mummification process was a vital part of that journey."

"Didn't I read somewhere that they used to disembowel them before they wrapped them up?" It was Tamara's turn to offer her insight.

The doctor nodded. "In a way, yes. You see, the heart was considered to be the most important organ in the body, and as such, the only one necessary to assist the dead in passing through the afterlife. Therefore, the Egyptians would remove most of the other organs – liver, lungs, stomach, intestines – and place them in special jars, called canopic jars, and leave them close by in the tomb."

"What about the brain?" Tamara continued, fascinated by the gory details.

"Well, as the Egyptians no longer believed the brain was necessary in death, they had a way of scooping it out through the corpse's nose and discarding it."

Some of the swans pulled faces as they listened to the vivid description.

Cynthia took the opportunity, while everyone else was engrossed, to turn around to check on Jacinda.

She and Stead were nowhere to be seen.

"So where are the jars for this mummy?" asked Felicity, determined to not be outdone by her younger sister.

The doctor turned and indicated towards the sarcophagus. "I'm sad to say we have no record of their being found. They were not in Professor Kautz's collection, nor were they listed when Anlet-Un-Ri's chamber was first discovered, adjacent to the boy-prince Mehet-Met-Too's tomb."

"Could she have been mummified without her internal organs being removed?" It was Mildred this time showing an interest.

"It's possible," replied the doctor, "although very unusual, if that were the case. Unfortunately, the mummification of this great lady was not recounted in the history books, so we really know very little about her death."

Cynthia tugged Sarah's sleeve, as she was the nearest girl to her.

As Sarah turned, she immediately saw the concern in Cynthia's expression.

She mouthed the word, "What?" so that Miss Ogilvy would not hear.

Chapter 29

Cynthia signalled over her shoulder, towards the spot where Jacinda and the guard had been moments before.

Sarah realised the cause for her friend's dismay, immediately. She held her hand over her open mouth, for fear of making a noise and alerting their teacher.

At that moment, Miss Parker made her way towards the group.

Sarah saw her approach and leaned in to tell Cynthia.

Miss Parker hovered behind the girls and waited for a suitable break in the doctor's speech before announcing to them that Miss Hedges had said it was time to leave.

The other girls turned at the sound of the PE teacher's words, and instantly saw the look of concern on their friends' faces.

Before they could make up an excuse, Danielle was already doing a head-count.

"Who's missing?" she enquired, double checking. "Where's Jacinda?"

Miss Ogilvy barged her way through the girls and stood shoulder to shoulder with her colleague. "Yes," she demanded, turning around to survey the area. "Where is Miss Singh?"

"She went to the bathroom a few moment ago," lied Cynthia, desperately trying to buy them all some time.

The toilets were housed near to the temporary bar area, not far from the security office, which was where they had last seen their friend talking to the guard.

"We'll find her," offered Cynthia, grabbing Sarah by the arm, and pulling her along before either teacher had a chance to object.

"Okay, then," sighed Danielle, "the rest of you grab your coats from the cloakroom and wait for me by the entrance."

The other girls scuttled off after their friends.

Danielle turned to her colleague. "Did they seem a little jumpy to you?" she enquired.

Miss Ogilvy sniffed the air. "Not at all," she said, confidently. "You can put your full trust in the swans, Miss Parker. They will never let the good name of the academy down."

With that, the maths teacher strode off haughtily towards the entrance.

"Fine," said Danielle sarcastically to herself, before making her own way towards the cloakroom.

Cynthia dragged Sarah through the remaining crowd towards the security office.

Once there, they both scanned the area for any sign of their friend.

"That guard should not be difficult to spot, even in this crowd," offered Sarah.

"That's what worries me," replied Cynthia. "Why can't we at least see him?"

They both decided to check out the ladies' toilet, just in case Jacinda had in fact gone in there. They went in through the two sets of swing doors, one after the other. Inside there were 10 separate cubicles, of which four were in use.

Sarah looked at her friend. "We can't stand here all night, waiting," she implored.

"Jacinda." Cynthia called out, "are you in there?"

There was no response, save a flush being activated further down.

They waited for that cubicle door to open, but as soon as they saw it was not their friend, they left.

"Where now?" asked Sarah, really starting to panic. "What if he's taken her upstairs to one of the upper floors? They could be anywhere. We need to tell the teachers."

Cynthia grabbed her friend by the wrist and sun her round to face her.

"Ow, that hurts," Sarah squealed.

"Are you insane?" Cynthia hissed. "How are we going to explain her disappearance to Miss Hedges?"

Chapter 29

"We could just say she must have wandered off to see another part of the museum," Sarah said sulkily, rubbing her wrist.

"And end up getting Jacinda in trouble?"

Sarah pouted. "I don't know. What else can we do?"

"We search for her ourselves," insisted Cynthia "We're supposed to look out for each other."

Just then, they heard something crash in the security room further along the passageway. It sounded to both of them like something falling on the floor.

Cynthia moved off, with Sarah close behind.

As they reached the office door, they could see movement behind the frosted glass panel.

Cynthia gently twisted the handle and pushed open the door.

Jacinda was lying on the large desk which dominated the room, with Bill Stead on top of her.

Her dress was up around her waist, revealing her bare legs, and one of Stead's hands was rubbing her naked thigh.

His face hovered above hers, and they could hear him begging their friend for a kiss.

Meanwhile, Jacinda had both hands on his shoulders, desperately trying to push him off her.

Without a word, Sarah sprang into action.

She leapt forward and grabbed hold of the table lamp that was lying on the floor and doubtless had been what the girls heard crashing down moments before.

Grabbing hold of it just above the heavy base Sarah brought it down on the back of the guard's head.

Stead screamed out, and immediately stood up, holding the back of his head.

The girls were suddenly all too aware of the guard's size as he towered over them, blocking their path to their friend.

Without stopping, Sarah swing the lamp in an upward arc,

managing to catch Stead on the chin. He immediately flung an arm across his face to protect himself.

Taking advantage of the situation, Cynthia ran around him and helped Jacinda off the desk.

Sarah readied herself for a roundhouse assault with the lamp.

But before she had a chance to swing, Jacinda pulled back her leg and kicked Stead straight between the legs.

The big guard dropped slowly to his knees, both hands now firmly pressed to his groin area.

Sarah, realising another attack was now unnecessary, dropped the lamp and helped Cynthia guide Jacinda out of the office.

Once outside, Cynthia was relieved to see that their little commotion had not been heard by those outside.

"Are you all right?" Sarah asked, concerned for her friend.

"I think I'm going to puke," replied Jacinda, wiping her mouth with the back of her hand.

"Please don't, darling," purred Cynthia. "That's awfully undignified."

"He shoved his filthy tongue in my mouth," Jacinda objected. "I'm entitled to throw up after that!"

"Can you at least hold it in until we get back?" sighed Cynthia. "It'll raise fewer questions; we can say it must have been something you ate."

Jacinda stared at her coldly. "Did anyone ever tell you you're all heart?"

Chapter Thirty

As the crowds slowly began to thin out at the end of the evening, Dawn started to wish that she had not agreed to the doctor's offer of a massage.

True, her back and ankle were both killing her and, if offered right this minute, she would jump at the chance of a soothing rubdown. But the doctor was still enchanting some of the remaining guests with tales of ancient Egypt and did not appear as if she was about to run out of steam any time soon.

The super had already left for the evening, and so had her DS, who did not so much as raise an eyebrow when she informed him of the reason why she no longer needed a lift home.

Indeed, Dawn, herself was still not one hundred per cent sure of what the evening might hold in store.

She had stopped drinking after her fourth glass of Champagne, which she knew was probably already three glasses too much, considering she was on duty, but at the time of the offer she was feeling a little light-headed and, she had to admit, more than a little intrigued by the doctor's suggestion.

Her thoughts were a jumble of possibilities.

When the doctor offered her a massage, was she doing so merely because she saw a fellow female in pain, and wanted to help relieve it?

Dawn had once known a woman she went to college with, who studied to be a chiropodist, and she used to carry a mini-chiropody kit with her everywhere she went. Dawn had lost count of how many times her friend had insisted on whipping out the kit and going to work on someone's feet, regardless of where they were or what company they had been in at the time.

Perhaps the doctor was cut from the same cloth.

Some people had an innate need to help others, often in the most bizarre circumstances.

On the other hand, Dawn could not help but wonder if the doctor was actually coming on to her. Dawn was not a lesbian and, unlike many of her female friends, she had never been curious enough to consider trying it. And, to be fair, she had had her fair share of offers.

A couple of her friends once told her that, consciously or otherwise, she gave off an aura which made her seem open to such an offer.

Whether that were true or not, would the doctor have picked up on it so fast?

Dawn supposed some women might.

Perhaps the leather biker's jacket had been a bad idea.

Dawn glanced sideways at the doctor who was speaking to a small group next to the sarcophagus. She had to admit she had a wonderful figure, and she definitely had an air of allure about her that was quite unmistakable.

If she were ever to consider dipping her toe in the lady-pool, she could make a much worse choice.

Dawn caught herself wondering what the doctor's skin would feel like once she took off her stunning dress.

"Champagne?"

Chapter 30

Dawn turned to see a waitress holding out a tray of Champagne flutes.

She could feel her cheeks glowing, as if the girl had somehow been able to read her thoughts and knew what she had been imagining.

"Thank you." Dawn took one without considering the options.

The girl smiled and moved on.

She really did not want another drink.

Or perhaps she did. After all, she could always say that, once the super left, she assumed she was off the clock.

Dawn sipped it slowly.

The effervescent bubbles skipped up her nose as she drank.

She allowed her eyes to follow the form of the doctor's tanned bare legs, from her thighs, all the way down to her formal, shiny black shoes.

For a moment, she considered how disappointed she would be if all the doctor wanted to give her was a massage.

On the drive to the hotel, Dawn asked if she could keep her window open, rather than have the air-conditioning on. She enjoyed the feel of the night breeze on her face and inhaling deeply helped dispel any feelings of drunkenness brought on by that final glass of bubbly.

She closed her eyes and sank back in her seat.

"Sorry," she said, apologetically. "You must think me very rude but, if I'm honest, I think I drank a tad too much tonight."

"Are you okay?" asked the doctor, concerned. "If you do not feel up to it, I can always just drop you home."

Dawn allowed her head to loll to one side. She opened her eyes so she could see the doctor. "Actually," she said, trying desperately not to slur her words. "I'm really looking forward to it."

Once they reached the hotel, the doctor handed her keys to

the parking valet outside, and the two women linked arms and walked in together.

Amina still had her room card on her, so they walked to the lifts and rode up to her floor.

Once inside the room, they felt the air-conditioning kick in. The cool breeze was a blessing after such a hot day, but they both agreed it did not compare to the real thing.

The doctor slipped off her shoes and kicked them to one side.

"That's better," she said, "I feel as if I've been standing for a week."

She sat down on the edge of the bed and rubbed her sore feet.

Dawn discarded her biker jacket and flung it over the back of a chair. Following Amina's lead, she kicked off her shoes, too, although her feet were nowhere near as sore as her back, which had really started to throb during the last hour of the exhibition.

Amina stood up from the bed. "How do you fancy a drink?" she asked, brightly.

Dawn held up her hand. "I'd really better not," she replied, "my head is already starting to spin."

As if to prove the point, she dropped down in one of the armchairs by the balcony door.

The doctor smiled and walked over to the mini-bar fridge. She opened it and perused the contents before turning back to Dawn. "Are you sure I can't tempt you to one more?"

Dawn shook her head. "No, really, but please, you go ahead – you've been on mineral water all evening."

Amina selected a half-bottle of Champagne, and stood up, closing the fridge door with her bare foot. "This is going to taste so good – I've been dying for a proper drink all evening."

"Were you not allowed a drink at the exhibition?" Dawn asked curiously.

Amina shrugged. "I doubt the curator would have objected,

Chapter 30

but I wanted to stay on top of my game, just in case, so all I dared do was take tiny sips."

She removed the gold foil from the top of the bottle, twisted the wire cage free and gripped the domed cork in her hand.

Dawn watched, amused, at the look of sheer determination on the doctor's face as she tried to loosen the cork.

After a moment, she gave up. "Aarrrg, stupid thing!"

She looked over at Dawn and the two women laughed.

Dawn stood up and walked towards her. "Here, let me," she offered, "you need to keep your hands for more delicate work."

Amina smiled, and handed over the bottle gratefully.

Dawn took a tea towel from on top of the fridge and gripped the cork with one hand while trying to turn the neck of the bottle with the other hand.

Eventually it began to move but, before she knew it, there was a loud pop and the cork flew up and bounced off the ceiling.

Before she could stop it, a small tidal wave of Champagne erupted from the neck of the bottle, and splashed over Amina's dress, soaking her front.

"Oh, my God, I'm so sorry," blurted Dawn, placing the now-settled bottle back on the fridge.

Amina laughed. "That's okay, accidents will happen," she said. "I was going to put it into the hotel's dry cleaners tomorrow anyway."

Dawn looked horrified. "But your beautiful dress," she pointed out, "it'll be ruined."

"Not at all," Amina assured her, wiping down her front with another towel from on top of the fridge.

"Oh, Doctor Anmali, I'm just so…"

Amina reached out and placed her finger over Dawn's lips. "My name is Amina," she informed her. "Now, is there enough left in that bottle at least to fill my glass?"

Dawn filled one of the glasses provided with what was left in the bottle. It was larger than a Champagne glass, so at least the spillage had not wasted too much.

When Dawn turned back to hand Amina her glass, she had already removed her wet dress, and was in the process of dropping it into the wash basket just inside the bathroom.

Dawn could not help but stare as the beautiful Egyptian walked towards her, her hand held out to receive her drink.

She was breathtakingly beautiful.

Their eyes locked as Amina began to drink. She took several long swallows before she next came up for air. Seconds after her last swallow, she quickly shot up her empty hand to cover her mouth.

Dawn heard a tiny burp escape from behind her hand.

"Sorry," Amina apologised, blushing. "This stuff's so fizzy."

"Don't I know it," agreed Dawn.

Once she was sure her digestion wasn't going to betray her again, Amina took another sip, but a smaller one this time.

"Right then," she said, placing her glass back on the fridge. "Let's get you out of that dress and we can begin work."

Before she had a chance to reply, Amina guided Dawn to face away from her and slowly began to unzip her dress.

The doctor helped ease the garment over Dawn's hips, after which Dawn stepped out of it and placed it on the chair with her jacket.

Dawn had never felt self-conscious about her body, but in the presence of the work of art that stood before her, she suddenly felt terribly out of shape.

She sucked in her stomach without realising it.

Amina pretended not to notice. "Could you fetch the large towel from the bathroom?" she asked. "We don't want the hotel complaining that we made a mess of their lovely bedspread."

While Dawn grabbed the towel, she noticed her reflection in the bathroom mirror.

She had a bit of a tan around her neck and down her arms

from the tee-shirt she wore last Saturday when she was out shopping. But other than that, she was pasty white all over. Had she known then that she was going to be in this position today, she would have paid for a spray tan to give her an even glow.

Compared with Amina, she looked like a sheet of typing paper.

As Dawn made her way back into the bedroom, Amina switched off the lights.

In the shadowy gloom, Dawn watched the petite woman walk across the floor towards the balcony, where she swept the curtains back to let in the light from outside.

There was a half-moon that night, which, combined with the starlight, bathed the room in a celestial glow, tinged with amber from the reflection of the car park's overhead lighting.

Amina walked back over to Dawn with her hands out, and together they spread the fluffy cotton towel over the bedspread.

"Lie down on your back for me," instructed Amina, "let's tackle that ankle first."

Dawn complied willingly, and lay back on the sumptuous mattress, feeling the soft texture of the towel embrace her.

She was ready to fall asleep, right then and there.

Her eyes closed, Dawn heard the cap of a bottle or jar being unscrewed.

"This is so much more effective than modern medicines." Amina spoke from the darkness. "And, unlike most of the shop-bought ones, this has no sting, no burning sensation, and it doesn't make you itch for hours afterwards."

Dawn suddenly felt her foot being gently lifted off the towel, and Amina's soft hands began to massage her swollen ankle.

Her caressing touch was so gentle that Dawn did not even wince as the other woman applied the ointment to her painful joint.

The doctor's hands were so soft, they made Dawn feel as if

she were wearing velvet gloves, as she rubbed them back and forth along her ankle.

Dawn let out a deep moan of pleasure and clutched the towel with both hands.

Although Amina was touching only her ankle, she could somehow feel a gush of euphoria within her, like an orgasm climbing to its peak.

She slid her other foot back along the towel, until it was resting just below her rump.

The urge to slip her middle finger under the elastic of her panties and down between her legs was overwhelming. But Dawn fought to keep her hands by her sides.

Suddenly, Amina gently returned her foot to the towel and let go.

Dawn felt the loss of her touch.

"Okay, that should do for that. Now let's have you on your tummy and we'll see if we can't sort out that back of yours."

Dawn shuffled on to her front and lay with her arms stretched out to her sides.

She heard the doctor retrieving something else from a drawer, but she could not be bothered to turn over to see what it was. She was still too overcome by the sensual effect of the first part of her massage.

Amina appeared beside her and placed something on the nightstand to her left.

Dawn half opened her eyes and saw the bright yellow flame as a match was struck.

She realised that Amina was lighting an incense stick, and she watched the plume of smoke rise into the air for a moment, before closing her eyes once more.

Without saying a word, Amina pulled Dawn's panties down her legs, and discarded them on the floor, before climbing on top of her and straddling her buttocks.

The doctor was so light that her weight barely registered on

Dawn's mind, as she felt the woman's smooth hands glide up her back, towards her shoulders, and back down again.

She had certainly been right about the balm having a soothing effect, and Dawn could feel every knot and cramped muscle in her back relaxing at Amina's touch.

The scent from the incense stick wafted through the air, and Dawn could smell sandalwood and burnt oak. The combination fused together, reminding Dawn of late-night camp fires in her garden when she was a child, when her parents would allow her and her younger sister to play camping.

The feeling she had experienced when Amina was massaging her ankle was now spreading through her tenfold. It was almost as if the doctor's hands were somehow slipping beneath her skin and delving deep inside her body to stimulate every erogenous zone she possessed.

Again, Dawn found herself unintentionally trying to move her hips to allow her moist opening to rub against the towel beneath her. Even with Amina on top of her, the petite Egyptian barely weighed enough to afford Dawn any resistance.

Amina's hands continued to glide effortlessly across Dawn's back and shoulders and as Dawn breathed in, she could smell a heady combination of the incense stick and something else that she could not quite place.

She breathed deeply, and soon realised that the other scent she could now smell emanated from Amina herself. Dawn surmised that it must be some form of body lotion that she applied to her skin, although it was odd that she had not noticed it until now.

It was too subtle to be perfume, but the aroma was intoxicating.

Dawn could feel her eyelids growing heavy.

She was aware of Amina saying something to her, but her voice sounded very far away, and Dawn could not make out the individual words.

The orgasm that flooded through her moments later stimulated every nerve ending in her body simultaneously.

It continued until she passed out.

Once Amina saw that Dawn was asleep, she carefully climbed off her, and patted her bare rump with her hand.

The doctor retrieved her Champagne from the fridge and walked over to the window to gaze outside while she enjoyed it.

The night was clear and inviting.

Since she turned down the air conditioning, and lit the incense stick, the air had grown a little close.

Amina opened the door that led out to the balcony and stepped outside.

She glanced around, just to make sure that no one else was out on their balconies to see her. When she saw that the coast was clear, she set her glass down on the outside table and began removing the grips that held her hair in place.

Once the last one was out, she ran her hands through her flowing locks, freeing them from the confines of the hairspray she had used to keep them in place.

She stood leaning against the railing, feeling the relief of the cool night air as it gently brushed against her naked torso and ruffled her hair.

Amina sipped her drink until it was gone, then she slipped into bed beside the sleeping detective and soon she, too, fell asleep.

Chapter Thirty-One

WHEN THEY ARRIVED BACK AT THE ACADEMY, THE swans thanked Miss Hedges and the other teachers politely for such a marvellous evening, and, on Cynthia's instructions, they declined the offer of a late-night supper, claiming fatigue.

It was vital to the success of tonight's operation that the teaching staff should be in bed and fast asleep as soon as possible.

Before lights-out. Cynthia gave everyone their instructions.

Instead of donning their nightwear, the girls all changed into their Seddon tracksuits, with the academy emblem emblazed across the back.

Colleen set her alarm for one hour, to allow the teachers ample time to fall asleep.

If truth be told, there was more than a touch of trepidation among the girls about Cynthia's latest idea. But none of them felt strong enough to question the validity of her scheme, so they all decided to just play along, and say nothing.

It seemed to be only seconds before Colleen's alarm woke them up.

The girls made their way across the hall to the lower sixth

dorm, and Carrie-Anne and Geraldine were given the job of going in and waking the ducklings.

Each girl took one side of the dorm room, making sure that they did not disturb any of the other pupils as they went about their task.

Meanwhile, Sarah and Josephine had been given the unenviable mission of breaking into Mr Franks' cottage and retrieving the keys to the minibus.

Franks' cottage lay on the outskirts of the academy grounds, far enough out of the way to be considered as isolated, but still within walking distance, so that he was always on call.

"I don't suppose there's any chance he left them in the ignition?" asked Josephine hopefully.

"No chance – life is never that easy," Sarah responded.

Josephine thought for a moment. "So how exactly are we supposed to break into his cottage without him knowing?"

"Well, according to Cynthia, our Mr Franks is partial to a drop of the hard stuff of an evening, so I'm hoping he's going to be asleep, or at least passed out by now."

Josephine nodded. "Yes, but how do we actually get inside? Breaking and entering are not exactly my forte."

"Or mine," Sarah agreed. "I guess we'll overcome that one when we get there."

Sarah could tell that her friend was not in the least bit convinced and, to be fair, neither was she. Her main hope was that the old man left his door unlocked as they were relatively secure within the academy's grounds.

When they came over the brow the hill and saw the cottage, both girls noticed that a light was still burning inside.

"Not a great sign," observed Josephine.

As they drew closer, both girls hunched over, just in case the caretaker happened to be looking out of his window. From this angle, it was impossible to tell for sure, especially with the flickering light in the background.

Chapter 31

The school minibus was parked to one side on the gravel drive.

Sarah tried the door but, as she feared, it was locked.

She jumped down from the step. "Come on, looks like it's plan B, after all."

They made their way around to the side of the cottage and edged forward slowly until they could see inside the lighted room.

The main curtain was open and, from close up, they could see through the net curtain that the light was from the television at the far end of the room.

Once she decided Franks was nowhere to be seen, Sarah raised herself up enough to be able to see inside properly.

There was an armchair with its back to them and, beside it, a small occasional table, on which stood a half-empty bottle of what appeared to be whiskey and a glass filled almost to the brim.

Sarah edged her way further along the window until she was able to make out an arm dangling from the right-hand side of the chair. She imagined Franks must be slumped in his armchair, watching the television. The only question was whether he was awake or asleep.

"What can you see?" whispered Josephine, still crouched down below the sill.

"He's there all right," Sarah confirmed. "But I can't tell from here if he's asleep or not."

"What shall we do?" Josephine was struggling to keep the tremor from her voice.

Sarah looked back at her and shrugged. "I suppose we have no choice. We'll have to try the front door."

Josephine looked around nervously. "Do we have to?" she whined. "Can't we just go back and tell Cynthia it was locked, and we couldn't get in?"

Sarah looked up at her, startled. "And end up having to

complete a double dare for being responsible for the plan not working? No, thank you!"

Both girls knew the rules. If a Swan was to blame for an initiation plan not working out, then she had to complete a double dare, which Cynthia would devise, ensuring that it was at least twice as bad as whatever the Swan had failed to complete in the first place.

The alternative was being dropped by the other girls, and that was unthinkable.

Josephine knew her friend was right, so she reluctantly turned on the spot and started to edge her way towards the front door.

She waited until Sarah had caught up.

The cottage was a 16th-century brick building, left behind from when the school grounds used to be farmland. The front door was solid oak, with an arched top, and black-painted metal door furniture.

There was only one keyhole, right beside a metal handle with a thumb grip above it of the kind called a Suffolk latch.

"Right, here we go," announced Sarah. She grabbed hold of the handle and placed her thumb on the thumb grip. Holding her breath, she depressed the grip, slowly, until she heard the metal catch inside the door lift out of its holder.

If the door was unlocked, all she would need to do was push it open.

If it was locked, then they had real problems.

Sarah pushed forward, but the door would not give.

She looked at Josephine, still holding the thumb release down, and tried again, this time placing her shoulder against the wooden door, for extra impetus.

To her surprise, the door flew open.

Sarah managed to stop herself from falling forward and braced her foot against the step to help keep herself upright.

The old door had been wedged solidly inside its frame, which is why it did not give immediately. The problem was, the noise it had made when Sarah forced it open, sounded loud enough to wake the dead, let alone the caretaker in the next room.

Both girls stood where they were for a moment, listening out for the sound of movement from the living room.

It was hard to tell over the sound of the television, but eventually they were both satisfied that their entry had not disturbed the slumbering Franks.

Sarah let out her breath slowly and under control then took several quick gulps of air to steady herself.

Just then, Josephine began gesturing, excitedly.

Sarah turned to see what her friend meant and noticed the chauffeur's jacket Franks had been wearing that evening, draped over the bannister at the bottom of the stairs.

Sarah turned back to her friend and nodded her understanding. She signalled to Josephine to hold the door open – the last thing they needed was for a freak gust of wind to slam it shut while she was still inside.

Josephine came forward and took over holding the door handle from Sarah.

Sarah looked down, but it was too dark to see what type of floor she was about to step on. She considered removing her shoes to help muffle any noise she might make, but then decided that the soles of her trainers would be safe enough.

She stepped forward, into the small hallway.

There was a slight rustle from the coarse mat just inside the door, but not enough to cause alarm.

Sarah took two careful steps forward which brought her close enough to the staircase to reach the jacket. She checked the two side pockets first, but both were empty. Taking the jacket off the bannister, she held it up so that she could investigate further.

The jacket had two inside pockets. The first was also empty. The second had what she imagined was an old handkerchief.

Sarah fumbled around inside, just to make sure the keys were not buried underneath the material.

Again, she came up empty.

She removed her hand from the pocket and draped the coat back over the newel post.

She gazed at her hand in the darkness.

The thought of having rummaged around with the old man's handkerchief suddenly made her feel ill. The only other man she had ever known who owned such an accessory was her grandfather, and she remembered him blowing his nose into it, and then replacing it in his pocket. Then repeating the operation several times throughout the day.

Sarah rubbed her hand back and forth several times against her joggers, squirming at the thought of where that handkerchief might have been.

Now what?

If old Franks had the keys in his trouser pocket, there was no way she was going to fumble around inside them. Even if she could do so without waking him up, which in itself would be a miracle, the mere thought made her want to throw up.

She turned back to face Josephine to break the bad news, and just then she spotted something on the wall, beside the doorway.

Sarah edged closer and saw that it was a wall-mounted key holder, and there, dangling from one of the hooks, was a set of keys, one of which was definitely a vehicle ignition key.

Sarah reached out and grabbed the bunch off the holder, before dangling them in front of Josephine.

The relief on her friend's face said it all.

Together they pulled the door shut, wincing as the wood scrapped against the frame once more. The other option had been to leave it open, but they both agreed that would look far more suspicious when Franks woke up and took himself to bed.

At least this way, the old man would not have reason to give the doorway more than a cursory glance, which in turn would mean that there was less chance of his noticing the missing keys.

Sarah knew that one of the reasons why she had been chosen for this task was because she was the only one with a full driving license. Her parents had booked her a comprehensive week of driving lessons, followed by the written and practical tests, as a surprise present during the Easter break.

Since then, she had driven only the Mini they had bought her the previous Christmas to practise in. The minibus would be an entirely different ball game.

The ducklings all stood together in a line while Carrie-Anne carried out an inspection of their attire.

Like the swans, they had all been ordered to dress in their school tracksuits for the night-time task.

Once Carrie-Anne was satisfied, she nodded her approval to Cynthia.

"Right then, little ducklings, tonight will be your final task to complete your initiation into the Seddon Swans."

The ducklings all looked at each other excitedly.

This day had been a long time coming.

"Now," Cynthia continued, "here's the plan of action for tonight, and I expect you all to work together as a team in order to bring it off, understand?"

The girls nodded their understanding.

Cynthia strolled casually up and down the line of girls as she relayed the sequence of events she had devised for them.

As she spoke, the girl's faces reflected the discomfort they were all feeling at hearing the plan.

When she was finished, Cynthia turned to the ducklings. "Any questions?" she asked. Before giving any of them a chance to answer properly, she continued. "Good. Then we're all set to go."

Just as Cynthia turned to lead the way out, Natalie Prewst stepped forward.

Cynthia noticed the movement in her peripheral vision, so she stopped and turned back. "Yes? Problem?" she asked sternly.

Natalie was visibly shaking where she stood.

Cynthia turned back and walked over until she was standing directly in front of the girl. "Well, speak up. We haven't got all night."

Natalie raised her head. Cynthia could see her tears brimming over and trickling down the girl's cheeks. "We... I... can't steal something. It's against the law."

Cynthia turned to the other swans and shrugged.

She focused back on Natalie. "Since when have you been such a goody two-shoes?"

Natalie wiped her eyes with the back of her hand. "I've never stolen anything in my life," she spluttered. "My father's a chief constable – he'd never forgive me if I brought shame on the family."

Cynthia seemed shocked by the response.

She threw her arms out in exasperation, before turning back to her fellow swans.

"Colleen," she called. "Isn't this one yours?"

Each of the swans was allocated at least one duckling and it was their responsibility to ensure that their charge adhered to the Swan code in all matters, and this refusal to complete an initiation task would be considered a blatant breach that would not be tolerated.

Colleen walked over. "Indeed she is," she replied.

"Well, can you please talk some sense into her?"

Colleen stood beside Cynthia and looked deeply into Natalie's eyes.

Natalie could not hold the senior girl's gaze, and looked back down at the floor, where her teardrops had started to form a puddle on the wooden flooring.

"Now, Natalie," Colleen began, softly. "You know full well that if you refuse to take part in the full initiation process, you cannot be made a Swan."

Natalie nodded her understanding, still keeping her head down.

"Now, I know deep down that you do not wish to spend all of next year as an ugly duckling, especially when you've come so far and done so well."

Colleen paused until Natalie shook her head.

She was making progress.

"I was only saying to the girls just the other day how proud I am to call you one of mine. You really are a credit to the ducklings."

She moved in closer and placed the side of her index finger under Natalie's chin, lifting the snivelling girl's head so that their eyes could meet.

Colleen held Natalie's gaze for a moment before continuing.

"Now," she continued, her tone tinged with an edge to convey her expectations. "You aren't going to let me down, are you?"

Natalie's entire body began to shiver, and a fresh batch of tears dribbled down her face.

Colleen's gaze hardened. She could feel herself losing her charge.

Finally, Natalie blurted out: "I can't steal something, I just can't, please don't make me…" She collapsed to the floor in a heap, loud sobs racking her body, as she hugged herself with both arms.

Colleen looked over to Cynthia, who shook her head.

Gazing down at the blubbering girl, Colleen kicked Natalie with the side of her foot. Not hard enough to cause her pain, but enough to impress on the younger girl her disappointment in her.

"Get back to bed," Colleen barked. "I'll deal with you in the morning."

"And don't you dare tell anyone about what we have planned for tonight, or else," threatened Cynthia.

They waited in silence for Natalie to pick herself up off the floor.

With her head bowed, the young girl ran out of the room, still hugging herself and sobbing.

Once her sobs could no longer be heard, Cynthia turned to the rest of the line-up.

"Anyone else care to join the ugly duckling?" she asked, not attempting to disguise the venom in her question.

The other ducklings stayed in place, not answering.

"Good, then let's go."

Chapter Thirty-Two

"IT'S THE NEXT TURNING ON THE RIGHT," SCRAPPER called out, checking the directions on his mobile. "We should be able to see it when we turn."

The recovery driver had taken far longer to reach them than expected, but at least the actual repair did not take long. The cause of the breakdown was a problem with the power to the fuel pump, which, according to the chatty repairman from the motoring organisation, was relatively common in the make of van Jeremy was driving.

Reluctantly, Scrapper texted Len Bixby to inform him of the delay.

He considered just leaving it. After all, Len had not given them a specific time to be there, just a rough estimate of how long the journey should take.

But in hindsight, Scrapper realised that if they took too long and the bloke at the other end grew impatient and called Len himself, then Len might think that Scrapper was trying to pull a fast one and lose his rag with him.

He decided the explanation would sound much better coming from him first.

Len had actually been surprisingly understanding. He told Scrapper that he would call ahead to the receiver and not to worry about it.

Scrapper was relieved, but he still apologised over and over until Len cut the call off.

It was almost midnight when they turned into the street where the museum stood.

Jeremy parked up outside, while Scrapper sent a text to the number Len had supplied him to say they had arrived.

They waited.

The street was well lit and, after a while, Scrapper began to grow annoyed at being left out in the open for so long. A police car could cruise by at any moment, and then what would they say they were doing this far from home?

If the coppers grew suspicious and decided to search the van, the game would definitely be up.

Scrapper stared down at his phone. "Come on yer bastard, call me back," he demanded.

In the front seat, Jeremy turned to his cousin. "I don't like this, we're too exposed out here, should I find somewhere more secluded to park?"

Before Phil had a chance to answer, Scrapper called out from the back.

"Shut up and keep yer eyes open. I'll decide if we need to move."

Phil looked over his shoulder to see Scrapper concentrating on his mobile once more.

He looked at his cousin and gave him a knowing smile. Regardless of whether or not he stuck with Scrapper after this, there was no way he was dragging Jeremy in again.

He would just make up a story that Jeremy had his license lifted for speeding or something equally believable. Their paths did not need to cross again.

Scrapper's screen lit up with the words, "Come in," in

response to his text.

He leaned forward so that he could see out of Jeremy's side window and, from his vantage point, he could not see an access route.

Just then, the large security gates began to swing open.

Jeremy drove in as Scrapper relayed the instructions and parked up next to the staff entrance.

The gates swung shut behind them with a loud clang.

The noise of the gates slamming shut made Scrapper jump around in the back of the van. He realised that they were trapped, and his mind began to reel.

What if this was a set-up?

Suppose Len had done a deal with the coppers, and they were waiting inside to rush them?

There was no way out!

Even if Jeremy's piece of shit van was to ram the gates, they looked solid enough to withstand more than they had to throw at them.

The van would probably crumple upon impact.

Scrapper's paranoia was taking over. He began slamming himself against the back of Jeremy's seat, demanding that he let him out. At least then, if necessary, he could make a break for it and try to climb over the gates.

"Let me out, now!" he screamed, grabbing Jeremy by the shoulders and shoving him forward violently.

Phil turned back to his mate. "What's goin' on Scrapper?" he demanded. "What's yer hurry? Shouldn't we sit 'ere and wait for further instructions?"

"No, I want out, now!"

They all looked over as the staff door opened, and Bill Stead stuck his head out.

When he saw the van, he signalled for them to come inside.

The sight of the huge security guard appeared to have a

calming effect on Scrapper and he immediately stopped his attack on Jeremy and sat back in his seat.

They all stayed put for a moment, Phil and Jeremy awaiting their orders.

In the back, Scrapper was breathing heavily, as if he had just finished running a 400-metre dash.

Phil looked back out of his window, and saw Stead signalling frantically for them to follow him. "Shall we go in?" he asked, looking over his shoulder.

Scrapper was breathing normally now. "Yeah," he replied. "Come on."

They all climbed out of the van. Scrapper had the bag the courier had given him slung over his shoulder, which almost made him fall over as he tried to alight.

Jeremy saw this and reached out to grab him to stop him falling.

"Cheers," said Scrapper as he readjusted the bag.

They walked towards the open door and, without introductions, Stead ushered them all in, and pulled the door shut behind them.

Amin Salah turned around when he heard the door slam shut. Even though it was at the far end of the museum, the sound echoed through the empty building, causing him to freeze where he was, and wait.

During the exhibition, he had managed to hide himself on one of the upper floors and waited until the last of the guests had left.

He had assumed that security would make a final sweep of the building to ensure all the guests were accounted for and, sure enough, after about half an hour, he watched from above as a uniformed guard climbed the stairs to check the upper floors.

Chapter 32

He remained hidden while the security man made his rounds, holding his breath when he passed close by him.

After that, he waited patiently, listening out for any movement from below until he was sure that only the night guard remained.

He planned to bide his time and give the man a chance to fall asleep as he watched his television inside his small office before he ventured back downstairs to commence his mission.

Everything had gone to plan thus far.

Once he had crept back down to the ground floor, Salah moved silently over to where the security office was located, just close enough so that he could tell if anyone was moving around inside.

There was nothing, apart from the sound from the television.

He was confident the guard had had ample time to fall asleep, as such men do when they had to perform mundane duties such as this.

Carefully, he edged his way back through the next room, until he came to the new exhibition area.

That was when he heard the door slamming.

He was not fazed. So it seemed the man was not asleep yet. He'd probably ordered a take-away for dinner which was why he had to open the staff door, to collect it from the driver.

It would not be long now.

Once he had stuffed his face with his chosen junk food, Salah was confident the man would doze off in minutes.

Either way, he did not intend making any noise while he worked, so being this far away from the security office, Salah was content to continue with his task.

He made his way over to the sarcophagus.

Once more, he gazed up in awe at the mighty mummy.

Standing this close to it, surrounded by the artefacts discovered in the professor's home, he could almost appreciate why Kasim held felt obliged to recite the ancient text from the scrolls. They were, after all, considered by some to be a form of worship and submission. But they also contained hidden messages that bestowed mystical powers and were not be treated lightly or carelessly by the user.

Such disrespect could just as easily have been interpreted as provocation by the spirits and the results could be catastrophic.

Instead, Salah merely crossed his arms in an x-shape and bowed three times to prove his subservience.

After that, he moved in closer to inspect the ancient covering.

He apologised to the mummy before he started to prod at the breast area, in an attempt to locate a protrusion which might indicate the presence of the sacred Eye of Aken.

The bandages had naturally frayed over time, and in some places, they had worn apart completely, but since several layers had been used, the inner ones still seemed mostly intact.

Salah had hoped to be able to carry out his task without leaving evidence of his interference. However, he now realised that such a quest teetered on the edge of impossibility.

He pressed a little harder against the outer covering, but there were no obvious signs of the ancient relic.

Salah knew that, although still encased in bandages, the skeleton inside was more than 3,000 years old and had already been exposed to heaven knows what since first being removed from its burial chamber. Therefore, if he were to exert too much pressure from the outside, the skeleton could give way, which would mean that the sacred artefact, if present, could fall inside the skeletal frame.

That would leave him only one option.

He would have to remove all the bandages until he located it. And that would leave no doubt in anyone's mind that the mummy had been interfered with.

Salah decided to play it safe.

He already knew from listening to the doctor's address

earlier in the evening, that she had taken samples from the bandages and sent them off for testing. If Salah was careful, he believed that he could follow those cuts in the fabric and make a few incisions of his own that would not be detected at first glance.

His aim was to prise the bandages away from one side of the mummy, so that he could insert his hand far enough under the wrappings without disturbing the actual skeleton.

It would take time and great patience, but he was confident that he could accomplish the task within the time he had allowed.

Salah removed his dinner jacket and cufflinks and rolled up his sleeves.

He took the scalpel he had brought with him from his inside pocket before placing his jacket over the nearest display cabinet.

Before commencing the operation, Salah grabbed a pair of latex gloves from his trouser pocket and pulled them on, then took the protective cover off the scalpel blade.

Taking a deep breath, he stepped up to the mummy once more.

His head barely reached its sternum so, as he attempted to locate the best place to start cutting the fabric, he was not aware of the mummy's eyes slowly opening.

Salah followed a path across the mummy's chest with his hand, until he located the end piece of a torn bandage.

Moving closer, he inspected the area to ascertain if it was a suitable candidate for attempting his operation.

Anlet-Un-Ri's right hand grabbed him at the back of his neck.

Before he had a chance to respond, the mummy pulled him back so that he could stare into her malevolent black eyes.

Salah dropped his scalpel, and it clanged on the wooden floor.

The noise sounded to him further away than it should have.

Instinctively, Salah raised his arm in an attempt to free himself from the mummy's grasp, but it was in vain.

Salah could feel his feet leaving the floor, as Anlet-Un-Ri raised him off the ground with one hand.

He felt something begin to crack in his neck.

His arms and legs swung around wildly, as he tried to escape the mummy's hand as it clamped ever tighter.

He watched in horror as the mummy's left hand came slowly up to the level of his throat. It remained there for a few seconds, as Salah felt his eyelids growing heavy.

He tried to scream, but the sound was caught in his throat.

The mummy moved its left hand under his chin, the fingers overlapping those from its right hand.

Salah strained to lift his weary arms so that he could grab hold of those of the mummy, in an effort to yank them off him. But they felt like lead weights.

As the image before him faded into darkness, he heard his neck snap.

Chapter Thirty-Three

AMINA SAT UP IN BED, WITH A START. HER ENTIRE body was covered in a film of perspiration, and her heart felt as if it were trying to break out of her chest.

She placed the palm of her hand against her heaving bosom and waited for her breathing to regulate itself.

Beside her, Dawn stirred. Turning on her side, she unwittingly wrapped her leg over Amina's hips, pinning her down.

Amina knew instinctively that the mummy had been woken once again.

A ripple of trepidation spread throughout her body.

This seemed much worse than the last time, when Kasim had used incantations from the Egyptian book of the dead to wake the mummy.

This time, Anlet-Un-Ri would not be satisfied with just taking revenge on the one who disturbed her ancient slumber. Her spirit was unsettled, and her vengeance cried out for blood.

Amina knew that she could not lie there and pretend she was not aware of what was going on. This was her destiny, as foretold to her by her maternal grandmother when she was still a child.

The ancient Egyptians knew that when a person was denied their inherent burial rights, their spirit could not be at peace in the afterlife until they had taken their revenge on those who had wronged them, and that included anyone who desecrated their tomb.

Amina knew that now she had been awakened, Anlet-Un-Ri would consider any living being who crossed her path as a representative of those who had caused her death.

The fact that more than 3,000 years had passed since she died would count as nothing to the vengeful spirit.

To her, it would be as if mere minutes had elapsed before she was woken.

As for the individual who released her, they would be the target of her wrath for initially disturbing her and denying her the chance to rest at peace.

Amina had always suspected that the mummy had taken care of Kasim, and now she had doubtless already focused her anger on whomever had disturbed her once more.

The museum would not be able to contain the mummy, and Amina knew that once she broke out, no one would be safe.

This was the very set of circumstances her superiors had ordered her to prevent.

Her responsibility was clear.

Amina leaned over to push Dawn back off her. The police officer was a good deal larger and heavier than Amina, and it took her several attempts before she was able to slide her tiny frame out from underneath her sleeping companion.

Once she was free, Amina stumbled around the room in the dark, trying to make her way over to the wardrobe to find something to wear. The dress she had worn to the opening was neither practical nor understated enough for the occasion.

She chose a black polo neck, and a pair of black trousers. Her underwear was all neatly folded in the chest of drawers opposite the foot of the bed. But Amina feared that sliding the drawers open and closed to retrieve them, might make too much noise and wake Dawn up, so she decided she could do without them.

Amina slipped on a pair of black pumps. They felt strange without socks on, but again, those were in the drawers with her underwear.

Now all she needed were her car keys.

Amina stopped and thought for a moment.

She remembered walking into the hotel with Dawn, and riding in the lift to her room. Her room card was in her purse, and she imagined herself walking into the room and trying to remember what she did with it, because the chances were that her car keys were in the same place.

Cautiously, she crept across the room to where she remembered leaving her purse.

As she flipped the clasp open, the room was suddenly flooded with light.

"What are you doing?" said a sleepy voice from the bed.

Amina turned to see Dawn raised up on one elbow, yawning and rubbing sleep from her eyes.

"Nothing," she lied. "You go back to sleep – I won't be long."

Dawn stopped rubbing her eyes and focused on the doctor.

"Why are you dressed? Are you leaving?" she asked curiously.

Amina released a pent-up breath. "I need to go somewhere, quickly, but I'll be back before you know it."

She knew what she had said would not satisfy Dawn's inquisitive police-officer mind, but she had no time for explanations as she could feel the threat from the mummy growing by the minute.

Just as she had feared, Dawn was not buying her vague words.

Before Amina had a chance to make for the door, Dawn

swung her legs over the side of the bed and walked over to where she was standing. Even naked, she was a formidable presence.

Hands on hips, she looked down at Amina.

"Please tell me what's going on. I know there's something you're hiding."

Amina gazed up at her and sighed.

Although well versed in the art of hypnosis, Amina found herself not wanting to use her skills on the officer.

The truth, however, would sound too ridiculous for words, but she felt she had been left with little choice.

"I'm going to confront your killer," she explained.

Dawn took an instinctive step backwards. "Excuse me!" she replied, shocked by the doctor's announcement. "Is this some kind of joke, because, if it is…"

Amina held up her hands. "I know I sound ridiculous," she admitted, "but I really think I know who killed that Egyptian man in the museum the other day."

Dawn held her ground. "So, you were just going to head off on your own and confront them, is that it?"

"It's not as straightforward as all that, but I need you to trust me."

"I do trust you, odd as it seems right at this moment, but you cannot expect me to let you wander off to find a killer on your own. That's my job, don't you think?"

Amina knew that they were wasting valuable time, but by the same token, short of making a break for it, she knew that Dawn was not going to allow her to leave without a proper explanation.

Finally, she gave in. "Look, just get dressed and come with me," she suggested. "I'll fill you in on the way. How's that?"

Dawn stayed where she was for a moment, pondering the offer.

It was not ideal, by any means, but Amina seemed intent on

Chapter 33

leaving the hotel, so at least Dawn would have time to consider her explanation on route to wherever they were headed.

"Okay, fine," she agreed, and turned to look for her clothes.

While she struggled back into her evening dress, Amina grabbed a band and pulled her long hair back into a pony-tail.

She continued to search for her car keys, but to no avail.

"I don't suppose you remember where I put my car keys, do you?" she asked over her shoulder.

Dawn thought for a moment. "Didn't you hand them to that parking valet when we came in?"

Amina slapped her palm against her forehead. "Of course I did," she agreed ruefully. "Are you ready?"

Dawn finished struggling into her dress.

She lifted her hair up from the back of her neck. "Zip me up, please."

Amina complied. "How are the back and ankle feeling?"

Dawn turned back and pressed her foot down hard on the carpet.

"Feels great," she enthused. Next, she stood up straight and bent from side to side. "Amazing," she admitted, smiling. "You should market that."

Amina smiled. "My ancestors would turn in their graves. Ready?"

Dawn nodded. "Should I call for back-up?" she asked, half-jokingly.

"Let's hope we don't need them," Amina replied, looking serious, as she turned towards the door.

"I can't wait to hear your theory," Dawn called from behind, following the petite Egyptian out.

"Don't say later that I didn't warn you," Amina called back over her shoulder.

Sarah manoeuvred the mini-bus through the town, narrowly escaping collisions against parked cars on two separate occasions.

Nervous as she was about driving such a large vehicle, she was also secretly very proud of herself, considering her Mini was the size of car she was used to.

The screaming from some of the girls on the bus when Sarah veered too close to parked vehicles was both annoying and off-putting. In the end, Cynthia had to demand silence for the rest of the journey, although she too had her concerns about how her fellow Swan was handling the bus.

When the minibus finally turned into the street at the back of the museum, there was an audible sigh of relief from some of the girls.

Sarah parked in front of the gates and turned off the engine.

Cynthia turned back to face the passengers. "Now, you all know the plan, yes?"

There were nods from all parties, although she could tell from the expressions on some of their faces that they were not at all happy about tonight's escapade.

Cynthia turned to Geraldine. "Okay, you're up. Don't let the side down."

Sarah released the locking mechanism, and the door slid open.

Without speaking, Geraldine exited the bus and made her way over to the intercom by the double gates. The security box was unmanned, just as Stead had told Jacinda it would be tonight.

Geraldine took a deep breath, then pressed the call button.

She waited, but there was no response from the other side.

She turned back to the bus and shrugged her shoulders.

Perhaps the big security guard had lied to Jacinda about him being the only one on duty tonight. Maybe there were no night guards, and he had only said that to her in the hope that she might agree to stay behind with him once everyone else had gone.

Jacinda said he was a creep, so it was not beyond the realms of possibility.

Geraldine could see Cynthia indicating for her to try again.

This time, she kept her finger on the buzzer a little longer, just in case the guard inside – if he was there – had fallen asleep.

It did the trick. This time, a gruff voice answered. "Yes?"

Geraldine used her most seductive voice when she answered. "Hello, I'm terribly sorry, but I was a guest here tonight, and I seem to have lost my bracelet. It's very valuable and, if I can't find it, Daddy is going to be awfully cross. I was wondering if I might pop in and have a quick look for it, please?"

There was a slight pause. "No, sorry, you'll 'ave to come back when we're open."

"Oh, please, if you let me just have a tiny peek, I'd be ever so grateful, I promise I won't be long. I brought a few of my friends from the academy to help me search, so it really won't take that long."

"'ang on, are you one of those girls from the school that was in 'ere tonight?"

"That's right," Geraldine replied sweetly.

Cynthia was right – the mere mention of the academy was enough to pique the guard's interest. He had already tried it on with Jacinda and, even though Sarah had given him what for, he was definitely the kind of bloke who thought himself God's gift.

There followed another pause.

Geraldine could hear the sound of heavy breathing over the intercom.

"All right, come in and park. I'll be out in a minute."

Before she had a chance to thank him, Stead had switched off his mic.

Geraldine made her way back to the bus and ran up the steps excitedly.

"The old Simms charm – works every time," she announced, proudly.

The heavy iron gates clattered open.

Sarah started up the engine and waited for them to be fully parted before she drove in.

"Park as close to the entrance as you can," Cynthia reminded her.

"Will do."

Cynthia turned back. "Right, you lot, duck down until I give you the signal, got it?"

The ducklings all obeyed without question.

Jacinda, too, shuffled down in her seat, out of sight. It had been decided that since she, Cynthia and Sarah had already crossed swords with the guard, they would stay back, out of sight. The last thing they wanted was to antagonise him, or he might change his mind about granting Geraldine and the others entry.

Once she had parked up, Sarah moved to one of the seats behind her, and slid down out of sight.

The lights inside the bus were off, so it would already be virtually impossible for anyone outside to see who was there, but Cynthia did not want to take any chances, so she too, kept her head down.

Carrie Anne and Colleen moved up towards the front to join Geraldine and together they waited to disembark.

After a few moments, the staff door opened with a crash, and Bill Stead filled the opening.

"Let's go," called Geraldine, and the three of them left the bus and sashayed over to the open doorway.

Bill Stead eyed them suspiciously. "Now which one of you silly girls lost her bracelet, then, eh?"

Geraldine turned her head to one side and pretended to be overcome with coyness.

"That's me, I'm afraid," she said bashfully. "Daddy will be so

Chapter 33

upset if I don't find it. It's very kind of you to allow my friends and me to come in and look for it."

She took a step closer to the guard, and slowly lifted her head as if she were taking in the magnificence of his huge chest, before gazing into his eyes and pouting.

Stead flushed. "Right, er, okay. Well, follow me then, an' we'll see if we can find it."

Stead turned and made his way back into the museum.

The girls had banked on him not being a gentleman, and he had proved them right.

Leaving the three of them to walk in after him allowed Colleen the opportunity to bend down and slip the rubber doorstop she had brought with her into the grooves of the door frame.

She kicked it in place and rammed it home with the heel of her trainer before she quickly piled in behind the others.

"I really can't thank you enough," said Geraldine, linking arms with Stead. "Oh," she exclaimed, "you are a big boy," and with that, she placed her free hand on his bicep and gave it a gentle squeeze.

The ruse worked, and Stead did not notice that the staff door remained slightly ajar.

From inside the bus, Cynthia peered through her nearest window. She watched as Colleen jammed the stopper in place, and waited for the door to swing back, before she ordered the ducklings to make their move.

Cynthia led the remaining ducklings out of the bus, pressing her index finger against her lips to demand silence.

They followed her over to the staff door, and waited in a line behind her, while she checked that the coast was clear.

Once she was content, Cynthia turned back to face them. "Now, you all know what is expected of you and, if you work together as a team, this should hardly take any time at all."

There were a few uncertain nods, but most of the girls just looked too scared to respond.

"Remember, you just need to steal one item, regardless of how small it is, from one of the glass cabinets, then it's all over. Ready?"

This time, she did not wait for a response.

Cynthia pushed the door open a little further and ushered the ducklings inside.

She watched from the safety of the entrance, until they had all disappeared around the nearest corner. Then she made her way back to the bus.

Chapter Thirty-Four

Danielle finished drying her hands on the roller towel and pulled it down so the next person to use it had a fresh piece.

Not having an en-suite room was one of the minor inconveniences she, and several of the most recent arrivals, had to put up with, but at least she did not have to trek to another floor to use a lavatory.

She crept along the corridor in her bare feet, back towards her room at the far end.

As she neared the entrance to the lower-sixth dorm, she could hear a noise coming from behind the wooden door.

Danielle pressed her ear against the wood and listened.

The sound was muffled behind the door but it sounded to her as if one of the girls was crying.

It was not uncommon amongst the younger girls, especially. For some of them, this was their first experience of living away from home, so it was only natural that they would sometimes feel uncomfortable in such unfamiliar surroundings.

That aside, it was a little out of the ordinary to have one of the older girls crying themselves to sleep. But there was no denying the sound she heard.

Miss Hedges had always instructed the staff not to respond to such an event, for fear that to do so might encourage girls to do it again to win attention or even inspire some of the other girls to imitate the behaviour. But, unlike the headmistress, Danielle did not feel comfortable hearing a young girl sobbing her heart out without doing something about it.

Not wishing to wake everyone else in the dorm, Danielle did not bother to knock. Instead, she slowly turned the handle and pushed the door inwards.

To her surprise, only one bed appeared to be occupied.

Each lower-sixth dorm housed six beds, plus individual wardrobes, writing desks and

chairs, plus an assortment of full-length and half-sized mirrors.

There were no partitions between the beds, which allowed teachers to scan the entire room without having to leave the doorway.

Danielle blinked several times to help her focus in the gloom of the darkened room. She looked at each bed in turn, but there was no mistake – only one was occupied, and the girl huddled under the covers was the one she had heard crying from outside.

Danielle edged her way towards the occupied bed, not wishing to scare the girl.

A creaking floorboard announced her presence, and Natalie Prewst suddenly sat up with a start, and looked back towards the source of the noise. When she saw it was Danielle approaching, she immediately calmed down and wiped her eyes with the back of her hand.

Danielle sat on the edge of her bed and smiled at her warmly.

She realised that the young girl would doubtless be embarrassed at being discovered crying under her bedclothes

Chapter 34

and so might not wish to admit why she was in a such a state to begin with.

Danielle's biggest concern was that Natalie had been a victim of a Swan initiation prank again, and, if that were the case, then this time she was going to insist that Miss Hedges take immediate, and decisive, action.

Danielle placed her hand on Natalie's calf, through the bedding, and rubbed it back and forth. "So, what's up kiddo? Care to let your old teacher in on the drama?"

Straight away she could tell that Natalie felt awkward about the situation. The young girl hung her head and shook it from side to side.

The PE teacher slid further up the bed, so that she could put her arm on the young girl's shoulder. "Come on, I promise you whatever it is, it's not half as bad as you think."

Natalie looked up and shrugged. "It's nothing," she said unconvincingly.

"Well, if it were just nothing, you wouldn't be so upset about it, would you?"

Another shrug. "I suppose not."

Danielle could see that she was going to have to do most of the work herself. If Natalie really did not want to talk about whatever was upsetting her, then she would have to drop it. After all, forcing the girl to talk might only exacerbate her melancholia.

Danielle glanced around the room. "Where is everybody?" she asked, keeping her tone purposely casual.

Natalie sniffed. "They're on an initiation jaunt."

"So how come you're in here? Have you already finished all of yours?"

The girls shook her head slowly. "No, I refused to go, so I'm no longer a potential Swan. I'll just be an ugly duckling next year, for everyone to make fun of and laugh at."

A fresh flood of tears sprang from her eyes, and her tiny frame began to jerk with the sobs.

Danielle moved closer and put her arms around the poor girl, allowing her to cry on her shoulder. She waited until the worst of the tears had subsided, before she eased the grief-stricken girl off her.

"What made you change your mind about joining the swans?" Danielle asked, wiping away some of the girl's tears with her thumb. "I thought they were supposed to be the bee's knees around here."

Natalie reached over to the table beside her bed, and pulled open the top drawer, removing a tissue from the box within. She blew her nose, hard, and wiped the end, before discarding the used Kleenex in the bin next to her bed.

"I couldn't do what they were asking of us, so they threw me out."

Danielle nodded. "I see, and what exactly did they want you to do? Was it something personal you did not like the sound of?"

Natalie shook her head, once more. "Not exactly. It's just that with my father being a senior police officer, if we were caught, he would end up hearing about it, and he'd never forgive me."

Danielle liked the sound of this less and less.

She thought for a moment.

Why would Natalie's father, copper or not, care what stupid childish pranks the girls embarked on?

Unless.

"Natalie, the thing they wanted you to do, was it something illegal?"

The girl looked up immediately and her cheeks grew red.

"It was, wasn't it?" pressed Danielle. "Please tell me where they are, and what they're up to."

Natalie shuffled back against the wall behind her.

Chapter 34

She looked to Danielle as if she wished she could somehow dissolve into the wall and disappear.

The PE teacher's heart went out to the poor girl. She knew only too well how possessive some of the older girls could be about their precious Swan society but this was more important than any code of conduct among the girls.

If they were really doing something stupid enough that it might result in their being arrested, or worse, then even Miss Hedges would want to know about it.

After all, if any of their actions were to bring the good name of the academy into disrepute, the headmistress would probably burst a blood vessel and die on the spot.

Extracting the information form Natalie, however, was not going to be an easy task.

Anxious as she was to find out what was going on, Danielle did not want to resort to threats of punishment – the teenager had obviously been through enough already.

"Natalie," she began, keeping her voice steady, "if there's a chance the girls might end up in serious trouble, you know you won't be able to forgive yourself if you could have said something to help prevent it, don't you?"

The girl dropped her gaze once more and gave a slight nod.

"So please tell me what they are up to before it's too late to help them."

Minutes later, Danielle was striding down the corridor, back to her room. Once there, she quickly dressed and, grabbing her car keys, she left, closing the door gently so as not to wake up anyone else on the floor.

As she reached the top of the stairs, she stopped and turned back.

On reflection, she decided she needed some support, and there was only one colleague she could trust to keep her mouth shut, if it came to it.

Danielle made her way back past her own bedroom and

around the corner towards the fire exit. At the last room on the right, she stopped and gently knocked on the door.

No sound came from inside, so she knocked again, slightly harder this time.

As there was still no response, she decided to grab the bull by the horns. Danielle opened the door and snuck inside, closing it behind her.

Ruffled up in the sheets lay her colleague, Pascale Bouvier. The young French teacher was the closest to a friend she had made since joining the teaching staff.

Not wishing to alarm her, Danielle moved to the end of the bed, where she could see one of Pascale's bare feet poking out from beneath the crumpled bedding.

"Hey," she whispered, holding the woman's big toe between her thumb and forefinger, and shaking it gently.

The French mistress moaned and turned over on to her other side.

Her bare foot disappeared back under the bedclothes as she moved.

Running out of patience, Danielle moved to the top of the bed and shook her friend by the shoulder. "Oi, sleepy-head, I need you," she said, keeping her voice down, just in case someone might be awake in the adjoining room.

This time, Pascale opened one eye and squinted up at her colleague. "What's wrong?" she asked with a yawn. "You had one of those wet dreams about me again. I told you, you're not my type."

The French teacher closed her eye and hugged her pillow.

Without saying a word, Danielle drew back the covers, exposing Pascale's naked form and swatted her on the backside.

Pascale sat up with a yelp. "Ow, that hurt!"

Danielle put her finger to her mouth. "Shh, it was meant to. Now get up – I need your help."

"What?" Pascale swung her legs over the side of the bed. Her

Chapter 34

usually immaculate hair was strewn across her face. She yawned loudly and stretched her arms above her head.

Danielle could not help but notice the woman's perfectly rounded bosoms as she lifted her arms.

"I'm watching you!" Pascale warned.

Danielle felt her cheeks go warm. "Will you shut up and get dressed," she commanded.

"Where are we going?" Pascale demanded, clearly not impressed at having her sleep disrupted.

"I'll tell you on the way," Danielle promised. "Now please, for the love of all that's holy, will you move your butt?"

Bill Stead burst through the security office door, making Scrapper jump to his feet so fast, he upended his chair, sending it flying backwards.

From the look on his face, Phil gathered he had something exciting to announce.

"Hey lads," he began, breathlessly, "have I got a surprise for you!"

Scrapper lifted his chair off the floor and shoved it back into place. He pretended as if his reaction to Stead's entrance had been perfectly normal, and not in any way out of the ordinary.

"What's that, then?" asked Phil.

The big security guard's smile spread across his face. "There's three gorgeous-looking creatures just come into the museum, looking for something one of them dropped earlier. And now they're locked in, can't get out without me."

"Oh, yeah," said Scrapper excitedly.

Stead nodded.

Phil's brow furrowed. "So what?"

Scrapper turned on him. His eyes wide open and staring

menacingly. "So, it sounds as if there might be some pussy on offer, that's what!"

"Exactly," agreed Stead. "I've already chosen mine, so you three can either fight over the other two or take it in turns with 'em – I'm not bothered."

Phil held up his hands. "Wait a minute, we came here to do a job." He turned to Stead. "So, if you'd like to just check you're happy with your merchandise, we'll be off."

Scrapper ran forward and grabbed him by the collar. "What are you talkin' about? You gone soft or something?"

Phil stayed calm. "Listen Scrapper, we don't want no trouble, yeah? This ain't our manor so we need to be careful."

"Yes," agreed Jeremy, still seated off to one side. "I need to get back to London, I've got work in the morning."

Scrapper leapt across the room and caught Jeremy on the chin with a wild uppercut.

Jeremy rocked backwards and took his chair with him.

He landed on the floor, smacking the back of his head against a metal filing cabinet.

Phil rushed over to his cousin. For a minute he thought he was out cold, but when he reached him, Jeremy moved his head from side to side, moaning.

Phil helped him back up to his feet. "What the hell was that for?" he yelled at Scrapper. "Have you forgotten? Without him you wouldn't even have been able to deliver this shit."

Scrapper strode over to his mate, until they were only inches apart. "Look, I don't need no one's help. It's thanks to me that you and 'im 'ave a taste of the big time, so stop whinging an' let's go an' look at some skirt."

Ignoring Jeremy, Scrapper put his arm around Phil's shoulders.

Phil shrugged him off. "No thanks. I think we'll be leaving, now."

Scrapper was livid. Phil could see that behind his stare, his old friend was gone. He had seen it coming for a while now, because of all the gear Scrapper insisted he could take without any ill effects. But there had been no point in trying to reason with his friend – he did not want to listen.

To his surprise, Scrapper began to pat Jeremy down, as if he were trying to dust him off after his fall.

Suddenly, he stuck his hand inside Jeremy's jacket, and pulled out his van keys.

"Oi," yelled Jeremy, grabbing for his keys, but missing as Scrapper yanked them out of his reach.

He held them up, like a new owner toying with a puppy. "Now no one leaves without me, got it?"

Before Phil had a chance to remonstrate with him again, Scrapper turned to Stead.

"Right then," he said, shoving the van keys deep down inside his jeans pocket, and patting them. "Where's this pussy, then?"

Jeremy went to rush forward, but Phil stopped him, and shook his head.

He knew it would not be worth the fight.

Scrapper followed the security guard back outside.

Chapter Thirty-Five

"I can't see anything from here," Suzi Ansbach whispered.

The ducklings were all lined up along the balcony of one of the upper floors of the museum. When Cynthia had first let them in, they began to follow the signs that led to the new Egyptian exhibition but, halfway along the corridor, Greta Clarke, who was in the lead, saw Bill Stead walking back towards his office, so, in a panic, they all ran for the nearest staircase.

"Do you think he's gone?" asked Joanne South, timidly.

Suzi turned to her and pulled a face. "How would I know? I just said I couldn't see anything."

Joanne pouted, and turned back to look over the railing once more.

After a while, Janice Cooper said. "There's no movement down there at the moment and we can't stay here all night. I say we make our way along to the other side of the floor and see if there's another staircase at that end to take us down."

She looked along the line and waited for the others to nod their agreement.

Chapter 35

Since their arrival, someone had turned on the downstairs lights, which they presumed was probably the guard who let the others in. But upstairs still had only the emergency lights on, which meant that the girls had to move a little more cautiously, to avoid bumping into things.

Janice and Suzi led the vanguard and the other girls fell in behind, in pairs, with the exception of Joanie Vintner, who brought up the rear alone.

Even with the assistance of the downstairs lights, the museum felt creepy in the dim light, and several of the ducklings were beginning to wish they had showed the same spirit as Natalie and refused to come along.

Joanie especially kept thinking how much happier she would be if she were tucked up in her own bed right now.

Perhaps, if they had all stood together and refused, the initiation task would have been cancelled.

After all, what would Cynthia and the others have done to them – dropped them all?

That would mean no swans at all next year, and that would never do.

An audible click from somewhere in the darkness behind her, made Joanie swing round, and a tiny yelp escaped her lips before she could block it.

The others stopped and looked back towards their colleague.

"What's the matter?" asked Rose Dyson in a hushed tone. She and her partner Lesley Smith were the closest pair to Joanie.

"I thought I heard something back there," Joanie pointed into the darkness behind her.

"Oh, don't say that," whispered Lesley. "This place gives me enough of the creeps as it is." She shivered involuntarily.

The other girls came forward and huddled up.

"What's going on?" asked Greta, shuffling forward to get a better view.

"Joanie thought she heard something behind us," offered Rose.

"I did," insisted Joanie. "It was a loud clicking sound, as if someone were cocking a pistol, like on the telly."

Joanne backed into Suzi.

"Ow, that's my foot, dozy," she scolded, pushing Joanne back off her.

"I'm sorry," Joanne murmured. "Oh, I wish we'd never agreed to this stupid thing in the first place. We all need our heads tested."

"Me too," agreed Rose.

"And me," Lesley chimed in.

"Look," Janice countered, doing her best to keep her voice under control, "we all agreed to this, so it's a bit late now to be complaining, don't you think?" Her question was aimed at the group at large, but Joanne, Rose and Lesley, could not help but feel it was really aimed at them.

"Janice is right," agreed Suzi. "None of us wants to be here, but here we are, so we'd better just get on with it. The sooner we grab something, the sooner we can all go back to bed."

"Why can't we just take something from up here?" offered Joanie. "They'll never know – it's all the same rubbish."

"She's got a point," Suzi agreed. "One chunk of rock looks pretty much the same as another."

"Cynthia would know," mumbled Janice, "I think she expects us to nick something a bit more valuable than a lump of stone."

"She didn't specify anything," argued Rose. "I think it's a terrific idea. We should vote."

Janice sighed and turned back to see what Suzi thought, as she was the one the others normally turned to at times such as this.

Suzi shrugged. "Fine by me, but it'll have to be something generic-looking, otherwise Cynthia and the others will know it's not from the new exhibition."

Chapter 35

Janice turned back to the others. "Okay, so it's agreed, now all of you spread out and start looking for something."

The others were not enamoured at the prospect of splitting up, but as it seemed to be a consequence of not having to waste any more time navigating their way back downstairs, they reluctantly began their individual searches.

On the ground floor, Geraldine, Carrie Anne and Colleen were all awaiting Stead's return. He had left them searching for Colleen's imaginary bracelet while he slipped back to the entrance to switch on some more lights for them.

"How much longer do we need to hang around here?" asked Colleen, rubbing her hands up and down her arms. "It's bloody freezing."

"They have to keep the temperature down overnight because of some of the exhibits," replied Carrie Anne.

"How'd you know that?" Geraldine piped up.

"I heard that doctor talking about it earlier. Some of us were actually listening."

Geraldine stuck her tongue out playfully.

"Your boyfriend's taking his time," Colleen observed.

Geraldine gawped. "Er, excuse me, he's nothing of the kind, thank you."

"Well, the way you were holding on to him when we came in here, you could've fooled me."

"Shush, I hear someone coming," said Carrie Anne.

They all turned back towards the partition behind them.

Geraldine, remembering her part, slipped her bracelet out of her pocket, and slid it over her hand.

Bill Stead turned the last corner, with Scrapper by his side.

The pair looked almost comical due to their difference in height and stature.

"Now then, ladies," Stead began, "let's see if we can't find that bracelet o' yours."

"No need," Geraldine chirped up, "we found it, see." She offered out her arm with the bracelet dangling from it.

Stead looked at Scrapper, but the smaller man was too busy eyeing up the three girls.

"Well, that's a bit of luck," said Stead. "What say we celebrate and have a little drinky? I've got a lovely drop of brandy in my desk drawer."

"Oh, no thank you," replied Colleen, "we really need to get back."

The three girls began to walk back in the direction Stead and Scrapper had just appeared from.

As Geraldine reached Stead, he grabbed her by the wrist, and held it tightly.

"Ow, you're hurting me," Geraldine yelled at him. "Let me go!"

Stead ignored her objection and pulled her closer. "Not until I get a little kiss first," he said, leering at her.

"Hey, stop that now," said Carrie Anne, moving in to rescue her friend.

"Not so fast, missy," hissed Scrapper, lunging at her before she had a chance to reach Geraldine.

Scrapper wrapped his arms around Carrie-Anne's slender waist and held her close to him. She could smell his tobacco breath as he laughed raucously. She turned her face away and tried to pull herself free, but Scrapper was too strong for her.

"Come on," he urged her. "I've come a long way for this."

All of a sudden, she felt wetness on the side of her face and realised, to her horror, that Scrapper was licking her.

Carrie-Anne started to gag.

Colleen felt trapped between trying to help her friends or running back out to grab reinforcements. She looked around for something to use as a weapon, in an attempt to try and make the men release her friends.

She looked on helplessly, as Scrapper managed to drag Carrie

Anne down on the floor with him. The poor girl was struggling to break free, but he seemed in total control of the situation as he pinned her arms down and slid his body on top of her.

To the side, Colleen noticed one of the roped-off barriers which separated them from the next corridor. She quickly unhitched the rope and grabbed the metal stand with both hands.

At first, it was heavier than she had anticipated, so she was unable to lift it. But on her second try she raised it high enough so that she could bring it down on Scrapper's back.

Colleen was afraid that she might hurt Carrie Anne in the process, but she was short on options, so she swung it down, landing the heavy round foot of the stand square in the middle of his back.

Scrapper cried out in pain and shock.

His body slumped down on top of Carrie Anne like a dead weight.

Geraldine, meanwhile, was having less success in preventing Stead from forcing a kiss from her. He held her head between his two massive hands and forced his mouth against hers.

Colleen lifted the metal frame once more, and balanced it on her right shoulder, as she carried it over towards Stead's exposed back.

As she prepared to swing it again, Stead caught sight of her, and spun around so that Geraldine would take the brunt of the blow.

Colleen managed to stop herself just in time.

Stead grinned at her while still holding on to Geraldine. "So, what yer gonna do now, then?" he sneered.

"Leave her be," Colleen demanded, "or I'm calling the police right now!"

Colleen's hand went down to her pocket, just as she remembered that she had not thought to bring her mobile with her.

She gazed back up to see the big security guard grinning, broadly.

Changing tactic, Colleen went back to Carrie Anne, who was still trying, unsuccessfully, to push Scrapper off her.

Colleen discarded her weapon, and bent down, grabbing Scrapper by his shirt. She yanked back with all her might, but only managed to rip the cheap fabric. The momentum from her action sent Colleen flying back into one of the glass stands, which then toppled over and smashed against the stone floor.

The artefacts from within the casing scattered around the area.

Hearing the sound of breaking glass, Stead turned his attention away from the helpless Geraldine and glared down at Colleen instead.

"You stupid fuckin' bitch," he roared. "What've you done?"

Colleen looked up at the big man as he cast Geraldine to one side, sending her sliding across the floor, and advanced on her.

"I… I…" Colleen was too petrified to find the words.

Then, from behind, they all heard the sarcophagus that held the mummy of Anlet-Un-Ri, begin to shake where it stood, as the enormous mummy stepped forth on to the floor.

They all stayed frozen to the spot, as the mummy turned its mighty head first one way, then back to face them.

The mummy took its first step towards the five of them, as Geraldine screamed from the top of her lungs.

None of them could believe what they were witnessing, yet at the same time it was all happening right in front of them.

"What the fuck?" said Stead, turning so that he was facing the approaching mummy head on. "What's goin' on 'ere?"

Scrapper scrabbled to his feet, finally freeing Carrie Anne. From her angle, trapped beneath her assailant, she could only see what was happening behind her from the corner of one eye. Now that she was able to sit up, she experienced the full horror of what was going on.

Chapter 35

"Is this some kind of fuckin' joke?" demanded Scrapper, seeing but not believing what was taking place. He pointed to the approaching mummy. "Is that fucker for real?"

Colleen snapped to her senses. She reached over and grabbed Carrie Anne by the wrist and pulled her close. The two girls hugged each other as they watched Anlet-Un-Ri take another stride towards them.

Colleen slowly began to steer her friend around the frozen figure of the security guard, and towards Geraldine, who was still lying on the floor, unable to move.

When they reached her, they both helped her to her feet, all the time keeping their gaze fixed on the mummy.

Their minds raced as they watched Scrapper back away from the oncoming monstrosity. He finally stopped when he was close enough to Stead to feel safe. Whatever was going through his drug-addled mind, he felt sure that his new friend would protect him.

The three girls all began to move back slowly, in unison.

Each was afraid that if they made any sudden movements, the mummy would notice and lurch forward, after them.

For now, the big security guard seemed to be holding his ground.

As Anlet-Un-Ri drew closer, he realised that she was far bigger than he had first thought. With each approaching step, her stature seemed grow taller and wider, until she was close enough that he felt himself grow weak at the knees.

Pushing Scrapper away from him, Stead turned on his heel to run. As he did so, he accidentally put his foot down on a small artefact that had spilled from the display case Colleen had knocked over.

He slipped sideways. Unable to regain his balance in time, Stead fell, crashing head-first against the base supporting another cabinet. The force of the blow was not enough to render him unconscious, but the glass cabinet that fell directly on top of his head as a result served the purpose just as efficiently.

The force of Stead's shove sent Scrapper careering across the polished floor, directly towards the mummy.

Before he had a chance to recover his balance, Anlet-Un-Ri leaned over and placed her enormous hands around Scrapper's scrawny neck, lifting him up off the floor, before holding him up to her eye level.

Scrapper jerked around in the mummy's grasp like an executioner's victim dangling from a rope. He swung his arms around in an arc, taking wild punches at the mummy's head in an effort to free himself, but even those that landed made no impact.

His legs danced and kicked underneath him, but to no avail.

The girls heard an audible crack echo through the enclosure where they stood as Scrapper's neck broke.

The girls broke into a run, heading back the way they had come in earlier.

They did not dare look back, for fear the mummy might be gaining on them, like in some nightmarish dream where, the faster you try and run, the less ground you cover.

Anlet-Un-Ri waited until Scrapper had stopped moving altogether, before hurling his lifeless body behind the scenery backdrop to her right, where it dropped on top of that of Amin Salah.

The mummy turned her attention to the fallen security guard.

She could sense that he was not dead yet, but for his part in the desecration of her final resting place, he must suffer.

As she strode purposefully towards his prone body, the guard began to move.

He opened his eyes and blinked several times, trying to bring his eyes back into focus. His head throbbed from the impact of the falling glass cabinet, and he could feel fragments of broken glass in his mouth.

It took him a few moments to remember why he was fleeing in such a hurry before his accident. As his memory returned, he moved his head over and stared straight back at the feet of Anlet-Un-Ri.

Without allowing him time to move into a more advantageous position, the mummy lifted one of her colossal legs, and clamped her foot across the neck of the security guard.

Stead choked and spluttered, fighting desperately to free himself as the mummy bore down with her full weight on his throat.

The force of her enormous weight on his windpipe prevented him from drawing another full breath and, as much as he kicked and fought to break free, there was no letting up from his attacker.

As the blackness started to take over his mind, Stead felt his own neck crack and splinter like so much dry wood on an open log fire.

Chapter Thirty-Six

AMINA SWUNG HER CAR AROUND THE FINAL BEND AND pulled up directly in front of the museum gates. Before Dawn had a chance to say anything to her, she jumped out of the driver's seat and ran to the intercom, jabbing the button several times, without waiting for a response.

On the drive over, Amina had explained to Dawn about the legend of Anlet-Un-Ri, and why she was convinced that the dead warrior's mummy had come back to life and killed Kasim.

Under ordinary circumstances, Dawn would have laughed off the doctor's explanation. But there was a sincerity in her voice that made Dawn feel as if Amina at least believed that what she was saying was the truth.

Even so, walking mummies and spirits being summoned back from the afterlife were all a little too 'Hammer House of Horrors' for her to take seriously. But rather than question it, she decided just to respect Amina's conviction and wait and see for herself.

She left the car and joined Amina at the intercom.

Dawn saw the doctor jabbing the button, and she could hear

Chapter 36

the faint sound of the buzzer coming through the small silver microphone grate.

"No one answering?" she asked.

Amina shook her head. "No. I only hope I'm not too late."

Dawn thought for a moment. "Perhaps the guard is on a patrol and can't hear the buzzer from where he is," she offered helpfully.

"I hope that is the only reason," replied Amina.

At that moment, a voice came back through the grate. "Yes."

The voice sounded irritated, but also, to Dawn's trained ear, a little timid.

"Yes, hello, this is Doctor Anmali. I work here – could you please let me in?"

They waited, but no reply came.

Eventually, Amina hit the buzzer again. This time, she kept her finger on the button until it was answered.

"I'm sorry, the guard is not here at the moment, he's on a patrol. You'll have to wait until I can find him."

Dawn leaned forward. "Now listen to me," she said, the authority from her years of police training automatically kicking in. "This is Detective Inspector Dawn Cummings, County Police, and I need you to buzz us in, immediately."

There was a slight pause, before the voice answered: "Just give me a moment – I don't know how this system works… I won't be long."

Inside the security office, Jeremy turned to his cousin, shaking. "What the hell are we going to do now? The police are outside."

"I told you not to answer that thing, didn't I?" replied Phil angrily.

"I'm sorry, I thought it was just kids playing around."

"Yeah well, it looks like you were wrong, doesn't it?"

Phil rubbed his head, thinking.

Now that Jeremy had given their position away, they were

trapped. If that really was the police outside, there would be questions they could not answer without landing themselves in it, and if they searched the office, which they were bound to, they would find the bag of drugs they had brought with them, and then it would really be all over for them.

"Phil," pleaded Jeremy, "what are we going to do?"

Phil held his hand up to stop his cousin's pleading. If he were being honest with himself, he felt responsible for landing them in this situation. He knew that Jeremy would do anything he asked, so dragging him along was all down to him.

How was he ever going to explain to Jeremy's parents that their son might end up in prison because of him?

The buzzer went off again.

Jeremy looked at the intercom microphone as if it were a bomb about to explode.

Sweat ran down his face, and he was shaking visibly.

"Calm down," Phil told him. "It's gonna be all right. You stay in here. I'm going out to speak to whoever's at the gate."

"But then they'll see you," cried Jeremy. "And once the police see your face…"

"We don't know that they are the police, do we? Maybe it's someone playing a practical joke. Either way, we can't leave them out there all night without some kind of explanation. If they are the police, that'll just make them more suspicious."

Jeremy considered his cousin's analysis and nodded his head.

As if to emphasise the urgency of the matter, the buzzer sounded once more.

"I'll be back as soon as I can," Phil assured Jeremy. "If Scrapper and that guard show up, tell them to wait here for me, okay?"

Jeremy nodded, unconvinced. He knew that he was the last person in the world that Scrapper would ever listen to, so he secretly hoped Phil would return first.

Phil made his way back towards the staff entrance.

Chapter 36

In the distance, he thought he heard something that sounded like glass breaking.

He considered heading in that general direction to see if he could locate Scrapper and that guard himself. But then he decided that whoever was outside, sitting on the buzzer, required more urgent attention.

When he reached the door, he noticed that it was not properly secured.

A sudden chill went through him.

Had someone broken in?

Were they lurking the in shadows, waiting for a chance to strike?

He shook it off. Being stuck in such a gloomy building in the early hours was enough to give anyone the willies.

Phil decided that the guard must have left the door ajar when he let those girls in.

He pushed it open, and straight away saw the reason why it had not closed properly.

Phil kicked the rubber stopper sticking up from the groove in the frame. It held fast. In a way he was glad, at least it would mean that the door could not swing shut and lock him out in the process.

As soon as he walked outside, Phil noticed the minibus parked next to the entrance.

Reading the logo on the side, he presumed it must have been what the girls arrived in.

For a second, he was sure he caught sight of a shadow moving inside, but he decided to ignore it. The two women waiting impatiently by the gate needed his immediate attention.

Phil strode over to the gate, trying to appear casual and in no way anxious.

He sized up the two women as he grew nearer.

Neither one particularly screamed copper to him, but then he knew that looks could be deceptive.

As he neared the gate, he smiled, broadly. "Hello," he said, cheerfully, "can I help you?"

Dawn stayed quiet and let Amina speak.

"My name is Doctor Amina Anmali, and I work at the museum as a guest of the curator, Mr Unwin." She held up her museum identification card. "Would you please open these gates and let us in."

Phil gave the card a cursory glance, then looked back up. "I'm really sorry," he said, apologetically. "But the night guard is still on patrol, and only he knows how to operate the controls."

"Can't you contact him on his radio?" asked Amina, impatiently.

Phil shrugged. "He left it in the office. I don't think he was expecting any visitors."

Dawn had heard enough.

She lifted her warrant card. "I'm DI Cummins," she stated, formally, "County Police, and I need you to open these gates immediately."

Phil looked physically sick.

So, she had not been lying before. Now things were becoming serious.

He held out his hands, for emphasis. "Officer, I'm telling you the truth," he said meekly, "my cousin and I are with a friend who knows the guard here. He's taken him on a tour of the museum, and neither my cousin nor I know how to operate the gates."

His excuse did have a ring of plausibility to it.

"Okay, listen, I believe you, millions wouldn't," said Dawn. "How about you try that security box and see if there's a lever or button in there?"

Phil turned and saw the guard's station.

He turned back and nodded, before making his way over to it.

Chapter 36

His mind was reeling. He knew that, either way, this was not going to end well.

If only Scrapper had not grabbed the van keys, he and Jeremy could at least make a break for it if he managed to open the gates. He no longer cared about his friend. Scrapper was acting far too irrationally for even Phil to cope with, so if this copper and the doctor caught him and the security bloke shagging those girls, that was their problem. He just wanted out.

But how was he going to achieve that without retrieving the keys first?

When Phil reached the security box, he grabbed the handle, and pulled.

The door was locked.

He tried several times just to emphasise the situation to the two women, who were watching him, intently through the wire grid of the gates.

"It's locked," he called back. "The guard must have the key."

Just then, a car came screeching around the corner, and pulled up outside the gates.

Dawn and Amina both turned around to see who had just arrived.

As Danielle and Pascale emerged from their car, Dawn decided she needed to assert her authority in order to find out what the latest arrivals wanted, fast.

She flashed her badge. "Good evening, ladies. May I ask what business you have here at this hour?"

Both women were clearly taken aback by the presence of a police officer.

Regardless of the circumstances, neither wanted to land the girls in trouble unnecessarily, so Danielle decided to try and explain things without going into too much detail.

"We're both teachers from Seddon Academy," she began, "and we believe that some of the upper sixth girls may have tried to come here tonight as a prank."

"Look, there," said Danielle, pointing to the mini-bus.

Dawn glanced over at the bus. "Is that them?" she asked.

"I believe so," replied Danielle. "I'm really sorry if they have caused any trouble, but I'm sure we can straighten everything out without any fuss," she offered hopefully.

Dawn looked back at Phil. "What do you know about this?" she asked sternly.

Phil tried to think up a feasible story, but then decided to go with the truth.

He did not want to dig them in any deeper.

"The guard told us some girls had arrived to search for a necklace, or ring, or something, that one of them lost in the museum earlier. Our friend went with him, I haven't seen them since."

"How long ago was that?" asked Danielle, anxiously.

Phil shrugged. "About ten minutes or so, maybe a bit longer."

"So why did you tell me he was on patrol?" demanded Dawn.

Phil shook his head. "I'm sorry," he said, dejectedly. "I just didn't want to get anyone in trouble. My cousin and I were only giving our friend a lift, we didn't realise things would end up like this."

"I need you to open this gate, right away," insisted Danielle. "I need to take the girls back to the academy now."

Before Phil had a chance to reply, there came a scream from behind him.

He spun round in time to see Colleen, Carrie Anne and Geraldine, emerge from the building, holding on to each other in an effort to keep themselves upright.

"Girls," screamed Pascale at the top of her voice. "Come here this instant!"

The three girls either did not hear their teacher or were just too focused on their task to bother responding.

Chapter 36

They ran straight for the mini-bus and disappeared inside.

All those gathered at the gate could see shadows moving around inside the minibus, and there was distinct shouting and screaming coming from within.

"What's going on?" demanded Danielle. She pointed her finger at Phil. "If you, or one of your friends, has done anything to harm those girls…"

Phil held his hands out, again. "No, listen, this is the first time I've actually seen them. I was in the security office when they arrived – it's nothing to do with me."

"Then why are they screaming and running for their lives?" shouted Pascale.

"I don't know," insisted Phil.

Dawn held up her hands. "All right, all right," she called. She looked at Phil. "You, get back inside, find that security guard, and get these fucking gates open. I'm starting to lose my patience here."

"Okay, okay," Phil assured her. "I'm going in right now and I'll find him, wherever he is. Just remember, I did try to open them myself – it's not my fault the guard's door was locked."

Phil turned away and began walking back towards the museum.

"And please tell the girls on the bus to come out here, immediately," called Danielle.

Phil raised his hand in acknowledgement without turning back.

He was halfway towards the bus when the mummy of Anlet-Un-Ri appeared at the staff entrance.

Chapter Thirty-Seven

"What the hell was that?" asked Lesley, looking over at Joanie who was standing at a glass cabinet, a couple of feet away.

"I don't know," replied Joanie, glancing over towards the balcony. "It sounded like glass shattering."

Joanie walked over to stand next to her friend. Suddenly, she did not feel safe on her own.

"Let's go and find out," suggested Lesley, tugging at Joanie's sleeve.

"What! Are you mad? You want us to go down there, alone?"

Lesley rolled her eyes. "No, dummy, I mean let's go and look over the balcony and see if we can work out what that noise was."

Joanie felt foolish. "Oh, okay then."

The pair made their way towards the balcony ledge and leaned against the polished brass railing to see over.

The majority of the space below was obscured by the tops of the various display cases that were dotted around the museum. There was no initial evidence to show what might have caused the crash they had both heard, but that hardly surprised either of them, considering the layout of the displays.

They stayed there for a couple of moments.

"Oh, well," said Lesley, "whatever it was, we can't see anything from here. Might as well get back to the job at hand."

"This place really gives me the creeps," Joanie admitted. "I can't wait for this stupid thing to be over."

Just then, they heard a scream.

It came from somewhere below, echoing up from one of the ground-floor galleries.

The two girls stared at each other in shock.

"What the hell was that?" asked Lesley rhetorically. "It sounded like a scream."

"It must be one of the girls who came in before us. What if they're in trouble?"

"Serves them right for making us do this."

Joanie glared at her friend. "You don't mean that, surely."

"I suppose not," Lesley replied dejectedly.

From behind they heard a scuffle of feet on the carpet. They both turned to see the rest of the ducklings approaching from various angles across the floor.

The girls crowded around them.

Greta was the first to speak. "What the hell was that? It sounded like a scream from over there."

The others nodded their agreement.

"That's what we thought," said Joanie, "but you can't see anything from up here – the cabinets are in the way."

The rest of the girls huddled around, leaning against the railing.

They scanned the floor below.

Seconds later, they heard another scream, only this time it came from more than just one person.

The girls looked at each other for guidance.

"Do you think it could be Geraldine and the others?" enquired Janice.

"That's what we were thinking," replied Lesley, looking at Joanie for confirmation.

"What're we going to do?" asked Suzi, sounding desperate. "They sound as if they're in trouble."

The next scream sounded much closer, and the girls returned to scouring what they could see of the floor below.

Within seconds, Geraldine, Carrie Anne and Colleen all emerged from behind a partition, frantically running between the cabinets, while simultaneously appearing to be attempting to hold each other up.

They skidded across the polished floor, half-tripping in their haste to make it back to the staff entrance.

"Hey, girls." Suzi called out. "We're up here." But her call was lost on them.

As the three swans disappeared from view, Janice grabbed Suzi's hand to attract her attention. "I think we need to get out of here," she urged. "Something must be up for them to be acting like that. And whatever it is, it has got to be more serious than this stupid initiation gig."

Her friend did not need convincing.

Suzi nodded. "Come on girls, I think we've overstayed our welcome."

They all turned to leave as one.

As they did so, they heard Rose cry out: "Oh my God, what the hell is that?"

The girls crowded back to the railing to see what their friend might be talking about.

At that moment, they all witnessed Anlet-Un-Ri striding through the room the three swans had vacated moments before. Instead of weaving her way through the display cabinets, the mummy simply shoved them out of her way, sending them crashing to the ground.

Chapter 37

Joanie and Lesley looked at each other, both suddenly realising what that earlier sound, which first drew their attention to the lower floor, must have been.

Some of the girls covered their mouths to prevent themselves from screaming. As terrified as they were at the sight of the mummy, it did not seem prudent to draw attention to the fact that they were all only a few feet above it.

They all watched in silence as the mummy moved through to the next partition, and finally out of their line of vision.

Their stunned silence continued for a while after the mummy disappeared.

Finally, Greta remarked. "Please someone tell me this is just some stupid Hallowe'en prank, that was just someone in costume, right?"

"It's too early for Halloween," Rose responded absentmindedly.

"Even so," Greta continued, "please don't tell me that was supposed to be a real Egyptian mummy come to life, or I might just throw myself off this balcony and end it all."

Suzi took in a deep breath. "I've no idea what we just saw, but whatever it was, the girls were mighty afraid of it, and I think it would be prudent for us to be, too."

"I want out of this place, now," said Joanne, her voice trembling.

"Good call," offered Suzi. "I suggest that we go the other way and look for a fire escape, I really cannot see the fun in making our way back downstairs towards that thing, whatever it is."

The others mumbled their agreement, and together they all moved off towards the far side of the balcony.

"What in the name of all that is holy are we looking at?" asked Pascale, staring across the museum car park at the huge mummy that was blocking the staff entrance.

Amina shot Dawn a look, as if to try and convey to her that they needed to act immediately.

The question was, what could they do? Especially as they were stuck outside the gates.

"Hey," Dawn called out to Phil, signalling for him to make his way back to the gate.

Phil complied, walking backwards so that he could keep his eyes on the mummy, in case it made a sudden dash towards him.

When he was close enough, Dawn said. "You said you had a friend in there, yes?"

Phil half turned and nodded.

"Can you call him, and ask him if he can find a way to get this gate open?"

Phil took out his phone, mechanically. He scrolled through his contacts and hit Scrapper's number. He waited while the phone connected, then heard it ringing on the other side.

He waited until he could hear loud R&B coming through his speaker, followed closely by Scrapper's message.

He glanced back towards Dawn.

Then he remembered Jeremy. He called him and waited with bated breath for him to reply. Seeing the huge mummy blocking the doorway, Phil could not help but wonder if it had already crashed its way through the museum, destroying the security office on route.

"Yeah, where are you? What's going on?" Jeremy's voice demanded.

Phil heaved a sigh of relief. "Listen to me, and listen good," he began, the urgency in his voice conveying the fact that there was no time to waste. "There's something weird going on here, and I need you to figure out how to operate these gates from that office – there must be a control panel or something."

"I can't see anything," admitted Jeremy. "What happened with the police, are they still there? Why don't you come back in and we can look for the panel together?"

"There isn't time, Jeremy. Just do what I ask and look for yourself."

After a moment, he came back. "There's nothing obvious, but what do you mean there's something strange going on? I thought I heard a scream earlier. Do you think Scrapper and that guard are hurting those girls? Maybe we should go and investigate."

"No!" yelled Phil. "Don't come out. I need you to find that control and open these gates before it's too late."

"Oh my God!" It was Danielle who cried out.

Phil turned to her, then followed her gaze back towards the staff entrance.

The mummy had begun to walk towards the minibus.

"The girls, the girls," Danielle shouted, looking at Phil, "you must get them out of there."

"Jeremy, find that fucking release button, now!" Phil disconnected the call without waiting for his cousin to reply.

The four women had started hammering on the metal gates, screaming for the girls to get off the bus before it was too late.

Phil realised he was their only hope. But what could he do?

That mummy, or whatever it was, looked enormous, and how the hell do you fight off one of those things, anyway?

The mummy had now reached the bus and was hammering on the locked door.

There was the sound of shattering glass as the mummy thrust its massive hand through one of the bus's windows.

They could hear the screams coming from the girls inside.

Phil scoured the area around him. Off to one side, next to

the security box, lay a pile of junk that looked as if it had been discarded by the workmen when they fitted the gate.

Phil picked up a length of metal tubing about two feet long. Under normal circumstances it would make a perfect weapon. But his adversary made the situation anything but normal.

He held the pipe tightly in his hands and began running towards the bus. He hoped that the momentum behind his strike might help to tip the balance in his favour.

The mummy again shot its hand through the glass in the door, so now it was able to grab hold of the metal frame, which it used to tear the door off its hinges.

As the mummy turned to discard the frame of mangled metal and broken glass, Phil struck home with his makeshift weapon, smashing it across the mummy's broad back.

The blow hardly registered with the mummy, although Phil felt the vibration of it shudder through his hands, almost making him drop his weapon.

Anlet-Un-Ri turned slowly and stared down at Phil.

Phil could feel his legs wanting to give way underneath him, but he managed to stand his ground and held the metal tube up for another go.

The mummy did not move.

It was almost as if it were challenging Phil to try another strike.

Inside the bus, the girls' screaming was reaching fever pitch, and he knew that he was the only thing that stood between them and the mummy.

Phil had never seen himself as the hero type. In fact, he had always dreamed of a quiet life with a steady job, a flat and a girlfriend. But if the rest of his life was to be determined by this moment, he knew exactly what he had to do.

Raising his weapon above his head, he screamed out from the pit of his stomach, as he launched himself at the mummy.

With a speed that belied her size, Anlet-Un-Ri grabbed the

Chapter 37

steel tubing on its downward journey, and clamped an enormous hand around it, before wrenching it free from Phil's grasp and throwing it across the car park.

Before he had time to react, the mummy grabbed Phil by the throat, and lifted him off the floor, shaking him until his body went limp, and then throwing him to one side, out of the way.

Phil hit the concrete hard and rolled over a couple of times before hitting the museum wall and lolling against it.

The four women at the gate looked on in horror at the speed with which the mummy had dispatched their one hope for the girls trapped on the bus.

The mummy turned its attention back to the open doorway of the bus and ducked its head under the roof to allow it entry.

Chapter Thirty-Eight

THE DUCKLINGS MADE THEIR WAY CAUTIOUSLY ALONG the carpeted upper floor until they could go no further. At the end of the passageway, they saw a sign that announced the way to the nearest fire exit.

Relieved, they pushed through the swing doors, and found themselves in a high corridor that led to their right.

Greta and Suzi led the way along the passage that stretched around a corner, out of sight. From the grumbling voices behind, they knew that some of the girls were not happy with their surroundings, but what other option did they have?

At the end of the corridor, they turned left, following the sign, and found themselves at the top of a flight of stairs.

The lighting in this part of the passage was particularly dim, so Greta and Suzi exchanged a glance for a second, before silently agreeing to venture on.

With the structure of the balcony lying horizontally across their eyeline, from this angle it was impossible to tell what awaited them down below. So, halfway down, Suzi crouched down as low as she could, until she could see what lay ahead.

The bottom of the stairs opened on to another passage but,

Chapter 38

from her vantage point, Suzi could see the fire-exit doors at the far end.

She stood up and turned back. "It's okay, girls – the fire exit is at the end of the next corridor."

A cheer went up, which Greta shushed. They were still far from being out of the woods, as far as she was concerned.

They made their way towards the fire exit together.

Unable to wait, Joanie rushed forward and hit the release bars hard.

The two doors swung open, then stopped a few inches out.

A large thick-linked metal chain held the two release bars together, with a stout padlock securing the ends.

Unable to process the situation, Joanie continued pushing against the bars, as if by doing so, she would somehow, miraculously, be able to break the chain.

The others, realising immediately that their friend was losing control, tried to comfort her as best they could with kind words and soothing gestures.

Eventually, Joanie ceased her onslaught and pressed her back against the doors, before slumping to the floor. She placed her face between her bended knees and clasped her hands over the back of her head. They could hear her sobbing.

Lesley and Rose moved in on either side, and sat down beside her, placing their arms across her shaking shoulders.

"Shouldn't this thing be open by law?" asked Joanne, exasperated. "We should report them to the police, or at least the council. This isn't on."

"I doubt they keep it locked during opening hours," replied Janice, "but they probably weren't expecting anybody to be dumb enough to break in overnight."

They all waited together in the semi-darkness.

It seemed to have been a long journey from where they first saw the mummy to where they were now, and the thought of having to retrace their steps did not appeal to any of them at that moment.

Eventually, it was Greta who found the courage to say what they were all thinking.

"Well, we're certainly not going to get out this way. And I don't know about the rest of you, but I don't fancy being blocked in this tiny corridor if that thing decides to come looking for us."

She noticed a shudder pass through some of the girls at the mere mention of the mummy.

"I can't go back out there," Joanie protested, shuddering and pressing her knees together tightly.

"Of course you can," insisted Joanne. "We're stuck in this together, and we need each other to get through."

"Damn straight," agreed Suzi. "We leave no man behind – whatever's out there, we face it together."

"She's right," said Janice "Whatever we saw, we need to get back up on the upper floor. At least there are places to hide up there. And if we can find another way out, even better."

Joanie dried her eyes on her sleeves. "But what if we can't find another way out?"

Janice held out her arms in front of her to encourage Joanie to stand up. "Then who knows? Maybe that thing has already left the building and is halfway down the street by now. Either way, we don't want to end up trapped down here, so come on, let's get moving."

Encouraged by her friend's words, Joanie stood up with help from Rose and Lesley.

Greta waited until everyone was ready, then she said, "Forward, troops," and started back towards the stairs.

When they reached the upper floor of the museum again, Suzi ushered everyone back, and edged forward to see through the door, just to make sure there was no ugly surprise waiting for them on the other side.

Chapter 38

Once she was satisfied the going was clear, she looked back and mouthed the words, then she led them back on to the floor.

The girls all poured out through the door and gathered in a group on the upper level.

They waited for a moment, hoping that inspiration would strike one of them. But, in the end, Greta merely shrugged her shoulders and announced that they should start moving back towards the staircase they used initially to gain access to this level.

They moved silently across the floor, being careful to avoid bumping into any of the display cases or cabinets along the way.

As they approached the top of the stairs, Janice and Greta volunteered to head down first, to ensure that the way was clear.

Some of the girls objected to them risking it alone, but they insisted.

The two girls crept down the stairs, listening intently for any sound that might indicate the presence of the mummy. Each held on to the bannister rail nearest her and neither said anything as they made their descent, to help them to concentrate.

As they neared the bottom, the area before them was open-plan, which allowed them to see that no one was hiding, waiting to pounce on them.

To their left, they could see the security office. The door was closed but the light inside was on.

The two girls looked at each other. "Should we go and see if that security guard is in there?" whispered Janice. "You know, the big one who let the others in."

Greta shook her head. "I think the quicker we get out of here the better. And now I come to think of it, what if that was him dressed up in costume that we saw chasing the girls out."

Janice looked sceptical. "Do you think?"

Greta shrugged. "We only saw it from above. The angle might have deceived us."

Janice thought for a moment.

She supposed there was some merit in Greta's explanation. After all, it made more sense than a live mummy rampaging through the museum.

At the far end of the area they were standing in, they could see the staff door.

It still seemed to be open, which was a relief after the fire exit.

They were still too far away to hear the commotion taking place outside.

"Should we go back and call the others before we go any further?" asked Janice.

Just then, the security office door burst open, and a man came rushing out, stopping directly in front of them. He seemed to have a long-barrelled torch which he was holding above his head like a weapon.

Greta reacted without thinking. She spun around in an arc and landed her clenched fist right in the middle of Jeremy's nose.

They both yelled, "Ow!" simultaneously.

Jeremy dropped his torch, and the lens front shattered on the hard floor.

Greta stepped back, rubbing her fist with her free hand.

Joanne grabbed the torch from the floor and held it like a weapon.

"Who are you?" she demanded.

Jeremy, still holding his nose with both hands, whimpered: "Jeremy. Why did you hit me?"

"Well, what do you expect when you come charging out at innocent girls like that."

Jeremy removed his hands for a moment, and both girls could see blood smeared all over his face. He looked at his hands and saw the mess, before reaching in his pocket and pulling out a wad of tissues, which he pressed against his nose.

"I think you broke my nose," he mumbled, looking at Greta reproachfully.

She shook her hand to help ease the pain. "Sorry," she said, "you scared me. Who are you? One of the security team?"

Jeremy looked on, dejectedly.

For a moment the girls thought he was not going to answer.

Then he shook his head. "No, I'm just here with my cousin. We dropped in with a friend, but something weird is going on here."

"How do you mean weird?" asked Janice, glancing nervously at her companion.

Jeremy examined his tissues, then, seeing the amount of blood on them, shuffled some of the cleaner ones to the front, and placed them back on his nose.

He looked up. "I don't know," he replied. "Just weird. I mean, my cousin went out ages ago to speak to some coppers at the front gates, but he hasn't come back yet. And then he phoned me and yelled at me to find a way to open the gates, but I can't find the controls in there, and now he's not answering his phone."

"Did you say the police were outside?" asked Greta, excitedly.

Jeremy nodded. "Yeah, there was some policewoman shouting down the intercom at me, and I think she had a doctor with her."

Greta grabbed Janice by the arm. "We're saved. You stay here with the walking wounded, I'm going back for the others."

Janice nodded, nervously, but before she had a chance to object, Greta was sprinting back for the stairs.

The four women locked outside the gates could see the minibus starting to rock from side to side as the mummy squeezed its gigantic frame inside.

Pascale put her hands to her mouth to supress a scream. She desperately wanted to look away, but somehow felt it was her responsibility to watch her girls.

Danielle stood back and looked up at the gates. She saw the curled spikes of metal along the top, specifically designed to keep intruders out.

Even from down here, she could tell how sharp they must be.

On either side of the gates, the solid brick walls stood a good couple of feet higher than the metal spikes, but there did not appear to be anything protruding from them.

At least, not that she could see.

The wall was impossible to climb unaided, and there was certainly no time to drive back to the academy to retrieve a ladder or a climbing rope.

Danielle turned back to study the gates.

Although the way at the top was barred, the actual gates themselves were constructed from a mass of grids, with holes just big enough to allow her fingers through.

It would be risky, but what other choice did she have?

Without saying anything, Danielle took a few steps back, and made a run for the gate, leaping as high as she could to secure an initial hold.

Her body thudded against the metal, sending vibrations through her body, but she managed to wrap her fingers through the metal grid, and push with the soles of her trainers hard enough to gain purchase.

She stayed like that for a moment, bracing herself for the climb.

"Oh, my God," called Pascale, stunned by her colleague's agility. "Please be careful – it is a long way down."

Chapter 38

Dawn looked up at the teacher hanging off the gate.

She was as strong and fit now as she ever had been in her career, but even she knew her limitations, and this was definitely something out of her league.

All the same, as the only police officer on the scene, she felt as if she should be doing something other than just looking on.

She pulled out her phone.

Amina saw what she was doing and put her hand on Dawn's arm. "What are you going to do?" she asked, staring into Dawn's eyes.

"I'm calling dispatch for back-up. Whatever that thing is over there, we aren't going to be able to take it down alone."

"Please don't," Amina pleaded. "They cannot help, and it will only make things worse."

Dawn starred at her. "So what do you suggest?"

Amina squeezed her arm. "If I can get inside, I think I may have something that can stop the mummy and send it back to where it came from."

Dawn looked up at Danielle. She was making progress but it was slow going, from what she could see.

Dawn turned back to Amina. "And just how do you intend to get inside? Because, unless you can do that," she pointed at Danielle, "there doesn't appear to be any other way in."

Amina glanced up. "I am hoping that once our friend here gets over the gate, she will be resourceful enough to find a way of opening these gates."

She could see that Dawn was not convinced, but she smiled at her when she slipped her mobile back in her pocket.

Dawn looked back out over the carpark.

The mummy had now managed to climb inside the bus.

It would only be seconds now before it reached the girls.

She had never felt so useless in all her life.

Inside the bus, the girls were all cowering at the back, as the mummy struggled to manoeuvre itself through the rows of seats.

Cynthia had the girls behind her, and was holding her arms out to her sides, as if to protect them. She had no idea what was going on, but she felt responsible nonetheless for insisting they all came on this merry jaunt.

Behind her, she could hear some of the girls whimpering as they huddled into the smallest space they could manage.

Some prayed, others cried but, at least thus far, none of them had passed out.

Cynthia stared into the dead, black eyes of their approaching assailant. She had already seen how easily it had dispatched the bloke outside who tried to defend them with a piece of metal. So she knew they had little hope of survival if it caught up to them.

Their one saving grace at the moment was that the bus was way too small for the colossal size of the mummy.

But metal seat frames were no barrier for Anlet-Un-Ri.

The mummy, frustrated by her lack of progress, gripped hold of the top of the nearest seat, and pulled it clean away from its base.

Fortunately, this still left the bottom half of the frame fixed to the floor, so her progress was still hampered for the moment.

Bending down as far as the bus would allow, the mummy gripped the seat from underneath, and pulled back until the steel frame gave way. She threw the twisted hunk of metal behind her towards the front of the bus.

This allowed the mummy to move forward at least a couple of inches, and Cynthia could tell by its demeanour that it was satisfied with its progress, now that it had figured out how to eliminate such obstructions.

In panic, Cynthia began looking around the bus for some form of weapon, but there was nothing to hand. The bag racks above their heads were constructed of long metal poles, which might make excellent spears. But she knew that she would need strength equal to that of the mummy to remove one from its mounts.

She turned around and looked at the other girls.

Colleen, Carrie-Anne and Geraldine looked to be still recovering from their ordeal inside the museum. Jacinda, Josephine, Sarah and Connie did not look as if they had any fight left in them, either.

Cynthia called over to Connie, who was the nearest to the emergency exit.

"Connie, please try the emergency exit – it's our only hope," she pleaded with her.

"It's jammed – we've tried it already," the girl spoke through her tears.

"I know, I know," replied Cynthia, desperately trying to keep calm. "But just have another go. You never know, you might suddenly release the door and save us all."

Connie struggled round to face backwards, and Cynthia watched the girl take a firm hold on the release lever.

She pulled it with all she had to offer, but it would not give.

"Come on, girls," Cynthia intervened, "give her a hand, team effort, chop, chop."

She watched as Josephine and Sarah, the two closest to her, turned their attention to the emergency exit and also took hold of the lever, heaving with all their might together.

It still would not budge.

Meanwhile, the mummy was busy dismantling another seat to get closer to them.

Cynthia looked at the windows. This was an air-conditioned bus, so the windows did not open, but if they had something solid enough, then perhaps they could shatter the glass, and possibly climb out.

Even if they managed to let only one girl escape, there was a possibility she could open the back door from outside. Surely there must be a release handle or something.

At least it would be worth a try, but once again they were hampered by not having anything they could use as a weapon.

The three girls at the back continued to struggle with the emergency door, but it all appeared to be in vain.

With their focus on their companions, none of the girls in the van noticed their PE teacher reaching the top of the security gates.

Danielle was on the last handhold before she reached the coiled spikes waiting to rip her flesh at the top.

She paused for a moment to catch her breath.

She was proud of herself for making it this far, and she could not afford to blow her progress by mistiming her final assault.

The nearest wall to which the gates were fixed was only a few feet to her left.

She eased her way along the gate, keeping her balance by digging in her rubber soles. Her hands felt like sandpaper, but that was the least of her worries for now. She had to make it over the wall and somehow find a way to open the gate before the mummy reached the girls.

Once she was close enough, Danielle reached over with her left hand, and gripped the edge of the wall. She held her breath, and released the gate with the other hand, using the momentum of her body to bring her closer to the wall. She grabbed hold of the edge of the capping and held on tight as her legs slid away from the gate.

Once she had a firm hold with both hands, Danielle hoisted herself up and swung her right leg over the wall, using the action to boost the rest of her body up.

She sat straddling the wall and looked down at the other three women, giving them a thumbs-up.

Danielle glanced over towards the bus, and she could see from her vantage point that the mummy had already broken in.

Leaning over, she grabbed the top of the wall with both hands and lifted her other leg over. Lowering herself down as far

Chapter 38

as she could, Danielle dangled from the edge of the wall. She estimated the drop to be about sixteen feet, straight on to hard concrete.

Pushing herself away from the wall, Danielle dropped to the ground.

She bent her legs to help cushion the landing and finished with a forward roll.

Chapter Thirty-Nine

Suzi was the first of the ducklings to poke her head through the open doorway. The other girls were huddled behind her, with Jeremy bringing up the rear.

Some of the girls had still been reluctant to venture outside, but the option of remaining inside the museum, possibly for what was left of the night, also did not appeal. So, on balance, they all decided it would be best to stick together and leave.

The sight that met Suzi's eyes when she focused on the dimly lit car park was enough to make her stop dead in her tracks.

She could see the mangled remains of the minibus's door discarded on the ground, next to the prone body of a man. The man was not moving and the thought that he might actually be dead caused a ripple of disquiet to flow through her body.

Off in the distance, she heard the sound of metal being crashed against metal.

Suzi strained to see and realised it was their PE teacher, Miss Parker.

The teacher was hammering against the door of the security

cubicle with what appeared, from this distance, to be a metal pole.

Before she had a chance to switch her gaze towards the bus, to see what was taking place in there, some of the other girls behind her began to push forward, eager to see what was happening outside.

Suzi moved to allow them to join her.

Lesley was the first to scream when she saw what was taking place inside the damaged bus.

Her scream alerted the rest of the ducklings to the fate of their fellow students, trapped inside the vehicle with the mummy gaining ground by the second.

Suddenly, Janice broke free from the crowd, and ran towards the bus. Before anyone could stop her, she hopped up the stairs that led to the driver's compartment and yanked hard on the release lever that controlled the emergency exit door.

It took her several attempts to force the lever to move but finally she managed it and, before they realised what was going on, the back door of the bus flew open, and several of the swans spilled out on to the asphalt.

Cynthia, who was still the furthest back from the door, heard the commotion behind her, and turned to see that the door was finally open.

She looked back for a spilt second, just as Anlet-Un-Ri ripped out the last seat-casing that stood between them.

The mummy lunged for the petrified girl, but Cynthia allowed herself to fall backwards, out of reach. She scooted back along the ground as the frustrated creature grabbed hold of thin air, and just managed to shimmy backwards and out of reach before the mummy attempted another grab for her.

Once more Anlet-Un-Ri found herself caught between another row of seats as she watched her precious prize being helped out through the back door by some of the other girls.

The mummy released a wail of anger and frustration that

echoed through the car park and sounded to those within earshot like nothing on earth.

Cynthia and the rest of the swans gathered themselves together, still unable to fathom how they had managed to open the back door in the nick of time.

Meanwhile, Janice jumped from the bus and re-joined her fellow ducklings.

"Oh, my God," shrieked Joanie, "how did you know to do that?"

Janice shrugged. "I've watched old Franks do it loads of times."

"You could have been killed," Lesley yelled.

"Well, someone had to do something," Janice reasoned.

"Now what?" asked Greta, staring directly at the bus. "That thing looks pretty pissed off."

"You're not wrong there," agreed Rose. "I say we follow the others." She pointed towards the older girls who were now running towards the main gates, where Danielle was still attempting, unsuccessfully, to gain access to the security booth.

As Jeremy squeezed through the girls to see what was happening, he saw the man lying on his front up against the side wall, and immediately recognised him as his cousin.

"Phil," he called out, pushing past the others and running over to see to him.

Jeremy knelt down beside Phil, and tentatively reached out a hand to grab the top of his shoulder.

He shook him. First gently, then, when he received no response, more violently.

Phil stirred and moaned softly. But at least, to Jeremy's relief, he was still alive.

"Come on, mate, we've got to get you out of here, now," Jeremy insisted.

He tried to pull his cousin towards him, but he was too heavy, and did not appear to be able to assist in his own rescue.

"Come on, Phil, for goodness' sake, you have to help me." But Phil was still too groggy to respond and, when Jeremy let go, he slumped back against the wall.

Jeremy heard approaching feet behind him.

He turned to see Greta, Janice and Suzi looking down on him.

"I can't get him up," Jeremy explained.

"Are you sure he's still alive?" Suzi enquired hesitantly.

"I heard him moan when I tried to move him," Jeremy said. "He has to be alive."

They heard another thunderous roar that froze them all in their tracks.

Turning, they saw to their horror that Anlet-Un-Ri had managed to break free from what was left of the mini-bus.

The mummy stood outside the open emergency door, with its arms held out towards the girls, as if offering to hug them. But all those gathered knew instantly that, if they were the ones caught within such an embrace, their lives would be over.

The swans had, by now, reached the metal gates, and some of them were hammering against them with their fists, screaming and crying to be let out.

The three women outside the gates looked on helplessly, while doing their best to calm the girls down.

"Well, we're not going to make our escape through them in a hurry," Janice observed, pointing towards the melee taking place at the far end of the car park.

"There must be some way of opening them," suggested Greta.

"Perhaps they are on a timer," offered Suzi. Then she thought about what she had just said. "Mind you, that wouldn't make much sense if there was a fire, or something. How would the brigade get in?"

Janice spun around and grabbed her friend's arm. "Brilliant," she announced, excitedly. "We can set off a fire alarm, even if the gates don't open automatically, the fire brigade must be able to smash their way in."

"There's a release button in the security office."

They all looked down at Jeremy, who had made the sudden announcement.

He was still trying to revive his cousin, without making much progress.

The three girls exchanged curious glances.

"Are you sure?" Suzi, asked.

Jeremy nodded.

Suzi squatted down beside him. "Can you show us where it is?"

Jeremy looked back. His cheeks had turned red. "I don't know exactly, but when we arrived, the guard on duty opened and closed them from inside somehow. And when your friends first arrived, he said that he had locked us all in, so he must have been able to control them from inside his office."

Jeremy did not sound as positive as the girls had hoped he would.

But it made perfect sense that the controls would be housed inside the security office.

Suzi patted Jeremy on the back and stood back up.

She turned to the others. "Well, it's worth a try, what do you think?"

Greta and Janice, were in agreement.

"What about them?" Greta mouthed, pointing down at the two men.

Janice squatted down and urged Jeremy to help her lift Phil off the floor.

Between the four of them, they managed to lift him and carry him back to the entrance. Once there, they told their friends who were all still crowded just inside the doorway their plan.

No one wanted to stay any longer than was absolutely

necessary. But, by the same token, they realised there was no point in their heading towards the locked gates.

Especially as that appeared to be where the mummy was heading right now.

Back at the gates, Danielle reluctantly gave up in trying to break into the security box.

Her hands throbbed from the vibrations that ran through the steel tube each time she smashed it against the door handle.

The handle was looking the worse for wear from the occasions when she was on target, but it still refused to yield.

Her initial idea when she climbed the fence was to try and help the girls on the bus to break out. But, now that they had, without her assistance, they were still left with the problem of how to escape.

Even Danielle would have been hard pushed to climb back over the wall. But there was no way she could help the girls over, and equally no way she could leave them behind, so she was out of options.

She turned back to check on the mummy's progress.

Fortunately, the creature shuffled unsteadily, but it was still gaining ground and heading straight for them.

"Miss, what are we going to do?" It was Connie Cole who cried out as she left the rest of the pack and ran over to Danielle.

The girl had twin streams running down her cheeks, and Daniele could see from this distance that her sports top was already wet where they had been falling.

Danielle reached out and hugged the girl with one arm, her other hand still holding the steel pipe. "It'll be okay," she assured her unconvincingly.

She looked over at the three women outside pleadingly.

Amina waved at her frantically, from outside, signalling for her to come over.

Danielle let go of Connie and trotted over.

"There's another entrance at the front of the museum," Amina shouted, trying to make herself heard above the cacophony of screams and cries coming from the swans.

Danielle held her hand up against her ear, as if to show that she was finding it difficult to hear over the noise.

"Did you say another entrance?"

Amina nodded. "Yes, it's probably locked as well, but it's somewhere else to run to, to get away from the mummy. Perhaps the gate there is easier to scale."

It was a thought and right now Danielle was all out of ideas of her own.

She turned back.

The mummy was no more than twenty feet away and closing in.

Daniele took in a deep breath and yelled at the top of her lungs: "Now listen to me, there's another entrance at the front of this building. So, when I give the word, I want half of you to go left, the others to go right, and get around the mummy. Then head for the front entrance and I'll join you there. Got it?"

Cynthia and Jacinda nodded their understanding, and quickly tried to divide their friends into two groups. It took some pulling and shaking, and Jacinda even had to slap Josephine around the face to bring her back to earth, but eventually they achieved their goal.

Once they appeared ready, Danielle spun back around.

The mummy drew closer.

"On three," ordered Danielle. "One… Two… Three, go!" With that, she held the heavy metal tube over her head with both hands and hurled it straight at the approaching mummy.

The pipe flew through the air, turning over and over, until it crashed straight into the mummy's chest.

The impact had about as much effect as a ping-pong-ball, and it clattered to the ground, barely halting the mummy's progress for a split second.

But the girls were off and running, most screaming as they went.

Anlet-Un-Ri turned from one side to the other as the girls made their way passed, too far out of reach for the mummy's shambling posture .

"The gate," Amina called out from behind, "we need to open the gate."

Danielle held her hand up to acknowledge the doctor's words, but she kept her focus firmly on the mummy, taking her moment to dash around it, following the swans.

Off to her left, she noticed Sarah slip.

Danielle swerved to try and prevent the girl from falling, but she was too late, and Sarah slammed down on the asphalt with a sickening thud.

Colleen, who had also noticed her comrade fall, stopped to help her.

"Keep going," Danielle screamed. "I'll get her."

She bent over and grabbed the girl under her armpits, hoisting her to her feet.

"Are you okay?" she asked, concerned.

Sarah nodded. "I think so – grazed my knee, that's all."

Danielle slapped her rump. "Go, keep moving," she ordered.

Sarah continued on her way.

Danielle checked behind her. The mummy it appeared, had no interest in those outside the compound. Instead, it had turned back, and was now shuffling back towards the museum.

Danielle ran back to the staff entrance.

She looked along the side of the building and saw the last of the swans disappear around the corner.

At least they had a good head start. She just hoped it would be enough.

Danielle was positive she had seen some of the ducklings huddled around the entrance earlier but, from her angle at the security hut, it was not possible to tell who exactly it had been.

Now they were nowhere to be seen, so she suspected they had gone back into the building.

She was torn between trying to protect both sets of girls. But she reasoned that at least the older girls were outside and, she hoped, even now discovering another way out of the grounds.

But, if the younger girls were still inside, their danger was more imminent.

Danielle checked over her shoulder.

The mummy had once more reached the wreckage that had once been the school minibus and seemed to be heading her way.

She stepped back inside the entrance and pulled the door closed.

Something was not right. The door would not lock.

Danielle reopened them and checked all around the inside of the framework. There was no obvious sign of what might be causing the door to malfunction.

She slammed them shut again.

Still they refused to lock into place.

Throwing them open, once more, Danielle could see that the mummy appeared to be inspecting the remains of the bus, almost as if it suspected that someone was hiding inside.

Danielle was positive that none of the girls had jumped back in. Why would they?

Unless one of the ducklings had dodged in, after the mummy had fought its way out of the vehicle.

A cold feeling sank down to the pit of her stomach. If one of the younger girls happened to be inside, she needed to warn them.

She looked on helplessly, while the mummy surveyed the metal shell.

Lowering herself to the floor, Danielle slid her fingers along the inside of the door frame. Her fingers suddenly struck what appeared to be a rubber wedge.

Chapter 39

The sound of glass splintering made her look up.

Anlet-Un-Ri had shoved a mighty fist through the nearest piece of glass left intact on the bus, and followed up by grabbing the inside of the frame with both hands and shaking the vehicle with such force that it rocked back and forth on its wheels.

Keeping half an eye on the bus, just in case one of the girls should appear, Danielle used her fingers to try to prise the rubber stopper free, but to no avail.

She sat up and slapped her hands against her pockets, until she could feel her car keys inside. Retrieving them, Danielle used the metal edge to lift out the stopper, just far enough so she could grab hold of it, before yanking it free.

The mummy was still fully engaged in its work.

Danielle watched for long enough to convince herself that the creature merely wished to destroy their vehicle in case they attempted to use it to escape.

So long as none of her girls were trapped inside, she did not really care what the mummy did to the bus.

She closed the door and heaved a sigh of relief when she heard the satisfying sound of the locks engaging.

Chapter Forty

Dawn, Amina and Pascale watched from behind the metal grate as Anlet-Un-Ri ripped the side panel from the mini-bus and discarded it over to one side. The huge chunk of metal rolled and scraped along the tarmac, before finally coming to rest, near to where Phil had been lying until moments earlier.

Apparently still unsatisfied, the mummy continued to go to work on the vehicle by grabbing the underside and lifting what was left of the shell off the ground on one side, then over completely.

The remaining glass in the widows shattered on impact with the ground.

It was only then that the mummy turned its attention back to the museum.

"What is that thing's beef with the bus?" asked Dawn, turning towards Amina.

"I'm not sure," the doctor admitted. "Unless she wants to make sure that no one gets away in it."

"What are we going to do about the girls?" Pascale asked, gripping the metal mesh of the gates in both hands, and squeezing. She was feeling pretty hopeless having watched her colleague scale the wall and help the girls to escape from the mummy's clutches.

"They should be safe for now," replied Amina. "Who knows, they might even have found another way out by now."

"I really think I should call this in," insisted Dawn. "Even if they manage to open the gates, we are still going to need back-up."

Amina snapped her head around and stared into Dawn's eyes, holding her gaze.

"If they manage to open the gates, I promise you, I will deal with the mummy," she assured her.

Ordinarily, Dawn would have ignored Amina's protestations and just made the call. But Amina's gaze was mesmerising, and once again, she found herself unable to resist.

Her biggest fear right now was that something bad would happen to one of the people inside the museum and, as a result, she would be accused of being negligent.

Her entire career could be on the line, not to mention the fact that the death of any of those girls would stay on her conscience for the rest of her life.

The three women watched as the mummy, finally finished with destroying the bus, made its way back over towards the staff entrance.

From this distance, they could not tell whether Danielle had locked the door or not.

But it seemed to make no difference as the mummy forced its way in, shoving the door against its locking mechanism and ripping it off out of its frame.

Amina supressed a scream, as she rattled the gates. "I need to get inside, why don't these stupid things just open?" she yelled.

As if in answer to a prayer, the motor for the gates began to whine, and seconds later, they began to open.

Inside the museum, Danielle could see Jeremy up ahead, sitting next to his cousin on the floor where the girls had placed him after carrying him back inside.

She rushed over to them. "Is he okay?" she asked, concerned by Phil's obvious state of semi-consciousness.

Jeremy shook his head. "I don't know, he keeps coming around, but then falls back asleep again. Did you see what happened to him?"

Danielle nodded. "He was trying to save the girls from being attacked by the mummy."

"He needs a doctor," Jeremy insisted. "We have to get him out of here."

Danielle leaned over and patted his shoulder. "And we will, just as soon as we figure out how to open those stupid gates."

Jeremy looked over at the security office. "I told the others that there was a control panel inside there, they've gone to try and figure it out."

"Good. You stay here – I'll be right back."

Danielle ran to the security office and shoved against the door.

It was locked from the inside.

She banged on the wood with her fist. "Open up, it's me, Miss Parker."

She could hear scuffling and furniture scraping inside, as if someone were moving something away from blocking the door.

Joanie Vintner opened the door, just enough to see out. Then, on seeing Danielle, she threw it open wide, and ran into Danielle's arms.

"Oh Miss Parker," she cried. "It's all been so horrible, and now we're trapped in here with that horrible thing outside."

Daniele tried to comfort the sobbing girl.

She looked over the girl's head and saw the rest of the

ducklings crowded inside the cramped office. Suzi, Greta and Janice all appeared to be studying the laptop on the main table with intense interest.

"Is everyone okay?"

Lesley, Rose, and Joanne huddled inside the open doorway, nodding.

They could see that their teacher's attention was focused on their shaking colleague but decided they could all do with a little comfort, so they bundled themselves through the door and wrapped their arms around the PE teacher.

From inside the office, they heard a triumphant cry from Suzi: "Got it!"

Before Danielle had a chance to ask the girl what she had achieved, they all heard a tremendous crash echoing down the corridor.

Danielle looked back towards the staff entrance, just in time to see the mummy rip the double doors off their hinges.

―――

Amina sprang through the opening before the other two women had a chance to attempt it.

She sprinted across the car park towards the gaping maw that had, only seconds before, been the staff entrance.

Dawn and Pascale gave chase, with the French teacher veering off to one side of the building, in pursuit of the swans.

"Wait!" Dawn yelled after Amina, unable to keep up with the lithe Egyptian.

The mummy had disappeared back inside the museum, but Dawn feared it might be waiting just inside the entrance, ready to attack the first victim who entered behind it.

But such thoughts clearly had not entered Amina's mind, as Dawn watched her charge through the doorway without even slowing down.

Dawn put her head down and ran for the doorway, all thoughts of the agony she had been in the previous evening with her ankle now a distant memory.

She wished Amina had waited for her. It was her job as the police officer to lead the charge, regardless of the circumstances.

Or, if she was being honest with herself, was she simply worried about what might happen to Amina before she had a chance to save her?

———

The four schoolgirls held on to their teacher for dear life as they watched the mummy lurching towards them.

Danielle knew she did not have the luxury of devising a plan, she needed to act fast.

She could see Jeremy desperately attempting to move his cousin out of the mummy's path, but it was obviously to no avail. He just did not have the strength to lift his cousin on his own.

Danielle frantically looked around her.

At the far end of the corridor, she spotted the bottom of the staircase leading to the upper floor. She eased herself away from the four girls, who by now, were bordering on becoming hysterical.

"Quick," she ordered, "run for those stairs." She looked at the three girls still hiding inside the office. "You lot, too. Come on – there's no time to waste," she urged.

Suzi, Greta and Janice did not need to be told twice. They rushed through the open door, almost knocking Danielle over in their haste.

Once the girls had all reached the stairs, Danielle turned back towards the mummy.

The creature was within a few feet of the two men huddled together on the floor.

Chapter 40

Danielle took an automatic step towards them but realised that she had no chance of reaching them before the mummy.

She spun around, desperately trying to find a weapon so that she could at least make an attempt at a rescue.

Deep down, she knew it was futile, especially after the fiasco with the metal tubing out in the car park. But she had to do something. She could not bear the thought of standing by while the mummy attacked the two young men.

"Anlet-Un-Ri!" The cry came from behind the mummy.

Danielle looked over and saw the tiny frame of Amina standing in the open doorway.

The mummy stopped dead in its tracks.

It was almost as if it somehow recognised the voice of the doctor.

As it slowly turned to face her, Amina slipped her hand in her pocket, and pulled out her locker key. She ran over to the lockers set out by the cloakroom and opened hers. She took out the Eye of Aken, which she had discovered, much to her surprise, hidden in the mummy's sarcophagus during her initial inspection.

She held the sacred artefact above her head, so that the mummy could see it clearly.

Danielle looked on, as the mummy stayed in position, almost as if it were suddenly frozen to the spot.

For a moment, nobody moved.

Then, Amina began slowly to advance towards the mummy, repeating scripture from the ancient scrolls as she stared into the creature's black eyes.

The diminutive form of the Egyptian looked quite ridiculous in comparison to the gigantic stature of Anlet-Un-Ri. But she moved closer, nonetheless, proud and unafraid.

Just then, Dawn appeared at the doorway.

Her eyes took in the scene before her, and she understood

immediately that Amina was planning to sacrifice herself to the mummy.

She called out. "Amina. No!"

Her scream broke the doctor's concentration, and she stopped and turned to face the officer.

As if also released from a spell, the mummy took a step towards Amina.

Amina indicated the sacred jewel in her hand. "It's all right," she assured Dawn, evidently touched by the officer's concern for her wellbeing. "I have the power to stop her, just let me finish the incantation and you will see."

Amina smiled at Dawn, then turned to face the mummy once more.

The close proximity of the mummy took her by surprise, and before Amina had a chance to retreat, Anlet-Un-Ri shot forward one of her arms and grabbed the Egyptian by the throat.

Amina's eyes bulged in their sockets as she felt her feet leaving the floor.

The sacred artefact slipped from her grasp, and bounced along the concrete floor, coming to rest several feet away.

Seeing the situation which she had caused by her interference, Dawn ran forward and grabbed Amina's rising body around the waist. She desperately wanted to yank her free of the mummy's grip, but at the same time she was afraid to pull too hard, for fear she might end up causing the woman's death by strangulation.

She could hear Amina gasping for breath.

Dawn let go of the woman and moved to her side, reaching up and wrapping her hands around the mummy's arm. She pulled with all she had until she too was left dangling off the ground, suspended from the same arm which held Amina aloft.

Danielle ran forward, without any real plan of attack. All she could think to do was charge the mummy from behind, in the

Chapter 40

hope that she might be able to knock her off balance and, in the process, free the two women.

But, before she reached her goal, Jeremy leaped to his feet, and ran head-first at the mummy, crashing into its back at full speed.

The force of the blow caused Jeremy to fall back on to the ground.

He looked up in terror, as the mummy slowly turned to see who had dared attack her from behind.

But his assault achieved the desired effect. As the mummy turned to face her new foe, she released the two suspended women.

Dawn fell back on her behind, with Amina landing in her lap.

The doctor coughed and spluttered, gasping for breath now her airway was finally open once more.

Realising his impeding peril, Jeremy scooted back along the floor, desperate to keep away from the mummy's grasp.

The gargantuan creature loomed over him, coming closer with each step.

When he finally managed to regain his feet, Jeremy felt faint, and his legs no longer seemed able to support him. He attempted to run, but his sense of direction had deserted him, and he crashed into the security office, just managing to stay upright by using the open door for support.

Danielle kept her gaze fixed on the spot where the sacred artefact had fallen.

Seizing her chance, she side-stepped the mummy's advance, and sprinted over to where it lay.

Grabbing it, she carried it over to where Dawn was trying to help Amina back to her feet.

Danielle took one arm and Dawn the other, and together they helped the doctor stand.

Amina held up a hand to thank them, then bent over with her hands on her knees while she continued to clear her throat.

Danielle glanced back over towards Jeremy.

Miraculously, he had managed to stay out of the mummy's grasp. But it was obvious to her that it was only a matter of time before he collapsed to the floor again.

Amina stood up, placed her hand over her mouth, and coughed.

She held out her other hand to Danielle, and the teacher placed the bejewelled artefact in her hand.

Once more, Amina held it aloft, and began reciting the ancient scripture.

The mummy came to a sudden halt once more and turned slowly to face the doctor.

As it advanced towards where the three women stood, Danielle nervously grabbed Dawn by the sleeve, and mouthed the words, "What should we do?"

The police officer shook her head.

This time she knew that, whatever happened, she must not disturb Amina in her prayer.

Reluctantly, Dawn moved away to one side, taking Danielle with her.

Amina stayed put, reciting the scripture from memory while the enormous mummy of Anlet-Un-Ri advanced until it towered over her,.

Just as it seemed as if the mummy was going to trample Amina underfoot, it veered off to one side and began to walk back towards the area where the exhibition was housed.

Amina followed close behind, her lips moving constantly as she walked.

Dawn and Danielle trailed behind, both anxious to see how this scene was going to play out.

Once they were back at the main exhibition area, the

mummy obediently climbed back inside its sarcophagus, and leaned back, crossing its mighty arms over its chest.

Amina continued speaking the ancient language for several minutes after the mummy had settled, before she finally stopped and announced: "It is done."

Chapter Forty-One

THEY DISCOVERED THE MANGLED REMAINS OF Scrapper, Bill, and Amin Salah discarded behind one of the fixtures near the mummy's sarcophagus.

Were it not for the dead bodies, Dawn had considered keeping the night's events secret.

Even though she now knew who the guilty party was behind the murder of Kasim, this was one report she did not look forward to making.

When she made the call, it was DI Ampstead who arrived on the scene first. He seemed genuinely concerned about Dawn's safety, which, although touching to begin with, was quickly replaced by smirking and laughter amongst the rest of his squad, when Dawn gave her evidence.

The mere fact that everyone else in attendance gave the same eye-witness report still did not convince Ampstead that they were telling the truth.

Later that morning, Dawn spent a very awkward hour being grilled by Superintendent Jacks, which even resulted in threats of Dawn being suspended if she refused to take the investigation seriously, as Jacks put it.

Chapter 41

In the end, she had to agree to undertake a psychological evaluation to ensure that she was fit for duty, which suited her fine.

She was tired of retelling the same story to people who refused to believe her, in spite of the fact that more than 20 civilian witnesses backed her up.

As the first available appointment with the force's psychiatrist was two weeks away, under the circumstances, Jacks ordered Dawn to stay at home, at least until then.

She did not bother to argue with the superintendent's decision, and instead just treated it as a paid holiday.

Several changes were instituted at the Seddon academy. Having discussed the traumatising events the swans and the ducklings had endured, Marigold Hedges wrote to each parent personally, explaining the events that had taken place, and offering them the chance to remove their daughters from the academy with a full refund for the year.

Fortunately for her and the school, all the girls wished to remain.

The swans no longer felt themselves so superior, having discovered a new respect for their younger counterparts, so they and the school staff decided that, henceforth, the privilege of becoming a Swan carried with it a new mission.

Danielle and Pascale were put in charge of deciding what the new regime was to be.

Gone were the initiation ceremonies, the bullying and the belittling. From now on, the duty of a swan was to tutor and mentor the girls in the year below. They were charged with helping the younger girls choose which subjects they were best suited to for the next level. Besides that, they were required to give them help and advice on everything from the correct etiquette at social events to make-up and relationship issues.

Once word got out, Stanley Unwin found himself being bombarded with requests from the press and television companies, all hoping for an exclusive story about the ancient mummy that, apparently, came back to life.

The poor curator had no taste for dealing with such people but, try as he might, he could not avoid them, as they followed him wherever he went, badgering him to the point of distraction.

Finally, the museum board hired a liaison officer who managed to secure a very profitable deal for the museum, for which Stanley received most of the credit.

The holdall containing the drugs lay undiscovered inside Bill Stead's locker for close to a month.

Eventually, the job of clearing out the locker was given to the security company, who in turn handed it over to one of the cleaners, with strict instructions to box up anything personal for Stead's wife.

When Sarah Janu came across the holdall, she almost did not bother to open it. But, when she pulled back the zip and realised what the contents were, she hid them inside her own locker, and just shoved Stead's porn magazines and DVDs inside instead.

Having no experience with drugs, she bided her time, watching the odd comings and goings of some of her fellow tenants, especially the ones she had witnessed Stead visiting in the past.

Finally, she found a buyer.

Whether or not he could be trusted to offer her a fair price, she did not care. She sold the drugs a bag at a time. The buyer did not ask, or seem to care, where the merchandise came from, but seemed more than happy to hand over £500 in cash for each purchase.

In total, Sarah made more than £10,000 from the deal.

One day she left the area with a full bank account to start a new life.

Phil recovered from his injuries and he and Jeremy returned home to London.

Chapter 41

From what Scrapper had told him, Len Bixby had already been paid by money transfer from Bill Stead before they made their delivery, so Phil had no concerns that members of Len's clan would turn up at his door one day, demanding to know what happened to the merchandise.

Both he and Jeremy had watched Bill Stead shove the holdall into his locker that night, and their biggest fear was that, when it was discovered, the police might come knocking. So Phil told his cousin that, if it came to it, all they had to say was that they did not know anything about any drugs, and that they were merely tagging along with Scrapper, who wanted to catch up with an old friend.

After all, neither of their prints would be discovered on the gear.

That knock at the door never came.

The police arranged their own forensic examination of the mummy, to ascertain what, if any, evidence there might be to suggest that it had come to life.

Amina was not allowed anywhere near the operation, for fear of contamination of evidence.

The doctor in charge of the operation confided to his colleagues that he believed the examination would prove to be fruitless, which ultimately it was.

The only anomaly discovered was that the soles of the mummy's feet seemed to have dust particles, mud and dirt that matched samples taken from the museum floor and the car park.

Once the examination was complete, and the doctor's report collated, the mummy of Anlet-Un-Ri was returned to the museum, where it took pride of place, once more, at the centre of the exhibition.

The Eye of Aken was given its own display cabinet, with a full description of its supposed powers written by Amina.

The words of the ancient text that Amina had recited in order to return the mummy to the afterlife, and from which the power to raise the mummy also came, she decided to keep to herself.

The night after the incident at the museum, Dawn and Amina lay together in her hotel room, drenched with perspiration from their lovemaking.

They had ordered champagne and smoked-salmon sandwiches from room service and ate on the balcony, watching the sun set.

Exhausted from having had no sleep the previous night, they drifted to bed with heavy eyes. But, once there, they undressed each other before falling on to the luxurious king-sized divan, locked in a passionate embrace.

Where their energy came from, neither of them could say, but each managed to bring the other to orgasm twice before they were done.

The End

Dear reader,

We hope you enjoyed reading *Dawn of the Mummy*. Please take a moment to leave a review, even if it's a short one. Your opinion is important to us.

Discover more books by Mark L'Estrange at https://www.nextchapter.pub/authors/mark-lestrange

Want to know when one of our books is free or discounted? Join the newsletter at http://eepurl.com/bqqB3H

Best regards,

Mark L'Estrange and the Next Chapter Team

You might also like:
Ghost Song by Mark L'Estrange

To read the first chapter for free, please head to:
https://www.nextchapter.pub/books/ghost-song

Printed in Great Britain
by Amazon

55181655R00211